WHEN PIPING WAS STRONG

WHEN PIPING WAS STRONG

*Tradition, Change and the Bagpipe
in South Uist*

Joshua Dickson

JOHN DONALD

First published in 2006 by
John Donald Publishers
an imprint of
Birlinn Limited
West Newington House
10 Newington Road
Edinburgh
EH9 1QS

www.birlinn.co.uk

Copyright © Joshua Dickson 2006

The moral right of Joshua Dickson to be identified as the author of this work has been asserted by him in accordance with the Copyright, Designs and Patents Act 1988

All rights reserved. No part of this publication may be reproduced, stored or transmitted in any form without the express written permission of the publisher.

ISBN10: 1 904607 52 7
ISBN13: 978 1 904607 52 6

British Library Cataloguing-in-Publication Data
A catalogue record for this book is available from the British Library

The Publisher acknowledges subsidy from
The Carnegie Trust for the Universities of Scotland
The John MacFadyen Trust
The MacRobert Trust
South Uist Estates Inc.
towards the publication of this book

Printed and bound by Antony Rowe Ltd, Chippenham

∼

Dedicated to the memory of Angus Campbell of Frobost, Neil MacDonald of Garryhellie and Seonaid 'Jessie' MacAulay of Smerclate, all consummate bearers of the culture of music in South Uist, whose generosity in word and melody allowed this work to take shape.

And to my mother and father, for sending me on my way.

∼

CONTENTS

Acknowledgements x
Abbreviations xii
List of Plates xiii
List of Figures xv
Map of South Uist, Benbecula, Eriskay and Barra xviii

1 INTRODUCTION 1
    Aims and Issues 2
    Methodology 4
    Guide to Musical Terms 7

PART ONE: CONTEXT AND INFLUENCE

2 '*Thòisich an gille air seinn na pìobadh*':
   PIPING AND THE ORAL TRADITION IN SOUTH UIST 13
    Between Words and Music 18
    Pìobairean Smearclait and Other Tales 24
    The Ceilidh 32

3 '*A multitude of papists*':
   CATHOLICISM AND THE PRESERVATION OF TRADITION IN SOUTH UIST . . . 38
    Catholic Beginnings 39
    Protestant Inroads 46
    Tradition Preserved 48

4 '*We followed the old pipe-playing in the new country*':
   FROM SOUTH UIST TO THE NEW WORLD, 1772–1923 57
    Major Emigrations from Uist 60
    Old Pipe-playing in the New Country 67

5 *'We had the gratification of good cheer and excellent piping'*:
   South Uist and Clanranald, c. 1630 – 1900 73

   Patronage 74
   The Martial Tradition 91
   Piping in the Community 96

PART TWO: TRADITION AND CHANGE

6 *'Interest in piping in South Uist is getting keener than ever'*:
   The Age of Improvement, 1900–58 105

   The State of Piping, c. 1900 107
   Two Societies, One Goal 116
   The Instructors and their Legacy 123

7 South Uist, Clanranald and Ceòl Mór 138

   Continuity of Tradition 138
   Tunes Associated with Uist and Clanranald 146

8 *'You could catch it by the ear'*:
   Pipers and the Piping Family in Twentieth-Century South Uist . . . 154

   The MacDonalds of Garryhellie 155
   The Campbells of Frobost 161
   The MacDonalds of Daliburgh 167
   The Morrisons of Loch Eynort 169
   Seonaid 'Jessie' MacAulay née Macintyre of Smerclate 171
   Calum Beaton of Stoneybridge 176

9 *'Nowhere in Scotland do the pipers come foward in such numbers'*:
   The Highland Games in South Uist 181

   Beginnings 183
   Sports and Dancing as Elements of Conservatism 187
   Piping at the Games: Local v. Mainland 190

10 *'A credit to the Hebrides, which has given of its best sons'*:
   South Uist Piping and the Great War 200

11 '*B' fheàrr leotha fear a bha cluichd leis a' chluas*':
    AESTHETICS AND TRANSMISSION IN SOUTH UIST PIPING 207

    Traditional Dance 208
    Toward a Local Aesthetic 211
    The Voiced and the Unvoiced 220
    By the Ear v. By the Book: Attitudes and Repertoires 227

12 CONCLUSION 236

Notes 241
Appendix: South Uist Games' Piping Results, 1898–1999 279
Discography 297
Bibliography 300
Index 313

ACKNOWLEDGEMENTS

There are many to whom I am indebted for their support, advice, encouragement and corrections throughout the long development of this ethnography into its present form.

For his continual and unerring guidance over the past several years, my thanks go firstly to Dr John Shaw, who acted as my principal supervisor during my doctoral studies in Celtic and Scottish Studies, Edinburgh University. I also thank Dr Mark Trewin, formerly of Edinburgh University, for his help with the more ethnomusicological aspects of the present work, and Dr Roderick Cannon for reading of the thesis and his very helpful suggestions. I thank the staffs of several archive and library institutions, among them Edinburgh University Main Library Special Collections, the National Library of Scotland, the National Archives of Scotland, Dr Christine Johnstone of Columba House Catholic Archives, Dr Donald MacLeod of the Free Church College and Col. Angus Fairrie of the Queen's Own Highlanders' Regimental Museum at Fort George, for kindly allowing me to conduct research at their facilities.

For help with photograph and notation scanning, access to sound archive sources and permission to reproduce images, my thanks go to Dr Margaret MacKay, Mr Ian MacKenzie, Mr Stewart Smith and Dr Cathlin MacAulay, all of Celtic and Scottish Studies, Edinburgh University; to Ms Anona Lyons of the Department of Geography, Edinburgh University, for producing the map of South Uist, Benbecula, Barra and Eriskay; and to Mr Robert Wallace and Miss Jeannie Campbell of the College of Piping, Glasgow, for access to images and permission to reproduce them here. I am also greatly indebted to Iain MacInnes of Ceolmor Software Ltd for his arrangements of the musical examples into their present format. The examples were created using Piobmaster 2.3 notation software.

For financial support toward this publication, my sincere thanks go to the trustees of the John MacFadyen Trust, in particular to Mr Neil Fraser, Dr Angus MacDonald and Mrs Emily MacDonald; to South Uist Estates Inc, in particular to Mr Tim Atkinson, former factor of South Uist; and to the Carnegie Trust for the Universities of Scotland. I also thank the Faculty of Arts (University of

Edinburgh) and the Catherine McCaig Trust for their financial support during my studies at the postgraduate stage.

Special thanks go to the late Dr Margaret Fay Shaw Campbell of Canna for permission to reproduce a selection of her photographs, and to Neil Fraser once again for arranging for their use in this publication.

I also extend my gratitude to several others in the business of piping and scholarship for their informal, but no less valued and insightful, conversation and support over the past few years in relation to the present work: Allan MacDonald of Glenuig; Hugh Cheape, Curator, the National Museums of Scotland; Dr John Gibson of Judique, Nova Scotia; Roderick J. MacLeod, Principal of the National Piping Centre; Dr Gary West, Lecturer in Scottish Ethnology, University of Edinburgh and host of BBC Radio Scotland's *Pipeline*; and Dr Mike Paterson, features editor, *Piping Today*.

Lastly, my heartfelt thanks go to the pipers, and others, of the South Uist community who have been so supportive of my interest in the piping tradition of the southern Outer Hebrides. Those who acted as informants in the conduct of ethnographic research include the late Seonaid 'Jessie' MacAulay, Louis Morrison, Rona Lightfoot, her brother the late Neil MacDonald, Ronald MacDonald, Neil Johnstone, the late Angus Campbell, his wife the late Bell Morrison and, most especially, Calum Beaton. They gave of their time generously and patiently. In a similar vein I also thank Angus Johnstone of the South End Piping Club, who joined me in jaunts round Uist and in practice chanter sessions on the CalMac ferries to while away the hours, and to many others in Uist who gave freely of their advice and enthusiasm.

I cannot conclude this list without expressing heartfelt gratitude to my wife Nicole, for her fortitude, and to my parents, for their pride.

To all – *Mòran taing, a chàirdean*.

JHD
Edinburgh
September 2005

ABBREVIATIONS

AC	Angus Campbell, informant
Acc	Accession number for manuscripts at the National Library of Scotland
Adv	Advocates Library manuscript, National Library of Scotland
CB	Calum Beaton, informant
HSL	Highland Society of London
JM	Seonaid 'Jessie' MacAulay, informant
MSR	March, Strathspey and Reel (tunes played as a single set in competition)
NM	Neil MacDonald, informant
OT	*Oban Times*
PS	Piobaireachd Society
PT	*Piping Times*
QOCH	Queen's Own Cameron Highlanders
RL	Rona Lightfoot, informant
SA	Sound Archives housed at Celtic and Scottish Studies, University of Edinburgh
SC	Sound Cassette
Stat Acc	*Statistical Account of Scotland*
TGSI	*Transactions of the Gaelic Society of Inverness*
WHFP	*West Highland Free Press*

PLATES

1. Army piper at the Uist games in Askernish, probably local, c. 1930–31.
2. Pipe Major Neil MacLennan of Lochboisdale with his sisters Ina and Mona c. 1930.
3. The remains of the old MacMhuirich steading in Stilligarry, opposite Loch Skipport to the east.
4. The low hill in Smerclate is known locally as *An Claigeann*, or The Skull, upon which Clanranald's MacIntyre pipers are said to have resided.
5. Angus MacAulay (*Aonghus Sheòrais*) of Benbecula, playing at the games on Askernish machair, c. 1931.
6. John MacDonald, Inverness, at the Lochboisdale Hotel in South Uist, c. 1932.
7. John MacDonald, Inverness, and Seton Gordon travelling by ferry in the Hebrides, c. 1930s.
8. Rona MacDonald (Lightfoot), Garryhellie, on the pipes as her brother Neil helps tune her drones, early 1950s, Glasgow.
9. Rona MacDonald (Lightfoot) as a young girl on the practice chanter in Daliburgh, c. late 1940s.
10. Angus Campbell, Frobost, as a boy before the Great War, preparing to compete at the Askernish games.
11. Angus Campbell, Frobost, with pipes, in military dress and kilt.
12. Pipe Major John MacDonald, or *Seonaidh Roidein*, of Daliburgh and Glasgow, c. 1940s.
13. Roderick MacDonald, or *Ruairidh Roidein*, of Daliburgh and Glasgow, c. 1940s.
14. The late Seonaid 'Jessie' MacAulay, née MacIntyre, in Uist House, Daliburgh, 1998.

15. Calum Beaton and his youngest son, Calum Antony Beaton, on the croft in Stoneybridge, with Beinn Mhór in the background, 1998.

16. Unidentified piper competing at the South Uist games on Askernish machair, 1981.

17. Pipers and judges posing at the Askernish games, 1954.

18. Pipes and drums of the 4th/5th Battalion Queen's Own Cameron Highlanders, taken in Aldershot, 1953.

19. The South End Piping Club practising in Daliburgh Drill Hall, April 1999.

20. A trio of pipers, South Uist, c. 1930–31.

FIGURES

1. 'Fhir a' Chinn Duibh' (Alasdair Boyd) 22
2. 'Lament for the Children', Variation 2 (Kilbery) 22
3. 'Patrick Òg' (MacDonald) 143
4. 'Patrick Òg' (MacKay) 143
5. 'Patrick Òg' (Piobaireachd Society) 144
6. a. 'Patrick Òg' (Calum Beaton)
   b. 'Mary MacLeod' (Calum Beaton) 144

Nuair a bha pìobaireachd a' dol gu làidir ann an Uibhist – a' dol fada roimhidh sin, ro'n chogadh mu dheireadh ach nuair thòisich mi fhìn air pìobadh, 's ann as deaghaidh an Darna Cogadh is thòisich na games *as ùr ann an Uibhist – bha móran phìobairean matha ann an Uibhist an uairsin. Bha an ceòl a bh' aca, chanainn-sa gu robh an ceòl aig muinntir Uibhist ann a sheo na bu chruaidhe, fhios agad; 's e daoine a bh' ann, bha iad ag obair daonnan air a' chruit is àiteachan eile, is bha na corragan aca na bu chruaidhe. Gheobhadh tu an ceòl aig an fheadhainn nach robh ag obair le 'n lamhan – ged a bha iad uamhasach fileanta, bha an ceòl aca car bog air choireiginn. Cha robh e tighinn suas idir ris a' cheòl chruaidh a chluinneadh tu aig muinntir Uibhist.*

When piping was strong in Uist – since long before the last war but when I started piping myself, which was after the Second World War and the Uist games started anew – there were many good players in Uist then. I would say that the music that the Uist people had here was harder, you see; the people here, they were working on the croft and other places, and their fingers were harder. You would get the music of those who didn't work with their hands – although they were very skilled, their music was somewhat soft. It just wasn't up to the hard music that you would hear the Uist folk playing.

Calum Beaton
Stoneybridge, South Uist
November 2000

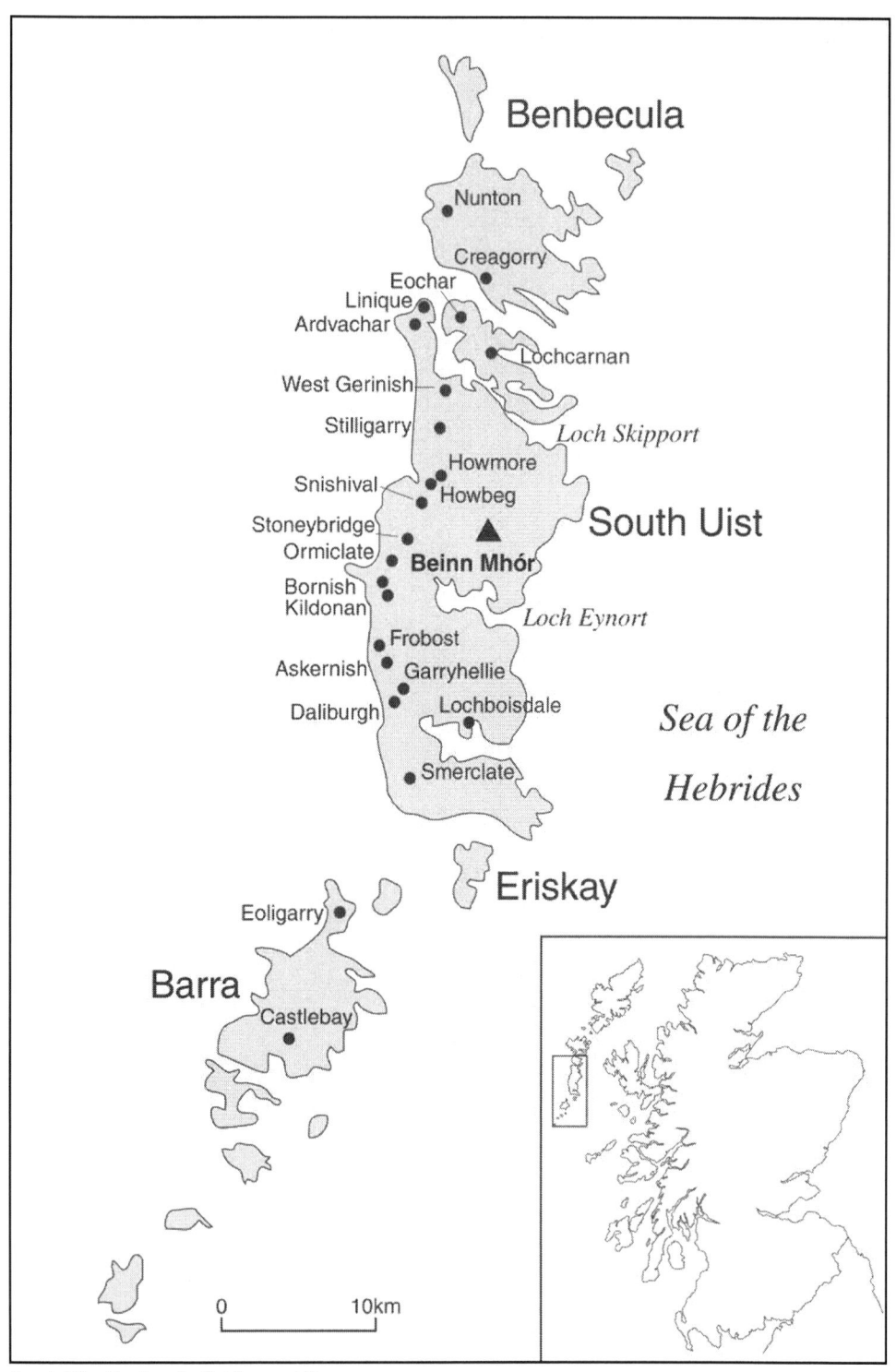

South Uist, Benbecula, Eriskay and Barra

CHAPTER 1

INTRODUCTION

This is a social history of piping in South Uist from as much of the 'insider' perspective as it is possible for the outside observer to apprehend. Some considerable obstacles confront such an approach: the language barrier is the most immediate, followed by the reluctance against open discussion which can often colour relations between an island community and an outsider. But I have enjoyed one or two advantages in my studies which make relations, and therefore research, easier. I learned Gaelic as an undergraduate student at Aberdeen University, and although my command is far from perfect, sources by and large have tended to appreciate the effort and communicate with more openness than may otherwise have been the case. Of course, the subject matter itself may have had something to do with it; piping is remarkably free from taboo in the Hebrides compared to, say, religion, where even the local Gaelic-speaking researcher has had problems uncovering local sentiments in the past. Equal to or even more relevant than my knowledge of Gaelic, however, was my acquaintance with the bagpipe. There is a fraternity to piping which often transcends social barriers. My being a piper first, and a researcher later, has without question been my key entrée into the community because piping – perhaps more from the Gaelic perspective than the English – is a nation with few internal borders. I say more so from the Gaelic perspective because the English-speaking world of piping is mountainous with exalted institutions – the Piobaireachd Society, the competition system, quantifiable standards upon which to judge and be judged – while the landscape of old-world Hebridean piping is comparatively flat for all the grass roots. And within the juxtaposition of these worlds lies the present work's primary importance: to explore the traditional Gaelic context of piping in relation to that of the mainstream community is to understand more fully why piping is the way it is.

AIMS AND ISSUES

The internal Gaelic aspect of the 'national music' has gone largely untouched by modern scholarship for reasons practical as well as political, since few are both inclined and qualified (linguistically and academically) to combine the necessary disciplines. On another level, though, the Gaelic point of view simply doesn't matter very much in mainstream piping. Previous writers have tended to address institutional aspects like the involvement of the Highland Societies of London and Scotland and the rise of formal competition in the nineteenth century[1] or the oft-touted esoteric nature of *ceòl mór* and its supposed exclusivity to those within a select body of disciples, to whom alone the 'authentic' tradition has been passed down.[2] These are all valid topics. There is nothing inauthentic about mainstream piping as it has developed over the past two centuries; as with any tradition, it is authentic within its own context. But its emphasis in modern scholarship means that Highland piping is rarely considered with regard to the old-world Gaelic social culture which occasioned its development as an art form.

Of course, there are notable exceptions. It began perhaps with ethnomusicologist Peter Cooke's 1972 watershed analysis of the difficulties associated empirically with the written notation of pibroch tunes, using 'MacCrimmon's Sweetheart', or *'Maol Donn'*, as a case study. Cooke was perhaps the first to set the pibroch tradition consciously in the context of Gaelic song, comparing scores from several sources over the past two centuries with extant song variants in order to identify a melodic relationship. As time wore on, a keener regard for the Gaelic perspective and piping's cultural roots began to emerge among scholars, particularly in the last decade. Allan MacDonald built upon Cooke's work by addressing in depth the melodic and rhythmic relationship between *ceòl mór* and popular Gaelic song at about the same time that Roderick Cannon produced a new edition of Joseph MacDonald's c. 1760 treatise, bringing to new light a crucial snapshot of classical piping in the post-Jacobite era and a fund of lost Gaelic nomenclature.[3] Shaw and Gibson, meanwhile, have laid the groundwork on the internal Gaelic aesthetic by describing piping within Gaeldom's wider social framework.[4] But this side of piping represents a cultural and functional environ far removed from that of the institutions mentioned above and, consequently, doesn't often enter the imagination of the performing and academic community. The Gael, in the minds of many, is still possessed of that tribal character, or peripheral ethnicity, which is the normal preoccupation of anthropologists but not of mainstream pipers or documentary historians; in short, the Highland pipes are no longer thought of as a Gaelic instrument. To an extent, of course, this is true – they are not *purely* Gaelic but are imbued with a pan-Scottish identity, and rightly so, in the eyes of the many nationalities who now play them, including the Scots themselves. But just as John Lorne Campbell once railed against historians of the Forty-Five who remained ignorant of the language and sentiments of the common Highlanders forming its bedrock,[5] cannot modern piping studies also benefit from an approach which considers the language and sentiments of those under whom Highland piping first evolved? Language, after all, is the door to culture, and in turn to the cultural compulsions which dictate tradition.

With this in view, the present work addresses the nature of piping in a Gaelic-speaking island community and how it has changed over the course of time. It is divided into two parts following a loose chronology. The first explores the contexts which underlay the South Uist tradition from the seventeenth to the twentieth centuries: we locate piping's place in the community's oral traditions and social culture in Chapter 2 so as to better grasp the complementarity which characterises the Gaelic arts; we then deal in Chapter 3 with the conflicting elements of Catholicism and Presbyterianism against the backdrop of the turbulent seventeenth century, and how the religious context has since profoundly affected piping in Uist and throughout the Hebrides. Chapter 4 traces the island's major emigrations, forced and unforced, to call attention to emigrant pipers from Uist to North America; and Chapter 5 assesses what oral and documentary records can tell us of piping in the Outer Hebridean quarter in relation to the patronage and martial affiliations of the old Clanranald aristocracy.

The second part of the present work traces the latter-day influence of mainstream literacy and the modern competitive era on local transmission and aesthetics. Chapter 6 addresses the impact of piping societies geared toward 'improvement' on South Uist's non-literate dance-piping tradition from about 1900. In Chapter 7, I make the case for the survival of a remnant of eighteenth- and nineteenth-century *ceòl mór* performance style in the community up to the 1940s; I also take time to look at tunes in the classical repertoire which carry traditional associations with Clanranald and South Uist. In Chatper 8, I offer brief biographies of prominent piping families and individuals in South Uist, bringing to light many aspects of the culture of transmission and how it has changed over the course of the past century. In Chapter 9, we deal with the history of the Highland games in South Uist and their role as both a preserver

3

of tradition and a leverage for mainsteam influence. Chapter 10 addresses the effects of the 1914–18 War on local traditional life and the piping community; the Second World War is given less of a priority here because the effects concerned were already long established by then. Finally, Chapter 11 analyses the nature of the aural idiom in South Uist, its survival in the era of staff notation and its implications for the apprehension of music among Uist's piping community.

A priority given to the indigenous perspective throughout allows us to witness these influences through the eyes of those who felt them, and to hear the testimony of those whose opinions are a key element in understanding the nature of Gaelic music in traditional Highland society – an environ far removed from the mainstream aspects of piping and which, arguably, only South Uist and its adjacent isles are capable of reflecting even sporadically at this late date. In another generation, these memorates will be available only as archive recordings. The present work's real contribution to current scholarship, therefore, is the testimony of a Gaelic community for whom the transition from the old world to the new is still within living memory.

∾ METHODOLOGY ∾

In assessing the South Uist tradition and its influences, the guiding methodological principle has been to utilise oral historical accounts and documentary records to their mutual best advantage. This helps to create a more dynamic picture of local piping in the sense that first-hand oral accounts, whether from conversation with living informants or from early accounts noted in manuscripts, can add immediacy and cultural perspective to documentary evidence, while documents used to establish a basic thread of history can support the validity of the oral accounts. This approach is by no means novel. The Rev. William Matheson, Gaelic scholar and valued tradition-bearer, was a tireless proponent of the legitimacy of oral tradition and its relevance to the study of Highland history. On the character of historical information preserved in oral tradition, he observed:

> Subtract this element from the materials to be used for the writing of Highland history, and you take away much of its human interest. The question now arises whether this is what the serious historian must do. Many who regard themselves as serious historians would say that it is. They would contrast this kind of material, the credibility of which they would rate very low, with contemporary evidence and the confidence that can be placed in it. But it is not as simple as that. Historical traditions orally preserved are far from being free from error, but the contemporary document also can err . . . What we are offered, in fact, is not certainty from one

kind of source and uncertainty from the other, but varying degrees of probability. Therefore I would hold that we cannot exclude historical traditions orally preserved from the material to be used for the study of history. But, naturally, techniques appropriate to the nature of such traditions must be used, in the same way that the study of MS sources has its own appropriate techniques.[6]

Of course, the present work is not concerned purely with history, but the principle of historical relevance and the agenda of the internal Gaelic point of view applies here just as surely. And the present work utilises to a greater extent a source of material heretofore rarely tapped in this field – that is, the Gaelic-speakers themselves. Interviews with eight informants of South Uist origin were conducted in all, seven of them pipers and only one not actually residing in Uist. A small amount of material dates back to a research trip in the summer of 1995, during my final year as an undergraduate at Aberdeen University, but most of it was produced during trips from 1998 to 2000 while I was a postgraduate student in Edinburgh.

My interviews generally took the form of open-ended discussions and participant observation, assuming in most cases a teacher–pupil relationship common among pipers. This is a method not without precedent in ethnomusicological research: Timothy Rice's study of the Bulgarian *gaida* tradition, for example, hinged on his apprenticeship under a highly regarded master player, from which vantage point he was able to assess the role of piper and singer within the settings of family, village and wider Bulgarian society.[7] The subject of piping proved a similar advantage to my own studies as it allowed for the adoption of clearly defined roles between observer and observed. My South Uist sources would often slip into the role of tutor when discussing performance style or related local customs, reach for the practice chanter or the pipes and give examples as one would to a student; they might also have felt more at ease discussing their memories and opinions with a fellow piper rather than with one who does not share, at least to some extent, a musical tradition with which they readily identify themselves. In either case, I believe that the teacher–pupil model created a template in which the interaction, musical or otherwise, more naturally reflected the environment under scrutiny.

Although such participant observation has tended to prioritise the subjects' own point of view, that is not to say that their word is regarded as final. The trap of foregoing all analysis of ethnographic material due to the inherent 'truth' of an informant's perspective – a tenet, more or less, of the naturalist approach to ethnographic research – has been criticised elsewhere as lacking in academic rigour.[8] Neither, however, can I entirely espouse the positivist approach, which in many ways mirrors the methods of the physical sciences and demands a controlled and standardised environment for research in order to reach quantitative conclusions.[9] Aside from the fact that this approach goes against the spirit of my stated aims, it is simply unfeasible under present conditions in South Uist. It is universally acknowledged both in and beyond the island that piping there is not what it once was; reports in 1910 that every father and two or more sons were 'able to discourse on the national instrument', as one *Oban Times* correspondent put it, paint a very different picture from what can be observed today, as popular media and entertainment continue to erode hitherto traditional pastimes. South Uist is certainly not lacking in pipers, but a sense of past glories and future misgivings pervades the community. Piping is simply no longer as universal a part of daily life as it used to be. A collective memory still exists among those of the elder generation, however, and the best living sources available on the local tradition, past and present – those recognised by their neighbours as skilled and experienced pipers and as sensitive observers of the cultural ebb and flow – tend to come from their ranks. So the relatively small number of informants featured in the present work reflects a consolidation, as it were, of the most qualified sources that the community has to offer. Their emphasis ensures that the present work is largely qualitative; but this being a combination of oral and written records and an analysis of contexts, the 'truth' contained in their views is never left unassessed.

Two among these sources have made particularly important contributions and warrant special note here. Calum Beaton, or *Calum Eairdsidh Choinnich* of Stoneybridge, gave freely of his time and was always eager to pass on the music he had learned and the observations he had made of life as a piper in his community. The late Seonaid 'Jessie' MacAulay, or *Seonaid Dhòmhnaill Chorodail* of Smerclate, was similarly generous. A retired schoolteacher and a frequent source of local lore and oral history, she could recall vivid scenes of local ceilidh piping from as early as the 1920s. Her perspective, like Calum's, was of immense value when assessing the changing character of musical transmission over the past century.

A word may be necessary on some aspects of text and translation. Words in Gaelic are everywhere italicised, such as *ceòl mór*, *canntaireachd* and *pìobaireachd*, except where they occur as proper names in mainstream usage, such as Patrick Mór, the Campbell Canntaireachd or the Piobaireachd Society, or when quoting a written source that does not italicise them. Gaelic place-names within otherwise English text are also left in regular font and are spelled according to anglicised convention, e.g. Eochar for *Iochdar* and Ardavachar for *Aird a' Mhachair*. Translations of informants' material are entirely my own. As for quotes from Gaelic publications, archive transcriptions or manuscripts, translations are mine except where noted. Notes to the text are found at the end of the book.

As the present work is not primarily concerned with musicological analysis, illustrations of staff notation will be found only in Chapters 2 and 7 in order to demonstrate stylistic points made in the text; tunes otherwise mentioned are widely known among piping circles and are referenced for source.

∽ GUIDE TO MUSICAL TERMS ∽

The reader unfamiliar with piping or its Gaelic nomenclature may appreciate a cursory guide to the terms used throughout this work. Fuller descriptions of the Highland bagpipe itself, and the various aspects of its music, are readily available in other published works currently in print.[10]

Ceòl mór

This translates literally as 'big music' and is generally considered the 'classical' music of the pipes due to its ceremonial and courtly associations. *Ceòl mór* came to fruition in the West Highlands of the sixteenth century, a development somewhat concurrent with the rise in status of the bagpipe itself as the preferred music of the Gaelic aristocracy during *Linn nan Creach*, or the 'Age of Forays', when internecine feuding and conflict between clans was common due to the vacuum of power left by the forfeiture of the Lordship of the Isles in 1493. Thanks to the distancing of the Gaelic aristocracy from their roots in the post-Jacobite era, the social *raison d' être* of this subtle and sophisticated class of music gradually fell away. The natural bearers of the tradition and repertoire – the pipers themselves – carried on regardless, however, in the retention and transmission of music by both oral, and to an extent, literate means, but the changes sweeping Scotland in the late eighteenth century nonetheless had a profound effect on its development as an art form. A watershed mark occurred in 1781, when the Highland Society of London established competitions, a decidedly artificial intervention, for the expressed purpose of preserving *ceòl mór* from oblivion. Whether affairs then were really so dire is debatable, but such was the conventional wisdom of the time. Many consider its composition to have been a lost art since approximately the mid-nineteenth century, if not earlier; an indication in itself of the distance that has grown between the music's cultural origins and those who now perform it.

Ceòl mór consists of a theme, called the *ùrlar* or 'ground', followed by variations embellished with increasingly complex gracenote patterns. The tunes which form the surviving repertoire fall under a range of categories – 'laments', 'salutes', 'gatherings' and 'battle-tunes', among others – which reflect the pipes' functions in Gaelic society during the turbulent sixteenth to eighteenth centuries.

Ceòl beag

Literally 'small music', the term is meant relative to *ceòl mór*. It is most often referred to as the 'light music' of the pipes and encompasses the marches, strathspeys and reels played for competition as well as less-embellished strathspeys, reels, jigs and hornpipes played for dancing. It also refers to marches played for military functions. Some pipers or enthusiasts would stress that a third term, *ceòl meadhonach* or 'middle music' exists to describe slow airs and funeral dirges, but since the term is generally paid little heed and is of smaller scope than the classical music, for all practical purposes Highland piping today can be neatly divided between *ceòl mór* and *ceòl beag*.

Pìobaireachd

This word simply means 'piping' in its original Gaelic usage, but in mainstream convention it has come to be regarded as synonymous with *ceòl mór*. The spelling is often anglicised as 'pibroch', and this latter term is used occasionally in the present work, usually in the context of competition records and the Gaelic 'pibroch song' tradition.

Ceòl cluais

Literally translated as 'ear-music', this term, which I have encountered in living use only among the South Uist community, refers to piping learned aurally as opposed to literately; it also carries a fundamental association with the function of playing for dance. It most often connotes the style of dance-piping which characterises the Cape Breton tradition, where literacy rarely entered the musical equation until the mainstream influences of the post-Second World War era. That the term is used in South Uist, and that such an aural idiom of transmission and performance is still within living memory there, is testimony to the extent to which an indigenous Hebridean musical aesthetic has survived there in the modern age of staff notation and competition. In the present work the term is introduced in Chapter 2, is mentioned occasionally in subsequent chapters and receives a fuller analysis in Chapter 11.

Canntaireachd

Deriving from the same Latin root as in English 'chant', this term refers to the syllabic notation system used by pipers to transmit tunes vocally. It is associated primarily with *ceòl mór* and was the normal method for all pipers until music for the Highland bagpipe began to be written on the stave in the late eighteenth century, and literacy became increasingly prioritised through the nineteenth. Today it takes a definite back seat to staff notation and exists in a less structured and formal state than some believe it to have been in the pre-literate age. It is commonly maintained, however, that the use of *canntaireachd* in transmitting *ceòl mór* is still the proper – that is, the most 'authentic' – means of interpreting the music, a direct (if somewhat romanticised) nod to piping's Gaelic roots.

Puirt-à-beul

Meaning 'mouth-tunes', this phrase refers to short Gaelic songs[11] meant to provide rhythm for traditional Highland dancing, such as the Scotch Reel or Cape Breton step-dancing, in lieu of instruments. Their melodies are extant also as tunes on the bagpipe and fiddle, and it is really just the mode of performance – i.e. the use of the voice – that distinguishes *puirt-à-beul* from traditional Cape Breton fiddling or *ceòl cluais* piping as a musical idiom; they are all of a common cultural stock.

PART ONE

Context and Influence

CHAPTER 2

'Thòisich an gille air seinn na pìobadh'
PIPING AND THE ORAL TRADITION IN SOUTH UIST

In March 2002, I was asked to be an usher at the funeral of Hamish Henderson, folklorist, poet and revered father of Scotland's twentieth-century folk revival. I listened at the back of the congregation as several well-known singers and scholars (Henderson had once declared Scottish traditional music the most 'bookish' in the world) took part in the service at St Mary's in Edinburgh's New Town: Alison McMorland sang in Scots, Margaret Bennett in Gaelic; Timothy Neat spoke at length; and piping the coffin into and out of the church was Allan MacDonald of Glenuig. MacDonald was brought up in a Gaelic-speaking Moidart family with Uist connections on his mother's side and piping all around him, and is today known the world over both for his playing and for his scholarship on the melodic links between classical piping, or *ceòl mór*, and the Gaelic song tradition.

Unlike Bennett and McMorland, who sang songs, MacDonald played them. I recognised the melody to *'Latha dhan Fhinn am Beinn Iongnaidh'*, or 'The Fenians' Day on the Mountain of Wonder', an Ossianic ballad dating back to the twelfth century and recorded from the singing of Kate Campbell of South Uist in 1965. I then made out the repetitive phrasing of *'Tàladh Dhòmhnaill Ghuirm'*, or 'Blue-eyed Donald's Lullaby', with which his nurse is said to have lulled the young chief of the MacDonalds of Sleat to sleep as a boy in the 1530s.[1] The songs were ancient, and they were fresh: Allan's re-interpretation of them as instrumental laments was the immediate, living continuance of an overlapping between song and instrumental idioms long ubiquitous in Gaelic tradition.

Listening to Allan that day brought to mind the occasion when I first visited South Uist in 1995 and met the late Neil MacDonald, Kate's son, in Garryhellie. Like his sister, Rona, their father, Archie, and their uncles, cousins and forebears from Daliburgh to Frobost, Neil was a piper. He was in his sixties then and did not play often, but pipe music was never absent from his lips. He gave innumerable competition marches in *canntaireachd* and sang the verses of local *puirt-à-beul*, sung as often as piped in the ceilidhs of a generation ago. '*Drochaid Chlann 'ic Ruairidh*', or 'The Bridge Rory's Children Made', was a particular favourite: a song composed locally to satirise the construction of the Uist–Benbecula causeway in 1941, the late Roderick MacDonald of Daliburgh and the Glasgow Police popularised it as a two-part reel mainstream pipers recognise today as 'The Famous Bridge' – a compelling example of both the latter-day survival of village *aoir*, or satiric verse, and the fluidity with which a single musical idea can find multiple expressions among a community so inclined. Neil told me how he had piped at the funeral of local bard *Dòmhnall Ailean Dhòmhnaill na Bàn-fhighiche* three years earlier and, like Allan, had found the instrumentalisation of song to be the most fitting tribute. He had played the melody to one of the bard's most famous compositions, '*Ceud Fàilt' air Gach Gleann*'. As Neil recalled the air in conversation, the words themselves came easily and without hesitation:

Ceud fàilt' air gach gleann	A hundred greetings to every glen
'S air na beanntannan mór' –	And to the great mountains –
'S iad a chuimhnich dhomh an t-àm	They reminded me of the days
Ghabh mi sannt air bhith beò.[2]	When I hungered for life.

To Neil, lifelong *Uibhisteach* and witness to the ebb and flow of a tradition he himself enriched and perpetuated, and to Allan, scholar, Moidart Gaelic-speaker and heir to traditions both mainstream and aboriginal, words and melody were often indelibly intertwined.

The late Sorley MacLean once referred to this duality of words and music in traditional Gaelic culture as products of a 'simultaneous creation',[3] by which he referred to the melodic, stylistic and lyrical overlapping that occurs between these two faces of Gaelic orality. Each supports and complements the other within a framework wherein music and language share the same space; as a result, interdependent links are formed between songs, poetry, storytelling and instrumental music. Gaelic poetry, for instance, up until approximately the Second World War and the advent of the post-modern literary age, was rarely performed without being sung to an accompanying air selected and adapted from a stock repertoire. Vestiges of this ancient (re)compositional rule are still being documented among village bards in the West Highlands and Islands today.[4]

Waulking songs too dictated a tenacious synonymy between melody and lyric, as folklorist Margaret Fay Shaw found when living in South Uist in the late 1920s and early '30s. Among women waulking cloth in the township of Glendale, she observed that a single melody could well refer to a hundred different songs, and that the ostensibly meaningless vocables forming a song's refrain had to be given correctly if it were to be identified, implying a mnemonic function. She was later moved to reminisce on the effect of this on the parameters of Gaelic aesthetic thought:

> In folkmusic [sic], words and tunes are inseparable. A traditional Gaelic singer must be given the words to the air, or at least the chorus, before he or she can recognise the song. I was once told, when I said that a certain singer had the air but not the words, 'How could she have the song without the words?'[5]

The bagpipe inevitably shared in the mutual influence while vocal and instrumental music held a roughly equal premium in Gaelic social culture. As will be seen below, legends still current in Hebridean society occasionally admit circumstances in which pipe melody was imbued with lexical meaning, while many traditional Gaelic songs reflect, in their melodies, particular grounds or variations of *ceòl mór*.

This overlapping calls to mind an 'interrelationship of the arts', as the American ethnomusicologist Alan Merriam put it in 1964, that 'refers to the point of view that the arts stem from the same sources; that all the arts are really just one Art differently expressed because the materials are different.'[6] Such a holistic image, though overtly theoretical, finds resonance with the living practice of Gaelic tradition. John Shaw was perhaps the first to realise in diagrammatic form the interlocking and interdependent nature of the various narrative and musical 'arts', including piping, as performed in the ceilidh of the old-world Gael.[7] John Gibson, in like vein, found holisticity an implicit theme when commenting on the earliest definitive treatise on Highland pipe music. Written by Joseph MacDonald of Durness around the year 1760, *A Compleat Theory of the Scots Highland Bagpipe* was written with the tacit acknowledgement that the technicalities of dance (*ceòl beag*) and ceremonial (*ceòl mór*) idioms, otherwise so removed in style and function, were based on a common template. Gibson observed:

> The manuscript dealt primarily with *ceòl mór* for the simple reason that, according to MacDonald, it provided the most comprehensive and rational overview of Highland piping. All the fingerings for dance music fell automatically into the wider study, the *ceòl beag* grace-note clusters being but fractional parts of, if not identical to, the longer *ceòl mór* ones. Obviously, all Highland pipers saw both forms as part of a larger whole.[8]

Based on such depictions of a complementary nature, stemming, as Shaw asserts, from the ceilidh as its chief trasmissive context, one can well imagine the affinity connecting the 'different materials' of the Gaelic musical 'Art'.

For centuries, scholars have noted the importance of the complementarity of folk arts to traditional Gaelic culture generally, and to South Uist particularly. Martin Martin, in his *Description of the Western Isles of Scotland* written towards the end of the seventeenth century, described the innate musicality of the people of his native Skye in terms which would have applied to many a community in the *Gàidhealtachd* at the time:

> They have a great genius for music and mechanics. I have observed several of their children that before they could speak were capable to distinguish and make choice of one tune before another on the violin; for they appeared always uneasy until the tune which they fancied best was played, and then they expressed their satisfaction by the motion of their head and hands . . . Several of both sexes have a quick vein of poesy, and in their language (which is very emphatic) they compose rhyme and verse, both which powerfully affect the fancy . . . They have generally very retentive memories.[9]

He went on to set South Uist quite apart in its conservation of language and all that that implies as regards traditional culture, commenting that 'the natives speak the Irish tongue more perfectly here than in most other islands; partly because of the remoteness and the small number of those that speak English, and partly because some of them are scholars, and versed in the Irish language.'[10] 'Scholars versed [i.e. literate] in the Irish language' was a reference to two dynastic families under Clanranald patronage who kept and composed Gaelic documents relevant to their professions – the Beatons, who were learned physicians,[11] and the MacMhuirichs, who, as bards and *seanchaidhean* (a combination of genealogist and historian) to Clanranald, were active in Uist from the sixteenth century to the mid-eighteenth. Originally an Irish family whose appearance in Scotland is dated to the early thirteenth century in Islay and Kintyre, the MacMhuirichs produced the Red and Black Books of Clanranald, a compilation of genealogy, history and poetry which chronicles the Clanranald line up to the early eighteenth century.[12] Alexander Campbell, travelling through South Uist in search of material for his seminal collection of Highland music, *Albyn's Anthology*, enquired after the whereabouts of the Red Book to a MacMhuirich descendant in 1815; the man replied that Clanranald had taken it from his family and it had not been seen again. In fact, the Red Book had been entrusted by Neil Og MacMhuirich, the last bard and *seanchaidh* of note in that family, to the care of James MacPherson during the latter's collection of Ossianic songs and narrative in the Hebrides in 1760. It is a telling note on the post-Jacobite decline of the bardic family's fortunes that the descendant was himself unlettered, and was led nameless and cap in hand to an audience with the visiting collector. Although he proclaimed himself proudly as the twenty-second male MacMhuirich in succession and recited from memory examples of his forebears' song-poetry, he was in the end dismissed as nothing more than a 'clumsy, elderly lout'.[13]

In these families' hey-day, however, literacy was an indication of their élite professional and social status. Such was the MacMhuirichs' status in South Uist, in fact, that their hereditary lands in Stilligarry and Drimsdale were generally regarded as lawful sanctuary – at least, so we are led to believe by the storytellers.[14]

In 1860, South Uist's value to the study of traditional Gaelic culture was again called to the fore when folklorist John Francis Campbell, in compiling his *Popular Tales of the West Highlands*, discussed Ossianic tales. 'This is now the rarest of any [class of tale],' he wrote, 'and is commonest, so far as I know, in Barra and South Uist'.[15] His contemporary, Alexander Carmichael, was in Uist around the same time in pursuit of Gaelic oral literature which he felt had hitherto decayed in the wake of the Disruption in many other, predominantly Presbyterian, areas; literature which he claimed had been 'widely diffused, greatly abundant, and excellent in quality – in the opinion of scholars, unsurpassed by anything similar in the ancient classics of Greece and Rome'. He wrote in particular of the great fund of lore provided by one Hector MacIsaac and his wife:

> In September 1871, Iain F. (John Francis) Campbell and I went to see them . . . The wife knew many secular runes, sacred hymns, and fairy songs; while the husband had numerous heroic tales, poems, and ballads . . . The stories [he] went over during our visits to him would have filled several volumes. Mr. Campbell now and then put a leading question which brought out the storyteller's marvellous memory and extensive knowledge of folklore.[16]

The hymns, incantations and proverbs he collected in Uist and Benbecula during the 1860s and '70s would ultimately form the bulk of his influential six-volume *Carmina Gadelica* (1928–71).

South Uist's remoteness and conservation of tradition continued to attract folklorists well into the twentieth century. The work of the late Margaret Fay Shaw and that of her late husband John Lorne Campbell have proved most influential; Campbell in particular is noted for pioneering field recording techniques while collecting in Uist, and in 1964 he re-affirmed the area's continuing value in his introduction to Frederick Rea's *A School in South Uist: Reminiscences of a Hebridean Schoolmaster, 1890–1913*. 'Impoverished though many of the people then were,' wrote Campbell, 'their lives contained many elements of interest to the folklorist and the general historian: in many ways Uist was still a microcosm of the Highlands of the eighteenth century: even today it preserves a greater amount of Gaelic tradition than any other part of Scotland.'[17] It is a testimony to Uist's cultural fortitude that, in the dawn of the twenty-first century, it continues to do so with arguably greater self-consciousness than ever before; a fact no doubt stemming as much from an increasingly sophisticated sense of economic opportunity (as the recent boom in *feisean* will attest) as from Gaelic's diminishing overall census figures.

∽ BETWEEN WORDS AND MUSIC ∽

The interrelationship between vocal and instrumental music in Gaelic tradition is a result of their serving very much the same function, to the point that they seem at times entirely interchangeable. Eighteenth-century writers such as Knox and Burt observed singers as well as pipers providing rhythm for group labour on the western coast and the Isle of Skye. Their counterpart of the 1830s, James Logan – a writer of romanticised Highland lore and a man of some importance to piping historiography by his authorship of the notes to MacKay's *Collection* of 1838 – drew further attention to this unity of function when he remarked that 'at all rural occasions in the Highlands it has been observed that labour is accompanied by singing. Where music can be had, it is preferred. A piper is often regularly engaged in harvest to animate the reapers, and he generally keeps behind the slowest worker.'[18] The functional versatility shared by vocal and instrumental music was never restricted to the drudgery of labour. Alexander Campbell, during his Hebridean sojourn in 1815, was bemused to discover *puirt-à-beul* singers in North Uist providing the precise rhythmic requirements for dancing that he had previously associated only with instrumentalists:

> While at Lochmaddie I writ down four original airs with part of the words from the mouth of Mrs. Campbell, daughter of Capt. Cameron. While here, I witnessed for the first time, persons singing at the same time they dance: and this is called dancing to port-na-beul, being a succedaneous contrivance to supply the want of a musical instrument. This effect is droll enough; and gives an idea of what one might conceive to be customary among tribes but little removed from a state of Nature. What renders the illusion more probable is the mode in which these merry Islanders perform the double exercise of singing and dancing: – thus the men and women sing a bar of the tune alternately; by which they preserve the accent and *rhythms* [sic] quite accurately – the effect is animating: and having words correspondent to the characters of the measure – there seems to be a 3-fold species of gratification arising from the union of song and dance – rude, it is confessed – but such as pleases the vulgar; and not displeasant to one who feels disposed to join in rustic pleasures, or innocent amusement.[19]

Vowel lengths and other elements of the Gaelic language corresponded with the dance-step rhythms (or in the case of group labour, with the repetitive motions of tasks such as waulking cloth or rowing) in the same way as a piper or a fiddler would articulate the rhythms of a strathspey or reel.[20]

The scene Campbell described in North Uist mirrors in some important respects the reminiscences of one of this work's primary oral sources, Seonaid 'Jessie' MacAulay, née MacIntyre, of Smerclate, South Uist, who passed away in March 2002. Born around 1913, MacAulay was a schoolteacher, long retired by the time I had met her, whose vivid memories of local piping in the 1920s and '30s are invaluable to an understanding of piping's place in the community's wider grass-roots oral tradition. Brought up listening to her father, an ear-learned piper, and later taught in the literate idiom during Uist's era of organised instruction by professional tutors, MacAulay was able and well-placed to articulate her observations of dancing to *puirt-à-beul*, the survival of the interchangeability described above, and the nature of aural transmission in the ceilidhs of her youth:

> *Bhiodh iad a' dannsa leis a' phìob . . . is puirt-à-beul nuair nach biodh pìob aca; bha iad a' dèanamh dannsa leis an òran . . . Gu leòr dhen a' cheòl cluais, 's e òrain a bh' ann originally, fhios agaibh. Cluinneadh tu strathspey no reel, bha iadsan 'nan ceòl cluais, a chionn 's e òrain a bh' ann. Bhiodh iad a' dannsa leis a sin, nuair nach robh pìob aca no sian, bhiodh iad a' dannsa leis na h-òrain.* Mouth-tunes, *puirt-à-beul*.[21]

> They would dance to the pipes . . . and to mouth-music when they didn't have pipes; they would dance to the song . . . Much of the ear-music was songs originally, you know. You would hear a strathspey or a reel, they were ear-music, because they were songs. They would dance to them, when they hadn't the pipes or anything, they would dance to the songs. Mouth-tunes, *puirt-à-beul*.

MacAulay's testimony, and examples collected from local singers like Alasdair Boyd (who was also a piper) and Kate MacDonald,[22] put the *puirt-à-beul* tradition's continuance in South Uist well into the twentieth century.

Mention was made earlier of Gaelic songs which correspond melodically to extant pieces in the *ceòl mór* repertoire. These are by custom called pibroch songs[23] and are another example of the verbal-melodic (or vocal-instrumental) affinity in Gaelic music. Sometimes *ceòl mór*'s Gaelic origins are fossilised in the English-language rhetoric of mainstream piping circles; the phrase 'get the song out of the tune', for example, is nowadays a clichéd piece of advice from master to pupil which scholars such as Allan MacDonald[24] believe to be an anachronism from the days when *ceòl mór* was taught solely through *canntaireachd*, and is meant to help one attain an 'authentic' interpretation of the tune despite having learned it from staff notation. Jessie MacAulay, among many other Uist pipers, believed the expression of the 'song' in the tune to be a common quality heard in the performance of *ceòl mór* locally in the early decades of the twentieth century. In conversation in 1998, she recalled that Angus Campbell of Frobost, a local authority on *ceòl mór*, used to give this advice in his playing and teaching days; no doubt he'd been told the same thing by his own teacher, John MacDonald of Inverness:

> *Fhios agad, sin agad Aonghus Caimbeul à seo, chanadh e daonnan,* 'First learn the song, then you can start the pibroch!' *'S ann mar sin a bha daoine a' cluichd aig an àm sin.* Like a traditional music.[25]
>
> You know, you have Angus Campbell from here, he would always say, 'First learn the song, then you can start the pibroch!' That's how people played at that time. Like a traditional music.

Two pibroch songs commonly known in the west Highlands, '*Colla Mo Rùin*' ('O Colla, My Beloved') and '*Dà Làimh 'sa Phìob*' ('Two Hands on the Pipes') were recorded by Margaret Fay Shaw from South Uist informants in 1948.[26] '*Dà Làimh*' has no known equivalent in the surviving *ceòl mór* repertoire; it shares the same story background with one tune, 'The Cave of Gold', but they do not seem melodically related. The cognate tune to '*Colla Mo Rùin*', on the other hand, is widely recognised and is recorded in the annals of the repertoire under the title 'The Piper's Warning to his Master', which can be seen as a reflection on the tune's legendary origins. The story behind '*Colla*', both the song and the tune, is well known: *Colla Ciotach*, or 'Left-handed Colla', the MacDonald chief famed for his exploits in the early seventeenth century, led an expedition to capture Castle Dunniveg (the castle varies with the many different versions of the tale) which was being held by a garrison of Campbells, with whom Clan Donald feuded during *Linn nan Creach*, or the Age of Forays. The advance party was captured, but the garrison's commander permitted the piper among them to play a tune before being hanged. Illustrating the phenomenon in Gaelic cosmology in which instrumental music is occasionally imbued with lexical meaning, it is said that the very notes of the tune he played formed the words of a warning, allowing Colla and the rest of the MacDonalds to escape. Collector Donald John MacDonald of Pininerine, a valued tradition-bearer in his own right, recorded verses to '*Colla*' peculiar to Uist from his uncle, Neil MacDonald, in 1953:

A Cholla, cuir umad	Colla, push away
Bi ullamh gu falbh	Be ready to flee
A Cholla, cuir umad	Colla, push away
Bi ullamh gu falbh	Be ready to flee

O fàg Dùn Naomhaig	Oh leave Dunniveg
Ràmh is taoman	With oar and baler
Fàg Dùn Naomhaig	Leave Dunniveg
Ràmh is taoman	With oar and baler.
A Cholla nan cleas (x 3)	Colla of the war-feats (x 3)
Gabh an taobh deas	Take the south side
Tha mise làimh.	I'm in their hands.
A Cholla na [sic] *rùin* (x 3)	Colla of the loved one (x 3)
Seachainn na caoil	Avoid the strait
Tha mise làimh.	I'm in their hands.
A bhrathair ghaolaich ghabh iad mi (x 3)	Loving brother, they caught me (x 3)
Chan ann nam aonar ghabh iad mi.	I'm not alone, they caught me.
A bhrathair ghaolaich ghabh iad mi (x 3)	Loving brother, they caught me (x 3)
Am beul an aonaich ghabh iad mi.[27]	In the lee of the hill, they caught me.

The occasion of the song's (and tune's) origin, whether entirely fictional or based to some extent on an actual event, highlights the concept of musical instrumentation conveying verbal messages in the 'music-culture' of the Gael; and while sources for the '*Colla*' legend do not extend earlier than the nineteenth century, enough orally transmitted anecdotes of a similar nature are on record – particularly in relation to piping[28] – to give the impression that the phenomenon has underpinned Gaelic oral tradition for a very long time.

A lesser-known song, but one equally demonstrative of the affinity in question, is '*Fhir a' Chinn Duibh*', or 'The Black-haired Lad', recorded for the School of Scottish Studies by the aforementioned piper, Alasdair Boyd. Boyd was born in Eochar, South Uist, in 1889 and piped during the 1914–18 War with the 5th Cameron Highlanders. He had a tremendous knowledge of local songs and folklore, as well as having been an excellent player of dance and martial tunes in his day. Between 1953 and his death in 1970 he recorded over seventy songs for the School's sound archives.[29] In the year of his death he recorded '*Fhir a' Chinn Duibh*' for researchers Morag MacLeod and Dr Peter Cooke at his home in Oban:

Fhir a' chinn duibh, thug mi gaol dhuit	Lad of the black hair, I gave you love
Fhir a' chinn duibh, thug mi gràdh dhuit	Lad of the black hair, I adored you.
Thug mi gaol, is thug mi gràdh dhuit	I loved you, I adored you
Thug mi gaol nach tug mi 'chàch dhuit	I gave you love that I didn't give to the rest.
Fhir a' chinn duibh, thug mi gràdh dhuit.	Lad of the black hair, I adored you.

Figure 1. Fhir a' Chinn Duibh, sung by Alasdair Boyd (SA 1970.7.1)

It is, at its core, a simple and quite generic love song, its plaintive falling and peaking over the F sharp a melodic archetype in the stock repertoire which constituted the Gaelic song tradition and consequently reminiscent of many other Gaelic songs and instrumental pieces – including a themal variant in the pibroch *Cumha na Cloinne*, or 'The Lament for the Children'.[30] Boyd, a piper, made a direct connection between the song and the pibroch by way of a common origin tale, believing that both derive from the lamentations of Patrick Mór MacCrimmon, piper to MacLeod of Dunvegan in the seventeenth century, who is said to have lost seven of his eight sons to fever in a single year; one in particular supposedly loved more dearly than the rest. The themal variant in the pibroch is usually played today as it was edited by Archibald Campbell, a founder of the Piobaireachd Society, in his *Kilberry Book of Ceòl Mór*.

Figure 2. 'Lament for the Children', Line 1, Variation 2 (Campbell, 1948)

Boyd claimed to have learned the 'pibroch words and tunes' as childhood lullabies from his mother and his uncle's wife Annie MacDonald who, significantly, was known as *Anna nighean a' Phìobaire* (Ann daughter of the Piper) and who would often sing pibroch songs while sewing. After singing the song for MacLeod and Cooke, he sang the *canntaireachd* vocables of the pibroch variation; in light of this, it may surprise some to note that he never played much *ceòl mór* himself.

The overlapping of speech and song does not only present itself in a musical performance, but can be implied in the everyday language of its native community.

Lambert pointed out the importance placed on vowel length in the storytelling tradition of Donegal, noting that 'with this emphasis on saying the story properly, the northern request for a song is *Abair amhran*. This is translated in English as "say a song" . . .'[31] The phenomenon has parallels in the South Uist tradition. Leaving aside the obvious parallel to be drawn from the phrase 'get the song out of the tune' as Jessie MacAulay noted above, which I believe is more relevant nowadays to the English-language rhetoric of mainstream usage, my conversations with pipers in Uist afforded the opportunity to record Gaelic grammatical constructions and inferences which I have rarely encountered elsewhere, in living usage or in print. Most striking perhaps were the expressions offered by Neil MacDonald of Garryhellie in our discussions in 1998. I asked him, at one point, if he felt the Gaelic language influenced a piper's performance style:

> JD: *Carson a tha difir ann am pìobair le Gàidhlig is pìobair gun Ghàidhlig idir? A bheil difir sam bith idir ann?*
> NM: *Chan eil sian a dh' fhios 'am ach chanainn gun toir iad **barrachd blas**[32] **bhon a' phìobaireachd**. Chan eil mi a' cantail gu bheil dona idir duine sam bith nach **cluichd a' Ghàidhlig** [sic], ach 's ann 'ga h-ionnsachadh – tha thusa ag ionnsachadh pìobaireachd, tha mi smaointinn ma tha Gàidhlig a' tighinn a-staigh . . . car math airson . . . thu 'ga seinn ann an òran Gàidhlig. Agus tha thu 'ga canntaireachd, is tha a' channtaireachd na's fhas' a dhèanamh anns a' Ghàidhlig . . . Mar a tha mi fhìn a' dèanamh a-mach, gu bheil cuideachadh mór ann a bhith **bruidhinn Gàidhlig leis a' phìob**.*[33]
>
> JD: Why is there a difference between a piper who speaks Gaelic and a piper who doesn't? Is there any difference at all?
> NM: I haven't a clue, but I would say that they give **more of an accent from the piping**. I'm not saying that anyone who doesn't **play Gaelic** is necessarily bad, but it's in the learning of it – you're learning piping, I think it is good if Gaelic is involved because you are singing it in the manner of a Gaelic song. And you are chanting it, and the *canntaireachd* is easier to do in Gaelic . . . As I myself see it, it's a big help to be **speaking Gaelic with the pipes**.

The point of view that the Gaelic language is a fundamental property of *canntaireachd* was reinforced, then expanded, by MacDonald's surviving sister and fellow piper, Rona Lightfoot. Rona is today recognised more often as a singer of traditional Gaelic songs than as a piper, but she came of age amidst the same social and musical influences as did Neil and when she emerged, along with her brother, onto the competitive platform of the local Uist games in the 1950s, her reputation as the finest female piper in Scotland quickly spread. When I visited her at her home in Inverness in 1996 she portrayed *canntaireachd* as an act of communication embodying several contexts in turn:

Fhios agad mar a' channtaireachd a th' ann an leabhar a' Phiobaireachd Society? ... *Cha dèan mise ceann no casan dheth* ... *Cha ruig mi leas siud. Cumaidh mi canntaireachd agam fhéin. Thuigeadh Aonghus e, thuigeadh mo bhràthair e, thuigeadh a h-uile duine ann an Uibhist e. Thuigeadh a h-uile duine am Barraigh no àite sam bith, ma tha Gàidhlig aca. Tha e mar gun dèanadh tu facal dha* note.[34]

You know how the *canntaireachd* is in the Piobaireachd Society book? ... I can't make head nor tail of it ... I have no need of it. I keep my own *canntaireachd*. [My teacher] Angus [Campbell] would understand it, my brother would understand it, everyone in Uist would undestand it. Everyone in Barra or anywhere else would understand it, so long as they speak Gaelic. It's as if you make a word of the note.

Here, in remarkably succinct terms, is the layered affinity between words and music in the eyes of a performer well-placed to observe, over time, the dynamics of her native tradition. *Canntaireachd*, as an act of communication, is portrayed as first and foremost a personal one, an expression of self; it is then, upon consideration, a familial one, inherited by listening to one's teacher and perhaps father or mother (in Uist, one's first teacher was almost always a parent); its meanings expand radially to encompasses region, a nod to the wider culture and aesthetic parameters from which one first absorbed the tradition; but in the end its provenance – as an act of communication, of piping transmitted vocally – is portrayed as supremely Gaelic.

∼ *Piobairean Smearclait* and other tales ∼

In 1955, Donald John MacDonald recorded a story from his neighbour, Mary Ann MacInnes of Stoneybridge. It concerned a baby in a cradle who would cry all day and all night and would appear not to grow or be satiated no matter how much his mother gave him to eat. A tailor who was busy making clothes in the house suspected that the child was a changeling – a mischievous, shape-shifting fairy – and asked the mother to go out harvesting for the day so that he could deal with the problem alone. While she was away, he took a menacing tone to the noisy child in the cradle and threatened to put a pair of scissors in the little one's throat if he continued to cry. This promptly shut him up, but not for long:

Bha an tàillear ag obair air fuaigheal agus e-fhéin a' gabhail port, agus ann am meadhon gnothaich, có a thogadh a ghuth ach am fear a bh' anns a' chreathail. Thug an tàillear leum a-nùll ga dh' ionnsaigh.

'Feuch a-nis dhuinn pàirt dhe d' cheòl sìthe fhéin,' ars' esan, 'air neo bidh an siosar ud anns a' mhionach agad.'

> *Leis an eagal a ghabh am fear eile roimh'n tàillear, agus fios aige gum marbhadh an tàillear e, thog e pìob a bh' aige anns a' chreathail, agus thòisich e air cluichd. Cha robh duine timcheall nach cuala an ceòl a b' àille 's bu bhinne a chuala cluas riamh; agus cha robh fios aca bho'n t-saoghal có as a bha e tighinn neo có a bha ga chluichd.*

> The tailor was busily sewing and was humming a tune to himself when, all of a sudden, who should raise his voice but the one in the cradle. The tailor leaped over toward him.
>
> 'Try part of your fairy music for us now,' he said, 'or these scissors will be in your throat.'
>
> With the fear he had of the tailor, and knowing that the tailor would kill him, he took a bagpipe he had in the cradle and began to play. There wasn't anyone around who didn't hear the sweetest and most wonderful music that ever reached an ear, and they had no idea where in the world it was coming from or who was playing it.

When the mother returned home that evening, the tailor told her what had happened and advised her to take the changeling to the loch and fling him in. This she did, and when the child hit the water he became a grey-haired old man who swam to the far end and slinked away; she returned to find her own baby safe in the cradle.[35]

Variants of this 'Tailor and the Changeling' story have been collected from as far afield from South Uist as Kintalen and Kirkcudbright,[36] and as it suggests, the predominating theme that characterises Gaelic piping tales is an intervention into human affairs by fairies, or *na sìthichean*. This reflects an association between music and the otherworldly realm of magic in Gaelic folklore. We find it in the tale surrounding '*Dà Làimh 'sa Phìob*' mentioned above, which, like '*Uamh an Òir*' ('the Cave of Gold'), sees a piper descend into a cavern to find treasure and is never heard from again, though to this day one hears him playing his music from underground. We find it in the traditional belief that the *caoineadh* ('keening', or funerary chanting), or its instrumental equivalent on the pipes, originated from the chirping of birds.[37] And we find it in the many tales in which pipe music is a gift bestowed to mortals by the fairies in subterranean hills. The famed MacCrimmon genius, for example, is said to have been given to their progenitor by a fairy as a gift in the form of a magic reed or chanter that carried with it '*Buaidh na Pìobaireachd*', or the 'Gift of Piping'.[38]

Calum Beaton related to me in the autumn of 2000 the provenance of a tune he often played in terms which suggest that such belief is far from dead – at least in Stoneybridge – and which underline the role of vocal chanting as a bridge to the 'other world' in traditional Gaelic cosmology. As Beaton demonstrated for me a set of dance reels he often played for ceilidhs, one in particular caught my ear for its fine melody. '*Port Bean Aonghuis Ruaidh*', or 'Red-haired Angus's Wife's Tune', was so-called because Beaton had learned it from his neighbour as a young man, who in turn, the neighbour claimed, had learned it from a widow (Red-haired Angus's wife) living alone nearby. The woman had claimed with all sincerity to have received the tune in *canntaireachd* from the fairies.[39] Some scholars have hitherto observed that non-lexical vocal music is perceived to function as a communicative bridge between this world and the next in Gaelic folklore; the *caoineadh*'s association with the chirping of birds and the stated connection of '*Port Bean Aonghuis Ruaidh*' to the fairies suggest that such an association between music and magic is still relevant in twentieth-century Hebridean tradition.

Just as MacCrimmon lore eminates from Skye, South Uist too has its indigenous body of tales surrounding a family whose pipe music was bestowed to them by the fairies. These were the Pipers of Smerclate, or *Pìobairean Smearclait*, to whom most sources attribute the name MacIntyre. The name is significant, for it ties the *Smearclait* story to a family who are known to have served as pipers to Clanranald until the beginning of the nineteenth century, as is discussed later in this work. The name MacIntyre was not attributed universally: Uist tradition-bearer Roderick Bowie called them MacRaes – '*Clann 'ic Rath Smearclait, daoine eireachdail foghainnteach sgairteil*'[40] ('the MacRaes of Smerclate, a beautiful, enduring, vigorous people') and Duncan MacDonald of Pininerine, Donald John's father, contended that a family of Johnstones in Loch Carnan were descended from that ilk.[41] Jessie MacAulay, who was herself from Smerclate and who belonged to a MacIntyre piping family, claimed that the folk of that township had their own name for the legendary pipers – *Pìobairean a' Chlaiginn*, or the Pipers of the Skull[42] – which is derived from the name of the hill upon which, according to Smerclate tradition, they lived; and that the pipers themselves may have been a family of MacNeils from Barra:

> JM: *Bha an t-ainm aca a' dol fada is farsaing, fhios agaibh. Tha feadhainn ag ràdh gur e MacNeils a bh' unnta, gur ann à Barraigh a thàinig iad . . . 's gur iad a bha 'Pìobairean a' Chlaiginn'. Chan eil fhios 'am, 's e rud cho sean, chan eil sian a dh' fhios againn an fhìrinn có bh' ann. 'S e 'an Claigeann' cnoc mór far a robh na pìobairean sin a' fuireachd, far a robh an taigh aca – 'Claigeann', a skull, a chanadh iad ris. 'Pìobairean a' Chlaiginn' a chanadh iad riubha. Chan eil 'Pìobairean Smearclait' ceart idir; 's e 'Pìobairean a' Chlaiginn' ann an Smearclait!*
> JD: *Am b' iad MacIntyres?*
> JM: *Chan eil fhios 'am.*[43]
> JM: Their name went far and wide, you know. There are those who say that they were MacNeils, who came from Barra, and that they were the 'Pipers of the

Skull'. I don't know, it's such an old thing, we have no idea who they really were. The 'Skull' is a big hill where those pipers stayed, where their house was – '*Claigeann*', a skull, is what they would call it. 'The Pipers of the Skull' is what they'd call them. 'The Pipers of Smerclate' isn't right at all; it was 'the Pipers of the Skull' in Smerclate!
JD: Were they MacIntyres?
JM: I don't know.

MacAulay's reference to a Barra MacNeil background to the family of lore may be explained on three accounts. It may stem from Smerclate's proximity, as a southern Uist township, to the former island; it may perhaps stem from a confusion arising from the years Robert MacIntyre, formerly piper to Clanranald, spent serving MacNeil of Barra around the turn of the nineteenth century; or it may allude to past intermingling between the two families. The Garrynamonie schoolmaster F.G. Rea noted down a variant of the tale concerning one '*Dòmhnall Ruadh Pìobaire*,' 'Red Donald the Piper', a MacIntyre, whom J.L. Campbell, the editor of Rea's memoirs, described as the great-great-grandfather of a woman living in Rea's time, called Janet MacNeil, of Cathaileith, Smerclate. Mrs MacNeil was born, he claimed, in 1810, putting *Dòmhnall Ruadh*'s day at approximately the end of the seventeenth century.[44]

Jessie MacAulay's testimony notwithstanding, the claims made by Roderick Bowie and Duncan MacDonald have proved exceptions to the legend's more frequent association with MacIntyres. The legend's near-universal association with Clanranald patronage[45] further suggests that it was based on this family, who, the written record indicates, served that function in Uist through the latter half of the eighteenth century, if not earlier.[46] The MacIntyre association was lent further credence when piper Calum Beaton of Stoneybridge declared of the legendary Smerclate family: '*Bha am foghlum os cionn Mhic Cruimein*' ('Their education, or musical instruction, was over and above that of the MacCrimmons'); Somerled MacMillan had stated the same phrase concerning the poet Donald Ruadh MacIntyre's paternal forebears who, in the opinion of the bard, came to Uist from Skye to become archers to Clanranald but who also, according to MacMillan, were excellent pipers.[47]

Through the natural course of oral narrative, about as many versions of their story are on record as there have been tellers of the tale.[48] The most commonly depicted setting is that at some point in the distant past, a father and his three or four sons lived in Smerclate and all were excellent pipers except the youngest boy, who was regarded as something of a simpleton and who, instead of piping, spent his time tending cattle. F.C. Carmichael[49] maintained that the father held 'the farm of Smearclaid' as Clanranald's personal musician, but did not name her sources. The late Archie MacDonald of Garryhellie (*Eairdsidh Raghnaill*), Neil and Rona's father and a prominent local piper in his day, told the story to collector Calum Maclean in 1953 and, unlike Beaton, began by conceding that the MacCrimmons were the most famous of all pipers at the time:

> *Tha naigheachd ri innse air pìobairean Uibhist a' Chinn a Deas. Tha Uibhist a' Chinn a Deas, tha e ainmeil airson phìobairean o chionn ùine mhór. Ach chan eil mi smaoineachadh a's an t-seann aimsir nach robh an t-Eilean Sgitheanach le Clann 'ac Cruimein na b'ainmeile na pìobairean eile bha air an t-saoghal aig an àm. Agus thachair seo an naigheachd a tha mi dol a dh' innis.*
>
> *O chionn ciad no dhà bliadhna bha pìobairean ann an Uibhist a' Chinn a Deas ris an canadh iad Pìobairean Smearclait. Bha an t-athair 's a cheathrar mhac bha iad math air fad go pìobaireachd. Ach bha aon fhear dhe'n cheathrair nach robh cho glic ri càch – cha robh ann ach leth-amadan, agus gu dé bha à ach a' buachailleachd cruidh an latha bh' ann a sheo.*[50]

There's an account to tell about the pipers of Uist's south end. The south end of Uist has been famous for its pipers for a long time. But I don't think in the old days that the MacCrimmons of the Isle of Skye were not more famous than other pipers of the world at the time. And this is how the story goes.

One or two hundred years ago there were pipers in the Uist's south end whom they called the Pipers of Smerclate. The father and his four sons were all good at piping. But there was one of the four who wasn't as clever as the others – he was nothing but a half-wit, and what was he doing but herding cattle on this particular day.

Another tradition-bearer, John Campbell, similarly described the youngest boy as *an gille luideach*,[51] or 'the bumpkin'. According to Duncan MacDonald, the boy's father evidently thought so little of him that he wasn't allowed to go near a chanter, and Donald Ruadh MacIntyre's rendering of the scene agrees:

> *Well a-nis mar a chuala mise, tha mi tuigsinn, bha 'ad uile gu léir 'nam pìobairean matha, Pìobairean Smearclait. Thàinig an gille bha seo dhachaidh an oidhch' ud, gille beag, fear a b' òige dhe'n chloinn. Agus cha robh e 'na phìobaire ro mhath, cha robh móran aig athair ma dheoghainn, cha robh e saoilsinn sian ma dheoghainn idir.*[52]

Well now as I heard it and understand it, they were all good pipers, the Pipers of Smerclate. This boy came home that night, the little boy, the youngest of the children. And he wasn't too good a piper, his father didn't have much regard for him, he didn't think anything of him at all.

While out tending cattle, or walking along the machair, or in some like circumstance, the boy receives the gift of piping from a fairy. This can take several forms: in E.C. Carmichael's account, the boy happens to be romantically involved with a fairy woman and she gives him a magic reed to put in his father's pipes; according to Duncan MacDonald, he encounters a fairy woman with light-coloured clothing and a white chanter – *'aodach liath oirre agus feadan gheal aice'* – who gives him not only the chanter but magic tunes to play on it. In most cases, however, the boy finds a *sìthean*, or fairy hill, with an open door in its lee and unearthly music pouring through. Attracted by the sounds, and investigating, he is confronted by one or more grey-haired old men.

The boy's encounter with the fairy in the hill is a key point in the tale, for here the mythological archetypes converge to symbolise the importance of orality in Gaelic tradition. The fairy must grant the boy a wish before he quits the hill, and of course that wish is to become a good piper. To receive the gift of music, many variants of the tale maintain that the boy must lay his fingers on the fingers of the fairy, and the boy's tongue must touch the fairy's tongue. Calum Beaton described the encounter along similar lines in 1995, asserting that the grey-haired man instructed the boy to put his tongue in the former's mouth and swish it around three times clockwise, or *deiseal*, in order to receive the musical gift.[53] 'The boy,' said Beaton with a smile, 'was understandably hesitant to do this.' Donald MacIntyre named the *sìthean* specifically and portrayed the ritual as involving not fingers, but feet:

> Mar a chuala mise tha sìthean a-muigh ann am mòinteach Smearclait ris an can 'ad Sìthean Mór a' Chreamailein . . . Chaidh an gille beag a-mach an oidhche bh' ann a sheo 's chaidh e chun an t-sìthein 's chual' e an ceòl a b' àille a's an t-sìthean, chual' e ceòl uamhasach fhéin breagha tighinn a-mach as an t-sìthean. Chunnaic e sin seann bhodach, o seann bhodach, sean, sean.
> Dh' fhoighneachd am bodach dheth, 'Dé bha thu 'g iarraidh?'
> 'Ah, Dhia Mhór,' ars [esan] ris, 'chan eil mis' ag iarraidh sìan,' ars esan, 'ach a bhith 'g éisdeachd ris a' cheòl.'
> 'Ciamar a chòrdadh e riut,' ars am bodach, 'nan dèanadh tu fhéin ceòl cho breagha ri sin?'
> 'Ah uill,' ars an gille, 'nach mis' a dhèanadh sin.'
> 'Well ma tà,' ars am bodach, 'cuir,' ars esan, 'snàthad mhór ann am beul an doriais ud thall,' ars esan, 'snàthad.' Chuir a-nis an gille snàthad no bior cruaidh air choireiginn. 'Trobhad,' ars esan, 'trobhad a-nise,' ars am bodach, 'agus cuir do chas,' ars esan, 'air muin mo choise-sa agus cuir do theanga 'nam bheul. Cuir do chas air muin mo choise,' ars esan, 'agus cuir do theanga 'nam bheul. Chan eil an diabhal sìan a chluinneas tu a-staigh ann a shin nach dèan thu fhéin a cheart cho math ris.'
> Rinn an gille sin. Sin ag' a-nis fear a' Phìobairean Smearclait a chuala mise . . . Ma bha e breugach a' tighinn ugam-sa tha e 'cheart cho breugach a' falbh bhuam ach siod mar a chuala mis' e.[54]
> As I heard it there is a fairy hill out on the Smerclate moorland that they call the Big Fairy Hill of the Creamailein . . . the little boy went out this night and he went

to the hill and he heard the most beautiful music in the hill, the most lovely music coming out of it. He saw there an old man, oh an old, old man.

The old man asked him, 'What do you want?'

'Ah, goodness,' he said to him, 'I don't want a thing except to be listening to the music.'

'How would you like it,' said the old man, 'if you yourself could make music as sweet as that?'

'Ah well,' said the boy, 'if only I could.'

'Well then,' said the old man, 'prop open the door there with a big needle,' he said, 'a needle.' Now the boy put a needle or hard point of something there. 'Come here,' he said, 'come here now,' said the old man, 'and put your feet on my feet and your tongue in my mouth. Put your feet on my feet,' he said, 'and your tongue in my mouth. There's nothing you'll hear inside there that you yourself won't make just as good.'

The boy did that. There you have now one of the Pipers of Smerclate that I heard about . . . If it was a lie coming to me, then it's just as much a lie going from me, but that's how I heard it.

The details of the encounter vary slightly with each teller, as is natural in oral narrative, but the symbolism remains constant.[55] The *gille luideach*, gifted now with music from the otherworld and able, as in the case of MacCrimmon lore, to command the emotions of others with his playing,[56] returns home. Fr. Allan McDonald of Eriskay, a pioneer in the collection of folklore in South Uist, noted a variant in which the boy, a Macintyre, returns home at night while his brothers are asleep, takes one brother's set of pipes to the barn and begins to play; woken by such ethereal tones, the brother exclaims *''S e glaodh amhaich mo phìob fhéin a th' ann!'* ('That's the throat's cry of my own pipes!') and the boy's supernatural prowess is revealed.[57]

In most other cases, the homecoming is the scene for what appears to be, if the legend is indeed based on the MacIntyres, a grass-roots comparison between the pipers to Clanranald and the pipers to MacLeod. Most variants of the tale describe a party of MacCrimmons travelling to South Uist to test the MacIntyres' skill, so as to see for themselves if the reputation that Clanranald's Smerclate pipers enjoy is justified. They are usually at the boy's house being entertained by his father when he arrives home. Calum Beaton gave a brief version in 1998 in which the boy instead meets two MacCrimmon pipers on the way back from the *sìthean* and, after assuring them that he is the worst in his family, plays music of mind-bending proportions; Beaton recited the MacCrimmons' response in lyrical, rhythmic Gaelic:

'Ma's tu-sa tha na's miosa, chan eil sinne 'dol na's fhàide.' Agus thàinig iad dhachaidh. Cha deach iad na b' fhàide na sin fhéin . . . Chan eil mi a' creidsinn facal dheth.[58]

'If you are the worst, we're not going any farther.' And they went home. They ventured no farther than that . . . I don't believe a word of it.

If the MacIntyre family first encounter the MacCrimmons at their home, the brothers are out, in many cases kelping on the shore – a detail that possibly dates the tale, or those versions of it, to the late eighteenth or early nineteenth century.[59] The boy offers to play for the esteemed guests until the brothers return, a suggestion at which the father scoffs; however, he has his way and everyone is astounded by his playing. Roderick Bowie illustrated once again the affinity between words and instrumental music in Gaelic tradition by singing words that were heard in the boy's tune, words that are these days sung as a milking song:

Ach co-dhiùbh n' air a thòisich an gille air seinn[60] na pìobadh – sin 's gu do dh' iarr iad air tòiseachadh 's e am port a chuir e air a' phìob:

> *'Till an crodh, far an crodh*
> *Till an crodh Dhòmhnaill*
> *Till an crodh, far an crodh*
> *Till an crodh Dhòmhnaill*
> *'S gheibh thu bean bhòidheach*
> *Till an crodh, far an crodh*
> *Till an crodh Dhòmhnaill*
> *'S gheibh thu bean ghaolach.'*

Bha trì no ceithir a thionndaidhean air . . . Cha chual' iad fhéin a leithid a' cheòl riamh.[61]

But anyway when the boy began to play the pipes – as they'd asked him to begin, this is the tune he put on the pipes:

> 'Bring in the cattle, look after the cattle
> Bring them in Donald
> Bring in the cattle, look after the cattle
> Bring them in Donald
> And you'll get a lovely wife
> Bring in the cattle, look after the cattle
> Bring them in Donald
> And you'll get a loving wife.'

There were three or four turns to it . . . They'd never heard the likes of such music before.

The tale comes to an end with the MacCrimmon pipers mortified by such skill and what it implies if the boy is indeed the worst of the lot; they hurriedly take their leave of the Smerclate pipers' home before the latter have a chance to ask them to play, since it would have been rude to refuse. According to Archie MacDonald's rendering they lost no time:

> 'A bheil thu ràdha,' ors fear dhiubh ris a' bhodach, 'gur e seo am pìobaire as miosa dhe na gillean agad?'
> 'O chan eil a-seo,' ors am bodach, 'ach leth-amadan. Tha na pìobairean cearta, tha iad 'sa chladach. Cluinnidh sibh pìobaireachd n' air a thig iad.'
> 'O ma tha,' ors pìobairean Dhun Bheagain, 'cha bhi sinne na's fhaide a-seo. Latha math leibh.' Is cha do dh'fhuirich iad gu d' thàinig na pìobairean cearta; thug iad an casan leotha . . . Cha robh gin aca a thigeadh suas ris an amadan.[62]

'Are you telling me,' said one of them to the father, 'that this is the worst piper among your sons?'
  'Oh this is nothing,' said the father, 'but a half-wit. The true pipers are on the shore. You'll hear real piping when they come back.'
  'Oh well then,' said the pipers of Dunvegan, 'we'll stay no longer. Good day to you.' And they didn't stick around until the true pipers returned; they quickly made tracks . . . They had nothing that would match the bumpkin.

From the above broad look at the place of piping in South Uist's folktales, the student of Gaelic fairy lore will have immediately recognised the constituent motifs as quite common in wider Highland tradition; E.C. Carmichael described the same basic framework in her treatment of MacCrimmon tales, for instance. As MacAulay's testimony concerning name variations according to locality suggests, the *Pìobairean Smearclait* tale is probably the surviving remnant of a basic storyline whose details were in the past adapted to whatever township it was being told in. One version, for instance, has been collected which is set in Bornish, to the north of Smerclate, and the place-names throughout reflect that area.[63] Whatever else it is – an oral document of past Hebridean patronage, a grass-roots regional variant of a wider archetypal cycle – I believe the *Smearclait* tale is above all a reflection of orality in Gaelic music and its survival into modern times in the South Uist tradition.

~ THE CEILIDH ~

The ceilidh is recognised as Gaelic tradition's trading post of sorts. It means literally a 'visit' or 'gathering' and, until the depression begun by the First World War, served as the primary social occasion when members of a community would meet at a designated house (the *taigh-céilidh*) to pass the winter evenings. In many areas the house would typically alternate through the week. This was the time and place when the songs, dancing and stories thus far illustrated were performed and all present were generally encouraged to contribute what they could within the parameters of traditional performance. They were known to last well into morning, occasionally until four or five a.m., when there was a good story being told or a particularly heated bout of dancing.[64] As is well known, the ceilidh has been largely superseded as evening entertainment in the Hebrides today by discos and the television, or at times by the modern development of a formal, paid-admission 'ceilidh' or '*bàl*' in the local community hall where a band will play Scottish country dance music and be finished by one or two in the morning; a far cry from the spirit of the earlier house-visits.

Folklorists describing Highland ceilidhs over the past hundred and fifty years reveal a cultural institution of remarkable structural consistency through space and time. Storytelling, singing and the playing of instrumental music, invariably for dancing, are always the main features, but the similarity of peripheral activities is equally striking: the initial small-talk and catching up with the latest news; the discussion of current events and politics; the men quietly playing cards or twining rope or fishnets while listening to the story, or the women knitting and sewing as a song is given; it suggests a tacitly formulaic rituality. Not everyone would agree with that conclusion. Canon John Angus MacDonald, in his treatise on the life and songs of Uist bard *Dòmhnall Ailein Dhòmhnaill na Bàn-Fhighiche* (at whose funeral in 1992 Neil MacDonald piped the melody to '*Ceud Fàilt' air Gach Gleann*'), emphasised the spontaneity of South Uist's traditional ceilidh as its defining feature and criticised the frequent depiction of the institution as following a 'fixed ritual'.[65] While I defer to Canon MacDonald insofar as he undoubtedly possesses greater first-hand experience of ceilidhs in traditional Gaelic society over a longer span of time, I believe there are indeed grounds to suggest an unspoken formulaic quality to ceilidhs where the type and breadth of activities are concerned. Canon MacDonald's own reference to the ceilidh as an 'institution', however informal, imbues it with essential parameters within which customs are perpetuated or, indeed, innovated.

Nineteenth-century folklorists waxed typically romantic. Take J.F. Campbell's record of a ceilidh in Barra in 1860, for instance, which depicts the atmosphere surrounding a recitation of Ossianic song-poetry. 'The audience was a numerous one on 10th September,' he writes, 'and we were highly attentive. One woman was industriously weaving in the corner, another was carding wool, and a girl was spinning dexterously with a distaff made of a rough forked birch-branch and a spindle which was little better than a splinter of fir . . . Old men and young lads, newly returned from the eastern fishing, sat about on benches fixed to the wall, and smoked and listened; and MacDonald sat on a low stool in the midst, and chanted forth his lays amidst suitable remarks and ejaculations of praise and sympathy.'⁶⁶ Compare this with Alexander Carmichael's reconstruction of the ceilidhs he had attended in his travels across the West Highland seaboard, which conveys the typical 'formula' over the course of the evening:

> The houseman is twisting twigs of heather into ropes to hold down thatch, a neighbour is twining quicken roots into cords to tie cows, while another is plaiting bent grass into baskets to hold meal. The housewife is spinning, a daughter is carding, another daughter is teazing, while a third daughter, supposed to be working, is away in the background conversing in low whispers with the son of a neighbouring crofter . . . The conversation is general: the local news, the weather, the price of cattle, these leading up to higher themes – the clearing of the glens, the war, the parliament, the effects of the sun upon the earth and the moon upon the tides . . . The stranger [i.e. Carmichael] asks the houseman to tell a story, and after a pause the man complies. The tale is full of incident, action and pathos . . . When the story is ended it is discussed and commented upon, and the different characters praised or blamed according to their merits and the views of the critics . . . If not late, proverbs, riddles, conundrums and songs follow.⁶⁷

Ceilidhs in the Gaelic-speaking emigrant communities in eastern Canada followed the same overall structure, and it is noteworthy how their descriptions bear witness to the cultural connection to the Scottish *Gàidhealtachd* maintained since the years of major emigration. At a gathering in Newfoundland in the late 1960s – a good hundred years or so after Carmichael's and Campbell's accounts – we find that 'the first half hour or so was usually spent in conversation with friends and neighbours, catching up with each other's news or telling amusing anecdotes they had heard since they last met. Before long, and usually with very little persuasion, someone would strike up a tune on one of the musical instruments. In no time at all then, the entertainment would be in full swing.'⁶⁸ Although it may be that instrumental music and dancing were a more prominent feature of this ceilidh than those of the West Highlands in the 1860s (if judging only by the above descriptions), the similarity in the order of events is significant. We see the same in the reminiscences of storytelling in the early twentieth century by Joe Neil MacNeil of Big Pond, Cape Breton, a community founded specifically by emigrants from Barra and South Uist:

> Long tales were most often recited on occasions when people called in at the houses and there was some encouragement . . . It was mostly during the long winter months that people engaged in this kind of activity . . . People didn't come just from one house or two houses for a house-visit; people would come from perhaps three or four houses, and some people would come over a distance as great as three miles . . . People would make small conversation at first, enquiring about happening in the vicinity and whether there was any news . . . [During the ceilidh,] things were going on but nothing was happening that would hinder or

interfere with the storyteller. Perhaps the woman of the house would be knitting socks or mittens; people would be working with knitting needles at the same time and twisting yarn, and the story was in no way interfered with by that.[69]

Personal accounts of the traditional ceilidh in South Uist follow the same tone so far depicted, pointing to a common conservatism among the Cape Breton and Hebridean *Gàidhealtachds* up to at least the first half of the twentieth century. The late Donald John MacDonald, collector, tradition-bearer and native of South Uist, famously depicted the ceilidh scene typical to his community in Pininerine up to about the Second World War in terms which accord considerably with scenes described above:

> *Ann an linn ar n-athraichean, 's gu h-àraid ar seanairean . . . cha robh baile gun a thigh-céilidh fhéin ann, far am biodh seanchas, naidheachdan, òrain is ceòl a' cur seachad na h-oidhche fhada gheamhraidh . . . Measgaichte ris a' chultur Cheilteach seo bhiodh gnìomhachas-làimh nam fear 's nam bàn: na fir a' snìomh fraoich no murain airson caochladh fheumannan agus na mnathan a' snìomh 's a' càrdadh, a' fighe 's a' fuaigheal: ach dèanadach 's gu robh gach fear is té, chumadh iad cluas gheur ri briathran an t-seanchaidh no an òranaiche.*[70]

> In our fathers' time, and especially in our grandfathers' . . . there was not a township without its ceilidh-house, where stories, news, songs and music would pass the long winter night . . . Mixed with the Celtic culture we had were the handicrafts of the men and women: the men spinning heather or grass for the repair of kelp nets and the women spinning, carding wool, knitting and sewing: but busy as each man and woman was, they would keep a sharp ear to the oration of the storyteller or singer.

A comparison between MacDonald's account and Jessie MacAulay's reminisensces of the typical house-visits to have occurred in Smerclate in the 1920s and '30s reveal that, as one might expect, the activities and traditional parameters of the ceilidh were, as one might expect, as broadly similar from township to township within Uist as they were from *Gàidhealtachd* to *Gàidhealtachd*. Such uniformity, however spontaneous in nature, was undoubtedly an essential factor in the transmission of Uist's bardic, narrative and instrumental arts.

JD: *Dé mar a bha céilidhean air oidhche gheamhraidh; an robh [daoine] a' tighinn cruinn?*

JM: *Bha iad a' cruinneachadh ann an aon taigh, fhios agaibh, ma dh' fhaoidte taigh mu seach – an taigh seo a-nochd, is an taigh eile an ath-oidhch' . . . Bha sgeulachdan is naigheachdan is* local gossip, *a h-uile sìan. Cuideachd, tha cuimhn' am fhéin na bodaich a' bruidhinn mu'n Phàrlamaid.* Away in London, you know. Especially the time when they were getting a pension for the first time. There was a lot of discussion. They got a paper a week old, you know, and it gave them a lot of topics ... *Bhiodh iad ag innseadh na sgeulachdan, is rud eile a bh'againn: toimhseachan,* puzzles. That was very popular too.[71]

JD: What were ceilidhs like on a winter night; did [people] come together?

JM: They gathered in one house, you see, perhaps in turns – in this house tonight, and in another house the next night ... There were stories, and news, and local gossip, everything. Away in London, you know. Especially the time when they were getting a pension for the first time. There was a lot of discussion. They got a paper a week old, you know, and it gave them a lot of topics ... They would tell stories, and another thing we had: puzzles. That was very popular too.

Environment has always proved a governing factor over transmission. So long as the ceilidh, piping's chief social context in South Uist up to the early twentieth century, remained in a traditional format in which the older Scotch Reels prevailed, so also would *ceòl cluais* remain a feature of local piping. *Ceòl cluais*, or 'ear-music', is what Uist pipers refer to as music learned and played solely through aural transmission and fundamentally associated with dance; as is discussed later in this work, one was the primary functional context for the other. Jessie MacAulay has mentioned earlier how *puirt-à-beul* would often be sung to provide music for ceilidh-dancing in the early years of the twentieth century when a bagpipe was not at hand; John Shaw has noted a parallel custom within the Cape Breton Gaelic fiddle tradition that was once widespread, pointing out also that '[*puirt-à-beul*] have often served as a device for musical instruction, recalling the earlier *canntaireachd* of the piping schools'.[72] Learning instrumental dance-tunes by the singing of *puirt-à-beul* has also been documented among the ceilidhs of the Newfoundland *Gàidhealtachd*[73] and, according to MacAulay, was a feature of piping transmission in the ceilidhs of her youth in South Uist:

JM: *Bha iad a' cluichd an fheadain, is cluichd na pìoba, is a' gabhail òrain ... Bhiodh iad a' dannsa leis a' phìob ... is puirt-à-beul nuair nach biodh pìob aca; bha iad a' dèanamh dannsa leis an òran ... Bhiodh tu ag ionnsachadh port aig an aon àm.*

JD: *An e sin dòigh a bh' aca airson na puirt a dh' ionnsachadh? Anns a' chéilidh, ag ionnsachadh puirt ùr' air a' phìob?*

JM: *'S e, 's e.*[74]

JM They were playing the chanter, and the pipes, and giving songs. They would dance to the pipes ... and mouth-music if they didn't have pipes; they would dance to the song. You'd be learning a tune at the same time.

JD: Is that a way they had to learn the tunes? In the céilidh, learning new tunes for the pipes?

JM: Yes, it is.

The perpetuation of *ceòl cluais* (what among Cape Breton fiddlers of a certain age would be referred to as *ceòl ceart*, or 'proper' music) was inevitably affected, at least in part, by the decline of the old-world ceilidh and the dances associated with it in South Uist during the era framed between the World Wars. By the time Calum Beaton came of age in the immediate post-Second World War era, the ceilidh was giving way to the *bàl*, or ball, as today's Scottish country-dance gatherings in the church or community hall are referred to in South Uist, an event whose origins go back to the high society of nineteenth-century mainland Britain[75] and which had evidently trickled down to grass-roots Hebridean custom by the mid-twentieth. The change in setting and the decline in the older, indigenous Scotch reels meant that the vocal resource of *puirt-à-beul*, functionally linked to the rhythms of such dances, was much less common as a form of transmission for piping. However, aural transmission itself was apparently as strong as ever as Calum Beaton recalls the playing of older pipers and their influence as a young man:

> *Cha bhithinn a' bodrachadh ris an fheadhainn a bhiodh a' dannsa 'sna bàltaichean [ach] ag èisdeachd ri có bha pìobadh, agus bha thu a' togail, a' togail an time, mar a bha iad-san a' cluichd. Bha beagan do dhifir seach mar a chluinneadh tu gu leòr ann an Glaschu . . . 's ann mar a bha e tighinn nàdar riut fhéin, mar a bha thu a' cluintinn nan seann phìobairean eile, na bu shine na bha thu fhéin, a chluichdeas mar a bha iad an uair ud airson dannsaichean no bàltaichean.*[76]

> I wouldn't bother with those who danced at the balls, [but would be] listening to who was piping, and you would pick up, pick up the time, like the way they were playing. It was a little different from what you'd hear often in Glasgow . . . It was as if it came natural to you, like you would hear the old pipers, older than yourself, who would play as they did then for dances or balls.

All in all, the ceilidh as a social institution is probably what most facilitated the interrelationships we have so far seen making up the Gaelic musical 'Art'. Pipers like Alasdair Boyd sang songs associated with the tunes, not knowing which came first; storytellers like Neil MacDonald of Pininerine sang words conveyed by the very notes of the bagpipe; and Donald Ruadh MacIntyre, piper and poet, told the tale of the fairy's gift in the distant past. The Hebridean ceilidh is certainly not now what it once was, even in Uist, but in its day it contributed to the versatility of Gaelic oral/aural tradition by its very nature as an inclusive social gathering, and as it changed, the nature of local piping – and its transmissive parameters – could not help but change with it. Later chapters explore this development in more detail; but there are other influences holding our attention before then.

CHAPTER 3

'A multitude of papists'
CATHOLICISM AND THE PRESERVATION OF TRADITION IN SOUTH UIST

'Popery is favourable to ceremony; and among ignorant nations, ceremony is the only preservative to tradition.' So wrote Samuel Johnson in 1773.[1] The post-Jacobite era was then just gaining steam: hopes of a Stewart monarchy had become safely unrealistic, political and ecclesiastical action was doing away with the old Highland order, and Gaelic society was renewing itself under the influence of British modernity. Johnson and Boswell had been concerned that under these conditions the old way of life in the Highlands would ere long disappear, and even at that early date their journey often proved their concerns well-founded. Johnson reflected that the few remaining Catholic islands, had they bothered to visit them, would have revealed more of that vanishing world: 'Since Protestantism was extended to the savage parts of Scotland, it has perhaps been one of the chief labours of the ministers to abolish stated observances, because they continued the remembrance of the former religion. We therefore who came to hear old traditions, and see antiquated manners, should probably have found them amongst the Papists.'

In the popular mind, the Catholic faith has a record of incorporating and encouraging indigenous tradition among Gaels (for reasons noble and not so noble), while the Presbyterian faith has come to possess a reputation, spurious or otherwise, for stamping it out from acceptable social behaviour in deference to a more ascetic spirituality. Samuel Johnson understood this; it allowed a grass-roots musical culture to continue in South Uist at a time when many other communities, wholly engaged in the dos-and-don'ts of the evangelical constitution, were compelled to shun such earthly matters. This continuity in turn allowed piping in Uist to flourish and mould itself into a distinct and recognised tradition in the twentieth century. Indeed it *was* distinctive – but only because it was part of a social culture accepted, even celebrated, in Catholic South Uist and eschewed where Presbyterianism ascended.

∾ CATHOLIC BEGINNINGS ∾

South Uist is a predominantly Catholic island, having been so according to local lore 'since the time of St Columba'.[2] This majority overshadows a Protestant presence which makes up about 20 to 25 per cent of the whole. The figure has changed with time: in 1755, the Society in Scotland for the Propagation of Christian Knowledge (SSPCK) received word from their appointed parish minister in South Uist that he 'went to every farm and took as exact a list as we could, and found of popists some scores more than two thousand souls – as for the Protestant Inhabitants I had an exact list of them I had taken in the year 1752, amounting to 165 souls'.[3] The population gap between Catholics and Protestants decreased over time as the island's population increased; by 1837, we find that 'out of a population of 6,890 . . . the number of . . . individuals . . . attending the Established Church [is] 980'.[4] By 1985, 'about 75 to 80 per cent of the population in the island of South Uist . . . belong to the Roman Catholic faith',[5] and this observation has applied since at least the turn of the twentieth century.

South Uist's Catholic majority, and the survival of the faith there in at least a nominal form after the Reformation of 1560, largely reflects the conservatism and traditionalism of the greater Clanranald, of whose territories Uist formed a part until its sale to Gordon of Cluny in 1838. Clanranald has been described as a 'solidly Catholic clan'[6] whose extensive lands along the west coast and islands formed the bedrock of Highland Catholicism in the seventeenth century. They encompassed Moidart, Ardnamurchan, Arisaig, North and South Morar and Knoydart – known collectively as *Na Garbh-Chrìochan*, or the 'Rough Bounds' – as well as the islands of Eigg, Canna and the southern half of the Outer Isles. The harsh and rocky terrain naturally encloses the mainland territory which made access and communication with surrounding lands difficult at that time (hence its name), and this isolation goes some way in explaining the conservativeness of language, social culture and religion found within. This at least was the opinion of Fr Charles MacDonald, a priest who lived and worked in Moidart for thirty years before his death in 1894. 'It is no doubt partly owing to this difficulty of access,' he wrote in his memoirs in the 1880s, 'that the inhabitants of these districts are about the most conservative in the kingdom – conservative in religion, conservative in those old-fashioned notions of loyalty to the crown and of respect for their landlords . . . When the old faith went down under the Revolution which swept over Scotland in the sixteenth century, the changes which were brought about can scarcely be said to have acquired a footing north of the river Shiel.'[7] Because of Clanranald's associations with the old faith, the 'Rough Bounds' were seen as a place of relative safety by priests and travelling missionaries throughout the turbulent seventeenth century, from the Irish Franciscans in the 1620s to the visitations of Bishop Gordon in 1707;[8] it was not until the aftermath of Culloden that the Clanranald line espoused for good, under duress, the Protestant doctrine of the national Church – bringing the days of *Na Garbh-Chrìochan* as a safe harbour to a close.

Clanranald's Catholic associations in Scotland can be traced back to at least 1337, when John, Lord of the Isles, from whose son the clan descended, applied to the Papal Court for permission to marry his kinswoman Amie MacRurie. However, really to explore the Catholicism of Clanranald – and in turn South Uist – we must look to their fundamental connection to Ireland.

The Clanranalds had always maintained close cultural links to the Irish northeast, through, among other things, their relations by marriage to the MacDonells of Antrim[9] and their ties to the O'Cathan family of Derry. In the latter case, Angus Òg MacDonald, Lord of the Isles, had married Àine Ní Cathan of Keenaght, County Derry, in the late thirteenth century. The wedding took place in South Uist. Àine's bridal retinue reportedly consisted of '140 men out of every surname in O'Cathan's territory', all of whom stayed and settled throughout the Highlands and Islands. Their descendants were referred to as *Tochradh Nighean a' Chathanaich*, or 'the Dowry of the Daughter of O'Cathan' and one of the present work's primary informants, Jessie MacAulay, counts herself a descendant of this group through her mother's side.[10]

The Clanranalds' cultural links with Ireland were further maintained in the subject matter of their hereditary bards, the MacMhuirichs, who were themselves descended from an Irish bard who migrated to Kintyre in the thirteenth century. Of all the celebrated bards in Scottish Gaeldom, the MacMhuirichs of Clanranald were uncommonly conservative of Catholic symbolism and Irish tradition. Among their elegies and histories contained in the Red Book of Clanranald, we find a chronology where the age of the world at the birth of Christ ('5,199') is the same as that given in the Irish *Annals of the Four Masters*; a genealogy of the Clanranald line going back to the Lords of the Isles and their descent from Irish nobility; and a storehouse of song-poetry exhibiting all the mythical themes of

Ossianic narrative. The stuff of Irish Gaelic lore – the Finn Cycle, Red Branch, Cuchulainn, Conn and the extension of the *Dal Riada* kingdom from Antrim to Argyll – lived in the repertoire of Clanranald's bards, and this can only be a reflection of their chiefs' own cultural leanings.[11]

Steady traffic between Clanranald's Hebridean territories and the north of Ireland in the sixteenth and seventeenth centuries would have continually renewed these cultural ties and, by extension, the people's attachment to the old faith after the Reformation. Men from Barra, for instance, were making pilgrimages to Croagh Phadruig in Mayo in 1593.[12] Another important crossing occurred in 1649, when Donald, son of Clanranald, set off from South Uist to Ireland at the head of 300 soldiers and gentry, many of whom were Irish, in order to support MacDonell of Antrim and in turn to secure Antrim's help in Scotland against the Covenanters; by then, Clanranald stood alone among the Hebridean chiefs in his resistance to Presbyterian government.[13] Eighteenth-century poet Alasdair MacMhaighstir Alasdair's well-known composition, '*Birlinn Chlann Raghnaill*', depicts a war party shoving off from Loch Eynort, South Uist, for the port of Carrickfergus in Antrim,[14] and this could easily have been based on an actual voyage. The crew in this song-poem made a ritual blessing of their boat and weapons before setting sail. One wonders if the Uist soldiers in 1649 or the Barra pilgrims in 1593 began their journey with a similar sea-prayer, such as this Catholic verse which invokes the Virgin and Christ for a safe return to the bosom of Clanranald:

Oigh chùbhr' na mara,	Perfumed Virgin of the sea,
Thu làn de na gràsan,	Full of graces,
'S an Righ mór-gheal maille riut,	And the great white King by your side,
Beannaicht' thu, beannaicht' thu,	You are blessed, you are blessed,
Beannaicht' thu a' measg nam ban.	You are blessed among women.
O guidh'! mo ghuidhe do Mhac Iosa,	Oh I beseech your Son Jesus,
E bhi mar rium,	He who is with us,
E bhi ri faire,	He who is on the horizon,
E bhi 'gar caithris,	He who watches over us,
E sgaoileadh tharuinn a chochuill bheannaicht	Who spreads over us his blessed mantle
O rà-soluis gu rà-soluis,	From ray of light to ray of light,
O shoills' òg-ghil a' chomhanaich	From the young white light of dawn
Gu soills' òr-buidh' an anamaich,	To the yellow-gold of dusk
'S ré na h-oidhche dùbhra dobhaidh,	And through tempestuous night,
E bhi 'gar còmhnadh,	He who helps us,
E bhi 'gar seòladh,	He who sails us,
E bhi 'gar steòrnadh,	He who guides us,
Le iuil agus glòir nan naoi gathanan gréine,	With the course and glory of the nine rays
Tro mhuir, tro chaol, tro chùmhlait,	Through sea, strait and channel,
Gus an ruig sinn Mùideart,	Till we reach Moidart,
O gus an ruig sinn Mùideart,	Oh till we reach Moidart,
'S deagh Mhac 'ic Ailein.	And the good *Mac 'ic Ailein*.[15]

In the shadow of the Episcopalian–Presbyterian conflicts within the Scottish Church that characterised the whole of the seventeenth century,[16] Ireland contributed in significant ways to the survival of Highland Catholicism, not least in Clanranald's Hebridean lands and particularly in South Uist. The most widely recognised of these efforts was the Franciscan mission to the West Highlands and Isles that began in 1619, lasted twenty-seven years and was reportedly responsible for 10,000 conversions and baptisms by 1633 alone[17] – all the more remarkable for the mere handful of missionaries involved. Following an initial observation of the area, four young priests were approved for the mission and in 1623 were sent off to win back the faithful: Frs Edmund McCann, Patrick Hegarty, Paul O'Neill and Cornelius Ward. We are concerned most with Ward and his travels through Moidart, Eigg, Canna, South Uist and Barra. His reports to Louvain, translated and summarised from Latin, shed a great deal of light on religious life in Clanranald's islands between the Reformation and its counter-movement and the natural predilection of the people toward Catholic ceremony, which was to work so much to the priests' advantage.

Cornelius Ward was in fact *Conchobhar Mac an Bhàird* ('Conor, son of the Bard'), a member of a prominent bardic family from Donegal and a skilled song-poet in his own right. This proved useful in his dealings with the laird of Muckairn when Ward's mission was still in its infancy: Campbell of Calder was notoriously difficult to gain an audience with, and knowing his weakness for flattery, Ward composed a poem in Campbell's honour and sang it in his presence, disguised as an itinerant bard. Ward spent three days in the guise before revealing himself to Campbell and convincing him to adopt Catholicism.[18] Matters were easier in Moidart, where he met Clanranald chief *Iain Mùideartach*. Iain was one of nine Hebridean chiefs who, under pressure from James VI, submitted to the discipline of the Church of Scotland as per the Statutes of Iona in 1609; this proved impossible to enforce, however, and he was happily 'reconciled' to the old faith by Paul O'Neill in 1624, the year before Ward's visit. Iain thereafter became so ardent a protagonist (some would say so skilful a strategist) that in 1626 he wrote to Pope Urban VIII offering to initiate a crusade to subdue all of Scotland in defence of Catholicism. Nothing came of it, but Clanranald made clear in his letter that the Irish were to be considered spiritual, political and military allies.[19]

We can glean from Ward's reports that the folk he encountered in Clanranald's islands retained strong elements of Catholic veneration despite generations of institutional neglect. This was not the fault of the Reformation: 'There were such long vacancies in the sees of Argyll and the Isles,' writes Donaldson, 'that, as we are told in 1529, those born in the more remote islands had not had baptism or other sacrament, not to speak of Christian teaching.'[20] By Ward's time, Eigg had not seen a priest in seventy years, and South Uist not in a hundred. But however blurred in memory and befuddled in pagan superstition they had become,[21] the elements of Catholicism were there. In Eigg, a church dedicated to St Donnan was still standing, though roofless, and in addition the saints Mary and Martin were still venerated. Local people carried their dead sunwise, or *deiseil*, round the church before burying them, and in later years the church was even reputed to be the last resting place of *Raghnall mac Ailein Oig*, 'Ranald son of Young Allan', a Morar chieftain famed as a piper and composer of *ceòl mór*.[22] In Canna, Ward found that St Columba was held in local esteem like 'a second God' and had entered into the realm of oral tradition: he was told that no frog or poisonous animal could exist there since Columba blessed the island, and that a toad which had wandered over from Rum not long afterwards had instantly turned to stone upon the shore. Once word of his travels had got around, Ward was invited to Uist's southern neighbour, Barra, by one of the MacNeill gentry who wished his child baptised – an indication that Catholicism had remained among the island's upper class as well as the lower – and there he found a roofless chapel dedicated to St Barr, a statue inside still venerated, and a grave nearby, which the islanders believed to be the saint's. Throughout these islands Ward continually encountered the remnants of strong Catholic practice which the long lapse in formalities had failed to dispel; coupled with pilgramages to holy sites in Ireland, it was enough to suggest that the old faith had never entirely broken down in this quarter of Clanranald territory.[23]

Ward reached South Uist in late October, 1625:

> From Canna Ward went to South Uist, which he reached at night after a rough crossing; there are no venomous animals there since St. Columba blessed the place; very early in the morning after his arrival Ward set out on his labours, accompanied by one of the leading men on the island; immediately rumour spread that a popish priest had arrived with the intention of winning over the people to his beliefs; as a result, next day, 28 October, a large crowd gathered, some anxious to learn about the faith, some merely curious; Ward was overjoyed; he sent a messenger to the leading men of the island to come and listen to him, and give an example to the people; they agreed to do so, and promised to accept the faith if they found Ward's arguments more convincing than those put forward by the ministers; Ward then preached on some of the fundamental truths of Catholicism; the people were in a dilemma; unless they accepted the faith they would find it difficult to be saved, and yet if they professed it, imprisonment and ruin would be their lot; they could flee to a foreign land and avoid persecution, but it would be impossible to bring their children; the gentry . . . said it was difficult to embrace Catholicism, seeing that no Catholic priest had visited them for about one hundred years, and that there was nobody to instruct the ignorant even if the people decided to become Catholics; Ward answered their objections and promised that he or some other

priest would visit them every year; on that condition, they accepted the faith, and asked for absolution; they said that bad fortune has been their lot since the tenets of the new faith were spread amongst them.[24]

From 30 October to 1 November, Ward claimed to have converted forty-one and baptised twelve out in the open among great crowds, and to have made a further 516 conversions and baptisms in South Uist by January 1626.[25] From his report we can cautiously infer several things: the first regards Ward's claim that, as in Canna, no venomous animals existed on the island 'since St Columba blessed the place'. It is quite possible that Ward was told this by an islander during his stay, perhaps by one of the 'leading men' (probably Clanranald gentry) who accompanied him after his arrival; if so, it suggests a Catholic veneration among the rank and file of the Uist community which had continued, as in Clanranald's other islands, long after formalities lapsed. The second is that, judging by the tone of the report, Ward had found in South Uist an accommodating audience who had gone through the motions of Protestant worship since the Reformation years out of fear of persecution by the Protestant bishop, his ministers and those they influenced. This again is identical to what Ward encountered in Eigg and in Colonsay, where the Bishop of the Isles was active despite the 'Catholic zeal' of Colla Ciotach MacDonald.[26] Third, it would appear that the majority of islanders in South Uist were quite willing to be reconciled back to Catholicism so long as they received some overdue acknowledgement – perhaps even something in the way of protection (though this is conjecture) – from Dublin and Rome.

The connection between Irish Catholicism and the West Highlands and Isles, particular Clanranald territory, can be observed throughout the remainder of the seventeenth century as missionary priests were periodically found at work in South Uist. This often involved great personal risk. Fr Patrick Hegarty, for instance, one of the four original Franciscan missionaries, was conducting mass in South Uist in 1630 when he was arrested by John Leslie, Bishop of the Isles, who had followed him to Uist from Iona earlier that year. Hegarty was rescued, however, by Ranald MacDonald of Benbecula, a 'staunch defender of Catholicism' and uncle and tutor to Donald MacDonald of Clanranald, at the head of thirty armed clansmen.[27] Hegarty was not the only one exposed to hazards. A priest named Donald MacDonald, in all probability a native of the isles, actively preached in and around Uist in 1650 despite having been captured and imprisoned in Edinburgh by Presbyterian authorities some time before. Two Jesuits from Ireland, Patrick O'Kerulan and Richard Arnot, were apprehended at the behest of the Synod of Argyll for conducting mass in South Uist and Barra in 1697. The written record also mentions a 'Mr. Mc O' Ure', a 'lustie bodied black haired young man' whom Allan MacDonald of Clanranald kept at Ormiclate as his resident priest around 1707 and who was complained against in a Synod report. 'Mc O' Ure' may have been an Irish Dominican priest whom Bishop Gordon is known to have translated to South Uist in 1708 following his visitation through the Hebrides.[28]

Anecdotes and tales that have survived in South Uist's oral tradition attest to the dangers faced by priests in those days and the community's sympathy for their work. In Loch a' Phuirt Ruaidh a secluded islet is known to this day as *Eilean an t-Sagairt*, 'the Priest's Island', ever since Fr James Devoyer, an Irish missionary recruited from Paris, hid there from Protestant authorities in the 1680s.[29] Also stemming from that era is a grisly tale of death and comeuppance. A priest on the run in Howmore is caught by a band of soldiers while still wearing the vestments for mass; the soldiers take him to a nearby hill and build a fire, into which his vestments are thrown:

> *A-nis nuair a bha an teine air gabhail suas gu math, dh' fhalbh fear do na saighdearan agus chàirich e a chas air muin culaidh an t-sagairt anns an teine airson agus gun loisgeadh i ceart, ach nuair a dh' fheuch e ri chas a thogail, cha robh rathad no innleachd aige air a gluasad as an àite anns an robh i. Thòisich e air slaodadh a choise cho math sa b' urrainn dha, ach cha tigeadh a chas as a sud, agus bha an teine a sìor-loisgeadh timchioll oirre. Mu dheireadh thòisich a theang' air tighinn a-mach air a bheul leis a' chràdh agus a chas 'ga gualadh. Chaidh càch air fad an sàs ann 'ga shlaodadh ach cha toireadh iad òirleach as a sud e. Mu dheireadh, thàinig a theang' a-mach leis is còrr air a bheul agus leagh a chas suas chun na glùine, gus mu dheireadh an do bhàsaich e agus a chas anns an teine.*
>
> *A-nis bha e na chleachdadh aig an àm ud, nuair a bhiodh tòradh sam bith ann, bhiodhte a' taghadh seann bhoireanach airson tuiream as deidh a ghiùlain. Bha cuid do bhoireanaich a bha ainmeil air tuiream agus bhiodh pàigheadh aig a h-uile té a dhèanadh tuiream air tòradh. Fhuaireadh seann bhoireannach anns an sgìreachd airson tuiream air tòradh an fhir a chaidh a loisgeadh, agus nuair a ghluaiseadh air falbh leis a' ghiùlain, thòisich a' chailleach air tuiream, agus seo an tuiream a bh' aice:*
>
> *'Cnàmhlach dubh air na maidean*
> *Do chas a' dol an giorrad*
> *'S do theang' a' dol am faidead*
> *Loisg thu culaidh an t-sagairt.*
> *Obara bob, adara dad*
> *Obara bob, bob bò i*
> *Cnàmhlach dubh air na maidean*
> *Obara bob, bob bò i.*[30]

Now when the fire was stoked up well, one of the soldiers went and put his leg over the priest's garments in the fire so that it would burn correctly, but when he tried to lift his leg, he had no way to move it from where it was. He started to pull his leg as hard as he could, but it wouldn't come out, and meanwhile the fire was burning all around it. Finally his tongue started to come out of his mouth with the pain of his charring leg. The others all pulled on it but they couldn't bring it out one inch. Finally, the rest of his tongue came out of his mouth and his leg melted up to the knee, till at last he died with his leg still in the fire.

Now as was customary at that time, when any burial took place, an old woman would be chosen to keen behind the procession. Several women were well-known for keening and anyone who would keen for a burial would be paid. An old woman from the area was got for the keening of the man who was burned, and when he was moved along with the procession, the old woman began to keen, and this is what she sang:

'Blackened skeleton on the firewood
Your leg getting shorter
And your tongue getting longer
You burned the vestments of the priest.
Obara bob, adara dad
Obara bob, bob bò i
Blackened skeleton on the firewood
Obara bob bob bò i.'

All in all, the reports of the Irish Franciscan mission and the character of certain local tales to have survived since that time suggest that elements of, and sympathy for, the Catholic faith were preserved in South Uist despite the breakdown of formalities in the sixteenth century. This was most likely to do with the island's geographic isolation and a cultural conservatism that was both local and reflective of the wider Clanranald territories; looking back, one must also conclude that Ireland's efforts toward the reintroduction of Catholicism in the Hebrides were equally important, and facilitated in no small way by the Irish north-east's linguistic and cultural ties to Clanranald.

~ PROTESTANT INROADS ~

After the upheaval of 1560, the Church of Scotland Reformed made what progress it could in the vast *Gàidhealtachd* of the period only by distributing resources, ministers and readers as widely as possible, and by directing most available funds toward that end at the expense of ministerial salaries.[31] So South Uist saw Protestant clergy in the late 1500s probably as rarely as they had Catholic clergy in the early 1500s; the Church was simply stretched too thin, especially considering their efforts to match the few Gaelic-speaking ministers with the many Gaelic-speaking regions. By the time of the Irish Franciscan counter-Reformation in the 1620s, Thomas Knox was Bishop of the Isles and, under his administration, nineteen ministers in all served the entire western seaboard. One of these was Ranald MacDonald, a native of the Hebrides and in charge of South Uist and probably Barra when Fr Ward arrived in 1625. MacDonald is conspicuous in local history for having been the first Calvinist minister *and* the first secular Catholic priest to reside in South Uist since the Reformation. Ward persuaded him to convert and train for the priesthood in January, 1626; he accompanied Ward back to Ireland and thence to Belgium, where he trained at the college in Louvain and was back in Uist at work for the old faith by c. 1631.[32]

Protestantism today owes its presence in South Uist mainly to the work of the Society in Scotland for the Propagation of Christian Knowledge (SSPCK), a Protestant body directed by their Majesties' Letters Patent in 1710 to 'erect and maintain schools in such places in Scotland, Especially the Highlands and Islands, as shall be found to need them most'.[33] If the track record of the previous century was any consideration, they must have felt South Uist to be in dire need. Three Catholic schools were already up and running in South Uist and Barra under Allan MacDonald of Clanranald's patronage around 1707, one of them in his own Ormiclate stronghold, and the SSPCK's committee records indicate that at least two 'popish schools' were still in operation in 1727.[34]

The first SSPCK school in South Uist was set up in March 1726, when Norman MacLeod was sent there to be certified and set to work as its headmaster.[35] Four years earlier, committee records show both an acknowledgement of Uist's Catholic majority and a petition (most likely coming from the Long Island presbytery, not Uist itself) for a Protestant school on the island: '4 January 1722 – The Committee reported that they had considered the petition of the presbytery of Zetland representing the need of a school in Fair Isle, and found that there are many other petitions for schools lying before them, particularly . . . for one in the Island of Southuist [sic] where the people are generally popish.'[36] But the prospect of an SSPCK school in South Uist languished in bureaucracy until 1725. In that year, the records show evidence of Protestant activity in Clanranald's Hebridean lands in which, as the Synod of Argyll stated, 'priests doe normally reside'.[37] This activity was undoubtedly to combat the 'discouragement that Protestants do meet with therein' by a 'multitude of papists' such as was found in the parishes of 'Kilmanivaig and Southuist'.[38] Four months before Norman MacLeod's departure to Uist,

> The Committee, having searched the Registers and considered the report of the Societies Correspondents as to the condition of their schools... shewed that they had ordered John Young [who had desired to be transported in respect of some Grievances] to succeed [Arthur Gregory of Corgraph] with his former Salary, and

they were of Opinion that Mr. Gregory's salary should be divided into two, one hundred pounds thereof to be given to a Schoolmaster in Southuist, and that the other one hundred pounds should be allowed for an itinerant school to the four isles of Egg, Roum, Mucka, and Cana, and that they had written to the presbyteries of Long Island and Skye to look out for and certifie fit persons to be Schoolmasters in those parts.[39]

The Protestant minority fostered by schools in South Uist such as MacLeod's were by no means silent and ineffectual in the eighteenth and nineteenth centuries. They had Scottish law and government behind them, after all, at least until the anti-sectarian Act of 1829.[40] The late folklorist and historian J. L. Campbell has written of the 'tight little oligarchy' – including the parish minister and exluding all Catholics – that managed community affairs during the land controversy of the late nineteenth century; he has also written of Daliburgh's school board as being systematically pro-Protestant and anti-Catholic in electoral and curricular matters until Fr Allan McDonald's election to the board and Bishop Angus MacDonald's entreaties to the Crofters' Commission in the 1880s.[41] Possibly the most destructive instance of religious influence in South Uist, from either faith, was the zeal of Colin MacDonald of Boisdale, cousin of Ranald MacDonald of Clanranald and co-owner of the island, who was brought up a Catholic but converted to Presbyterianism as an adult. Boisdale thereafter believed that his Catholic tenantry should follow his example, and persecuted them to such a brutal degree as resulted in Uist's first large wave of emigration to the New World in 1772.

Today Protestants exist in friendly relations with their Catholic neighbours, with an estimated 10 per cent of the main parish of Daliburgh attending the Church of Scotland.[42] In Benbecula the mix is more balanced, as was demonstrated in 1898 when twenty-four by thirty-two yards were added to the Nunton burial ground; when completed, a large group met at the site and neatly divided it into two equal parts – half for Catholics, half for Protestants.[43]

～ TRADITION PRESERVED ～

To the popular mind, the classic Protestant approach toward Hebridean folk culture is discernible in Martin Martin's impression of South Uist in 1695: 'The people residing here in summer say they sometimes hear a loud noise in the air like men speaking. I inquired if their priest had preached or argued against this superstitious custom. They told me he knew better things, and would not be guilty of dissuading men from doing their duty, which they doubted not he judged this to be . . . The Protestant minister hath often endeavoured to undeceive them, but in vain, because of an implicit faith they have in their priest; and when the topics of persuasion, though never so urgent, come from one they believe to be a heretic there is little hope of success.'[44] Perhaps the priest mentioned was O' Kerulan or Arnot, the Irish jesuits hunted by the Synod of Argyll in 1697. The SSPCK had more success in St Kilda in 1710, when we find that their schoolmaster, Alexander Buchan, claimed to have taken 'no small pains and trouble' to eradicate 'the pagan and popish superstitious customs so much yet in use among that people'.[45]

Their motive, of course, was a belief that the 'idolatry' inherent in Catholic or pagan symbolism detracted from a proper focus on Christian worship; anyone familiar with the First Commandment will understand the Protestants' reasoning. The approach of priests to this issue, however, was profoundly different. Instead of suppressing pagan customs in favour of a solidly ecclesiastical gamut – wiping the slate clean, as it were – they strove to incorporate these beliefs into an overtly Christian framework, thereby leaving something of the core of indigenous tradition intact. Looking back on seventeenth-century observations and missionary reports, one is led to wonder if their efforts were really for the sake of the eternal soul or merely to steer as many away from the reformed faith as possible, as if to fill a nominal quota of conversion at the expense of more substantial Christian persuasion. Consider, for instance, Martin's record of a priest's visit to Eigg:

> In the village on the south coast of this isle there is a well, called St. Katherine's well; the natives have it in great esteem, and believe it to be a Catholicon for diseases. They told me that it had been such ever since it was consecrated by one Father Hugh, a Popish priest, in the following manner: he obliged all the inhabitants to come to this well, and then employed them to bring together a great heap of stones at the head of the spring, by way of penance. This being done, he said mass at the well, and then consecrated it; he gave each of the inhabitants a piece of wax candle, which they lighted, and all of them made the dessil, of going round the well sunways, the priest leading them.[46]

The priest is said to have bade them repeat this ceremony every 15th April, and Dressler[47] has suggested that this was to undermine, in effect to replace, the islanders' hitherto usual custom of venerating a saint uncanonised by Rome (likely Donnan, Martin or Mary) every 17th April. This sort of thing undoubtedly took place in South Uist, where certain hymns and incantations collected among the folk by Carmichael in the nineteenth century indicate a like-minded incorporation of pagan rituality. Alexander MacBain, giving a paper on this material to the Gaelic Society of Inverness in 1890, observed that 'what is religious passes imperceptibly into what is purely superstitious, especially if the culture of the people is not high. Superstition is nearly all a survival of Paganism into Christian times; and in the incantations the names of Christ, his apostles, and the Virgin Mary took those of the old heathen gods.'[48] Many such verses survived into the twentieth century through local oral tradition; one in particular, collected in the 1950s, was invoked when smothering a fire before bed each night:

Smàlaidh mise nochd an teine	Tonight I smoor the fire
Mar a smàlas mac Muire	As does the son of Mary
Gu ma slàn an taigh 's an teine	Bless the house and the fire
Gu ma slàn a' chuideachd uile.	Bless all the people.
Mac Dé a dh' innseadh	The son of God who would tell
Aingeal geal a labhras	The white angel who speaks
Aingeal an doras gach tighe	An angel in the door of each house
Gus an tig an latha geal a-màireach.[49]	Till comes the morn's light.

Cornelius Ward, like Fr Hugh in Eigg, understood perfectly well how the superstitious nature of the folk in Clanranald's islands could be used to aid their reconciliation to Catholicism. We have already seen how Ward encountered such veneration of St Columba in South Uist and Canna to have digressed into superstition; in Barra also, pagan ceremony sat comfortably with Catholic awe. It was said, for instance, that dust from St Barr's grave calmed a storm at sea when thrown on the waters: 'For the sea,' writes Ward, 'as often as it is sprinkled with the dust of the grave of this saint is accustomed, as the inhabitants affirm, to cease from all storm.'[50] A Barra man of upstanding social rank even claimed to have had a vision which led many others to convert when they'd heard of it. He saw three friars, swathed in white and surrounded by light, approaching Barra; two said farewell and drifted elsewhere and the third landed on Barra's shore, where a great throng of people met him, eager to convert. This actually coincided with the meeting of Ward, O'Neill and Brady in Benbecula, upon which O'Neill and Brady left for Skye and Ward made for Barra. When he revisited the island after a further spell in Uist, the same man told him that an old woman had earlier seen two armies approaching Barra in a vision of her own: one clothed in 'shining raiment' and its leader 'more resplendid than the sun', the other clothed in darkness and led by a man of 'fearful countenance'.[51] The islanders interpreted the first army as that of Christ and the other that of Satan, and 116 people were reportedly terrified enough by this vision to have converted *en masse* at Ward's hand. Ward did nothing to dissuade them from a belief in second sight; like Fr Allan McDonald of Eriskay after him,[52] the 'Son of the Bard' probably identified with it culturally and did not think it at odds with Christian teaching. These and other instances when a superstitious belief persuaded many to convert[53] lead one to conclude that, when compared with the reformed ministers of the period, Catholic missionaries in and around South Uist were savvy in the art of conversion, more attuned culturally to the Hebridean way of life and quick to realise how powerful a Christianity made tangible with pagan ceremony could be among the West Highland Gaels. 'For this reason unbelievers are daily attracted to Catholicism,' writes Ward. 'It is impossible to say how great a number of people, for this reason alone, acquire a reverence for Catholic ceremonies.'[54]

The rise of evangelicalism in the early eighteenth century tended to bolster the ranks of secessionists in the Church of Scotland Reformed – those who grew more and more disgruntled with the state's right to nominate ministry, and the moderates' tolerance of it – and this culminated in the Disruption of 1843 when 451 clergy walked out of the General Assembly and established the Church of Scotland Free.[55] These evangelical ministers stressed the zeal of conversion, the godliness of temperance and the fellowship to be found in large revival-like gatherings such as the communion at Cambuslang in 1742. They embraced scholastic Calvinism and saw an over-importance being placed on 'earthly' rather than 'spiritual' matters for their taste; they dismissed moderate ministers as being 'indifferent to the morals of their people and being too tolerant', as Ansdell has observed.[56]

The Free Church became extremely popular in the Protestant Highlands. Their values, if anything, were more inclined toward strict social asceticism than the moderates' ever were, and so the evangelical movement has often been viewed as responsible for the decline of Gaelic oral literature and music in the Highlands and Islands, particularly in Lewis, since the nineteenth century. This is perpetuated in historical scholarship –

> The oral traditions, so carefully fostered by previous generations, were at one time actively discouraged by the Church, and most of them have been lost. Anything that savoured of the past was once frowned upon, and contemptuously referred to as *goraich* [sic], foolishness. In this way, much of the island's heritage of songs, stories, customs and beliefs came to be abandoned. Even the fiddle and the bagpipe had to give way to the *triomb*, Jew's harp.[57]

– as well as in postmodern Gaelic poetry, such as Lewis native Derick Thomson's *Bodaich-Rocais*, or 'Scarecrow', who 'came into the ceilidh-house / a tall, thin, black-haired man / wearing black clothes / . . . A woman was sitting on a stool / singing songs, and he took the goodness out of the music'.[58] Another classic example is Carmichael's introduction to the first published volume of *Carmina Gadelica*, in which he encapsulates his experiences in late nineteenth-century Lewis into a composite sketch. Visiting a Ness household, he asks the lady of the house:

'I suppose there is much fun and rejoicing in your marriages – music, dancing, singing, merry-making of many kinds?'

'Oh indeed no, our weddings are now quiet and becoming, not the foolish things they were in my young days. In my memory, weddings were great events, with singing and piping, dancing and amusements all night through, and generally for two or three nights in succession . . . It is long since we abandoned those foolish ways in Ness, and indeed throughout Lewis. In my young days there was hardly a house in Ness in which there was not one or two who could play the pipe, the fiddle, or the trump.'

'And why were they discontinued?'

'A blessed change came over the place and the people', replied the woman in earnestness, 'and the good men and the good ministers who arose did away with the songs and the stories, the music and the dancing . . . that were perverting the minds and ruining the souls of the people . . . They made the people break and burn their pipes and fiddles.'[59]

However, it would be wrong to conclude that the sort of tyrannical depravity implied in these albeit legitimate examples are typical of the entire Free Church or its principles. John Knox did not utterly condemn dancing, nor were Calvin's teachings ever against music, *per se*; if they were, there would be no tradition of psalmody in Gaelic Presbyterian communities today. Nor, for that matter, would the Lewis Pipe Band have been formed in Stornoway in 1904. In the 1930s, its Pipe Major, Murdo 'Bogey' MacLeod, a barber by profession, was known to whistle marches, strathspeys and reels while stropping the razor in his shop on Point Street, and would time his wrist turns to the progressively quicker tempi of the tunes.[60] Such functional musicality recalls the wider Gaelic tradition of waulking cloth to the beat of progressively quicker songs, or *òrain luaidh*, until the cloth is fulled and dry. These instances remind us that such innate and versatile musicality can be found in one form or another wherever Gaelic culture has thrived, regardless of religious persuasion; music, as the Gael believes, is 'in' you, and it must come out.

The difference in character between the social and musical environments of the southern as opposed to the northern Outer Hebrides may, in the end, refer simply to the strict Calvanist's association of piping with traditional Gaelic social culture – the dance, the ceilidh, the whisky – which he in turn regards as secular excess. Abraham Kuyper captured the essence of this philosophy in a lecture on 'Calvinism and Art' delivered at Princeton in 1898:

As Protestantism in general, but Calvinism more consistently, bridled the tutelage of the church, so also was music emancipated by it, and the way opened to its so splendid modern development. The men who arranged the music of the Psalm for the Calvinistic singing were the brave heroes who cut the strands that bound us to the Cantus firmus, and selected their melodies from the free world of music. To be sure, by doing this, they adopted the people's melodies, but as Douen rightly remarks, only in order that they might return these melodies to the people purified and baptised in Christian seriousness. The choir was abandoned; in the sanctuary the people themselves would sing, and therefore . . . the Calvinistic virtuosi . . . were bound to make the selections from the popular melodies, but with this end in view, viz, that now the people would no longer sing in the saloon or in the street, but in the sanctuary, and thus, in their melodies, cause the seriousness of the heart to triumph over the heat of the lower passions.[61]

Piety, restraint and a turning away from worldliness are the basic aims of Calvinism in the form of the Free Church; the obstacles to these things are anything that can be deemed a worldly excess, such as drinking, dancing, and merry-making in general. The 'people's melodies' are returned 'purified and baptised in Christian seriousness'.[62] Hebridean areas in which this religious climate prevails would find the merry-making that goes on 'in the saloon or in the street' – and by extension the *taigh-céilidh* – contrary to the dignity that comes with the observance of that faith's principles. And in traditional Gaelic social culture, with merry-making comes piping.

The assault on folk culture conveyed by the examples above are rather indicative of extreme lay groups within Free Church communities such as *Na Daoine* or *Na Bodaich* ('The Men' or 'The Elders'), those who take an active hand in preaching the Scriptures but who are not formal ministry; or else of the newly converted, whose fresh zeal had made them 'apt to be intemperate of speech and rash in action', as Carmichael commented.[63] Musical instruments were often the first to be sacrificed, even for those who were avid performers before conversion. This was the case with Donald Munro, blind fiddler and SSPCK catechist in Skye of the early nineteenth century, who never touched his fiddle after being converted.[64] So too with Sinclair Thomson, the 'Shetland Apostle', who until his conversion around 1816 often played the fiddle for dances.[65] It was also the case with John MacDonald of Ferintosh, the 'Apostle of the North' and the 'pet aversion of the old Moderates',[66] an excellent piper in his youth, whose father 'applied the axe to his son's bagpipes after the latter's mind was engaged in "higher matters" '.[67] The common view that the Free Church is based fundamentally on this kind of severe austerity is proof enough of *Na Daoine*'s influence at the grass-roots level of Hebridean Presbyterianism. Donald MacLeod, in his article in *The Realm of Reform*, tried to reconcile the extreme and the ordinary among those who expound the evangelical ideal:

> The human tendency to equate religion with asceticism has sometimes existed within Scottish Calvinism itself. The converted turn their backs on the world, regarding all secular activity as at best a necessary evil, to be abandoned as soon as possible in favour of church and prayer-meeting. There was nothing wrong

with the positive side of such a culture; certainly nothing wrong with a relish for Christian fellowship and a hunger for Christian teaching. What was wrong was that it became a rule for the Order – for example for 'the Men' of the Highlands – forbidding involvement in social, cultural, and political activities. Even the man who was over-enthusiastic in his crofting was frowned on as earthy (*talmhaidh*).[68]

From the above, one can imagine how a community given to the natural puritanism of the Free Church, and made more so by the asceticist influence of *Na Daoine*, would have little place for piping – a very 'social' and 'cultural' activity in the *Gàidhealtachd*.

It was a different climate altogether in South Uist. Religious occasions were a time not for ascetic solemnity, but for earthly jubilation: Carmichael observed during his tours of the southern Long Island that 'the Night of St. Michael is the night of the dance and the song, of the merry-making, of the love-making, and of the love-gifts';[69] Odo Blundell similarly found that in Uist, 'St. Andrew's Day was the beginning of the shinty season, which afforded endless amusement during the winter afternoons, whilst the evenings were enlivened with song and story, the bagpipe and the fiddle, several of which may still be seen in almost every cottage. Little wonder that Catholic Uist should have been a happy home where the ancient ballads survived better than elsewhere.'[70] Even the songs themselves reflected the people's temperament. In *Chan eil mi gun nì air m' aire* or 'I'm not free from thoughts that harass' in J.L. Campbell's transliteration, a waulking song most likely dating from the early eighteenth century, the Virgin Mary's name is invoked in the same breath as a reference to young men dancing at their weddings in the great hall of Ormiclate. In another, God, Mary and Christ are called on to bless a yew tree, and the singer describes her lover, a man named MacKay, as one who 'would dance neatly, nimbly and lively'.[71] There is even a tale collected by Calum Maclean in South Uist in 1959 of a woman with rheumatism whom the local priest cures by bringing out a fiddle and making her dance.[72] All this is a far cry from The Men's pious restraint; it testifies to a people who fundamentally associate Catholicism with Gaelic music and festivity.

Of course, there were always exceptions. Catholic Mary of Guise, for example, made the first attempt in Scotland to ban May-day or Beltane traditions, and other instances since then are known in Ireland and Cape Breton.[73] As for the Protestant church – 'Religion can never be divorced from the culture in which it takes root',[74] and accordingly we find instances of Protestantism looking kindly on pipe music in the *Gàidhealtachd*. Historically, this was widely accepted and by no means unheard of; tolerance of folk culture was just one of the faults the evangelicals found with moderates before the Disruption. Joseph MacDonald, author of *A Compleat Theory of the Scots Highland Bagpipe* (c. 1760), was the son of a moderate minister, and his brother Patrick, also a minister, played the fiddle all his life. More recently, in South Uist itself, the South End Piping Club was founded in Daliburgh in 1989 by a committee that included both the resident Catholic priest, Fr Roderick MacAulay, and the Church of Scotland minister, a Rev. Elliot. When asked why this minister in particular lent a hand in encouraging local piping, Club official Neil Johnstone simply replied that they were both aware that such matters as music and piping in the area were in a state of decline[75] – revealing a sympathy for local culture and an understanding of what the community finds important. Even in evangelicalism the lines can sometimes be blurred. This was the case with the aforementioned John MacDonald of Ferintosh, a fervent Presbyterian who had been an avid piper before conversion. The Rev. John Kennedy reveals a rare sympathy to Gaelic folk culture among evangelicals by means of a metaphor surrounding MacDonald's preaching:

> Duin' an Toir, as James MacKay of Proncy in Dornoch was called, was once giving an account of how he got on at Tain Communion . . . The season might be spoken of as a feill or feast. So might also a fair or market be described, and at these old markets there used to be piping and dancing. James said, 'Chaidh mi gu Baile-Dhubhthaich do'n fheill agus nuair a ràinig mi bha Ian a' pìobaireachd, is cha b'fhada nach robh mi fhìn anns an ruidhle.' ('I went to Tain to the fair, and when I reached it John was piping, and it was not long until I was in the reel.') When he reached Tain Dr. MacDonald was preaching, and he was not long a hearer until his heart was dancing to the music of the good news he was hearing. So our old worthies could shroud their meaning in a cloak of figures.[76]

So it would appear that in this case at least, Calvinism could not entirely divorce itself from the grass roots of Gaelic social culture.

With South Uist's association between Catholicism and indigenous Gaelic tradition in mind, it comes as no surprise that certain members of the clergy in Uist have encouraged piping out of a sense of community interest. This is almost certainly what Fr Roderick MacAulay had in mind when he helped to establish the South End Piping Club in 1989. In addition, Fr (later Canon) Alexander MacDougall, a piper himself, was a central figure in the founding of both the Highland games and the South Uist Piping Society in the beginning years of this century, as is discussed in greater detail in later chapters. Although his actions in hindsight betray an improver mentality, they nonetheless reflect the Catholic record of encouraging local tradition.[77] Others notable for their involvement in the indigenous arts include Fr Angus MacRae of Ardkenneth, who like MacDougall helped found the South Uist Highland games in Ardvachar in 1898; Fr MacIntosh, parish priest of Bornish, a member of the South Uist games committee around the year 1911; and Fr MacKellaig, parish priest of Bornish in the 1950s, who was a piper and founding member of the Bornish Pipe Band.

Perhaps the most noted of Uist's Catholic clergy in the encouragement of indigenous tradition, including piping, was Fr Allan McDonald (1859–1905). Resident of Daliburgh parish initially, latterly of Eriskay, and a contemporary of Fr MacDougall, *Maighstir Ailein* (or 'Father Allan' as he was known) was intensely interested in Uist's oral folklore and aided many scholars with their own studies of local traditions during his lifetime. His own pursuits in collecting and preserving the culture around him are widely acknowledged. It is said that he was first introduced to Uist's folklore by Fr Alexander Campbell (1820–93), who was formerly parish priest of Bornish but by the time of Fr Allan's arrival was retired and living in Daliburgh. Campbell was particularly helpful in introducing Fr Allan to local traditions and was listed among the latter's informants for his *Gaelic Words and Expressions from South Uist and Eriskay*.[78] Fr Allan's fondness for bagpipe music was well known. The Garrynamonie schoolmaster, F.G. Rea, wrote in his memoirs how the priest's 'eyes lighted up at the music of a strathspey, and, at a pibroch, his rugged weather-beaten countenance became suffused with colour and he drew himself up to his full six feet height at its warlike strains'.[79] His feelings as such reflected an abiding appreciation of Gaelic oral tradition as a whole, and nowhere is this more aptly demonstrated than in the Gaelic poetry which he himself composed:

Pìob 'ga spreigeadh, binn a feud leam,	Bagpipe inciting, sweet its whistle to me,
Is cha b'e sgread na fidhle;	It wasn't the screech of the fiddle;
Cridhe toirt breab as, 's e 'ga freagairt	Heart marking the beat, as it answers
Ann am beadradh inntinn.	By toying with the mind.
Air an fheasgair bhiodh na fleasgaich	In the evening the young would be
Ag comh-fhreagairt tìm dhi:	Keeping time to it:
Leam bu ghasda bhith 'nam faisge	As for me, it was fine just to be near
Dol ar teas an righlidh.[80]	Basking in the heat of the reel.

All in all, I believe it to be evident that religion has played an influential role in the nature of piping in South Uist, and certainly throughout the greater Hebrides. Different attitudes toward Gaelic social and musical culture that reflect distinct denominations of Christianity have fostered varying climates of tolerance. We have seen how Catholicism has survived in South Uist despite the neglect that characterised the sixteenth century and the founding of the evangelical Free Church in 1843; how, among Free Church communities, the severe asceticism of groups such as *Na Daoine* compounded the already restrictive social mores of the Calvinist ideal; and how Catholic clergy, in contrast, have acted with benevolence and encouragement toward South Uist's oral tradition in general, and piping tradition in particular.

CHAPTER 4

'We followed the old pipe-playing in the new country'
FROM SOUTH UIST TO THE NEW WORLD, 1772–1923

Emigration from South Uist in some form or another has been a constant theme in the island's history for over two hundred years. This has to do mainly with social, economic and agricultural conditions which men and women of each successive generation have either endured or escaped according to their means or inclination. Leaving can of course take several forms, the three most common, historically, being seasonal or permanent migration to the Lowlands in search of employment, joining the military and emigration to Canada.[1] The first of these has been an accepted facet of Uist life ever since the famine years of the 1840s,[2] and is a road travelled by a number of South Uist's well-known competitive pipers in the twentieth century, such as Rona Lightfoot, Willie Morrison, Ronald and Fred Morrison Sr, *Seonaidh* and *Ruairidh Roidein* and Calum Johnston, or *Calum Aonghuis Chaluim*. These pipers are discussed in greater detail elsewhere, as is the military's contribution. The task currently before us is to describe, albeit in broad terms, the emigration of local pipers to the Gaelic communities of Canada and to assess, to the extent that evidence allows, the impact of this on the home tradition.

Through the eighteenth century, the traditional Highland economy was gradually shifting from land-based to commercial-based. Writers have often attributed this to the latter half of the century as a reaction of landowners to the downfall of the clan system after the 1745 Jacobite rebellion.[3] In fact, commercialisation began as early as the 1730s with the introduction of kelp manufacture to the Western Isles, although to be fair, it was indeed the latter half of the century before kelping became notably renumerative. The industry rose on the west coast and islands as a product that was cheap to produce, renewable and easy to transport once prepared; these conditions, combined with a growing demand in the south and government sanctions against foreign substitutes until 1815, made the western Highlands and Islands the primary British source at the time. South Uist alone produced, on average, almost half the output of the entire west coast region by the end of the century.[4]

Hitherto, the economic basis of the Highland social order had been mainly subsistence agriculture complemented by the rearing and sale of cattle. Highland cattle were to become the main source of beef on the British market in the eighteenth century, so drovers would usually buy at least one or two cows per year from most tenants who owned livestock, part of the revenue from which tenants would use to supplement their crops' output. In this way, livestock was considered the 'principal wealth of the people'[5] until landowners' changing economic priorities forced their tenantry, by and large, to restrict pasturage and neglect animal husbandry in favour of the vastly more profitable kelp manufacture. The difference in returns was enormous. Towards the end of the eighteenth century, smallholders in South Uist and Benbecula were selling 450 to 480 head of cattle annually at £2.10s each in favourable conditions; compared with 1,100 tons of kelp sold annually from Uist around the same time at approximately £10 per ton,[6] the incentive to channel time and energy to the latter was clear – to the laird at least, to whom most of the proceeds went.

Scotland's union with England in 1707 started, for the Highlands, what the aftermath of the Forty-Five was merely to intensify: integration with the British money-based economy and commercialisation through agrarian improvement. These improvements began with the introduction of such crops as clover, rye-grass, turnips and potatoes upon arable Highland farms in the mid-eighteenth century, which was likely influenced by Lowland practice.[7] Improvements in crops and tilling procedures did not reach South Uist until the early nineteenth century, at which point they were a remarkable success.[8] However, improvement schemes were largely met, both in Uist and throughout the Highlands, with protest by tenantry because of a perceived threat to their way of life and, more specifically, a threat to their financial well-being; improvements on estate property generally meant a proportionate increase in rent, which in itself accounted for considerable discontent.[9] Under these conditions, the rigid class structure of a Highland estate allowed little if any social mobility: when a tenant's claim on land, no matter how ancient his family's occupancy, was merely tacit, the incentive to improve the land was lukewarm at best.

Economic instability south of the Highlands was also a source of unrest among tenantry and tacksmen alike. This is because some essentials of the Highland diet and livelihood were dependent on Lowland industry, and were therefore vulnerable to Lowland industrial depression. Meal, for instance, was imported to the Hebrides from Glasgow about four months of every year, to be consumed almost exclusively during that time; a cutback due to depression in the Central Belt would therefore have serious consequences for health and stability in the Highland areas relying on such essential imports.[10]

These factors represent the first half of the 'push–pull' argument, which maintains that emigration during the latter eighteenth century was primarily caused by general dissatisfaction among tacksmen and tenantry with radical improvement schemes and internal economic instability, combined with the lure of better opportunities overseas. The end of the Seven Years War in 1763 brought many former officers, often Highlanders, to settle lands that had been granted them by the Crown in return for service,[11] and the letters that they and other recent emigrants sent home to family and friends made glowing representations of life in Lower Canada and Upper America. In the midst of domestic hardship and economic upheaval, many Highlanders saw life in the New World as an escape, where there was said at the time to be no taxation, no landowners, no improvement schemes and high wages.[12] The end of the war also brought opportunities for labour in North America, preceding the American War of Independence, which cultivated an attactive environment for the out-of-work in Scotland.

Emigrations during this period, in the perception of those who braved new shores, were likely to have been the better of two unpalatable choices: to stay or to go. Until the end of the Napoleonic Wars in 1815, the landed class took the opposite view. The popular theory among most landowners and government officials in the late eighteenth century was that a higher population meant greater economic potential and a stronger military foundation.[13] There was also the view that Scotland would be losing a useful and industrious class of society; that is, there was a fear of labour shortage during a time of employment plenty.[14] After all, the kelping industry was taking off at that point and the returns of kelp manufacture, combined with rentals, constituted the principal sources of income to landowners by the turn of the century. The economic pressures on landowners at this time, and the domino-effect pressure on their tenants, would therefore have been enormous.

The sentiment of government and landowners was reflected in various attempts to discourage emigration indirectly, since an outright ban was never legally justifiable. The most official of these attempts was the Ships Passenger Act of 1803, which, under the guise of regulating dietary and medical provisions aboard transatlantic vessels, was designed to make emigration more troublesome and expensive than the alternative of staying at home. In addition to and preceding the Act, restrictions and regulations of land grants were conceived in 1774, though this was also partly due to instances of previous grantees making 'delusive proposals of encouragement' to prospective emigrants.[15] Both Clanranald and Lord MacDonald of Sleat, who held sway over North Uist, tried using legal loopholes to discourage emigration around the turn of the century. Clanranald himself – that is, the young Reginald George, whose father John had died in 1794 – approached the Judge Admiral in Edinburgh to issue warrants for the arrest of any man in South Uist caught trying to leave whose lease and contract for kelp manufacture were as yet unexpired.[16]

This sentiment was not to last. The year 1815 marked the end of the first era of emigration and the beginning of the second for one significant reason: the economic and industrial situation in post-Napoleonic Wars Britain had degraded sharply. Kelping, for instance, was no longer as remunerative as it once was, since cheaper materials were secured by government from abroad when trade was opened upon peacetime.[17] South Uist was unique in the early few decades of the nineteenth century for continuing to produce kelp in spite of losses in order to fend off rent arrears as long as possible, but this could not last forever.[18] Landowners were faced with a collapse of their hitherto staple income and a surplus of labour numbering in the thousands. In this new era, no longer were the Gaelic middle class and the larger tenants, in the main, voluntarily acting to preserve their way of life in a more liberal climate; the penniless, the vulnerable and the hungry came to be regarded as a liability, and most lairds began in response to feel emigration to be the only reasonable solution to the problem of a 'redundant population'.[19]

It was under these conditions that Reginald George MacDonald of Clanranald, in severe debt, put up South Uist and Benbecula for sale in 1838. By 1840, these islands, along with Barra, having been put up by the equally debt-ridden General Roderick MacNeil, 40th chief of his clan, were in the hands of Colonel John Gordon of Cluny.

～ MAJOR EMIGRATIONS FROM UIST ～

South Uist produced frequent emigrations to Canada during the period in question, the four most notable being that of the *Alexander* in 1772; 'Cluny's Clearances' between 1847 and 1853; the 'Cathcart Settlers' of 1883 and 1884 who founded a township in Saskatchewan; and those who boarded the *Marloch* in

1922 and 1923 for northern Alberta, occasioned by the Empire Settlement Act. The size of these ventures, and many others, varied considerably, as did the circumstances which prompted them.

The first emigration of note took place in 1772 aboard the *Alexander*. Much has been written about this venture to date,[20] particularly for being the only known Highland transatlantic movement of the late eighteenth century brought about by religious persecution. In this way it was also the only recorded instance of assisted passage for non-indentured emigrants up to the American War of Independence, and this in a period when emigration was systematically discouraged. The entire episode centred around the actions of Colin MacDonald of Boisdale, a cousin of Reginald George, the last of the Clanranalds to hold sway over South Uist. Boisdale was said to have been feared by tacksmen and to have had considerable influence over his chief; he himself held parts of South Uist in tack from his cousin, and received rent from between 250 and 300 families (comprising about a thousand individuals) who resided on his land, most of whom were Roman Catholic. Having been brought up a Catholic himself, Boisdale converted to Presbyterianism as an adult and in 1768 began to harass his tenantry in an attempt to see them converted as well. The trials he is said to have inflicted on his tenants include inviting them to send their children to attend a purpose-formed English-language Protestant school in 1770, at which he forced them to eat meat during Lent 'in contempt of the laws and practice of the Church in that holy season', as Bishop George Hay of Edinburgh put it the following year.[21] Correspondence exchanged by priests and bishops over this matter[22] state that Boisdale also made a practice of threatening local priests with bodily harm and threatening to dispossess his tenants of their land if they did not convert to the Established Church. He is even reported to have beaten one or more smallholders, in sectarian frustration, with an old cane – hence the nickname for Presbyterianism still heard in Uist today: *Creideamh a' Bhata Bhuidhe*, or the 'Religion of the Yellow Stick'.[23]

These things did not go unnoticed by the Scottish Catholic Church. Among the Church leadership, two bishops – the aforementioned Hay, of Edinburgh, and John MacDonald, who oversaw the Highland region – proposed sending the persecuted families to St John's Island (as Prince Edward Island was then known) as a way of establishing a colony for all harried Catholics. The leadership was divided on this point. We have already seen how emigration was opposed by government and landowners in this early period; some clerics argued that publicly espousing an emigration scheme would jeopardise the Church's precarious position, relative to the Protestant Establishment, throughout Scotland. It was agreed that a layman should nominally lead such a venture so as to divert publicity from the Church.

Such a layman was John MacDonald of Glenaladale, a Clanranald tacksman who was known to harbour misgivings toward his superiors' shifting priorities and was therefore a prime example of the Gaelic middle class's situation in the latter eighteenth century as discussed earlier. Educated in Germany by Benedictine monks, Glenaladale was known as *Mac Iain Òig*, being descended from a son of the first *Iain Mùideartach*; he was also staunchly Catholic and Jacobite, which all told made him an excellent candidate for the Church's design. Glenaladale was aware of the economic pressure and agricultural hardship building around him and, like the Church in this instance, saw emigration as a viable solution. In a letter written in March 1772 to Alexander MacDonald of Borrodale, to whom he sold his estate upon leaving for St John's Island, Glenaladale expressed his concerns:

> This with the situation I saw many of my friends whom I loved, like to fall into, and which their Children could not avoid, Unless Some other Path was struck out for them made me wish for a feasible method of leaving the inhospitable Part of the World, which has fallen to our share, along with them . . . Meal is scarce and our Cattle will be lost, and of Small Price under these Circumstances they have No reason to regret it who leave the Highlands.[24]

With the Church's private financial backing, Glenaladale managed to buy lot 36 on St John's Island, consisting of 20,000 acres, from Lord Advocate James Montgomery, who was indifferent to the emigrants' being Catholic.

Not until it came time to sail were the bishops and their disgruntled tacksman certain of the number of people involved in the venture. As mentioned earlier, certain members of the Catholic establishment were critical of the venture, thinking that only half of the people targeted by Boisdale's persecutions would be willing in the end to leave Uist. As it happened, out of 300 families given legal warning by Boisdale, only 36 were prepared to go; of these, 25 were eventually persuaded to stay.[25] Eleven persecuted Catholic families then, comprising about 55 people,[26] sailed from South Uist to settle on Tracadie, St John's Island, sponsored to the sum of £30 per family by the Catholic Church. The actual number of passengers aboard the *Alexander* was 214; the rest was made up of tenants from Barra, Eigg, Moidart and Arisaig, who were prosperous enough not to need financial support and who, instead of being the victims of religious persecution, left Scotland in response to the good things they were hearing about opportunities in the New World.

In response to this exodus of sorts, Boisdale appeared to have curbed his aggressions. Adams and Somerville point out, however, that due to harvest failures and destitution in that year and the next, another fifty families had opted among themselves to leave South Uist by July of 1773.[27] The authors cite no evidence of this, though, nor any of an actual venture.

Looking ahead a few years now, the period of relative peacetime between 1801 and 1803 which fell before the Napoleonic Wars and the Ships Passenger Act saw a surge in the out-movement which the American Revolution had interrupted. In these years, at least 6,803 passengers were recorded as leaving Scotland for the New World; of these, 4,855 were recorded as originating from the Western Highlands and Islands, of whom at least 900 set off directly from South Uist and Barra, while a further 424 were identified only as 'Papists from Scotland' and so suggests the southern Long Island as one source among others.[28] It would be unfair to say that ventures of such size and organisation originating from the Uist area were ten-a-penny in the nineteenth century, but it does appear that such ventures, when they did take place, corresponded roughly to seasons of relative scarcity such as in 1836 and 1843.

The most notorious period of scarcity in the nineteenth century was the Great Highland Famine, which left many of the crofting regions of the Western Highlands destitute and in need of charitable aid for perhaps the longest continuous period in that century, from 1846 to c. 1856. By the time of famine, kelping in South Uist had been discontinued even as a means of fending off rent arrears, while the increasing scarcity at harvest time left cattle in poor physical condition, causing a decline in price already low due to transport difficulties. Consequently the series of crop failures which afflicted many Highland districts, and which produced in South Uist a 'total' potato failure from 1848 to 1850,[29] really left the Uist tenantry with nowhere to turn but the various philanthropic organisations of the Central Belt and the island's proprietor, Colonel John Gordon of Cluny.

In his day, Cluny was one of the wealthiest proprietors in Scotland, if not in Britain, which was due more to his prior experience as a businessman than as a landowner. His motive for acquiring the titles to Barra, South Uist and Benbecula between 1838 and 1840 would seem a mystery, since the Uist estate was still in the aftermath of the 1836–7 crop failure and was certainly never considered an economically robust area. It could be that Cluny was simply looking for an inroad to the social and political circles open not to the wealthy, but to the landed wealthy. Land was, after all, the 'origin of rank' at that time and a prerequisite for further social and political influence.

As regards Cluny's response to the famine crisis, he left an unsavoury record. He was condemned by the Lord Advocate's Office and the Sheriff of Inverness contemporaneously, and by several histories latterly, for his inaction in the face of squalor and rumours of deaths in Barra,[30] and for his lack of concern for the well-being of those he forced to emigrate. However, he seems to have gone to great expense in feeding the hungry on his estate, albeit only when complaints grew loud enough.[31] Furthermore, he seems to have refused assistance from relief organisations in the south until about 1848, a good two seasons into the famine.[32] He was certainly independently wealthy enough to need little if any help in curbing the hunger of his tenantry in the crisis's first years – in a single sale, for instance, Cluny's factor paid over £1,000 to Captain J.R. Pole of the schooner *Enterprise* for 82¼ tons of meal, which speaks volumes about both the severity of the destitution and the Colonel's financial ability to combat it.[33]

Correspondence in 1847 between the Treasury, the Lord Advocate and the Sheriff of Inverness is notable for playing down the severity of destitution in South Uist while at the same time presenting alarming evidence of it. One such letter was written on 30 June by Sir Edward Coffin, of the Treasury, who thought generally ill of the whole clearance process, to Lord Advocate C.E. Trevalyan; it provides some testimony to the lack of resources open to the people, but argues that conditions at the time of writing were, after all, 'acceptable':

> [Some want had been anticipated] in the Long Island, in consequence of the detention of the *Rhadamanthus* on other service, and accordingly sent in the *Lightning* with [?] a small supply of Meal, which I found very acceptable on my arrival at Barra and South Uist. They were certainly ill off there, for a man sent by Dr. Boytan and myself with a message refused money for his trouble, and begged to have meal instead, because he could get none at any price, and we had scarcely anchored in Loch Boisdale when boats came alongside in quest of Meal, the people producing money to pay for it, and men offering 1/- a piece for bisquits, when they found that there would be some delay in the distribution for the meal. Capt. Baynton afterwards informed me, when I met him in Lochmaddy, that he had personally inspected many of the houses in Benbecula, and satisfied himself that the people were without other food than the cockles collected from the beach,[34] and showed signs of suffering from want, which I however did not anywhere perceive, and as the Local Committees had meal in their stores, it must have been chiefly the small part of the population not receiving an allowance from them which felt the temporary scarcity of food . . .
>
> They have at present no food of any kind on the Long Island, except their livestock, fish, and such as is imported from the Depots, or by dealers, the latter in very minute quantities, and at exorbitant prices, or already appropriated by the importers . . . At the same time, making all due allowance for W. Shaw's natural accuity about the condition of the people, I think that he has made rather more outcry than the occasion demanded. He could scarcely have been ignorant of the cause of the temporary interruption of the supply, and . . . it would have been no very extraordinary effort on the part of the gentlemen watching over the state of the people, if, on such an occasion, they had helped us out in a difficulty instead of complaining so loudly, and sent one or two small craft to the Depot for cargoes.[35]

In a memorial to the Home Secretary on 20 June 1849, Cluny finally appealed to the government for assistance in applying 'the remedy of an effectual emigration' to his destitute tenantry, which he described as about half of his population.[36] From that year through to 1851, Cluny forced the emigration of 2,906 individuals from Barra, South Uist and Benbecula to mainland Canada.[37] Many Uist emigrants during the famine years appear to have settled in the London and Williams townships of Ontario, others around Toronto and Hamilton;[38] this may have been because Cape Breton, hitherto the primary destination of Uist emigrants of that century, had been struck with its own potato blight in 1843 and was then no more agriculturally sound than the Western Highlands.[39] Whatever the case, most of these emigrants are recorded in contemporary newspapers and latter-day histories as having absolutely no resource open to them upon arrival in Canada, financial or otherwise, and dependent on the charity of the Ontario and Quebec public for survival.[40] Even a hundred years after the event, tales of Cluny's actions and the violent nature of his evictions and forced passages were being collected among the living memory of the South Uist and Benbecula community.[41] All told, Cluny's emigrations were the most severe in the Hebrides in terms of depopulation: from 1847 to 1853, some 2,906 came from South Uist, Barra and Benbecula under Cluny, while 234 came from North Uist under Lord MacDonald of Sleat; 2,279 came from Tiree and the Ross of Mull under the Duke of Argyll; and 2,337 came from Lewis, a far bigger and more populous island than South Uist, under Matheson.[42]

The next emigration of note took place in two parts, the first in 1883 and the second in the following year. In total, 287 individuals journeyed from townships in both South Uist and Benbecula to the Wapella district of Saskatchewan, Canada, and founded a settlement called 'St. Andrews and Benbecula' about ten miles south-west of Wapella town.

The most complete record of this double venture is a document written and printed in 1921 by James MacKinnon, a son of one of the emigrants, entitled 'The Cathcart Settlers'. This document is immensely valuable in that it gives not just the names (both in traditional Gaelic and in English) of the heads of families, but extensive biographical details as well, including religious affiliation. There is no explicit mention of why Emily Gordon Cathcart, Colonel Gordon's daughter-in-law and the estate's proprietrix at the time, financed this venture, as indeed appears to have been the case. The first man listed among the heads of families in 1883, for instance, a *Dòmhnall mac Dhiarmid* ('Donald son of Dermott'), had surveyed the territory the previous year to assess it 'as Lady Cathcart's agent'. Nor does the author explain really why the emigrants wished to go, for indeed it appears that the move was voluntary. A religious motive of the same type which spurred the 1772 venture can cautiously be ruled out, since both faiths were well represented: out of 287 individuals, 185 were Catholic and 102 Protestant. Occasionally one finds passing references to having been 'cooped up for ages' and having left 'cramped quarters for spacious ones', suggesting overpopulation and too much subdivision of crofting lands. The author also points out 'their decision to leave a place where a poor man has no chance to assert himself, and come for their children's sake, if not their own, to a country where every one has a good fair chance to do so',[43] which suggests a dissatisfaction with contemporary landholding and property policies which, ironically, were to be addressed that same year by the Napier Commission and by the Crofters (Scotland) Act of 1886.

The last major haemorrhage to occur in the South Uist community was in 1923 and 1924, when a total of 489 individuals (291 in the first year, 198 in the following) boarded the *Marloch* for Northern Alberta, Canada, in response to recurring economic and agricultural hardship and the opportunities presented by the Empire Settlement Act of 1922. Like the 1772 *Alexander* venture, South Uist's first bulk emigration, the Alberta venture was an attempt to establish a Catholic colony in the New World.[44] However, what made this venture different from those of the previous century-and-a-half was the outlook of the emigrants themselves. It appears that crofters had become much wiser to the limitations of the land once tenure was secured in the wake of 1886, and this was demonstrated by a pervasive, though not total, optimism among both emigrants and those they left behind on Lochboisdale pier. Some had grown savvy as well as wise, in that several emigrants from Barra and Uist made sure of retaining their crofts at home as insurance in case of failure in Alberta. This occasionally happened, as the late Duncan MacDonald of Pininerine remembered in 1956 concerning emigrants from his township:

> *Anns a' bhliadhna naoi ceud deug 's a trì air fhichead nuair a bha na daoine a' dol a-null gu ruige Ameriga anns an 'emigration scheme', dh' fhalbh Aonghus Mac Ruairidh ic an tàilleir á Peighinn nan Aoireann. 'S e esan an aon fhear a dh' fhalbh anns an 'emigration scheme' á Peighinn nan Aoirean ach Mac Nìll ic Dhòmhnaill ic Iain Òig. Fhad 's a bha Mac Nìll ic Dhòmhnaill ic Iain Òig ann an Ameriga, cha do chuir e bhuaidhe a chroit ann am Peighinn nan Aoireann idir, agus bha a' chroit aige 'ga h-àiteach aig Eachainn Mac Raghaill ic Eachainn. Thill Mac Nìll a-nall á Ameriga bliadhna neo dhà an déigh dha dhol a-null, agus tha e ann am Peighinn nan Aoireann fhathast, a' fuireach leis-fhéin anns an tigh thubhaidh a thog athair nuair thàinig iad do'n bhaile an tòiseach.*[45]

In 1923 when the people were going over to America in the 'emigration scheme', Angus son of Roderick son of the tailor left Pininerine. He was the only man to leave on the 'emigration scheme' from Pininerine except for the Son of Neil son of Donald son of Young John. While the Son of Neil was in America, he didn't rid himself of his croft in Pininerine at all, and it was worked by Hector Son of Ronald son of Hector. The Son of Neil returned from America a year or two after he went over, and he is in Pininerine yet, living on his own in the thatched house his father built when they first came to the township.

∼ OLD PIPE-PLAYING IN THE NEW COUNTRY ∼

But what of pipers? There are plenty of recorded instances of Gaels bringing piping to the New World, both from among the chiefly families and among the rank-and-file of Hebridean ceilidh life. Donald Ruadh MacCrimmon, who, with his brother Iain Dubh, presided over the demise of their family's piping school under the ebbing patronage of MacLeod of Dunvegan by 1770, served as a lieutenant in the British Legion during the American War of Independence, having quit Borreraig for North Carolina some years earlier. He later settled in Nova Scotia before returning in 1790 with hopes, ultimately fruitless, of restoring his family's dynastic institution in Skye.[46] The MacKays of Gairloch, pipers to the MacKenzies, were also not immune to the 'push–pull' economics of the age and the changes then taking place in the Highland social landscape. John MacKay (*Iain Ruadh mac Aonghuis ic Iain Doill ic Ruairidh*), grandson of the celebrated blind piper and bard Iain Dall MacKay, saw the writing on the wall and sailed with his family to Pictou County, Nova Scotia in 1805; there is also some speculation that his brother, also named John, was the unnamed piper who had sailed to Pictou aboard the *Hector* over thirty years earlier.[47] The historian Alexander MacKenzie noted, following an account by an émigré's descendant, a scene prefacing the 1773 voyage of the *Hector* from its point of departure at Lochbroom:

> As they were leaving, a piper came on board who had not paid his passage; the captain ordered him ashore, but the strains of the national instrument affected those on board so much that they pleaded to have him allowed to accompany them, and offered to share their own rations with him in exchange for his music during the passage. Their request was granted, and his performances aided in no small degree to cheer the noble band of pioneers in their long voyage of eleven weeks, in a miserable hulk, across the Atlantic. The pilgrim band kept up their spirits as best they could by song, pipe-music, dancing, wrestling, and other amusements, through the long and painful voyage.[48]

The MacCrimmon and Gairloch MacKay families notwithstanding, most piping to have crossed the Atlantic in the period in question was clearly among the unpatronised rank-and-file of Highland society. Among those who emigrated on the particularly well-documented voyages of 1774 and 1775, for example, six listed their occupation as 'piper'.[49]

Many pipers and piping families were among the emigrant groups who departed from South Uist's shores. The name MacIntyre, for instance, continually appears in the annals and reminiscences of emigrant pipers. As is discussed elsewhere, the hereditary pipers to the Menzies and Clanranald families were traditionally MacIntyres, and legend has it that Robert MacIntyre, piper to Clanranald in the closing years of the eighteenth century, left for America sometime between 1790 and 1804. He reportedly bequeathed the famous Bannockburn Pipes, which his family are said to have possessed for generations, to MacDonald of Kinlochmoidart, in whose possession the naturalist Seton Gordon observed the Pipes in 1930.[50] Similarly, the MacIntyre connection has enmeshed this emigration legend in some way with the fund of *Piobairean Smearclait* tales discussed in an earlier chapter; or so it appears, at any rate, from a Uist anecdote taken down by the parish priest of Eriskay, Fr Allan McDonald (1859–1905) from a local source, who referred to the Smerclate Pipers as emigrants to the New World. In a no-frills, workaday script recognised by many who have valued his work and followed in his scholarly footsteps, Father Allan transcribed the following:

> Neil MacRury of Kilpheder was a sailor. In one of his voyages to America he encountered another Uist man and they both went paddling about the bay in a yacht. They saw a beautiful 3-masted vessel and strange to say they heard the bagpipes played on board. As was natural they sailed toward the vessel and listened with pleasure to the wild music doubly dear so far from home. The piper asked them whence they came. They answered that they came from Uist. He asked if they knew Smerclate. They said they did. 'Did you ever hear of the Pipers of Smerclate?' They told him they had. 'Well,' says he, 'I am of the family. We followed the old pipe-playing in the new country. We have got on well. This vessel is my own and I sail about in it in fare [sic] weather.' He entertained the Uist men hospitably, and they departed realising the old proverb, '*Coinnichidh na daoine, ged nach coinnich a' chruinne*'.[51]

Other MacIntyre pipers appear in the emigrant record. Donald MacIntyre, or *Dòmhnall mac Thormaid* ('Donald son of Norman'), born around 1748, emigrated from South Uist c. 1820 and settled in Boisdale, Cape Breton County; his grandson *Dòmhnall Mór* ('Big Donald') and three great-grandsons were noted pipers. Another Donald MacIntyre is known to have left South Uist in 1826, settling at French Road, Cape Breton, and his descendants were also pipers of note in that area. The French Road MacIntyres have claimed descent from the hereditary pipers to Clanranald, and it has been suggested elsewhere that Donald may have been a son of Duncan MacIntyre, Piper to Clanranald during the 1750s.[52]

The late Jessie MacAulay, née MacIntyre, born into a piping family in Smerclate, described (as detailed elsewhere) her own ancestors' eviction from the Corodal area of South Uist at that time to make room for sheep pasturage. According to her, several other families of MacIntyres, pipers among them, were evicted from this area at the foot of Beinn Mhór in the 1820s to 1840s. While her great-grandfather settled with his wife in Smerclate, others were coerced to emigrate:

> *Chaidh feadhainn dhiubh gu* Nova Scotia *agus thug iad leoth' a' phìob. Agus tha cuimhn' am sgrìobh' a chuir iad gu m' athair anns na,* oh, nineteen-twenties. *Chunnaic iad an t-ainm againn anns a' phàipeir,* Oban Times, *sgrìobh iad aig an am, is chuir iad dealbh [de] phìob agus fear-gille, gille aca a' pìobaireachd.* They sent a photo of the boy, the young man, playing the pipes they had taken with them in the eighteen-forties; eighteen-twenties, thirties, or forties, the middle of the last century. *Tha mi 'smaoineadh gur e* Joe *an t-ainm a bh' air an gille,* Joseph, *no* Donald Joe, *no* Dan *an t-ainm air. Tha e cho fad air falbh.*[53]

> Some of them went to Nova Scotia and took the pipes with them. I remember a letter they sent to my father in the, oh, nineteen-twenties. They saw our name in the paper, the *Oban Times*, and they wrote to us, attaching a photograph of the pipes and a boy, a boy of theirs piping. They sent a photo of the boy, the young man, playing the pipes they had taken with them in the eighteen-forties; eighteen-twenties, thirties, or forties, the middle of the last century. I think the boy's name was Joe, Joseph, or Donald Joe, or Dan. It was so long ago.

MacAulay described her family, based in Smerclate these past 150 years, as having been 'pipers and archers to MacDonald of Clanranald' and as having relations in Boisdale, Cape Breton – both things that could indicate a close connection to the MacIntyre families of 1820 and 1826.

Other pipers from Uist appear on record. According to his descendants in Nova Scotia, a piper named Allan MacCormick emigrated from South Uist to Prince Edward Island sometime before 1808, and moved to Lake Ainslie, Cape Breton, in that year.[54] In addition, three people were recorded as pipers among the Cathcart Settlers on their journey to Saskatchewan. *Dòmhnall a' Bhanca* ('Donald MacDonald of the Bank') of Rudha a' Bhruich, a Protestant, was evidently an important member of his community, for 'in his early days no wedding or entertainment was complete without Donald and his pipes'. *Ruairidh mac Isaic* [sic], or Roderick MacIsaac of Uachdar, a Catholic, was 'a piper of some ability', evidently keeping 'the cares and worries of this vale of tears at a respectable distance'. Donald John, the son of *Raghnall Mór* ('Big Ronald

MacDonald') of Aird, another Catholic, was also a 'fine piper' who 'joined the forces in France during the war in that capacity' and who 'came home . . . with a complete fine Highland costume and an elaborate set of pipes.'[55]

It may interest some to note that piping seems not to have been as well-represented among this emigrant group as was traditional story-telling. Several indications among the biographical details of the heads of families hint at oral narrative skills and a continuance of traditional Gaelic social culture among the group. *Eoghainn beag* (Little Euan) MacKinnon of Eochar, for instance, was 'fond of the old Highland traditions and many a long winter's night he helped to shorten by his entertaining tales of long ago'. Ronald MacPhee, also of Eochar and known locally as *An Gobha Ruadh* ('The Red-Haired Smith'), was described as having a 'vivid imagination' which 'if cultivated by education in his youth would have made him a great romancer, as he could spin yarns by the yard at short notice, and keep it up indefinitely, while frequently the plow shares and the forge would be forgotten and burning as the smith yarned and the farmer listened'. *Raghaill mac Cormaig* (Ronald MacCormick) of Gramisdale was remembered for his 'good, long memory, and his fondness for telling the old Gaelic tales and traditions of his beloved Highlands'; and *Aonghus Dughallach* (Angus MacDougall), also of Gramisdale, had a 'great fund of stories about "ye good olden times" when men performed unbelievable feats in his native land'.[56] These romantic descriptions, written by a first-generation descendant and bearing witness to the dogged continuance of traditional pastimes and performance within the emigrant community, support the view that much emigration had taken place with the expressed intent of preserving old Highland culture in a freer social order.[57]

In 1907, the *Oban Times* reported the emigration to Canada of an E.C. MacRury of South Uist, an 'excellent musician who could play the violin and the bagpipe with grace and taste'. Assertions from many other sources that pipers in Cape Breton could often play the fiddle as well suggest a West Highland and Hebridean origin of the custom of multi-instrumentalism, which the case of MacRury, and others like him, supports.[58]

Passengers on board the *Marloch* in 1923 reportedly entertained themselves with 'concerts, whist parties' and 'dances',[59] among other things, and judging by the reminiscences of elderly pipers concerning the universality of piping in South Uist at that time, the bagpipe was certainly among instruments played to provide music. Piping was reported on Lochboisdale pier as the tug *Dunara Castle* ferried passengers to the main vessel.

How have these emigrations of pipers and piping families affected the home tradition? Realistically, not much. Transatlantic emigration may weaken the local tradition in theory, perhaps in the same way as wartime casualties weakened it during the Great War; a lessening or dispersing of sheer numbers under whose stewardship the tunes, styles and customs are maintained. In practice, however, whatever impact emigration had does not seem to have been widespread, permanent or debilitating to the tradition as a whole, and certainly not to the extent caused by the two World Wars. Emigrant pipers can be counted in individuals or families, not in whole communities. Countless references to the universality of the aural idiom in the early decades of this century, and of the literate throughout, prove the vitality of piping on the island despite emigration overseas.

In the end, we are left with a less tangible but no less real knowledge of the legacy which pipers of Uist or wider Hebridean origin have bestowed, through emigration, on their North American beneficiaries. This legacy has come full circle of late, since many Gaelic emigrant communities in Nova Scotia have been culturally conservative enough to ensure that what we know of traditional dance-piping pre-dating this century comes mainly from research into Cape Breton's inherited piping traditions. The most comprehensive body of such research to have come out in recent years is John Gibson's *Traditional Gaelic Bagpiping, 1745–1945* (1998) and *Old and New World Highland Bagpiping* (2002), both of which examine the history of Highland piping over the last two-and-a-half centuries from the perspective of old-world Gaelic social culture. Gibson offers a distinctly different point of view from that of most other histories. As I have mentioned elsewhere, they tend to deal exclusively with the institutional aspects of piping's modern development; he instead addresses the economic and cultural changes affecting Scottish Gaels in the eighteenth and nineteenth centuries and outlines in turn how this would have affected the indigenous functions and character of their music. The work of Barry Shears, piper-scholar of the Glace Bay area of Cape Breton, has also proved of immense value with regard to the collection and transcription of traditionally ear-learned tunes that were, for generations, staples of the Nova Scotia ceilidh piping repertoire.[60]

There is no doubt that such scholarly efforts to date which have brought the Cape Breton piping tradition to light have led to a growing interest in its repertoire and performance context among pipers in the old country in recent years. A considerable amount of experimentation has been under way from within the mainstream Scottish piping community – led most notably by piper and pipemaker Hamish Moore – in a self-conscious attempt to 'revive' the aural dance-piping style and repertoire of the eighteenth- and nineteenth-century Gaelic emigrant community. Separated by a gulf of time and culture, however, this has involved a significant degree of transformation in the process

– resulting, conversely, in genuine innovations observable in today's Highland piping tradition.[61] These and other examples of modern study and performance[62] show that emigration from South Uist and other Highland areas is not without a positive side; that its legacy to modern piping, at least, is the value with which scholars and performers alike have come to regard the North American *Gàidhealtachd* and all it has yet to teach us of Highland piping's roots.

CHAPTER 5

'We had the gratification of good cheer and excellent piping'
SOUTH UIST AND CLANRANALD, C. 1630–1900

Before moving on to the piping tradition as it developed in the twentieth century, let us look at what available sources can tell us about the island's piping in earlier times. Three areas are discussed that, all told, give a broad picture of the early modern piper in the southern Outer Hebrides: first, the patronage of Clanranald is juxtaposed against that of other chiefs and against other aspects of aristocratic traditionalism. Second, the piper's place in South Uist's (and Clanranald's) martial history, from *Linn nan Creach* to the Seven Years War, is explored. The third and final section offers specific and comparative evidence to depict the uses and functions of piping in South Uist's community life up to the turn of the twentieth century.

The sources used encompass both the oral and the written. Oral sources include the song and story traditions, where either focuses on piping or some other musical aspect of social or aristocratic culture. The song repertoire in the South Uist community is especially rich in references to pipe music. I have also used the recorded testimony of living Uist pipers where they support the above traditions' evidence. A variety of written sources complement and bolster the oral record. Clanranald's family muniments provide glimpses of patronised piping in times of both peace and war; contemporary tourist journals and other personal memoirs give rare observations of community life in the specified time period; competition records, music collections, letters and eighteenth-century government intelligence reports – all help to depict the place of the piper in pre-1900 South Uist.

~ PATRONAGE ~

In the last two chapters we have seen how the spread of strict Presbyterian religious values and the modernisation of economic and agrarian priorities in the eighteenth and nineteenth centuries fundamentally changed a clan chief's perception toward his land and people. This inevitably led to a decline in the old manners of chiefly patronage in the Hebrides, since under such conditions the foundation for aristocratic Gaelic tradition proved highly vulnerable. This was an age in which many contemporary observers were prompted to look upon the future of Highland music with acute pessimism: the Edinburgh-educated diarist John Ramsay of Ochtertyre, for instance, expressed concern in his introduction to Patrick MacDonald's *Highland Vocal Airs* in 1784, and his predictions of catastrophe were typical of popular thinking among the landed élite of the time. 'In less than twenty years it would be in vain to attempt a collection of Highland music,' he wrote. 'Perhaps it is rather late at present; but enough may be got to point out its genius and spirit.'[1] With these words Ramsay perpetuated the seductive point of view that where culture is concerned, with fragility and precariousness comes sublime nobility. Had he bothered to survey for himself the discourse of Gaelic music among its living bearers at the time – as the author of the very work he was prefacing had done – Ramsay might have contributed a more prescient treatise. His prediction was laid to rest in any case by the publication, thirty years later, of two further collections based, like MacDonald's, on the personal search for ethnographic material in the field.[2]

Ramsay made explicit mention of piping, and it is noteworthy that even as early as 1784, the rapidity of social changes had led him to perceive the tradition as deteriorating. 'Though the pipers have survived their brethren, the harpers, almost a century,' he wrote, 'they themselves will, ere long, share the same fate. The present ones are already inferior to their predecessors in knowledge and execution. Nor are they to expect encouragement from their chieftains and gentry, whose manners are formed on a new model: and the spirit of the commons is broken, and directed to objects very different from those of former times.'[3] Modern scholars tend to agree with Ramsay's assessment that the post-Jacobite climate of modernisation and shifting economic priorities threw the *raison d' être* of the classical music into doubt, but recent scholarship into published and manuscript collections compiled since then attests to the resilience with which *ceòl mór* retained a degree of vigour and traditional variability among what Donaldson in particular has coined 'the performer community' – that is, the pipers themselves – well into the twentieth century.[4] Pipers simply adapted to a new type of aristocracy and a new type of patronage with which to hand down what was handed to them. Literacy and competition were to play fundamental roles.

Fears that *ceòl mór* would not survive the decline in Gaelic aristocratic tradition reflected the sentiment of many landed gentlemen eager to preserve certain elements of Highland culture. This contributed, along with the drive for agrarian improvement, to the formation of the Highland Society of London in 1778. This was a society founded in order, among other things, to '[comprehend] the preservation of the music of the Highlands – much of it believed to belong to remote antiquity',[5] and they were led in this endeavour by the principle of cultural preservation through competition. An annual contest for the performance of *ceòl mór* was established under the auspices of the Society in 1781, first at the Falkirk Tryst and from 1784 in Edinburgh. In later years, both the HSL and its offshoot, the Highland Society of Scotland,[6] promoted literacy and sponsored the compiling of tunes into staff-notated collections throughout the first half of the nineteenth century. One of their earliest methods of promoting the 'scientific' transmission of pipe music was to award cash prizes at the annual contests to pipers who could produce their own written scores. The practice began around 1806 when one of the competitors was singled out:

> Sir J. Sinclair, by desire of the Committee, called Donald MacDonald, and informed him that a prize had been voted to him by the judges, for producing the greatest number of Pipe-tunes, set to music by himself; and it was recommended to him to continue his exertions in that way, and to instruct such others as might apply to him to be taught.[7]

MacDonald was a leading piper and pipemaker in Edinburgh at the time, and would later publish a seminal collection of tunes under the HSL's sponsorship around the year 1820.

Written settings of tunes gradually became the standard by which pipers were judged in these and other competitions, and as competition before a panel of one's social superiors grew more culturally central to the mainland piping tradition – itself a symptom of the decline in Gaelic tradition that characterised the post-Jacobite era[8] – the status and employability of the piper increasingly depended on a place in the prize-lists. They knew, after all, that potential employers – that is, landed gentlemen caught up in 'Celtic twilight' and eager to retain pipers on their estates – were in the audience.

These, in necessarily brief terms, were the circumstances which brought about mainstream literacy in the Highland bagpipe tradition. It was a gradual revolution in which the necessity of competition occasioned a shift from aural to literate transmission as the accepted standard of mainstream piping in the latter half of the nineteenth century.

In the days before the Highland Societies and the era of preservation, however, Highland chiefs were well known for their patronage of Gaelic vocal and instrumental music, including piping. The MacCrimmons, the MacArthurs and the Rankins, among others, were Hebridean piping families pre-eminent in the annals of seventeenth- and eighteenth-century musical patronage. So ubiquitous were their names in Hebridean society of the eighteenth century that John MacCodrum of North Uist (1693–1779), bard to MacDonald of Sleat, referred to all three in his c. 1760 composition '*Diomoladh Pìob Dhòmhnaill Bhàin*' or 'In Dispraise of Fair Donald's Pipes', wherein he satirised a neighbour for laying too much praise on a local piper of comparatively little skill. His reference to them conveyed a characteristially Hebridean familiarity:

A' chainnt a thuirt Iain	What Iain said
Gun labhair e ceàrr i,	He said it wrongly,
'S fheudar dhuinn àicheadh	We must deny it
Is pàigheadh dh' a chinn;	And put it right;
Dh' fhàg e MacCruimein,	He left out MacCrimmon,
Con-duiligh, is Teàrlach,	Condullie [Rankin] and Charles [MacArthur],
Is Dòmhnallan Bàn	And wee Donald
A tharraing gu prìs.[9]	He dragged to the top.

'*Air na pìobairean uile b'e MacCruimein an rìgh,*' intoned MacCodrum later in this famous piece; 'Of all the pipers, MacCrimmon was king.' On the one hand, this is a good contemporary indication of the family's standing in the opinion of grass-root Gaels in both MacCodrum's time and earlier; the MacCrimmons had served the hereditary office of piper to the MacLeods of Dunvegan from a time most likely prior to 1600 and would continue to do so until the dissolution of Gaelic aristocratic custom prompted a caustic severance in the early 1770s, and later writers did not spare the verbiage in their appraisal of the family as both the inventors of *ceòl mór* and its greatest exponents.[10] On the other hand, the text of MacCodrum's piece as a whole leaves no doubt that he referred primarily to individuals – pipers famed in their own right and on their own terms – and to their families' greatness rather by implication. As Matheson suggested, '*b'e MacCruimein an rìgh*' was probably a reference to Patrick Mór, in service to the MacLeods between roughly 1640 and 1670 and the reputed composer of 'I Got a Kiss of the King's Hand', among other classic tunes. Both the tune and the piper were associated with an incident meant to have taken place in May of 1651 during a muster of troops before King Charles II in which one manner of royalty was confronted with quite another. The incident's primary source, the Wardlaw manuscript, records that a 'John Macgurmen' or 'M'gyurmen' was seen surrounded on the field by eighty pipers, their hats off to him and his own head covered; the King, mystified by this spectacle and noting the deference shown to another by such a clamorous assemblage, enquired after it. He was reportedly told: 'Sir, yow are our King, and yonder old man in the middle is the Prince of Pipers.' King Charles 'cald him by name, and, comeing to the King, kneeling, his Majesty reacht him his hand to kiss; and he instantly played an extemporanian part Fuoris Pooge i spoge i Rhī [*Fhuaras pòg o spòg a' Righ*], I got a kiss of the kings hand; of which he and they were all vain.' Many consider the witness from whom the story descended to have misheard the name of the old man, and point further to the accepted authorship of the above pibroch as evidence that the 'Prince of Pipers' was, in fact, Patrick Mór MacCrimmon.

The MacArthurs were traditionally pipers to the MacDonalds of Sleat, a branch of Clan Donald known as *Mac Dhòmhnaill nan Eilean*, or 'MacDonald of the Isles', in virtue of their direct descent from the erstwhile Lords of the Isles. These MacDonalds historically held three territories and retained pipers in each: in Trotternish and North Uist, where the MacArthurs were situated, and in Sleat itself, a branch of the MacIntyre family.[11] The most celebrated of the MacArthur pipers was Charles (b. 1700), to whom MacCodrum referred above, who was taught by Patrick Og MacCrimmon – Patrick Mór's son – reputedly for eleven years and served three MacDonald chiefs in succession. He served at Duntulm Castle, MacDonald's Trotternish seat, and lived on a farm in Hunglater, near *Peighinn a' Ghobhainn* ('the Smith's Pennyland') rent-free by virtue of his office. Thomas Pennant, the naturalist, visited the MacDonald chief of the day during his tour through Scotland in 1772 and described his encounter with MacDonald's piper in Trotternish – believed to be Charles MacArthur, but could easily have been his son Donald, a piper of note at that time – in memorable terms. 'Take a repast at the house of Sir Alexander MacDonald's piper,' he wrote, 'who, according to ancient custom, holds his lands free. His dwelling, like many others in this country, consists of several apartments; the first for his cattle during winter, the second is his hall, the third for the reception of strangers, and the fourth for the lodging of his family; all the rooms within one another. The owner was quite master of his instrument, and treated us with several tunes.'[12] The year 1772 marks an age when, as we have seen, the piper's place in aristocratic Gaelic society was undergoing dramatic change, the famous piping schools – the MacCrimmons' and the MacArthurs' included – facing unceremonious demise. But Pennant's description of the piper to MacDonald of Sleat, whether Charles or Donald, evokes the image of a Hebridean musician at ease with his lot and his surroundings, 'master of his instrument', and of a patron consciously preserving this traditional service in uncertain times.

One gains the same impression reading of Samuel Johnson's encounter with MacLean of Coll and his piper, a Rankin, only a year later. '[MacLean] has the proper disposition of a Chieftain,' wrote Johnson of the young captain, 'and seems desirous to continue the customs of his house. The piper played regularly, when dinner was served, whose person and dress made a good appearance; and he brought no disgrace upon the family of *Rankin*, which has long supplied the Lairds of *Col* with hereditary musick.'[13] The piper in question was probably *Eoghainn mac Eachainn 'ic Chon-duiligh*, or Ewan Rankin, Protestant church elder and last of his family to preside over the famous Rankin school in Kilbrennan, which had closed in 1760; it had reportedly numbered seventeen pupils that year.[14] The Rankins in fact claimed common descent with the MacLeans of Duart in Mull and, according to tradition, had served as the MacLeans' pipers since 'time immemorial'.[15] The most celebrated of their lineage was Ewan's grandfather Condullie, who flourished in the early eighteenth century. If John MacCodrums's *bàrdachd* is anything to go by, Condullie's fame had clearly spread far beyond Mull's shores; probably, like Charles MacArthur, within his own lifetime. One wonders if he was still alive when MacCrodrum, around the year of the Rankin school's closure, warned his North Uist neighbour of the imprudence of dismissing the likes of the Rankin patriarch in no uncertain terms: *'Nan cluinnt' ann am Muile / Mar dh' fhàg thu Con-duiligh / Cha b' fhuilear leo t' fhuil / Bhith air mullach do chinn'* (Were it heard in Mull how you neglected Condullie, they would call for your blood to be on top of your head).

The late Ronald Morrison, a piper of deep Uist roots, had asserted that the MacArthurs maintained a footing in South Uist while enjoying the patronage of the MacDonalds of Sleat. The idea that MacArthur pipers were at least present in Uist at one time or another, and therefore in all probability influencing local repertoire and knowledge on the island, is supported on several accounts ranging from the anecdotal and traditional to the well-documented. One reference which, it has been suggested, supports a far earlier presence than is normally imagined is a song ascribed to Niall Mór MacMhuirich (c. 1550–c. 1630), bard and *seanchaidh* to Clanranald. Entitled '*Seanchas na Pìob' o Thùs*', or alternatively '*Seanchas Sloinnidh na Pìob' o Thùs*' ('The Pedigree of the Pipes from the Beginning'), the song is of the *aoir*, or satire, genre; a dispraise of the instrument, just as John MacCodrum's later piece, arguably a direct bardic descendant of *Seanchas*, was in dispraise of the performer. Thinly veiled as a history of the bagpipe's organological development, it ultimately focuses on two pipers, one of whom is explicitly identified as a MacArthur:

Éatroman muice o hó,	A pig's bladder *o hó*,
Air a shéideadh gu h-an-mhór,	Excessively blown
A' cheud mhàla nach raibh binn	The first bag that wasn't sweet
Thàinig o thùs na dìlinn.	Came from the beginning of the flood.
Bha seal re éatroman mhuc,	It was for a while of pigs' bladder,
Ga lìonadh suas as gach pluic;	Filled up from each cheek;
Craiceann sean mhuilt 'na dhiaidh sin	An old sheep's skin after that,
Re searbhadas is re dùrdail.	Harsh and buzzing.
Cha raibh 'n uair sin anns a' phìob	The pipe at that time had only
Ach siùnnsar agus aon lìop,	A chanter and one opening,
Agus maide chumadh na fuinn	And a stick that would keep the tune
Do'm [b'] cho-ainm an sumaire.	By the name of the *sumaire*.
Tamall doibh 'na dhiaidh sin	A while after that
Do fhuair ais-inntleachd inneil:	It got a backward device:
Feam fada leabhar garbh	A long thick rough tail
Do dhùrdan reamhar ro-shearbh.	A very bitter, deep, buzzing sound.
Ar faghail an dùrdain sheirbh	Upon resolving the bitter buzzing
Is a' ghoithinn gu loma-léir,	And the reed entirely,
Chraobh-sgaoil a' chrannaghail mar sin	The contraption spread like that
Re searbhadas is re dùrdan.	Harsh and humming.
Pìob sgreadain Iain Mhic Artuir	John MacArthur's screeching bagpipe
Mar eun curra air dol air n-ais,	Like a heron having gone backwards,
Làn ronn 's i labhar luirgneach,	Full of spittle, loud and spindly,
Com galair mar ghuilbrich ghlais.	An infected chest like a gray curlew.
Pìob Dhòmhnaill do cheòl na cruinne	Donald's pipe, of the world's music, is
Crannaghail bhreòite as breun roimh shluagh:	A bruised contraption, offensive to a crowd:
Cathadh a mhùin do'n mhàla ghrodaich,	Throwing its slavers through the rotten bag,
Fuidh 'n t-sùil ghainde robaich ruaidh.[16]	Under the ugly, sloppy, ruddy eye.

Some disagreement exists as to the identity of the composer. The eminent MacMhuirich scholar Derick Thomson maintained the authorship of Niall Mór, and pointed out that most printed versions of the piece, including MacKenzie's *Sàr-Obair nam Bàrd Gaelach* and the McLagan and MacNicol manuscripts, concur on this point; he tempered this conclusion, however, with the warning that these all probably stemmed from the same intermediate source, which taints the case somewhat.[17] Collinson ascribed it to Niall Mór's great-grandson Niall Og (c. 1630–1726), referring only to MacKenzie's *Sàr Obair* as his source; one is left with a suspicion that he may have confused the two in his researches.[18] The accomplished piper William MacDonald of Benbecula, for many years living in Inverness, referred to it as 'an old poem I used to hear when I was young' during a presentation at the Piobaireachd Society Conference of 1999 – an indication that the piece survived orally within South Uist's local bardic tradition – and attributed it to Niall Mór's son Lachlainn.[19] Far from merely surviving, MacDonald's evidence as a primary, living source illustrates the resiliency of oral transmission in the Uist community well into modern times; '*Seanchas Sloinnidh na Pìob*' apparently grew to forty-two verses in Uist vernacular Gaelic among the bards of the southern Outer Isles since the time of its composition, and MacDonald, by memory alone, quoted a refrain to the song not found in the manuscript sources.[20] However, Thomson's scholarship into the origins of the song, based on available manuscript evidence and a wider field of oral tradition, makes the most convincing and widely accepted case for the song's authorship as that of Niall Mór MacMhuirich.

One may infer that Niall Mór was not a great lover of the piping arts. '*Seanchas na Pìob' o Thùs*' may reflect the resentment of the professional bards toward the bagpipe's ascendancy over the harp (traditionally the bard's preferred accompaniment), which occurred over the course of the sixteenth century concurrent with the Age of Forays, or *Linn nan Creach*; alternatively, it may represent Niall Mór's specific malice towards the two pipers mentioned in the text. MacKenzie asserted that two MacArthur pipers, John and Donald, called on the MacMhuirich home in Stilligarry on a night when the *seanchaidh*, recently returned from bardic training in Ireland, was bedridden with smallpox, and that the sound of them tuning their pipes in the next room drove him to this invective barrage.[21] The scenario is plausible. The MacDonalds of Sleat and Clanranald would have periodically visited each other due to marriage and business ties, and each would have been attended by a retinue of courtly artists, including pipers. The MacArthurs mentioned could have quite reasonably visited the home of Clanranald's bards while the chiefs conferred at Nunton. As Niall Mór was meant to have composed it as a young man fresh from bardic college, it suggests a MacArthur presence in South Uist, however ephemeral, as early as the latter half of the sixteenth century.

Local oral tradition asserts that members of the MacArthur family ran a piping school in an area south-west of Gerinish,[22] a notion which at first seems doubtful. The MacArthurs' association with Skye and their service to the Lordship of the Isles remain their enduring legacy, and as shall be discussed below, the southern Outer Isles were in the hands of others. However, three historical references support local tradition in this regard, or at least render it plausible and point perhaps to a time-span within the eighteenth century: the first concerns Donald MacArthur, son of Charles; the second Donald's uncle, *Iain Bàn* or 'Fair John'; and the third concerns Archibald MacArthur and his unnamed brother, who may have been John's sons.

Charles MacArthur had two known sons. One, Alexander, was not an accomplished piper and emigrated to America after failing to convince his late father's employer, Lord MacDonald of Sleat, in 1800 to appoint him as his father's successor. The other son, Donald, is believed to have drowned some time earlier while ferrying cattle 'from Uist to Skye'.[23] Tragedy, it seems, followed tragedy: oral tradition has it that Donald's drowning took place even as his father's gravestone was under the mason's chisel. The local man Donald had hired is said to have abruptly put away his tools as soon as he had heard the news of his patron's death, fearing that he would no longer be paid. Looking upon the stone today – still neatly set in the cemetery of Kilmuir, near Charles's old farm in Hunglater, on the Trotternish coast – one is inclined to believe it: the epithet inscribed on it ends in mid-sentence. Donald had evidently achieved considerable status as a piper and had succeeded in drawing pupils from afar, as had his father. John Cumming, piper to the Laird of Grant in Lovat, had been sent to Donald MacArthur as a young man to serve an apprenticeship from 1770 to 1774, and in context MacArthur appears to have regarded his young charge with some favour.[24] It is unknown if Cumming was his only pupil at that time.

Donald most likely met his end in the late 1770s or early 1780s; certainly no later than the close of the eighteenth century, since his brother Alexander, in his petition to Lord MacDonald, described himself as the 'last Male representative of the family of MacArthurs formerly Pipers to Lord MacDonald's family'. With this claim he conspicuously distanced himself from his cousin Angus MacArthur, the Highland Society's offical piper in London at the time, who was a son of Charles's brother John. As the late Frans Buisman observed, Alexander probably did not consider Angus to be within the bounds of 'immediate family' where the Trotternish branch of MacDonald's pipers was concerned. Be that as it may, if the circumstances surrounding Donald's drowning are true, it suggests that he possessed a smallholding in Uist – perhaps near Gerinish.

The second account lending plausibility to the tradition of a MacArthur school, informal or otherwise, in Uist in the eighteenth century is the tenure of Donald's uncle *Iain Bàn* as piper to *Mac Dhòmhnaill nan Eilean* in North Uist. *Iain Bàn* was known to have resided in MacDonald's North Uist territory in 1745, earning a salary of £33 6s. 8d. that year.[25] Other references to a 'John MacArthur' appear in the lists of Lord MacDonald's expenditures in 1769 and 1771 but it need not be *Iain Bàn*; as Buisman pointed out, there is no mention of this

John being a piper.[26] Like his contemporary in North Uist, John MacCodrum, nothing is known of *Iain Bàn's* activities during the Forty-Five Jacobite rising, and we can guess little, for though his master's Hanoverian sympathies must be acknowledged, it is no indication of his piper's. It is tempting to surmise that if 'Fair John' MacArthur was stationed in MacDonald's Long Island territory for any length of time in the middle years of the eighteenth century, either he or members of his own immediate family could have easily made the trek to South Uist on occasion, whether on business for MacDonald of the Isles or simply to fraternise – in goodwill or in rivalry – with his counterparts the pipers to Clanranald. The world of piping, after all, has always been small. *Iain Bàn* died in or before 1779, leaving behind a widow, Marion MacLean, who remained thereafter in Trotternish.

Archibald MacArthur, possibly a son of *Iain Bàn* and Marion, was a noted prize-winner in the Highland Society of London *ceòl mór* competitions in Edinburgh. He took third place in 1804 but is perhaps remembered more for refusing second place in 1806, maintaining loudly that he should have won the contest outright. He had served as piper to Reginald MacDonald of Ulva and Staffa since the latter inherited those islands around 1800 from his father, Colin MacDonald of Boisdale, South Uist – he of *Creideamh a' Bhata Bhuidhe*, 'the Religion of the Yellow Stick'; the same Colin MacDonald who terrorised his Catholic tentants and caused the first major emigration of Uist families to the New World in 1772. William Gray, Pipe Major of the City of Glasgow Police Pipe Band from 1913 to 1932, claimed descent from the MacArthur pipers. He believed, according to family tradition, that Archibald and a brother both served as Colin MacDonald's pipers until his death, and the inheritance of his son Reginald, prompted the move to Ulva.[27] As a proposition, it cannot be substantiated; we have only the assertions of Pipe Major Gray, a Dunbartonshire man, to go by, and local oral tradition in Uist does not support it. All the same, it is fascinating. Taken together with the other historical accounts mentioned, it suggests that South Uist in the late eighteenth century saw influence from the classical MacArthur family via several sources: a formal MacArthur presence in Boisdale in the south, possibly a cattle-farm in the north, and occasional sojourns from North Uist. With reference to MacMhuirich's *'Seanchas Sloinnidh na Pìob'o Thùs'*, Buisman proposed that the Boisdale MacDonalds of the late eighteenth century may have been effectively rekindling formal ties between the MacArthurs and the Hebridean Clanranald MacDonalds from a far earlier time.[28] Looking at a map, one notices that Gerinish lies exactly midway between Boisdale and North Uist; and suddenly the notion of a MacArthur piping school of whatever sort, based in that area, is not so far-fetched.

The Clanranald line has been noted in particular for its tenacious hold on tradition in the face of change, and there is a wealth of examples from the South Uist community's song repertoire that illustrate Clanranald's patronage of Gaelic music in previous centuries. Some of these focus mainly on the work of bards,[29] but others clearly indicate the place of piping in a Clanranald chief's typical retinue. Angus Campbell of Benbecula, for instance, composed a lament for Captain Angus MacDonald of *Airigh a' Mhuilinn*, date unknown, which refers to him as '*Aonghuis òig riamhaich / Gu seinnte pìob leat*' (young handsome Angus, for whom a bagpipe would be played).[30] A rare reference to dance as a metaphor for war, involving both fiddling and piping, is found in a MacMhuirich song on the wounding of Angus MacDonald of Clanranald at the end of the sixteenth century:

Gum biodh fiodhall ga rusgadh	That a fiddle would be brought out
Pìob bu tartarach sionnsar	And a bagpipe of most clamorous chanter
Fuaim mhic talla ri chul sin	A sound echoing behind
Buidheann thaitneach air ùrlar	A fine group on the floor
'G iomart chleas air chrios cùil nam fear òga	Playing tricks on the rear guard of young men
'G iomart chleas air chrios cùil nam fear òga.[31]	Playing tricks on the rear guard of young men.

This was followed in 1618 by an elegy for Donald MacDonald of Clanranald, attributed to his widow Mary, which makes overt reference to her late husband's status as a patron of the highest order:

Is iomadh sgal pìobadh,	To every shrill cry of pipes,
Mar ri farrum nan dìsnean air clàr,	Just as to the clatter of dice on a board
Rinn mi éisdeachd a'd bhaile	And to the jibes and verses of the bards,
Mar ri éisg agus caithream nam bàrd.[32]	I listened in your household.

References to Clanranald pipers extend as far back as the mid-sixteenth century, so clearly the Clanranald line's patronage of piping was of very long standing. In spite of this, references to specific names (in particular those of South Uist and Benbecula origins) are relatively few. Our earliest such record is from 1636, when the 'Piper to the Captain of Clanranald' was complained against for taking part in the plundering, two years earlier, of the *Susanna*, an English barque laden with fruit and other perishables and bound for Limerick, which had been wrecked off the coast of Barra.[33] The piper mentioned was named John MacDonald; how long he held the office, and whether or not he received it hereditarily, is uncertain. However, evidence from available muniments and other documentary records, as well as surviving oral tradition regarding *Pìobairean Smearclait*, suggest that the office was held – through the turbulent eighteenth century at least – by a family of MacIntyres.

Documented records of MacIntyres as patronised musicians in Highland history place individuals, or families, of that name in Badenoch serving Clan Chattan, in Ulgary serving MacDonald of Kinlochmoidart, in Rannoch serving Menzies, in Sleat serving MacDonald of the Isles, in the Nether Lorn and Glenorchy regions serving Campbell of Breadalbane, in Barra serving MacNeil and in Uist serving Clanranald from the late seventeenth to the early nineteenth century.[34] Over the years, origin theories of varying strengths have been offered to reconcile the seemingly disparate strands. The historian Stewart has suggested that the MacIntyres of Rannoch in west Perthshire, pipers traditionally to Menzies of Menzies, were the pre-eminent 'root' family from which Clanranald's Uist pipers derived.[35] In the case of one late eighteenth-century piper, this would seem to have been the case – as will be discussed below – but Stewart did not take into account earlier references to MacIntyre pipers in many other Highland areas, including Uist itself. The Rannoch MacIntyres, in turn, were said by Henry Whyte (who wrote under the pen name 'Fionn') in 1904 to have originally served as bards to Clan Chattan in Badenoch.[36] Logan, in contrast, made the significant claim in 1838 that the MacIntyre pipers to Menzies were 'originally from the Isles'.[37] In the absence of more complete primary records, one can see how the strands very easily become convoluted. The late Ronald Morrison, who had been born in Gerinish, tried to link these references by suggesting that Clanranald's MacIntyres were originally a family of pipers from Moidart in the service of a cadet branch of Clanranald, who were brought by their chief to Bornish, South Uist, when the latter was given land there by *Mac 'ic Ailein*, and who eventually moved en masse from Bornish to Rannoch – presumably into the service of Menzies – at some point in the eighteenth century.[38] However, while local tradition does place a variant of the *Piobairean Smearclait* narrative in Bornish, Morrison seems to base his account not, as one might imagine, on local Gerinish or Uist tradition, but on Logan's brief anecdotal reference, and perpetuates too simple and linear a view. The documented records suggest not a single immediate, albeit mobile, family, but a widely-dispersed network of tradition-bearers in which multiple branches performed and composed contemporaneously for various patrons. On this basis, I contend that the MacIntyres were a much wider network of Gaelic tradition-bearers than can be accounted for by just one immediate family or one artistic discipline.

The case for placing a particular family of MacIntyres in South Uist in the eighteenth century as official pipers to Clanranald is based on the complementary nature of oral and written sources so far available to us. The oral record is comprised of both family lore and broader oral narrative. With regard to the latter, the cyle of *Piobairean Smearclait* tales collected in South Uist from the late nineteenth century to the present day is too consistent a strain of traditional narrative to be ignored utterly. While this rich corpus of anecdotes, legends and asides can be taken neither as historical fact nor its substitute, they do consistently depict a particular and indigenous family as hereditary pipers to MacDonald of Clanranald holding farmland in the south end of South Uist,[39] and can be seen as parallel to the narrative surrounding the MacCrimmons' service to MacLeod of Dunvegan. The vast majority of the *Smearclait* tales depict the family as MacIntyres. No date was ever explicitly fixed to them, but the details in their telling are at times reminiscent of *Linn nan Creach*, or the Age of Forays, suggesting that the tales go back as far as the sixteenth century.

Furthermore, one variant of the tale at least can be linked to a real person. *Dòmhnall Ruadh Pìobaire*, or 'Red Donald the Piper', was the subject of a local tale about the gift of piping bestowed to the first of his family to pipe for Clanranald. F.G. Rea, schoolmaster in Garrynamonie around the turn of the twentieth century, recounted the tale in his memoirs. Father Allan McDonald and John Lorne Campbell both identified *Dòmhnall Ruadh* as a MacIntyre and Janet MacNeil of Cathaileith, Smerclate, a very elderly woman in Rea's time, claimed to be *Dòmhnall Ruadh*'s great-great-granddaughter. MacNeil was born around the year 1810; Red Donald MacIntyre, therefore, would appear to have been born in approximately 1690. Gaelic oral tradition within families is often reliable for a basic, linear timeline of events and persons spanning several generations. On the basis of MacNeil's testimony in the 1890s, there is no reason to doubt that a man named Red Donald MacIntyre was indeed a piper in Smerclate in the late seventeenth century. That he piped for Clanranald at the time, or that his immediate family maintained the office hereditarily, is not at all certain; but in the context of the wider *Pìobairean Smearclait* tradition, such a notion cannot be dismissed out of hand.

For the same reason, it is also difficult to dismiss the testimony of modern Uist and Nova Scotia MacIntyre families who claim descent from Clanranald's hereditary pipers. In Cape Breton, where many families of the southern Outer Hebrides emigrated from 1772 to the 1840s, two MacIntyre families are known to have settled; one in Boisdale in 1820 and one in the French Road area in 1826. The descendants of both were noted pipers – leading one to suspect that the emigrants themselves were bearers of the tradition – and one family at least, the French Road MacIntyres, claimed descent from those in Clanranald's service.[40] Back in South Uist, Jessie MacAulay, née MacIntyre, of Smerclate, professed her family's background with characteristically Gaelic conviction, claiming that her paternal forebears were 'pipers and archers to MacDonald of Clanranald' who came originally from Skye; she also described having relations in Boisdale, Cape

Breton.[41] The reader may recall at this point the anecdote on the *Pìobairean Smearclait* theme discussed in an earlier chapter, noted down by Fr Allan McDonald in the 1890s, which referred to the Pipers of Smerclate as emigrants to the New World, following 'the old pipe-playing in the new country'.[42] While it is still by no means clear how the many strands of MacIntyre oral history can be reconciled into a neat timeline, or indeed whether they ever will be, the indisputable fact remains that an indigenous Uist family is immortalised in local oral tradition as having possessed the office of piper to Clanranald in hereditary succession for a significant period of time preceding the nineteenth century; a family most sources identify as MacIntyres.

The eminent nineteenth-century folklorist Alexander Carmichael's daughter, E.C. Carmichael, claimed in the *Celtic Review* of 1905 that two Uist MacIntyre pipers in the service of Clanranald were schooled by the MacCrimmons in Borreraig around 1745, and that 'four cows were said to be paid for their education there'.[43] She did not explicitly state her sources, but one imagines that she mined from *Smearclait* oral narrative material collected by her father. It is entirely within reason that Clanranald would send his piper(s) to a perceived centre of excellence such as the MacCrimmons' home in Borreraig for tuition; however, Carmichael's reference to cattle changing hands in payment for the two MacIntyres' apprenticeship, sourced undoubtedly from lore, is to my knowledge unique and may simply reflect the land-based economic world view of the storyteller(s) from whom the elder Carmichael's material derived. The account books of the noble families suggest that cash transactions for the instruction of pipers were the norm as early as the 1690s. The first Earl of Breadalbane, for instance, paid £40 to 'MacCrooman' and as much as £160 to Condullie Rankin for the schooling of 'Litle Johnie McIntyre the pyper' over several years c. 1697.[44] The Laird of Grant later paid a cash sum to Donald MacArthur in Skye for taking on his young piper, John Cumming, over a four-year period in the early 1770s.[45] Given the discrepancy over methods of payment and the lack of any corroborating evidence in Clanranald's written records, Carmichael's piece may not be historically accurate; but it is yet another link in the chain of oral traditional material suggesting the pre-eminence of the MacIntyre family among Clanranald's pipers.

Leaving aside the oral record for the moment, documentary evidence gives us only a handful of examples of MacIntyres (or possible MacIntyres, as the case may be) in the service of the Clanranald line, most of which have been broadly outlined elsewhere[46] and are not without their own ambiguities. They do, however, support the pre-eminence of the MacIntyre name in eighteenth-century Clanranald patronage. The first is 'A list of all the people of Benbeculla [sic], men, women, and young children past 12 yr old who are to be sworn September 29, 1738 for the extirpation of theft'. There includes in this list 'John the Piper', 'Helen his wife', 'Patrick his son' and 'Janett his daughter'.[47] The historian Stewart has postulated that this John was a MacIntyre on the basis that 'John the Piper' was the only man on this extensive list (which also includes two MacMhuirichs, quite plausibly surviving relatives of the famed Niall Òg) whose surname was not given, and further down the list there appears 'John MacIntyre' and 'Mary his spouse'; Stewart in effect proposes that 'the Piper' was used to differentiate between two men of the same family name. This is plausible, but tenuous. 'The Piper' or *a' phiobaire* was, and remains, a common appellative in Gaelic Hebridean tradition among those performing that function in tight-knit communities – to wit, *Domhnall Ruadh Pìobaire*, a MacIntyre, in Smerclate, born c. 1690; *Calum Pìobaire* of Barra, a MacNeil, piper to Roderick MacNeil of MacNeil at Quebec in 1759; and *Anna nighean a' Phìobaire*, a MacDonald, who nursed Alasdair Boyd as a boy in Eochar in the 1890s. It could well be that the compiler of the Benbecula list of 1738, be it a chamberlain or other functionary in Clanranald's Nunton household, simply referred to 'John the Piper' in the full understanding that this was the name by which all knew him; whether or not he was a MacIntyre is anyone's guess. One might counter this by pointing out, with reason, that there was probably more than one John playing the bagpipe in Benbecula at that time. But in the end the argument is of little use. Of greater significance to Stewart's proposition is the sheer improbability that a piper of high pedigree in the service of Clanranald could be banished for theft in 1738 and its only record be a Christian name on a list. The memory of such an incident would have likely survived in Uist's wider oral tradition or other MacIntyre-related lore. It must therefore remain conjectural that this John was a MacIntyre, and in turn that he was actually in the service of Clanranald.

The second and more concrete example from the written record is a charter drawn up in Nunton in October of 1759 and witnessed by three in attendance: Clanranald's gardener, the Benbecula schoolmaster, and 'Duncan MacIntyre, Piper to Clanranald'. A tack registration signed in Edinburgh in November of 1767 refers to the charter, and again mentions Duncan MacIntyre as its witness.[48]

The third and perhaps most enigmatic example surrounds one Robert MacIntyre, piper to John 'Moidartach' MacDonald of Clanranald, who, perhaps with others in his immediate family, is said to have emigrated to North America some time after 1790. In Robert's case – unlike Duncan and possibly other patronised MacIntyres before him – it would seem that Clanranald did indeed retain a member of the Rannoch family rather than one of Uist origin. One could speculate that the Uist family had not been immune to the economic changes taking place in the post-Jacobite era, and that John Moidartach was, by the 1780s, forced to look elsewhere for his piping; and furthermore, that by looking to Rannoch, he consciously sought to maintain his family's traditional link with the MacIntyres. Robert was the subject of praise poetry in his own lifetime: *Òran do Rob Dòmhnallach Mac an t-Saoir, Pìobaire Mhic 'ic Ailein*, or 'A Song for Robert MacDonald MacIntyre, Piper to Clanranald' was composed at Nunton prior to the chief's death in 1794 by the vernacular bard and catechist Alexander MacDonald of North Uist, a contemporary and one-time poetic sparring partner of John MacCodrum. Known locally as *An Dall Mór* or 'the Big Blind One' on account of a bout with smallpox as a youth, the bard has given us – intertwined with the ornate eulogising of his subject – the most local, most contemporary record of Robert's origins:

Rob Mac Dhòmhnaill Bhàin à Raineach,	Robert son of Fair Donald of Rannoch,
Bonaid is breacan an cuaich air:	Wearing a bonnet and plaid in folds:
Bha sùil leomhain 's i 'na aodainn,	He bore the eye of a lion in his visage,
Coltas caonnaig 'dol san ruaig air.	Turning a fight into a rout.
Chluich e 'corr-bheinn' air a' mhaighdinn	He played 'corr-bheinn' on the maiden [the bagpipe]
(Ceòl as caoimhneil' chaidh ri m' chluasan)	(The sweetest music that ever came to my ears),
Nach iarr biadh, no deoch, no èideadh	Who needs neither food, nor drink, nor clothing
Ach aon lèine chur mun cuairt dhi.	But a shirt wrapped round her.
Chluich e air maighdinn Chlann Raoghnaill,	He played the maiden of Clanranald,
Rob a leannan graidh 'ga pògadh	Rob's sweetheart, kissing his beloved,
Meal do mheodhair, meal do mheòirean;	Here's to your memory, here's to your fingers;
Meal do chuimhne is do glòir shiobalt'.[49]	Here's to your remembrance and your fine glory.

The *Dall Mór* proceeded to locate Clanranald's piper in the same league as the MacCrimmons and the MacArthurs – a formulaic comparison by then, but perhaps also a deliberate echo upon MacCodrum's 1760 satire.

As an oral document produced within the community in which Robert MacIntyre was then working and performing, its identification of the piper as the son of Donald Bàn of Rannoch undoubtedly lends greater credence to Logan's claims in his account of the Highland Society of London competitions in 1838. 'Robert MacIntyre, Piper to John MacDonald Esq of Clanranald' performed in the competition in 1785, took third place in the competition in 1787, second place in 1788 and won the prize pipe in 1790 playing 'The Duke of Hamilton's Lament', after which there is no trace of him in the records.[50] Logan mentions Clanranald's patronage of Robert, and the latter's emigration, in his 'Circumstantial Account' of the main hereditary families:

> These pipers lived in Rannach, but they were originally from the Isles. Donald Mór, the first [MacIntyre] of whom we have any account, was Piper to Menzies of Menzies. His son John learned from Patrick òg [MacCrimmon] at the college of Dunvegan ... His son Donald Bane followed the same profession, and left two sons, Robert and John. Robert became piper to the late MacDonald of Clanranald, after whose death he went to America.[51]

John MacDonald of Clanranald died in 1794, so from Logan's point of view the emigration would have taken place no earlier than this. But these competition records are really of little use in pinning down a date, for when Donald MacIntyre senior of Rannoch – quite probably the Donald Bàn in question – won the Prize Pipe for the second time in 1785, the Highland Society of London committee established a rule 'whereby a piper could only win a higher prize than he had previously gained, or nothing at all'.[52] So Robert's disappearance from the competition records after 1790, in this respect, proves nothing.

Robert remains absent from the written record until 1804, a decade after Clanranald's death. In that year, he is shown as having applied to Reginald George, John Moidartach's son and heir, for a tack of land in South Uist after serving some amount of time as piper to MacNeil of Barra.[53] In applying to his late ex-employer's son, he may have been planning an agricultural venture or perhaps even his retirement; but no indication of Clanranald's response has yet been discovered. In the light of the emigration tradition, however, it may well be that Robert was turned down.

Piper and historian Barry Shears has recently uncovered documentary evidence in Nova Scotia which appears to back this theory. Census returns taken in the Ballaches Point and Judique areas of Cape Breton in 1818 indicate that a Robert MacIntyre arrived from Scotland around the year 1813, and died in 1833. There was no written indication that this MacIntyre was a piper, though of course this is hardly conclusive. He was aged forty-nine at the time of the census, so if this was indeed the man himself then he would have been around twenty-one when he won the Prize Pipe in Edinburgh in 1790.[54] A gap still remains between 1804 and 1813; but in this respect we have only to look to MacDonald of Kinlochmoidart, Clanranald's cadet.

The naturalist and piping aficionado Seton Gordon was spurred to wax historical in an article to the *Oban Times* after visiting the home of Kinlochmoidart in 1930. The 'Bannockburn Pipes', wrote Gordon, 'were given to Donald MacDonald of Kinlochmoidart (direct ancestor of him who showed them to me) by the last representatives of the MacIntyres before they emigrated to America . . . in 1790'.[55] Nowhere does he mention the death of Clanranald, nor the name Robert. But Gordon did bring to light an ancient tradition on which, just as on the wider topic of the MacIntyres, Clanranald and Menzies are firmly linked. The so-called 'Bannockburn Pipes' is a single-drone set said to have been played at the Battle of Bannockburn in 1314 by a MacIntyre in the service of Menzies, and which was handed down thereafter as the Rannoch MacIntyres' most precious heirloom. But the set also turns up in the possession of a MacIntyre, or family of MacIntyres, who piped for Donald MacDonald of Kinlochmoidart in Ulgary, and who, upon emigration to the New World, bestowed the sacred relic upon his employer.

How to reconcile the old Menzies tradition with the fact that the famous pipes rested, for a time, in the possession of the Kinlochmoidart family? It is unlikely that the Rannoch MacIntyres moved en masse into the service of Kinlochmoidart, bringing their heirloom with them; the competition records contained in the same source show that at least two representatives of Menzies' MacIntyres, the elderly Donald senior and his son, Donald junior, were still active in Rannoch in the late 1780s. But Robert himself could have quite conceivably entered the employ of Clanranald's cousin if indeed he was refused a tack in South Uist. On the basis of all available sources, we may imagine the scenario suggested by Shears's discovery of the Cape Breton census entry to be the most plausible yet: Robert MacIntyre, a son of Donald senior or junior (either could have been the 'Donald Bàn' in question), is entrusted with the possession of the family heirloom; he moves for professional reasons from Rannoch to the employ of Clanranald until winning the Edinburgh contest of 1790 or until the chief's death in 1794; he moves thereafter into the service of MacNeil of Barra for a spell of years; he is refused a tack of land in South Uist by the foppish and puerile Reginald George in 1804; and finally he enters the employ of Kinlochmoidart in Ulgary before upping his stakes to seek a better life abroad around 1813, leaving the Bannockburn Pipes with his most recent master.

Robert, son of Donald Bàn – *maighstir gach pìobaire*, or 'the master of every piper' as the *Dall Mór* called him – is the last MacIntyre ever identified as Piper to MacDonald of Clanranald, and if he was indeed the last, then with his departure ended what oral, traditional and documentary evidence suggests was a long term of office for first the Outer Hebridean, and later the Rannoch, branches of that family. It is tempting to speculate that the piper to Hugh MacDonald of Boisdale, Colin's grandson, with whom itinerant music collector Alexander Campbell dined during his travels in South Uist in 1815, was a MacIntyre: 'During dinner, the pipe, as usual in lairds' houses, struck up and we had the double gratification of good cheer and excellent piping. Boisdale's piper being regularly initiated in the art, is an able Artist, and brilliant performer.'[56] It is equally plausible, however, that the piper in question was Archibald MacArthur or his brother. We will probably never know for certain.

The last chapter in the Clanranald line's patronage of piping centres around Donald MacKay of the Raasay MacKays, son of John and older brother of Angus. According to the HSL competition records, Donald took third place in 1820 as piper to MacLeod of Raasay; he was placed second the following year, listed then as 'Piper to Reginald George MacDonald, Esq of Clanranald', and won the prize pipe in 1822 playing, appropriately enough, 'Clanranald's Salute'. He remained in his position under Clanranald until 1829 and by 1838 was serving as piper to the Duke of Sussex (who was also the Earl of Inverness). So the Clanranalds were retaining pipers until just nine years before South Uist and its adjacent isles were sold to Colonel Gordon of Cluny. This is significant in the wider picture of Highland musical patronage: although Donald MacKay's appointment was a break from custom in the sense that he was not a native of Clanranald's holdings, as was the apparent succession of MacDonalds and MacIntyres that preceded him, it is a testimony to the family's conservatism of West Highland aristocratic tradition in an era of change.

～ THE MARTIAL TRADITION ～

Many pipers of South Uist origin have filled the ranks and bands of the Lovat Scouts and the erstwhile Queen's Own Cameron Highlanders in the twentieth century. This particular contribution of South Uist's to the piping of the British army will be discussed in later chapters; but one may justifiably enquire as to the conditions which led to such a contribution. There is no single straightforward answer. On one side it has to do with the affinity for piping in Uist's social culture; in the case of the Lovat Scouts at least, the island and the regiment shared a religious affiliation; and not least among prerequisite conditions is the island's martial tradition. As will be shown, the affinity among *Uibhistich* for military service is deeply rooted in the custom of Clanranald and the greater Highlands, and is an important context to the island's piping tradition, not simply for the sheer wealth of pipers who served in the late nineteenth and twentieth centuries, but because of the influence it inevitably had on attitudes regarding literately – and aurally – learned piping within the community.

The earliest references to martial piping in South Uist, in the oral record at least, concern Clanranald's involvement in the mainly sixteenth-century period known as *Linn nan Creach*, or the Age of Forays, when inter-clan warfare was rife due to the vacuum of power left after the forfeiture of the Lordship of the Isles in 1493. There is nothing of consequence in the written record which concerns Clanranald pipers' involvement in *Linn nan Creach*. However, for what it's worth, the historian Eyre-Todd wrote in 1923 of *Blàr nan Leine*, or the Battle of the Shirts (so called because the combatants stripped to their shirts in the heat of the summer day), when the first *Iain Muideartach*, or John of Moidart, led an attack on about 400 of Lord Lovat's men at the head of Loch Lochy in 1545. Eyre-Todd referred to 'the forces of John Moidartach descending upon him on the front and flank in seven columns with pipes playing and banners flying'.[57] However, no source for this account was given. Of the few *Pìobairean Smearclait* tales noted down by Fr Allan McDonald from living oral sources in Uist and Eriskay toward the end of the nineteenth century, one at least bears the telltale signs of originating in this period and refers to the journey of a piper from Smerclate to Ormiclate. 'On one occasion,' wrote McDonald, 'Clanranald was going on a foray to the mainland and he summoned the head piper of the family of the Smerclat pipers to appear at Ormiclat in good time so as to be ready to accompany the expedition.' On the journey to Ormiclate the piper encountered an old woman whose gift of a magic bannock rendered him invisible while he carried it on his person. He got rid of it only to find that 'Clanranald was particularly pained at the idea of an enchanted bannock being given up so easily as the invisible piper might have proved of notable value in any conflict that might occur'.[58]

Inter-clan strife of this type led Clanranald to become a conspicuous player in the Royalist forces during the Covenanters' War of the 1640s,[59] and his commitment to its prosecution is well-documented. He was said by his chronicler, Niall Mór MacMhuirich, in the Red Book of Clanranald, to have raised 'all the men of Uist, Eig, Moydart and Arasaig'[60] in anticipation of Alasdair MacColla's approach and alliance against the Campbells under Argyll in 1644 to a combined total of 800 men; he is also recorded as turning out a further 500 men of his clan under his son Donald to accompany MacColla in joining Montrose's forces as they neared Perth in 1645. These men, described as the 'truly fierce, very brave, powerfully spirited band of the Clanranald',[61] were to lead a charge against Covenanting forces at Kilsyth. They and the Glengarry contingent were noted as the 'main MacDonald strength' at the battle of Inverlochy, recorded at the time by the MacDonald bard *Iain Lom* as the 'great blood-letting' of Clan Campbell by Clan Donald.[62] And in 1648, Clanranald's son led an expedition from South Uist to Ireland to fight for the Irish Catholic cause, accompanied by those Irish soldiers who had fought for Clanranald during the Covenanters' War, as well as some 'Scottish gentlemen' – all told, about 300 men.[63]

It is reasonable to believe – indeed, it is a foregone conclusion – that men of South Uist were among those fighting under Clanranald's banner in all such conflicts. The numbers required by their chief, and the custom of hereditary jurisdiction which then prevailed, demanded it. The pipes surely went with them. The Earl of Lothian famously wrote in 1640 that the Covenanting forces were 'well provided of pipers';[64] why not the Royalist forces as well, what with the participation of the West Highland clans? Chiefs, when turning out men from their holdings to fight for Montrose and MacColla, would undoubtedly have been attended not only by men whose piping was incidental to their martial obligations, but by men whose piping was their living, pipers under their personal patronage – much like what was to occur the following century during the Fifteen, the Forty-Five and the Seven Years War.

Clanranald, and arguably clansmen-turned-soldiers (and pipers) of South Uist origin, were involved in all three of these conflicts. Allan MacDonald of Clanranald was made a colonel in the Earl of Mar's army during the rising of 1715, and is estimated to have commanded about 1,000 men. Although the records do not explicitly state it, natives of Uist were undoubtedly among this number. Allan was killed in November of that year at the battle of Sheriffmuir when a party of cavalry and foot under Lord Torphichen doubled back after a retreat and attacked; as is discussed elsewhere in the present work, some surrounding evidence suggests that his body may have been carried off the field by a Uist-born MacIntyre piper in his service.

Also present on the field was Allan's bard, Niall Òg MacMhuirich, the last to be patronised by the Clanranald line. As befitted his office, Niall composed an elegiac song praising his chief's generous character and old-world Highland values, and describing the effect of Allan's death on those close to him:

'S mór gàir ban do chinnidh,	Great was the cry of your kinswomen
O'n a thòisich an iomart,	Since the endeavour began,
An sgeul a fhuair iad chuir tiom orr',	They were daunted by the news
T' fhuil chraobhadh a' sileadh,	Of your blood gushing forth
'S i dòrtadh air mhire,	And spilling upon mirth,
Gun seòl air a pilleadh,	No way for you to return
Ged tha Raghall d' ionad,	Though Ranald was on by your side,
'S mór ar call ged a chinneadh an rìgh.[65]	We have lost much though the king did well.

The Jacobite army of 1745 has been called the 'valedictory manifestation of a martial culture peculiar to the Highlands of Scotland' in a recent assessment,[66] and regardless of its accuracy (for the latter-day contribution of Highland communities to British army regiments surely qualifies as a 'manifestation' of the old martial affinity), the Clanranald family's participation was considerable. The late Allan's grandsons, Ranald younger of Clanranald and Donald of Benbecula, reportedly raised an initial 250 men for the Pretender's army[67] from all corners of the Clanranald territories – including the Hebridean quarter, as contemporary bard Alasdair Mac Mhaighstir Alasdair expressed in what has survived as *òran luaidh*:

Mo chion a dhèanamh leat éiridh,	My hero would not fail thee,
Do Chaiptin fhéin Mac-Mhic-Ailein.	Thy own Captain, young Clanranald.
Gun theann e roimhe roimh chàch riut,	He joined thee before all others,
'S nì e fàs e, ach thig thairis.	And will again if thou comest.
Gach duine tha'n Uidhist 's am Muideart,	Every man in Uist and Moidart,
'S an Arasaig dhubh-ghorm a' bharraich.	And dark-green Arisaig of birchwoods.
An Canna, an Eige, 's am Mór-thìr,	In Canna, in Eigg, and in Morar,
Reisimeid chórr ud Shìol-Ailein!	The noble regiment of Clanranald![68]

Government intelligence reports and contemporary letters indicate Clanranald's, and in particular South Uist's, importance in tactical terms to Prince Charles's campaign. It is believed that the Prince stopped at South Uist before ever touching at Moidart or Glenfinnan, in order to enlist the aid of MacDonald of Boisdale, whom he regarded as an influential figure; that the Prince had indeed visited Uist beforehand is confirmed by the governor of Fort William, who wrote to the Duke of Argyll that the the Young Pretender's ship, having left Moidart, 'intended to *return* to Wist; if so Loch Boysdale or Loch Skipper are the only places such a ship can come into' [my emphasis].[69] The governor added that 'if there be any appearance of a considerable rising of the Clans near Moydart, then the arms, as it is said, are to be landed either at Arisaig, Clanronald's house, or at Uring Kenlochmoidart's house'. The Prince gained additional men from South Uist several months after raising his standard, as an unsigned letter dated 14 December 1745 indicates:

> Two Spanish ships from Ferrol arrived lately among the Western Islands of Scotland, touched at South Wiste, and brought from thence and some adjacent isles about 300 M'Donalds of Clanronald's men, and landed them on the mainland at Moidart, with 2,500 stand of small arms, 100 barrels of powder, with ball comform, and some chests of silver, supposed to contain 6000 [pounds], all which the said M'Donalds, with what further can be raised in that country from whence the Rebellion sprang, and to convey the said arms, ammunition and stores to Perth.[70]

That piping was heard under the Clanranald banner during the Forty-Five can be inferred from oral tradition, and in particular the titles and accompanying legends of various tunes in the classical repertoire of the bagpipe, which are discussed elsewhere. The Fort William governor's intelligence reports to Argyll provide a modest written record. When writing in August of the news that Ranald MacDonald younger of Clanranald, Donald MacDonald of Kinlochmoidart, Alexander MacDonald of Glenaladale and other Clanranald relatives had boarded the Prince's ship upon its arrival in Moidart, he noted that 'two of [his deputy's] servants saw this ship . . . where there is 15 fathom water, and saw Clanranald and others go out to that ship with pipers playing in their boat'.[71] This at least gives us a casual glimpse of one of piping's many functions as an accompaniment to affairs of state in old Highland aristocracy.

Both Ranald younger and his brother Donald of Benbecula obtained employment in the French army after the events of 1745. Both were to return to Scotland, however, and it is in association with Donald that the Clanranald line, and its pipers, make their first real contributions to British military tradition.

In response to the outbreak of the Seven Years War, three of the elder Clanranald's sons – Donald, William and Normond – received commissions in newly raised Highland regiments.[72] Donald was given command of a company in Fraser's 78th Highlanders and by 1757 was recruiting among his clansmen (tenants by this time) in Uist and Benbecula to fill the ranks. Seventy-two men of South Uist origin were in fact estimated to have fought in the Seven Years War; most, if not all, would have served under Donald.[73] Despite emerging social changes and legislation following the Forty-Five, the martial traditions of clanship were still a reality in the Highlands and Islands of the 1750s, and the fealty between classes often saw captains fill their companies with men from their own holdings. Since the 78th retained about fifteen pipers dispersed among ten to fifteen companies, one can safely assume that Donald was likely to have had at least one piper from his holdings accompany him to North America as part of the company. Donald was wounded in 1758 at Louisbourg in 'the taking of Cape Bretton (sic)',[74] after which he took over a grenadier company whose first commander, Charles Baillie, had been killed in combat; Donald's piper is believed to have followed him in the transfer.

As it happened, this piper disgraced himself at the Plains of Abraham in September 1759 for cowardice in combat – a rarely recorded occurrence in the annals of martial piping – and according to the company sergeant was ostracised for it by the men:

> Our company had but one piper and he was not provided with arms . . . When our line advanced the charge, General Townshend observing that the piper was missing, and he knowing well the value of one on such occasions, he sent in all directions for him and he was heard to say aloud, 'Where's the Highland Piper?' And, 'Five pounds for a piper', but de'il a bit did the Piper come forward . . . For this business the Piper was disgraced by the whole of the Regiment and the men would not speak to him, neither would they suffer his rations to be drawn with theirs, but had them served out by the commisary seperately and he was obliged to shift for himself as well as he could.[75]

The following year, Donald of Benbecula was killed at the Battle of Quebec but, auspiciously for the British military piping tradition, his unnamed piper was again present on the field and managed to redeem himself by staying and rallying the men. I say auspiciously because the piping of the Frasers at Quebec in 1760 was among the first instances of piping in British warfare to gain wide public acclaim, and therefore contributed directly to the modern image of the British army piper on the battlefield – which, among other things, influenced the formation of the Highland Society of London in 1778.[76] This then was the first significant contribution of the Uist piping tradition to that of the British army.

Other contributions were soon to follow. The (Old) *Statistical Account of Scotland* recorded that from 1772 to the last decade of that century, 'no less than 400 stout young fellows . . . have gone as recruits to the army and navy from the parish'. This is an enormous number of men within such a small population – estimated at the end of the century to have numbered 3,450 – to have left for military service in a twenty- to thirty-year span, even allowing for those who would eventually return; it is reasonable to believe that pipers were among them.

The next century saw the blossoming of the militia movement in Scotland, whereby units of officers and men for home defence were organised within specific counties. Reginald George MacDonald of Clanranald, last of the line to own South Uist, commanded the Long Island regiment of the Inverness-shire militia for many years until his death in 1873. With the territorial reforms of the Army in 1881, the militia formally became the reserve of the Regulars, each regiment adopting a regional recruiting district and assimilating that district's militia or volunteer unit; the Inverness-shire militia integrated with the Queen's Own Cameron Highlanders, a thoroughly Gaelic regiment, and became their 2nd – later 3rd – (Militia) Battalion. Many South Uist pipers are on record, both documentary and anecdotal, as having served in this and other battalions of the Camerons since at least the 1880s; several of them were noted prize-winners at regimental and civilian competitions, as will be discussed elsewhere in the present work.

~ PIPING IN THE COMMUNITY ~

Bagpipe music had a variety of uses and functions in the West Highland communities of previous centuries. Keeping time for group labour, whether it be launching or rowing a boat, roadworking, reaping harvest or waulking cloth, was a normal feature, as contemporary tourist journals and monographs on Highland culture illustrate: Knox, touring through Skye in 1786, noted that 'at this time the inhabitants were mostly engaged upon the roads in different parts of the island, under the inspection of the gentlemen and tacksmen, and accompanied, each party, by the bagpiper'.[77] Edward Burt spoke likewise of such western districts of the Highlands during his travels half a century earlier:

> In larger farms, belonging to gentlemen of the clan, where there are any of women employed in harvest-work, they all keep time together, by several barbarous tones of the voice; and stoop and rise together, as regularly as a rank of soldiers, when they ground their arms. Sometimes they are incited to their work by the sound of the bagpipe; and by either of these, they proceed with great alacrity, it being disgraceful for anyone to be out of time with the sickle. They use the same tone, or a piper, when they thicken the new-woven plaiding, instead of a fulling mill . . .
>
> . . . And among numbers of men, employed in any work that requires strength and joint labour, as the launching a large boat, or the like, they must have the piper to regulate their time, as well as usky, to keep up their spirits in the performance; for pay they often have little, or none at all.[78]

These writers portray bagpipe accompaniment to labour in communities outwith South Uist, but the time period and the social and cultural circumstances were the same; there is no reason to believe that the bagpipe did not have the same function in the southern half of the Long Island, an area widely acknowledged as having been more conservative of Gaelic culture than the mainland in subsequent generations.

Another facet of life in Uist is of course the funeral. Oral sources such as waulking songs and recorded memorates indicate that piping has long been used to accompany processions and burials; Donald John MacDonald testified to this in the middle years of the twentieth century in a summary of information obtained in South Uist during many visits,[79] and if we care to go further back, an indigenous waulking song believed to have been composed no later than c. 1700 describes a woman's last words before death:

Bheir iad mise leò air ghiùlain,	They will take me with them on a bier,
Air each gorm nan strian dùbailt . . .	On a gray horse with doubled reins . . .
'S truagh nach cluinninn siod, 's nach fhaicinn	A pity I wouldn't hear nor see it,
Farum do shluaigh, fuaim do bhrataich,	The noise of your people, the sound of your banner,
Glaodh do phìoba bhith 'dol seachad	The wail of your pipes as they go past
Air luing, 's air bàt' no air barca.[80]	On a ship, a boat, or a skiff.

These seventeenth-century *òrain luaidh* are among several oral and written sources which depict the pipes accompanying another major facet of community life in South Uist: dancing. Elsewhere in the present work, a number of informants claim that there was no instrumental music on the island in the early decades of the twentieth century other than that of the bagpipe, an exaggeration born of nostalgia for a time when piping was much more widespread. Contrary to present-day nostalgia, however, the surviving gamut of waulking songs depicts a vibrant multi-instrumental tradition in the South Uist of centuries past, presenting images of bagpipes, fiddles, harps and trumps all revolving around the act of dance in both common and aristocratic circles. The most comprehensive collection available of such songs is that published by John Lorne Campbell in 1969 based on the manuscript of Donald MacCormick of Kilpheder, South Uist, which the latter had first compiled in the 1890s. Campbell later collaborated with musicologist Francis Collinson to produce a second volume, forming a complete work of inestimable value to the study of oral and instrumental Hebridean tradition. In '*Cha dìrich mi an t-uchd le fonn* (I'll not climb the brae with song)', displaying Campbell's typically sensitive and ornate translation of Gaelic song titles, we find this verse:

Mo cheist maraiche nan tonn,	My darling sailor of the waves,
Chuireadh air an fhidhill fonn,	Who would play tunes on the fiddle,
Air an fhidhill, air an truimb,	The fiddle, the trump,
'S air a' phìob mhór nam feadan toll.[81]	And the bagpipe of hollow drones.

Another, '*'S mi m' aonaran am Beinn a' Cheothain* (I am alone on the misty mountain)', associates both fiddling and piping with Clanranald patronage:

Gu Ormaglaid nam ban teisteil,	To Ormiclate of the chaste women,
Far am bi crodh laoigh 'san eadradh,	Where the cattle are milked,
Ligeil fìona moch is feasgar,	Wine is poured early and late,
Fioghall 'ga seinn, pìob 'ga spreigeadh.[82]	And the fiddle played, and the pipes struck up.

'*An Spaidsearachd Bharrach* (The Barra Boasting)' depicts fiddling, piping and harp-playing among the pastimes in an upper-class Gaelic household;[83] and, unusually, '*Rinn mi mochéirigh gu éirigh* (Haste made I to rise all early)' illustrates the use of small-pipes as well as the big pipe for dancing in what was likely an aristocratic setting:

Rachainn leat ro' chùl-taigh dùinte,	I would accompany you to the enclosed chamber,
Far am faighinn modh is mùirne,	Where I would find manners and merriment,
Daoine uaisle mu bhòrdaibh dùmhail,	Gentlemen crowded round solid tables
Ruidhleadh mu seach air an ùrlar,	Reeling in turns on the floor,
Le pìob mhór nam feadan dùmhail,	With the big pipe of thick drones,
Le pìob bheag[84] *nam feadan siùbhlach.*[85]	With the small pipe of flowing tones.

This verse is interesting in that no tradition of small-pipe playing has existed in

South Uist within living memory. This song, along with '*'S mi m' aonaran*' and '*Spaidsearachd Bharrach*'' all demonstrate that Clanranald's pipers maintained a rich tradition of dance-music, supporting Gibson's point of view that a chief's piper's repertoire was never necessarily restricted to *ceòl mór*.[86]

Several nineteenth-century sources illustrate dancing to pipe music in South Uist and its adjoining area since the time of the songs. 'The people of Barray,' noted a local minister at about the time of Barra's sale to Gordon of Cluny in 1840, 'have no games or amusements but what are common to the surrounding islands. Dancing, with music of the bagpipe, is a favourite pastime.'[87] The reader may recall *Dòmhnall a' Bhanca*, or Donald MacDonald, the Protestant piper of Benbecula who emigrated to Canada aboard the *Buenos Ayrean* as one of the Cathcart Settlers of 1884; he was noted particularly for being in frequent demand for weddings or entertainment, as was another Donald whom Frederick Rea engaged to play for a school dance in the 1890s. 'I shall never forget that dance,' wrote Rea. 'I had engaged a special piper who came from a distance but was very popular at all weddings and parties – he was said to be the best player of reels on the island.'[88] Although Rea refers only to reels and does not mention the name of the dance, his description of the performance suggests that Donald played what has remained the typical Highland tempo progression of moderate strathspeys into quicker, more even-timed reels for an extended Scotch Foursome. In the Western Isles, then as now, the Scotch Reel was the supreme expression of social gaity, danced in two lines and changing, with little warning for the uninitiated, from the strathspey to the reel rhythm.

> The piper seeing that each at last had a partner immediately changed to a rousing reel tune. At once more than a hundred pairs of feet shod in heavy boots were thudding on the floor in some step of a reel, but all in time: all faces devoid of a smile, serious as though dancing were a business, the men looking upwards, and the girls with downcast eyes. The rhythm of the tune changed with an increase in time. With a loud yell the men now danced together in pairs – they whirled and sprang in a mad dance till, when they were pouring with perspiration, Donald slowed down his tune; it died away and the dancers were glad to rest – Donald knew his work![89]

A final example of dancing to pipe music in South Uist in the years before the turn of the twentieth century comes from Donald John MacDonald's interview with his father, acclaimed storyteller Duncan MacDonald, in Pininerine in 1956. In it Duncan describes the *Bàl Suitheadh*, or what might be termed a 'blackhouse ball', wherein members of a community would gather to hold a ceilidh of dancing, piping and often drinking. This tradition died out around the turn of the century, but had presumably thrived since much earlier times:

Bho chionn leth cheud bliadhna air ais, bhiodh dannsaichean air an cumail ann an tighean dubha ann an Uidhist. 'S e bàl a chainte ri cruinneachadh dannsa ann an Uidhist, agus 's e sin a chanar riutha fhathast cuideachd ... An-diugh chan eil a leithid sin a' dol ann an Uidhist idir. Tha cunntas mhór bhliadhnaichean bho'n nach robh bàl suitheadh ann an Uidhist ... Nuair a chruinneachadh na daoine uile gu léir, rachadh riarachadh liunn a chur mun cuairt air a h-uile duine, agus chuireadh am pìobaire a bha air fhasdadh aca suas a' phìob agus thòisicheadh an dannsa. Cha robh eagal sam bith gum faigh am pìobaire damaiste, o chionn bha pìobairean gu leòr anns an àite, agus bhiodh fear is fear mu seach a' toirt greis air a' phìob. Thòisicheadh an dannsa, agus nuair a dhèante trì neo ceithir do ruidhlighean dannsa, dh' iarrte air cuideigin anns a' chuideachd òran a ghabhail ... Chuirte an sin mun cuairt riarachadh liunn eile ... Rachadh an oidhche a chur seachad mar sin gu maduinn, eadar dannsa is òrain is òl.[90]

Fifty years ago, dances were held in blackhouses in Uist. Dance-gatherings in Uist were known as balls, and they still call them that ... Today there's no such thing going on in Uist at all. It's been a great many years since we had a blackhouse ball in Uist ... When the people would gather all together, beer would be distributed to everyone, and the piper who'd been waiting on them would put up his pipe and the dance would begin. There was no fear that the piper would tire out, because there were many pipers present, and they would take turns on the pipe. The dance would begin, and when three or four reels had been played, someone in the group would be asked to give a song ... More beer would then be passed around ... The night would be spent like that till morning, between dancing, singing and drinking.

MacDonald's lack of reference to any instrument on these occasions other than the bagpipe is entirely consistent with the reminiscences of my own informants, as will be seen in a later chapter. Some elements of the *bàl suitheadh* tradition yet survive. Calum Beaton, for instance, has used the word *bàltaichean* in conversation when speaking of dances in modern-day Uist; however, dances are held in town or church halls now and the circumstances are accordingly different. In a similar vein, Jessie MacAulay has spoken of the custom of pipers taking turns, '*a' toirt* turn *mu seach*', in the dances of her youth, but at the same time laments the rarity of such occasions today.[91]

PART TWO

Tradition and Change

CHAPTER 6

'Interest in piping in South Uist is getting keener than ever'
THE AGE OF IMPROVEMENT, 1900–58

By the turn of the twentieth century, South Uist had seen several important changes in its social and educational infrastructure. The entreaties of Bishop Angus MacDonald to the Napier Commission in 1883 had succeeded not only in securing a truer representation of the island's Catholic majority on the school board, but also in conveying the plight of Uist's crofters whatever their religion. 'Besides this special grievance,' he wrote, referring to the neglect of the Catholic majority's wishes, 'I believe that a statement of this case will tend to show the existence of a widespread evil, in the dependent and degrading position in which such tenants are apt to be placed – with no security of tenure, no guarantee against removal at will, and with the fear constantly hanging over them, that if they venture to assert their rights they may be made to suffer for it, without having the power to obtain redress.'[1] The Commission's report and the Crofters (Scotland) Act of 1886 duly placed redress for such grievances within tenants' reach, and gave the island's Catholics the means for proportional representation in their schools.

English-language schooling had become compulsory throughout the Isles in 1872, but by the turn of the century it seems to have had little effect on the general use of Gaelic, at least in the Outer Hebrides. An indication of this is the Duke of Atholl's complaint to the Scottish Education Department, dated 29 August 1901, in which he claimed that a sub-inspector who visited Pittagowan School in Perthshire the previous spring had advised the children to abstain from speaking Gaelic at all times except Sundays. The Duke, long an active supporter of Gaelic, was uncertain if the sub-inspector was acting of his own accord or through Scottish Education policy. In either case, he was incensed.

Through a series of letters, it was discovered that the sub-inspector had been 'joking' to the pupils, and his actions were evidently not representative of official policy; however, the initial reply of the head of the Department, Lord Balfour, reveals an implicit bias:

> My Dear Duke of Atholl,
> I have been away for a week in the Hebrides and therefore only received your letter on Saturday . . . From a purely Educational point of view, there is much to be said which runs counter to ideas of sentiment and of Highland Patriotism. In some parts of the west Highlands and Islands such as those where I was last week the continual existence of Gaelic as *the only* [sic] domestic language interposes a serious barrier to the well-being and prosperity of the rising generation.[2]

It therefore seems that under the Education Act of 1872, English was encouraged officially while Gaelic was discouraged unofficially. The evidence indicates that in these early days, as far as South Uist was concerned, neither policy was very successful.

South Uist at that time was undergoing a gradual decline in population, which was recorded in 1901 at just over five and a half thousand souls[3] – down over five hundred from ten years previously, but greater again than what the census would record the following decade. This decline was symptomatic of the perpetually poor economy which had caused much emigration in the previous century. Kelping, for example, had lain dormant since the post-Napoleonic Wars, and although it enjoyed a revival from the late 1850s, it again took a downturn in 1875 with the importation of iodine from Chile and Peru. The kelping industry would never again provide enough to sustain the population, which at the turn of the century held upwards of a thousand crofts at five to fifty acres each.[4] Numbers of livestock, such as sheep, horses and cattle, were plentiful at that time, as were crops such as potatoes, barley and turnips.

At the turn of the century, then, the South Uist community had seen great changes in some respects, and none in others: the population was in decline due to a poor economy and a language as yet irrelevant to their lives was being taught in their schools, but they were enjoying a renaissance of Catholic free-will and security of tenure; Gaelic remained the living tongue of the community. Where did the piping tradition fit into this picture? The written record, predominantly from the English-language point of view, can take us only so far in our search not only for facts and events, but for development of thought and cultural perspective at a certain point in time. When complemented by the predominantly Gaelic oral record, however, the judicious observer can discern a great deal of the state of the art and its idioms in the Uist community around the turn of the century, revealing it to be a pivotal period in which traditional functions and priorities did not so much change as fragment under the encroaching influence of modernity.

In looking for the root, and indeed the legacy, of such developments one must weigh the zeal for 'scientific improvement' that had gained momentum in the piping world throughout the previous century; the correspondingly increasing importance of competition and games culture to a piper's credibility; and the respectful deference with which literacy was regarded by the rank and file of Hebridean society up to the period in question. These influences converged in the form of two very literate and, in their own distinct ways, aristocratic, institutions: the mainland-based Piobaireachd Society of Scotland and the local South Uist Piping Society. These societies would make it their business to bring Uist's indigenous piping up to par with the technical and competitive innovations of Scotland's mainstream – that is, to 'improve' it in the same sense that Highland landowners had improved their tenants' agriculture in the light of the new economic priorities of the post-Jacobite era. Given the strength of these influences, a great many changes were inevitable.

THE STATE OF PIPING, C. 1900

Interest, if that word may be used, in piping was just as high at the beginning of the twentieth century as it had been for generations before then. The word 'interest' is deceptive; it is not meant in the western aesthetic sense, in which an objective psychic distance can exist between listener and performer, but in the sense that, as older pipers today remember, piping was an integral part of community life and taken fundamentally for granted. As the late Alexander MacAulay, himself a piper of Uist roots and a writer for the *Piping Times*, put it, 'If it was in you to be a piper, you would be a piper ... The house that couldn't produce at least one person playing the chanter was not of the South Uist way of life. They lived and breathed piping there.'[5] It was a noteworthy phenomenon even to contemporary observers, as the *Oban Times* of 1910 reported that 'the music of the historic "piob mhor" has always strongly appealed to the natives of the Outer Hebrides, and particularly to those of South Uist. There is hardly a family without its piper, and frequently one finds father and two or more sons able to discourse on the national instrument.'[6]

Older pipers today confirm that at that period it would have been considered unusual if a family didn't produce at least one piper; indeed, it is unanimously held by sources that the bagpipe was the only instrumental music available at the time. This would prove to be an exaggeration – though not by much – but it serves to illustrate the depth of feeling and nostalgia that the subject provokes. As the late Jessie MacAulay of Smerclate, born c. 1913, reminisced:

> JD: *Carson a thòisich thu air a' phìob?*
> JM: *Bha e cho furasda dhomh tòiseachadh ciùil! Bha a' phìob a' dol a-staigh againn daonnan tro a h-uile oidhche . . . is sin an aon cheòl a bh'ann airson a chluichd. Cha robh ach a' phìob a bh'ann. Sin mar a thòisich mi air a' phìob.*[7]
>
> JD: Why did you start (to learn) the pipes?
> JM: It was so easy for me to start the music! The bagpipe was going every night . . . and was the only music around for playing. There was nothing here but the bagpipe. That's how I started on the pipes.

Interestingly, the younger Calum Beaton expressed the same point of view that piping was, in his youth during the 1940s, the only music on the island. His contemporary, the late Neil MacDonald of Garryhellie, was similarly insistent:

> NM: *Dh'ionnsaich sinne nuair bha sinn òg, is bha pìobairean gu leòr mu chuairt a dh'ionnsaicheamaid. 'S e ceòl an eilein an uair ud co-dhiubh. An aon cheòl a bha 'san eilean.*
> JD: *An aon cheòl a-mhàin? Nach robh accordion, no fidheal, no . . . ?*
> NM: *Cha robh sian a' dol idir ach a' phìob.*[8]
>
> NM: We learned when we were young, and there were plenty of pipers around who would teach us. It was the music of the island at that point anyway. The only music on the island.
> JD: The only music? Weren't there accordions, or fiddles, or . . . ?
> NM: There was nothing at all but the pipes.

MacDonald was born in 1934, Beaton in 1931. They could only have been speaking of the late 1930s and '40s, long after the period in question; however, their viewpoint is very much the same as MacAulay's. It comes across as a slight exaggeration; informants' testimony and *Oban Times* records both mention the occasional use of the fiddle and the melodeon in the *taigh-cèilidh* around the turn of the century, and MacAulay once referred to the appearance of accordions in the 1940s.[9] But it suggests a remembrance born of nostalgia for a time when piping was more widespread. In this way the informants' descriptions are surely just as accurate for the beginning of the century as they are for the mid-point. Other sources lead to the same conclusion: the late Duncan MacDonald's description of the *bàl suitheadh*, or blackhouse ball, in the previous chapter was conspicuously devoid of any mention of instrumental music other than the pipes. At the dawn of the twentieth century, it seems, piping was everywhere and everything.

Both of the main branches of Highland pipe music, *ceòl mór* and *ceòl beag*, were extant at the time, though the indication is that the performance, if not knowledge, of *ceòl mór* had somewhat faded in the Hebridean community by then. This will be discussed later. As for *ceòl beag,* it is apparent that the piping tradition on the island had by then inherited two idioms of musical transmission: the literate and the aural. Each of these idioms implied different contextual functions. As has been discussed previously, the use of staff notation in piping had developed concurrently with, and in direct relation to, the rise of competition and a technical standard of fingerwork in the nineteenth century, an 'improvement' due largely to the efforts of the Highland Society of London; before the competitive function arose, however, piping in Gaelic society was passed on by ear and voice and, in South Uist, most often as dance-music in the ceilidh. The South Uist community refers to aurally-learned piping – particularly with regard to the dance function – as *ceòl cluais*, or 'ear-music'. A later chapter discusses the functions and aesthetics of piping in South Uist in greater depth, but for now, the pertinent issue is discovering the level to which both extended within the South Uist community at the beginning of the century, and the reasons why.

Literate transmission, or learning pipe music by staff notation, was known among individuals at least, if not communities. Gibson has maintained[10] that it was negligible in traditionally conservative areas like South Uist until the influences of the twentieth century came to bear; however, that is not to say that literacy, and its social acceptability in an otherwise ear-learned tradition, was entirely unknown on the island in the last half of the 1800s, when literate piping was becoming the established norm throughout Scotland. The MacGillivray pipers, who are said to have leased land in Barra in the 1880s, are reputed to have been literate in staff notation.

What most connected South Uist with literate piping in the latter half of the nineteenth century was the people's affinity for military service – a direct continuation of the martial tradition discussed earlier – which had led many Uist pipers into the British army, navy and militia since the eighteenth century. By the 1880s, some of these were quite literate and were noted prize-winners in local and regimental competitions.[11] Neil MacInnes and Lachlan MacCormick, for instance, joined the Queen's Own Cameron Highlanders in 1889; MacInnes as a regular and MacCormick in the Militia Battalion. In addition to winning the *ceòl mór* at the regimental Games in Malta in 1896, MacInnes took the Captain McLeod Medal for march, strathspey and reel playing and placed highly in the dancing.[12] MacCormick became Sergeant-Piper in the Camerons before latterly serving with the Lovat Scouts and is regarded by local sources as the pre-eminent competitive piper in Uist in the days before Piobaireachd Society involvement. He even acted as a judge of piping at the first Highland Games in South Uist in 1898, although this did not deter him from competing in subsequent Games.[13]

That the British army was a source of literate piping around this time is evinced in many ways. Up to the late eighteenth and early nineteenth centuries, there is nothing to indicate that the role of piping in the military required a literate standard,[14] but by then the Highland Societies of London and Scotland were heavily promoting the use of staff notation. Their efforts were nominally for purposes of 'preservation', but they were also heavily influenced by the army's need for pipers who could be taught tunes quickly and be sent off to face the French.[15] The fact that Highland regiments held competitions in the late nineteenth century is itself strong testimony, since competitive piping by and large implies literate piping. Literacy by this time was in most respects necessary for the military piper to carry out his duties, both as a solo ceremonial player and as a member of a regimental band.[16] Pipe Major William MacLean, for instance – twice gold medallist and resident of Benbecula around the turn of the century – hauled a blackboard around France during the Great War so that his pipers would be 'properly taught from music and not by ear'.[17] Similarly, Pipe Major Willie Ross is known to have made his army pupils write out their own manuscripts of tunes, 'laboriously transcribed by hand', in his course in Edinburgh Castle[18]; his example could hardly have been unique or original.

Examples like Willie Ross's can be found within the Uist tradition: the late Neil MacLennan of Lochboisdale, a well-known and respected local piper and Pipe Major in the Camerons, was known to teach solely 'by the book', and Neil Johnstone of Daliburgh, a former pupil, believes that MacLennan's dismissal of anything that smacked of ear-learning was due to his military influence.[19]

Such was their economic hardship in late nineteenth- and early twentieth-century South Uist that the military was often a piper's only recourse for literacy, since the published staff-notated collections were often too expensive for the unpatronised. Owning your own set of pipes was rare enough, which constituted another benefit of military service. As Jessie MacAulay recalled:

JM: *'S e ceòl cluais, 's ann mar sin a bha iad ag ionnsachadh aig an àm sin. [Ach bha] feadhainn . . . a' dol dhan Arm, is bha iad sin ag ionnsachadh a' chiùil as an leabhar;* pipe bands, *fhios agaibh. Sin fhéin an aon fheadhainn aig a robh na leabhraichean is a' phìob . . . 's ann nuair a chaidh iad dhan Arm a bha iad a' tòiseachadh leis na leabhraichean is na* pipe bands.

JD: *An ann 'san àite sin a bhiodh iad ag ionnsachadh ceòl a leughadh?*

JM: *'S ann, seadh, anns na* regiments. *Bha bràthair agam-sa, bha e a-mach anns na* Lovat Scouts, *gum faigheadh e pìob!* (laughs)

JD: *Am b'e sin dòigh airson fir òga pìob fhaighinn? A' dol dhan* Scouts?

JM: *Seadh, an* TA *is na* Scouts. *Bha* pipe band *aca.*
JD: *An robh pìoban daor aig an àm?*
JM: *Bha! Chan eil iad daor idir an-diugh, ach bha iad daor gu leòr an uairsin; fhios agaibh, cha robh móran airgead againn ann.*
JD: *Dh' fheumadh iad a dhol dhan* TA *no* Scouts *airson pìob a thoirt dhachaidh?*
JM: *'S e, 's e. Cha robh dà phìob 'san aon teaghlach idir, cha robh* [ach] *aon phìob.*[20]

JM: Ear-music, that's how they learned at that time. But some . . . went into the Army, and they were there learning the music from the book; pipe bands, you see. They were the only ones who had the books and the pipes . . . It's when they went to the Army that they began with the books and the pipe bands.
JD: Is that where they would learn to read music?
JM: Yes, in the regiments. My brother, he was out in the Lovat Scouts in order to get a bagpipe! (laughs)
JD: Was that a way for young men to get a set of pipes? Going into the Scouts?
JM: Yes, the TA (Territorial Army) and the Scouts. They had a pipe band.
JD: Were pipes dear at the time?
JM: Yes they were! They aren't at all expensive today, but they were dear enough back then; we didn't have much money around, you see.
JD: They would have to join the TA or Scouts in order to bring home a set of pipes?
JM: That's right. There weren't two sets of pipes in the one family, just one set.

MacAulay spoke first-hand of the 1920s at the earliest, but there is every reason to believe that the same was true of the years surrounding the turn of the century. Military activity, and military piping, were omnipresent then. Rarely was there a wintertime soirée or ball at which music by a local Cameron or Lovat piper did not feature highest on the bill.[21] In 1895, for example, 'an enjoyable soirée, concert and ball [was] given recently by Miss Fyffe, the energetic public school teacher of Balvanich, Benbecula, [for] the scholars attending the evening class. Selections on the bagpipes were given by Piper MacPhee, of the 2nd Battalion Queen's Own Cameron Highlanders. Dancing was kept up with high glee till the small hours of the morning.'[22]

The school in Kileravagh, Benbecula, held an annual end-of-year entertainment along similar lines, and in 1898 the Master of Ceremonies was Sergeant D. MacCorquodale of the Cameron Highlanders; piping was provided by fellow Camerons' Pipe Major MacPherson and Piper Angus MacLellan as well as civilian piper Alex MacRury. All were local. MacCorquodale and MacLellan danced the Highland Fling together 'in excellent style' and the Sergeant went on to give a few tunes on the melodeon.[23] About the same date, the evening continuation school in Torlum held a soiree at which Lachlan MacCormick himself, Angus MacPhee of the 2nd Battalion Camerons and a member of a well-known local piping family, Roderick MacMillan, gave selections on the pipes.[24]

The year 1906 marked the death of a young Torlum man, Roderick MacDonald of the 3rd Battalion Camerons. He was described in the *Oban Times* as a 'piper of no mean order' and was given a full military procession at his funeral in Inverness.[25]

Also in that year, the Lovat Scouts sponsored a ball in Eochar:

> [A] most enjoyable ball was given by the Lovat Scouts in the Iochdar Public School. Mr. Alex. Morrison, Merchant, Ardnamonie, called upon Piper Angus MacPhee, Lovat Scouts, for the '79th's Farewell to Gibraltar', and right well did Piper MacPhee respond to the invitation. The M.C., Lance-Corporal D.J. MacKay, Lovat Scouts, displayed his tact and ability in marshalling the couples for the Scotch Reels that followed. Country dances, quadrilles, lancers, the Highland Schottische, and refreshments all lent variety to the next part of the programme. Mr. Donald Ewan MacLean, Linique; Sergt. MacPherson, Lovat Scouts; and Mr. Peter MacKay, Kilauley, displayed their skill by dancing the Highland Fling, the Highland Laddie, and the Sailor's Hornpipe . . . The piping was much appreciated.[26]

This last reveals the difference in cultural character between a regimental ball and a traditional ceilidh of the period: the dancing of Scotch Reels notwithstanding, ear-learned dance-piping very likely had no place at that ball, where such Scottish Country dances as were mentioned were, and are, associated intrinsically with non-Gaelic influences. Moreover, the '79th's Farewell' is a standard tune in the military repertoire, and as MacAulay's testimony suggests, the military repertoire, as much then as now, implied literate transmission.

For a final example of the military's literate influence in South Uist, we need only look to the annual Highland Games at Askernish machair. In 1922 and 1923, the Games received generous financial support by the Lovat Scouts and the 4th Battalion Camerons, while the Lovats contributed further to the cost of the piping competition medals.[27] This is indirect influence at best, but it does reflect the regiments' point of view regarding competition and improvement.

To be fair, the fact of serving in the British army around the turn of the century does not prove conclusively that a piper was literate; there were always exceptions. Consider the case of Peter MacDonald, born in Inverness in 1837, who was unable to read or write when he enlisted in the 76th Highland Light Infantry in Arisaig, 16 January 1876, aged thirty-eight.[28] He served as a piper in the Militia for some years. His general illiteracy makes it improbable that he could read and write music on the stave, but there is a chance he was tutored in this, once enlisted. And in South Uist itself, Jessie MacAulay was able to recall an ear-learned piper from her youth, noted for his dance-piping skills, as being in the Lovat Scouts and playing in their band:

> JM: *Aonghus Caimbeul as an Iochdar – bha e sin 'na shuidhe 'sa* room *aige 'san sgoil agus a' cluichd a' chiùil . . . Bha esan cuideachd anns na* Lovat Scouts, is *a'* bhand. *Cha leughadh e an ceòl idir, ach bha e anns a'* phipe band.
> JD: *Cha b'urrainn dha leughadh?*
> JM: *Cha b'urra dha leugh', ach bha ceòl aige-san. Leis a' chluais.*[29]
>
> JM: Angus Campbell of Eochar – he was there sitting in his room in the school and playing the music . . . He was also in the Lovat Scouts, and the band. He couldn't read music, but he was in the pipe band.
> JD: He couldn't read?
> JM: He couldn't read, but he had music. With the ear.

MacAulay could recall little more of this Eochar man, memories of whom place him around the 1920s and '30s at the earliest. Calum Beaton recalled this man in conversation as well, saying that he was known locally by the name of 'Gighat' and that, as a great piper of dance music, he would often play seated on a low window sill, stomping both feet in unison to the rhythm of the tunes. That both Calum and Jessie recalled Angus Campbell of Eochar is important. It reminds us that although military and civilian (that is, ceilidh) modes of performance and transmission were growing increasingly polarised in this period between the literate and the aural, respectively, such emerging boundaries were not quite yet hard and fast in a society such as Uist's, where the traditional functions of piping were still ingrained in the wider social milieu. These exceptions notwithstanding, the written record indicates that in the early years of the twentieth century, literacy was extant among pipers in South Uist insofar as the Militia Battalions and the Lovat Scouts were involved.

Military pipers were always in the minority compared to the general musically inclined population. Informants state consistently that most piping in South Uist at the beginning of the century was learned aurally and within the context of dance, as it had been over earlier generations. This has proved to be yet another example of geography separating South Uist from the cultural happenings and trappings of less remote Highland areas. By the middle of the nineteenth century, it is certain that both idioms were in practice throughout greater Scotland, but the efforts of the Highland Society of London had by then steered the accepted standard of musical transmission firmly in the direction of literacy. Sir John Graham Dalyell was conspicuous in his use of the past tense when he noted in 1849 that 'the transmission of pipe music for this instrument otherwise than by oral tuition, or acquisition by ear, or by any semblance of notation, was probably unknown to our native musicians; and I presume, that teaching a pupil by language exclusively is a peculiarity in musical education'.[30]

South Uist, geographically peripheral and culturally conservative, largely avoided what was happening on the mainland up to the period in question. 'Literacy and staged competitiveness,' wrote Gibson, speaking of the 1800s, 'were aberrations unknown to, or eschewed by, Gaels who managed to go on living in places such as South Uist, North and South Morar, Moidart, places where tourists did not go.'[31] Excepting the instances of literate piping that the military presence suggests, testimony obtained from Uist informants concurs with this impression. As Jessie MacAulay recalled, ear-learning was quite the norm for her father's generation of pipers:

> *Bha mo bhràthair na dheagh phìobaire, agus dh'ionnsaich e an ceòl; bha m'athair na dheagh phìobaire cuideachd – cha do dh'ionnsaich am fear sin as an leabhar idir. Cha b'urrainn dha na puirt [a thoirt?] as an leabhar, ach bha e math air pìobaireachd 'na dheaghaidh sin. Cha robh cothrom aca co-dhiubh leabhar a dh' ionnsachadh. Bha aca 'nan cluais, fhios agaibh; cha robh leabhar idir aca ach an cluas is cha robh iad ag ionnsachadh as an leabhar cus idir.*[32]

> My brother was a good piper, and he learned the music; my father was also a good piper – he didn't learn from the book at all. He couldn't get the tunes from the book, but he was good at piping nonetheless. They never had the chance to learn from a book anyway; they had it in their ear, you see. They had no book at all but their ear and they weren't learning by the book at all.

Calum Beaton told a similar story regarding his own father, Archie, and the older generation of pipers in Stoneybridge:

> *Bha m'athair, chluichdeadh e a' phìob agus feadan, is bhiodh e 'ga chluichd tric gu leòr . . . Bha móran a chanadh* false fingering, *pìosan do phuirt is rudan an t-seòrsa sin. Agus bha gu leòr dhe na seann daoine mu chuairt, chluichdeadh iad co-dhiubh feadan is bha feadhainn aca a' cluichd air a' phìob, ach 's ann anns an aon dòigh mar sin a bha iad 'ga cluichd . . . Bha móran do phìobairean, mar a bha mi 'g ràdh riut, a chluichdeadh ceòl cluaiseadh; 's e a chanainn e.* Playing by ear.[33]

> My father, he would play the bagpipe and the chanter, and he'd play it quite often . . . What many would call false fingering, fragments of tunes and that sort of thing. And lots of the old people around, they would play the chanter at least and some of them were playing the bagpipe, but they would be playing in the same way as that . . . There were many pipers, like I told you, who played ear-music, as I would call it. Playing by ear.

The term 'false fingering' should grab one's attention. When a piper is taught by staff notation, he learns the grace notes and fingerings according to a precise template, whereas a piper taught by ear will position his fingers any which way in order to get what he perceives to be the right sound from his chanter. The literately taught piper necessarily regards such practice as shoddy or faulty; hence the term 'false fingering'. This was Calum Beaton's impression of his father's playing in 1940s Stoneybridge once he'd been taught by notation; the late Duncan Johnstone also had this in mind when describing the *ceòl cluais* pipers of Barra in the 1950s. 'When I visited Father John MacMillan on Barra during my holidays,' he once said, 'I used to go to see this old man with him. He was bedridden but he used to sit up when I took the practice chanter to him. He couldn't read music and his fingering was as false as Hell, but if you didn't look at the fingers and just listened the music was brilliant.'[34]

When those tradition-bearers in South Uist whom I interviewed spoke of *ceòl cluais* as played in their youth (between the 1920s and 1940s), their testimonies are often characterised, as in Beaton's above, by the mention of *na seann daoine mu chuairt an uairsin* – 'the old people around at that time'; they maintained that most ear-piping they had heard as children was performed by the elderly. This is a strong indication that the *ceòl cluais* tradition was becoming scarcer among the younger generation at the period in question, and that literate transmission was in turn becoming the more acceptable standard. By the time Calum, whose first exposure to piping was through Archie Beaton in the 1930s, was taught the bagpipe, it was through the latter method:

Bha m'athair, chluichdeadh e a' phìob... Bha mi smaoin' aig an àm gu robh e uamhasach math, nuair a bha mi anns an sgoil, ach nuair bhithinn-sa airson feuchainn air an fheadan, chanadh e rium, 'Cha dearg mis' air sian a theagasg dhuit idir, cha do dh'ionnsaich mi fhìn... a-riamh dòigheil.' Cha robh e airson 's gum bi mi ag obair air an fheadan ann an dòigh anns a robh e fhéin idir... Mar sin, cha do rinn mi móran gus an tig [sic] caraid, a thill dhachaidh as a' Chogadh – Alasdair Peutan... 'S e a thug dhomh a' chiad tòiseachadh air an fheadan, is fhuair mi leabhraichean – Robertson's Tutor, Logan's Tutor. *Bha mi fhìn a' togail gu leòr dheth cuideachd agus cha robh e uamhasach fada gus an rachadh agam air an ceòl a leughadh gu math fileanta.*[35]

My father played the pipes and the chanter... At the time, I thought that he was an excellent player, when I was in school, but when I myself wanted to try the chanter, he would say to me, 'I cannot teach you a thing, I never learned... properly.' He didn't want me to work on the chanter in the way that he himself did... So, I didn't do much until a relative returned home from the War – Alasdair Beaton... It was he who first started me on the chanter, and I got books – Robertson's Tutor, and Logan's Tutor. I picked up quite a bit too, and it wasn't long before I was able to read music quite fluently.

This snapshot of Beaton's earliest impressions is extremely valuable for what it reveals of the attitudes and perceptions toward aurally-learned and literately-learned music prevailing in South Uist by the 1940s. If his testimony can indeed be taken as reflecting the perceptions of the wider community at the time, and not just his family's, it would seem that the perception of *ceòl cluais* as an inferior idiom to the 'improved' competitive standard had become not just that of the up-and-coming, receiving generation, but was by then established to the point of being cross-generational; where even those among the elder generation, who had expounded the ear-learned tradition all their lives, began to feel that they had somehow learned *gu mì-dhòigheil* – ineptly.

What factors were involved in bringing about what appears to have been a significant change in South Uist's piping tradition from the nineteenth century to the twentieth? At the turn of the century, musical literacy was still a rare skill among *Uibhistich*, their long-standing affinity for military service notwithstanding. Another possible, though less accessible, avenue toward literate transmission would have been the increasing publication of music collections throughout the nineteenth century, which reflected the development of competition throughout Scotland and the consequent necessity attached to literacy. Beaton has referred above to collections like Robertson's and Logan's circulating in Uist in the 1930s and '40s. However, it is unlikely that there was sufficient demand in a place as far removed as rural South Uist for such written collections to have been made widely available at the beginning of the century, and informants' reminiscences have borne this out.

I believe the emphasis on literate transmission and its associated competitive function – which grew sufficiently widespread in South Uist to compel Beaton's ear-learned father to refrain from teaching his son – was compelled by two influences: the military, as shown, and latterly the involvement of the Piobaireachd Society in the instruction of South Uist's pipers from 1909. Their presence formed a landmark of change that ushered in an era of mainstream priorities and influenced the island's piping tradition for the rest of the century. But what were the circumstances behind their involvement? Why, indeed, did they become involved at all?

∽ TWO SOCIETIES, ONE GOAL ∽

In the closing years of the nineteenth century, piping throughout Scotland was vigorous and widespread, as it was in South Uist. The increasing role of the competition circuit and the military as piping's all-encompassing *raison d' être* by this time had ensured that *ceòl beag* was everywhere in a healthy state of development. However, a new class of piper was emerging in mainland Scotland – the 'skilled amateur piobaireachd player'[36], the landed Highland gentleman whose expertise was lent more readily to the study of the bagpipe than to the playing of it and who believed *ceòl mór* to be dying, its performed repertoire rapidly shrinking and knowledge of its interpretation under threat through a flawed competition system and a lack of sound judging practices. An anonymous series of articles in the *Oban Times* of September 1903, entitled 'The Passing of the Piobaireachd' and signed merely 'A.M.', lamented this state of affairs and sent out a clarion call to those who would affect change: 'Today there are thousands of players on the pipes, but of true pipers how many? The present writer knows of six who are worthy of the name. There are probably not more than ten in the whole world. Three hundred years ago ten as good, if not better, could have been mustered in Skye alone . . . Men are dying, tunes are vanishing, knowledge is waning.' 'A.M.' went on to conclude,

> The writer's purpose has not been to prove, for no proof is needed, but to draw attention to, the barbarous apathy with which our present generation treats the subject of piobaireachd music. He has reminded the reader how few piobaireachd are ever heard nowadays, and how pipers play piobaireachd solely in order to win prizes in competitions, judged frequently by men without the slightest elementary knowledge of the subject. He has tried to show that the fault lies, not with the present-day professional piper, but with those on whose patronage the piper is dependent.[37]

Recent scholarship has observed that, while the qualifications of men called to the bench at this time did indeed too frequently rest on social rank, with no regard for any real knowledge of the classical piping, the above sentimentality of doom was not generally shared by pipers themselves – the living bearers, and indeed interpreters, of the tradition.[38] The vision of the 'skilled amateur piobaireachd player', however, was prosecuted quite independently of them. In the 1770s and 80s the perceived climate had led Highland aristocrats with an interest in such matters to form the Highland Society of London, which in later years encouraged the cultural preservation of piping based on the principles of management, literacy and competition.[39] In 1903 a handful of like-minded gentlemen and military officers (one of whom was in fact 'A.M.',[40] whose writings were uncannily reminiscent of John Ramsay's in 1784) perceived that the very system which their forebears had established was leading to the downfall of its original goal as regards the preservation of *ceòl mór*. Competition needed reforming. In answer to this concern, they founded the Piobaireachd Society.

After initial enquiries at the Argyllshire Gathering at Oban the previous summer, the group met in Edinburgh on 19 January 1903. Their objectives were set down formally:

a) The Encouragement, Study and Playing of Piobaireachd Music on the Highland Bagpipe.
b) To collect Piobaireachd MSS and Legends, and publish tunes which have never before been published, and to correct, when possible, tunes already in print which are known to be wrong.
c) The general advancement and diffusion of knowledge of this ancient Highland music.
d) Eventually, by offering adequate money prizes, to hold Piobaireachd Competitions, to be judged by Members of the Society, a list of tunes to be played to such competitions to be selected by the Society.[41]

One may look quizzically at the fourth objective and note that the competition system was earlier derided for its failures by the very people who now wished to continue it. In fact, Society members saw a problem not with competition itself, but with the conditions under which pipers competed. They believed that the rules of the day not only allowed incompetence among judges, but complacency among performers – in that one had only to learn half a dozen or so tunes and could thereafter compete with the same tunes all his life. The system gave no incentive to broaden one's repertoire. The fledgeling Society's view in this matter was made clear in one of their own circulars printed on the day of their formation, 19 January, explaining the need for change:

In the Competitions for Piobaireachd playing, held under the existing rules, many of the most beautiful of the old Piobaireachds are never played at all; the reason being that at present it is only necessary for a piper to give a list of from 3 to 8 Piobaireachds to the judges, and many pipers give the same list year after year. The result of this is, that out of nearly 300 Piobaireachds which are in existence, only about 20 are ever played at Competitions . . . The Society believe that the falling off of Piobaireachd playing is largely due to 2 reasons. First, That so many pipers have different settings of the same tune, and they are afraid to play certain settings, in case their setting may be different to that which the judges think the correct setting. Second, That many tunes are so long that the pipers are afraid to play them, as a long tune is a much greater strain on both the fingers and on the pipes than a short one. A set of pipes might stand splendidly for 'Glengarry's Lament', but would go all out of tune in playing 'Donald Ban MacCrimmon's Lament'.[42]

Hence the Society's intention to have competitions judged by their own members (who at least at first would be eminently competent[43]) and to prescribe ever-changing lists of tunes so as to challenge the pipers' skills continually.

In 1908 or very early 1909, the South Uist Piping Society was formed in

Lochboisdale. This was a group founded by several local gentlemen, among whom were Simon MacKenzie of the Lochboisdale Hotel and Fr Alexander MacDougall of Daliburgh. It was established in the interest (and here I mean 'interest' in the clear western aesthetic) of raising the literate standard of pipe music on the island through large-scale organised tuition; particularly *ceòl mór*, but also the gamut of competitive marches, strathspeys and reels. Their exact reasons for this are obscure as few records survive, but, as is discussed below, there are grounds for believing that the demand for pipers of a certain technical standard in the British army, as the First World War loomed, probably had something to do with it. It is fair also to believe that they were prompted by the same drive for improvement which had forged competition and literacy in the nineteenth century and which had recently prompted the formation of the Piobaireachd Society in Edinburgh.

These Uist gentlemen saw the vitality of dance-piping all around them in kitchens, ceilidhs and weddings. The folklorist Margaret Fay Shaw, for instance, famously described a Glendale wedding party in the 1930s as resounding with 'the firing of guns and the skirling of bagpipes, which, playing the fine tune "Highland Wedding", led the procession home to the wedding breakfast. The celebration continued through the day and night . . . Dancing began with a Scots foursome reel for the bride and groom and best man and first bridesmaid. Then the guests joined them on the floor and danced until morning. South Uist is famous for its pipers and a great delight of such a day was to listen to their perfect playing and their timing of the lovely tunes.'[44] The Garrynamonie schoolmaster Frederick Rea had earlier participated in a similar Scots foursome wedding reel in the kitchen of Fr Allan McDonald's own house around the turn of the century. 'The swirl of the air set up in this little kitchen seemed to grip me up and whirl me around with its rousing rhythm, and as the ripples of the notes rose and fell,' wrote Rea of the piping, 'they made my toes ache to dance.'[45] The gentlemen members of the South Uist Piping Society, however, saw the ear-learned dance music around them as little more than the raw potential of a community lacking in the literate tuition required by the competitive and military idiom.

Simon MacKenzie's son Finlay, who succeeded him as hotelier, was also a key member and active patron of the Society. It is difficult to distinguish who else, if any, made up the Uist Society's founding committee because no records of the Society's beginnings appear to have survived; local oral tradition alone tells us that MacKenzie Sr and MacDougall became associated in their mutual interest in piping, but others with an interest in cultural and community affairs were probably involved. The late Alex MacAulay suspected that the island's factor at the time, a John MacDonald, had a hand in it[46] and this is supported by a correspondent of the *Oban Times* of 16 June 1923, who attributed the formation of the Society to 'Mr. Simon MacKenzie, Lochboisdale; Mr. John MacDonald, Askernish; and Father MacDougall, Daliburgh'. The resident priest of Bornish, a Fr MacIntosh, may also have been a member.[47] Whoever else may have been involved in the group's formation, with Simon MacKenzie and Alexander MacDougall we are on solid ground. Through their concerted efforts, the Piobaireachd Society was contacted, who in turn sent instructors to South Uist on a yearly basis for nearly fifty years – interrupted only by bureaucracy and two world wars. This period of institutionalised instruction would cement the foundation for mainstream piping for which South Uist has been celebrated ever since.

Simon MacKenzie was born in the middle years of the nineteenth century in Ross-shire, and died around the year 1928. He managed the Castlebay Hotel in Barra from 1881 to 1908, but took over the Lochboisdale Hotel some time before 1897.[48] He was a keen amateur piper, but is remembered today more for his patronage then his playing: the machair of Askernish, for instance, was leased to Lochboisdale Hotel at the time, and MacKenzie donated it for use by the Highland Games every July from 1909, before which time they were most often held on Nunton machair, Benbecula.

His son Finlay was born in 1883, most likely in Barra, and is remembered as having been an avid piper in his youth. He spent time with the Mounted Police in Canada in the years after 1900, so he was probably not among the Society's founders. He returned home, however, at the outbreak of the Great War and served with the Royal Scots Greys, with whom he obtained the rank of Major. He took over Lochboisdale Hotel around 1920, and it was from this time that he began to assert himself as a strong patron in the tradition of his father. The junior MacKenzie became a frequent contributor to the Games and was often voted Honorary President or Secretary of the South Uist Piping Society during his life.[49] In time he achieved lasting recognition in this capacity outwith South Uist, aided in no small measure by the Uist Society's functional association over the years with the Piobaireachd Society. An extract from the Piobaireachd Society minutes of 1948 shows his typical standing among mainstream piping circles:

> The Honorary Secretary submitted a letter from Mr. Norman MacKillop, Deraclate, Harris, requesting the assistance of the Society in giving tuition to young lads in the district. The Committee was of the opinion that the applicants should get in touch with the Piping Society of South Uist and particularly Major Finlay MacKenzie of Lochboisdale. If satisfactory arrangements can be made for the giving of tuition by the Piping Society of South Uist, the Society will consider the question of giving financial assistance toward a class of tuition.[50]

Nothing seems to have come of this intital proposal, but it serves to illustrate the confidence placed by that time in MacKenzie as a patron and organiser, and in the South Uist Piping Society as a legitimate body in matters of professional tuition in the Hebrides.

It was in Major MacKenzie's capacity as manager of Lochboisdale Hotel that his support of piping was most practically accomplished, though in this respect it must be said that his support was most often geared toward attracting mainland pipers, well known in competition circles, to the South Uist games. The anticipation of his hospitality – among competitors and judges alike – became as much of an incentive to make the journey as was the potential prize-money on offer; as Rona Lightfoot remarked in conversation in 1996:

Aig an àm ud, nuair bha mise òg, bha mòran, mòran do dheagh phìobairean a' dol a-mach chun na games an Uibhist . . . Bha am fear aig a robh Hotel Loch Baghasdal, Fionnlagh MacChoinnich an t-ainm a bh'air, 's bha leithid do notion *aige fhéin 's do ghaol aig' air a' phìob. Bha na pìobairean a' faighinn trì laithean [air feadh na games] anns an hotel is cha robh e 'cosg sìan. An asgaidh.*[51]

At that time, when I was young, there were many many good pipers going out to the Uist games . . . The man who owned Lochboisdale Hotel, Finlay MacKenzie was his name, and he had such an affection and love for piping. The pipers would get three days [during the games] in the hotel and it wouldn't cost them a thing. It was free.

Major MacKenzie's martial spirit was revived at the outbreak of war in 1939, and he is said to have recruited many soldiers and pipers among his neighbours for the cause. He accompanied the Uist contingent all the way to the Cameron Barracks in Inverness, intent on commanding them himself during the War, but was turned away as too old by that time for active service.[52] In 1961, after forty years as a central figure in South Uist's mainstream piping activities, he sold the Lochboisdale Hotel and moved with his wife to Belfast, where he died three years later.

Before leaving South Uist, as a final gesture of patronage for the tradition to which he had so long been witness, he bequeathed £2,500 as a contribution to the island's piping under the trusteeship of Colonel Charles Cameron, Pipe Major Neil MacLennan and Alasdair MacMillan – Uist men prominent in the military and business world. The trustees chose one promising young piper each year for several years following and used the money to buy him or her a new set of pipes. They announced the recipient and bestowed the gift on the occasion of the Flora MacDonald Cup, a competition strictly for locals which was established in the early 1950s and which has continued nearly every year since. Such recipients of the 'Finlay MacKenzie Memorial Pipes' include Willie Morrison of Loch Eynort and Glasgow, Neil MacDonald of Garryhellie and Calum Beaton of Stoneybridge.

The Rev. Fr Alexander MacDougall, known to his Uist parishioners as *Maighstir Alasdair*, emerges as a key figure in the introduction of organised piping tuition and Highland Games to South Uist in these early years of the twentieth century. He was born in Morar in 1859 and educated in England and at the Scots College of Douai in France.[53] After studying philosophy and theology at St Peter's College, Glasgow, he was ordained in 1890. Church records indicate that his first charge was the mission of Eriskay,[54] but this is puzzling because Eriskay was not considered a separate mission from Daliburgh until 1894, at which point Fr Allan McDonald was put in sole charge. The two even stood shoulder to shoulder in a group photograph commemorating the opening of the island's new church in that year: McDonald tall and straight-backed, gazing off into the distance; MacDougall stouter, eyes groundward, a cigarette dangling between two fingers.[55] If he was indeed sent to Eriskay in 1890, its non-status would explain the brevity of his tenure; before the year's end he was sent to Benbecula, where he served for thirteen years. He finally arrived at the Daliburgh mission in 1903, where he was to stay until 1920.

Alex MacAulay believed that Fr MacDougall had played the pipes during his college days in Glasgow, and was forever after 'religiously devoted to the finer art of piping'.[56] His devotion to community events began early: he spearheaded a campaign for the construction of Petersport Pier in Benbecula in 1904[57] and was instrumental, it appears, in introducing Highland Games complete with piping competitions in Ardvachar in 1898 (at which he judged the piping events along with *Lachlainn Bàn* MacCormick). In Daliburgh he is remembered chiefly for his involvement in soliciting tuition from the Piobaireachd Society in 1909, as non-piper Ronald MacDonald illustrated in conversation eighty-six years later:

> *Bha na daoine bha sin, tha fhios agad, bha am* music *aca ach cha robh e cho math aca. Cha robh duine ann a dh' ionnsachadh gu leughadh iad i à leabhar. Ach thachair sagart a bha seo ri Dalabrog, agus bha* interest *aige anns na daoine agus sa' cheòl. Fhuair e pìobaire bha siud, pìobaire cho ainmeil 's a bh' ann,* Pipe Major John MacDonald, Inverness . . . *'S e sagart a bha seo a thug e ann a sheo,* Father Alexander MacDougall. *'S ann à tìr mór a bha e . . . is bha e gu math* keen *air pìobaireachd . . . Bha* John MacDonald, Inverness *a' tighinn a h-uile bliadhna, a h-uile samhradh, a' tighinn chun na* games, *'s e am fear a dh' ionnsaich a h-uile pìobaire bh' ann, a thug dhaibh . . . Seonaidh Roidein, Ruairidh Roidein, Dòmhnall Nill, Eairdsidh* Lindsay, *Aonghus Nill, Seonaidh* Steele, *Angaidh MacQuarrie, Calum* Walker, *Aonghus Alec Mhóir; a h-uile pìobaire math bha sin, bha tòrr dhiubh. 'S ann bhon duine sin a thàinig an ceòl mór.*[58]

The people here, you see, they had music but they didn't have it so well. There was no one around to teach them to read it from a book. But this priest came to Daliburgh, and he had an interest in the people and in the music. He got a piper, the most famous piper around, Pipe Major John MacDonald, Inverness . . . It was the priest who brought him here, Fr Alexander MacDougall. He was from the mainland . . . and he was quite keen on piping . . . John MacDonald, Inverness would come every year, every summer, he would come to the games, and he's the one who taught every piper around, who taught them . . . John and Roddy MacDonald, Donald son of Neil, Archie Lindsay, Angus [Campbell] son of Neil, John Steele, Angus MacQuarrie, Calum Walker, Angus son of Big Alec; every good piper, there were loads of them. The pibroch came from that man.

After moving on to missions in Glenfinnan, Castlebay and Inverie, MacDougall retired on the eve of the Second World War and returned to his childhood home in Morar. He died a canon, in 1944, in his eighty-fifth year.

∽ THE INSTRUCTORS AND THEIR LEGACY ∽

On 15 December 1903, the Piobaireachd Society's General Committee heard that 'one of the objects of the Society should eventually be the appointment of Piobaireachd teachers in different parts of Scotland, and the Society to financially assist likely pupils to obtain instruction from them'.[59] This was not just a measure of their intent toward the 'diffusion of knowledge of this ancient Highland music'; it was their way of establishing one definitive setting for each tune they prescribed in competitors' lists. The Society felt that there were too many variant settings of tunes extant at the time to make for fair and straightforward judging: 'So many pipers have different settings of the same tune,' their honorary secretary stated in a printed circular, '[that] they are afraid to play certain settings, in case their setting may be different to that which the judges think the correct setting.'[60] Sweeping away all the traditional variation that made *ceòl mór* a living art, therefore, and authorising one version only for each tune played in competition, simplified the whole business for players and judges alike. This was modern management and efficiency in action.

It would be another nine years before the objective was set down as a formal rule of the Society,[61] but the committee began to establish courses and hire professional tutors to teach their settings as early as 1907. In that year, three instructors were picked from the top competitive field of the day to give twelve lessons to four pupils each in their respective cities. These instructors were John MacDonald of Inverness, John MacDougall Gillies of Glasgow and John MacColl of Oban. The pupils were approved by application to the committee, and evidently met with some success in the Games circuit that season.[62] This provided the Society with the impetus to repeat the courses the following year and to appoint a fourth instructor, Gavin MacDougall (a member of a long-established family of pipemakers and champion competitors), to teach in Aberfeldy.[63]

This is the background to the Piobaireachd Society's motives in answering the South Uist Piping Society's call for assistance; they were magnanimously diffusing knowledge of the 'ancient music', but they were also laying the foundation for their own reformed competitive tradition. The call was made and it was answered: on 5 July 1909, the Society congregated for their annual general meeting, where the secretary reported that

> By instructions of the President, a sum of £14 had been contributed towards the expense of a class of 6 weeks' duration in March and April last arranged for in South Uist by a committee of local gentlemen of which Pipe Major John MacDonald, Inverness, was Instructor and the Committee confirmed this payment. It was resolved to hold similar classes during the Autumn and Winter of 1909–10 in the Inverness, Oban, Glasgow, Aberfeldy, and Arisaig and Fort William Districts and also to contribute a sum not exceeding £10 towards the expense of a class in South Uist should the local committee again arrange for such being held.[64]

The president mentioned was in fact Lord Lovat, whose private regiment, the Lovat Scouts, had been recruiting in South Uist since 1900. As such, it is a matter of academic interest that the man who had greatly contributed to South Uist's one avenue towards the literate idiom up to that point – its military presence – would also be instrumental in ushering the island even further into the age of improvement and literacy. The Piobaireachd Society sent four instructors in all to South Uist from 1909 to 1958: Pipe Majors John MacDonald (Inverness), William Lawrie, William Ross and Robert Nicol. MacDonald's influence was arguably the greatest and longest lived, and weight will therefore be given to his involvement, but each made his mark in his own way. Let us explore the circumstances surrounding each instructor's involvement in turn, that we may consider, in the end, the legacy they have left behind.

John MacDonald, Inverness

John MacDonald was born in Glentruim in 1865 to a notable Gaelic-speaking piping family. His father Alexander, piper to the laird of Glentruim, had won the gold medal for *ceòl mór* at the Northern Meeting in Inverness in 1860 and his uncle William had won the same award, coveted above all others in the piping world, in 1868. William was serving as piper to the Prince of Wales at the time. Pipe Major MacDonald enjoyed the reputation of being one of the strongest links with the teaching of the MacCrimmons in his day. This is because although MacDonald's playing derived from several great piping figures of the nineteenth century, it came most notably from Malcolm MacPherson of Cat Lodge, Badenoch, also known as Calum Piobair (1833–98), and from Colin and Alexander Cameron, Jr, sons of Donald Cameron, a mainland piping authority who died in the same year MacDonald's uncle William won the Gold at the Northern Meeting. Calum Piobair was taught originally by his father, who is said to have been a pupil of Iain Dubh MacCrimmon.[65] He is also said to have received instruction from Angus MacKay (author of the *Collection* of 1838), son of John MacKay of Raasay, the latter having been a pupil of both Donald Ruadh and Iain Dubh MacCrimmon in the early 1800s; and from Alexander Munro of Oban, piper to Glengarry and composer of 'Glengarry's Lament', who also had roots in the MacCrimmon school. Donald Cameron, who had taught his sons Colin and Alexander, had been the star pupil of John Ban MacKenzie, who was himself a pupil of John MacKay of Raasay.[66] John MacDonald was therefore purported to have received MacCrimmon piping via two separate branches, albeit linked through the MacKay school. With such a piping genealogy, his status as a supreme authority was rarely questioned by contemporaries, still less by piping circles today. Still less by his South Uist pupils. He won over two thousand prizes in his competitive career,[67] and in recognition of his status he was made a Member of the Order of the British Empire (MBE) in 1932.

In March of 1909, a gale had reportedly blown the mailboat carrying MacDonald from Oban off-course, and it was many hours late in arriving at Lochboisdale pier. He received an eager welcome: 'Youth and youngsters of all ages flocked to him,' wrote Alex MacAulay, 'and few, if any, of those who attended the initial classes were mere learners. Some were already accomplished pipers.'[68] This meant, presumably, that some of the older pupils in his first class had already received some literate training in the militia battalions and had competed, which we know to have been true of Lachlan MacCormick, John Steele, Neil MacInnes and others. The spectacle which greeted MacDonald at Daliburgh School, the course's venue, was undoubtedly a memorable one: according to Piobaireachd Society records, no less than forty-six pupils – twenty-one adults and twenty-five boys – attended; compared to twelve pupils taught by the Society's tutors in all of Scotland in 1907, and sixteen in 1908 and 1909, this speaks volumes for the breadth of piping in the South Uist community at the beginning of the century. Ronald Morrison has claimed that the youngest among them was ten, and the oldest sixty.[69]

Pipe Major Neil MacLennan of Lochboisdale referred to MacDonald's first course during the presentation of the Finlay MacKenzie Pipes at the Flora MacDonald Cup in 1966. He had in his possession a photograph, taken by MacDonald himself, of all the boys on the class's first day, showing that everyone 'with the exception of one member who borrowed his granny's boots for the occasion' was barefoot. It is therefore a touching indication of economy and cultural priority in Uist at the time that all the younger members of the class would have possessed home-made practice chanters, cut and bored by an older relative with reeds cut from barley straw, but could not afford to wear shoes. [70]

The honorary secretary to the Piobaireachd Society reported that 'the progress made . . . was considered most satisfactory' and a correspondent to the *Oban Times* agreed. 'The marked improvement noticeable in piping,' the writer observed in a report on the Askernish games which followed the course, 'was due to the pains taken by Pipe Major MacDonald, who held classes at Daliburgh last spring.'[71] This was the *Oban Times'* first mention of John MacDonald in connection with South Uist instruction. The Uist Society's committee were evidently satisfied enough to press for MacDonald's return, and with enough subscriptions and financial help from locals, as well as the £10 the Piobaireachd Society had set aside earlier for the purpose, the second class duly took place in February and March of 1910. 'The classes have been a great success,' reported the Uist committee's secretary after MacDonald's tuition that year, 'and the local Committee is highly pleased with the progress which has been made, and are [sic] of the opinion that the money has been well spent.'[72] 'Progress' was exactly the feeling of the day. Soon after the end of the second class in Daliburgh, which numbered thirty-one pupils as opposed to sixteen on the mainland that year, the Uist committee made an appeal in the *Oban Times* for more contributions to secure a third session, and from this piece we can identify several important aspects to the early years of Piobaireachd Society involvement:

PIOBAIREACHD CLASSES IN SOUTH UIST

A NURSERY OF PIPERS

The music of the historic 'piob mhor' has always strongly appealed to the natives of the Outer Hebrides, and particularly to those of South Uist. There is hardly a family without its piper, and frequently one finds father and two or more sons able to discourse on the national instrument. Last year a few local gentlemen formed themselves into a Committee to encourage the young men of the district to take up bagpipe playing systematically, and to play from music. With this idea in view, they appealed to the Piobaireachd Society for financial help and to friends in and beyond the Isles for subscriptions in order to secure the services of a professional piper to teach the young men and boys.

Pipe Major John MacDonald, Inverness, was accordingly engaged for six weeks last year. The result of his tuition was so satisfactory that the Committee decided to have him again this winter, and thus a second session has been concluded with still better results. Now some of the young men are able to play several piobaireachds, marches, strathspeys and reels with perfect accuracy. The younger members of the class – boys eleven and twelve years of age – can read the music like their ordinary schoolbooks, and can render it with effect and precision on the practising chanter.

The Committee are convinced that large numbers of the public outside the Outer Isles would be glad to help to promote the success of the school. Up till now, the classes have been carried on through the assistance of the Piobaireachd Society, augmented by local contributions, and the Committee now appeal for further outside aid to enable them to continue their efforts to improve and promote the cult of the pipes in South Uist.[73]

The South Uist Piping Society's motives in organising large-scale tuiton were clearly to improve local piping from a backwater tradition to a modern one, where the pipes are played 'systematically' and 'from music', that is, by literate transmission. The Piobaireachd Society, in turn, needed to have their own settings as widely diffused as possible among the performers of the day for their competitions to be credible. Working together, the two societies tapped into a community of pipers whose raw musical material probably exceeded everyone's expectations; one wonders if Pipe Major MacDonald was really prepared to face forty-six pupils, chanter in hand and mostly barefoot, in Daliburgh School that first season. The *ObanTimes* piece also reveals that he taught competition *ceòl beag* in the Uist course as well as *ceòl mór*, which is confirmed by Jessie MacAulay's reminiscences in a later chapter.

The courses continued. MacDonald composed a report on the class of 1913 which the Society added to the minutes of their general meeting on 11 September. In it he attests to the facility with which his pupils had learned the use of staff notation and their tendency to join the military once of age:

The number of pupils attending this class was twenty-four. Of that number four were beginners this year, as the Committee thought it advisable to further advance the pupils of former years. The result is that nineteen of these are capable of doing for themselves in the reading and playing of music. The interest in piping in South Uist is getting keener than ever, and the Committee are desirous of carrying on this class another year, and in the event of their being able to do so, their idea is that, instead of starting another class of beginners, to continue instruction of the present class, confining it entirely to Piobaireachd, as they are sufficiently up in Marches, Strathspey and Reel playing. Personally, I think this is a very good idea, as there is very good material in the class, and I am certain that the majority of them would become good Piobaireachd players. I may mention that since the classes were started four of those who had tuition have joined the Regular Army, two Special Reserve and three the Lovat Scouts, and I can see that the tendency for the younger boys who are at present learning the Pipes is to join one or other of these branches, which will eventually lead to their joining either of the Highland Regiments of the line.[74]

One cannot help but suspect that the pipers' instruction in notation and their subsequent military service are in some way related, considering the army's promotion of literate piping and the many high-ranking officers among the Piobaireachd Society's core membership. The reader will recall that the Highland Society of London, who also had their fair share of military members, promoted the army as an attractive career for literately-taught pipers during the Napoleonic Wars. It seems a fair assessment that as the First World War loomed, the Piobaireachd Society and their South Uist counterpart tacitly followed their predecessor's example. MacDonald himself would have proved a fine role model for his South Uist pupils, having held the part-time post of Pipe Major to the 1st (later 4th) Volunteer Battalion of the Queen's Own Cameron Highlanders since 1890.[75] We can also see from his report that only twenty-four people attended his course in Daliburgh that year, a sharp drop from forty-six in 1909; but as he makes clear, the Uist committee had thought it better to consolidate the learners' tuition in *ceòl mór* rather than start an entirely new class of beginners.

Tuition was interrupted in 1914 by the Great War. He was not to return to South Uist as their tutor until the early 1930s, although other tutors were engaged in the meantime and he returned often as a judge and sponsor of piping at the games. He resumed instruction from 1931 or 1932 and it was not long after this point that the Piobaireachd Society was paying MacDonald an annual subsidy of £100 and giving him the freedom to hold classes wherever and whenever he saw fit; by this time he was in his sixties, and the older he grew, the more venerable he became and the more discretion he was given as to his teaching schedule. The South Uist classes were sporadic at best throughout the 1930s owing to ill-health and other work requirements,[76] and he made his final crossing to Lochboisdale pier on the eve of the Second World War. It was evidently common knowledge that this trip would be his last: the Pipe Major was presented at the end of the course with an antique cabinet, inside which were four tumblers and a decanter. A silver plaque was placed on its top, inscribed 'To John MacDonald, Inverness, from the piobaireachd pupils of South Uist, 1939'.

WILLIAM LAWRIE

Pipe Major MacDonald's annual course in Daliburgh was successful enough that by 1913, a committee modelled on that of the South Uist Piping Society was formed in Benbecula, with William MacLean as honorary secretary, for the purpose of organising tuition in Balivanich. The Piobaireachd Society had proposed that new courses be arranged for the following year in Benbecula and Aberdeen,[77] so they agreed to subscribe £15 toward the Balivanich course but left the work of finding a tutor to the local committee. A month after this decision, their general committee heard that William MacLean would engage Pipe Major William Lawrie, of the 8th Argyll and Sutherland Highlanders, as instructor.[78] Lawrie was born in Ballachulish in 1882 and, like MacDonald, was an experienced prize-winner, having won both the gold medals at Inverness and Oban in 1910 and the clasp at Inverness in 1911.

This course was not a success. Admittedly, Pipe Major Lawrie was a fully qualified instructor under the employ of the Piobaireachd Society, like Pipe Major MacDonald, and enjoyed the full confidence of the Benbecula committee. He had been confirmed as their instructor in September 1913 after they had reported the class a success and intended to continue it the following spring. However, the course was cut short after one season due to the outbreak of war in 1914, and Lawrie, on active service with the 8th Argylls, died from an illness aggravated by wounds in November, 1916. It also appears that despite the committee's report, the piping school in Balivanich was not received as eagerly as was MacDonald's school. This, in any case, is the impression gained from the results of the 1914 games, on which the *Oban Times* remarked that 'the Committee had expected that some of Pipe Major Lawrie's pupils from Benbecula would have attended, as special arrangements had been made to have some of the events confined to them and to Pipe Major MacDonald's pupils, and much regret was felt that none of the former came forward'.[79]

As the Balivanich school, like the Daliburgh school, was an enterprise in the competitive idiom, it stands to reason that a measure of its success would be competition turn-out and results; neither of which were got from Pipe Major Lawrie's 1914 course. However, the seeds were planted, and a course would again be held in Benbecula by succeeding instructors.

Willie Ross

The Great War caused a break in the Piobaireachd Society courses for much longer than actual wartime. Such was the depressed atmosphere in South Uist following hostilities that the summer games were not reinstated until 1922.[80] It was not until the spring of 1923 that the South Uist Piping Society reassembled to engage the Piobaireachd Society for renewed tuition. They sent their first instructor since Pipe Major Lawrie nine years earlier: this was Willie Ross, who later that same year issued the first of five volumes of competition-standard *ceòl beag* in unprecedented detail of gracing and expression.[81] He was without doubt the top competitor in Scotland at the time.

Pipe Major Ross was born in 1879 in Strathfarrar and served with the Scots Guards from 1896 to 1920. Upon his retirement from the Guards, Lord Lovat appointed him Pipe Major of his Scouts, a post which he held until 1933. The year 1920 also marked his appointment as head of the Army School of Piping at Edinburgh Castle. By the time of his arrival in Lochboisdale as instructor of the Piobaireachd Society course, he had taken the Oban and Inverness gold medals and had won the Inverness Clasp, for former winners of the Gold, seven times; as such, he brought the same qualities of military example and competitive success to his tutelage in South Uist as did his two predecessors.

Ross held classes in Daliburgh in 1923 and 1924, in Benbecula in 1925 and in Barra in 1926 and 1927. He spent three weeks with his pupils, as opposed to MacDonald's six, but the Society seemed every bit as appreciative of Ross's tuition. He no doubt endeared himself to committee and community alike through his methodical instruction and personal charm; this at least is the image gained from the *Oban Times*' description of his last two evenings in Daliburgh in 1923:

> After holding piping classes in Islay, Pipe Major Ross proceeded to South Uist, where large and enthusiastic classes were held every evening from May 15th to June 8th. Pipe Major Ross proved a most capable teacher. Accompanied by their friends the pupils assembled in Daliburgh School on the evening of June 7th and passed a most enjoyable evening of dancing and piping. Almost every man present was a piper. Mr. F.S. MacKenzie, honorary secretary of the South Uist Piobaireachd Society, presented Pipe Major Ross, on behalf of the pipers attending his classes, with a wallet of Treasury notes, thanking him in the name of his pupils for the care and patience he had exercised in instructing them.
>
> On June 8th a smoking concert was held in Daliburgh School, and Pipe Major Ross was the guest of the evening. His entertainers were the members of the South Uist Piobaireachd Society, who wished to express how much they valued the honour of having the foremost piper in Scotland coming to instruct the youth of Uist.
>
> Looking back, the Chairman said, to a period of about forty years, it appeared that piping would soon be a lost art. About that time there were three or four first-class pipers appearing at all the Highland Gatherings, but no young pipers were coming forward. Then the Piobaireachd Society was formed, and in time owing to the interest taken in piping by Mr. Simon MacKenzie, Lochboisdale, Mr. John MacDonald, Askernish, and Father MacDougall, Daliburgh, a Piobaireachd Society was formed in South Uist. For a time they had been successful in securing the services of that king of pipers and instructors, Pipe Major John MacDonald, for a few months every year, and the young pipers of Uist had just begun to make a name for themselves when the War broke out and the local Piobaireachd Society had to cease activities. The Society has been revived, and owing to the kindess of

the Scottish Piobaireachd Society they had been able to recommence their classes. Pipe Major Ross had shown himself a worthy successor of Pipe Major MacDonald as instructor of piping.

Pipe Major Ross replied, thanking the Chairman for his kind words. He said that he felt it easy to work in such a piping 'atmosphere' and with the conviction that he was among friends.

The evening passed with selections on the bagpipes and reminiscences of old pipers and bygone contests with many a hint to young pipers interspersed. Too soon they had to say goodbye for Pipe Major Ross was leaving Lochboisdale by steamer at midnight. The pleasure of having met Pipe Major Ross is one which none of those present will ever forget.[82]

Ross's classes in Barra prompted enough pipers from that island to compete in the 1927 and 1928 Games for the *Oban Times* to remark that 'they will not be long in securing places on the prize list'.[83] Alas, the Barra contingent had to satisfy themselves with Calum Johnstone's first place in the *ceòl mór* event of 1924; as the *Oban Times* published those words, several pre-war pupils of John MacDonald from Uist and Benbecula – Angus Campbell, Angus MacAulay, Archie Lindsay and Angus MacQuarrie, among others – were building a competitive oligarchy that would span twenty years and more. This is discussed further elsewhere.

Robert Nicol

The Second World War interrupted what might have continued through the 1940s, and as a result – much like the time of the Great War – it took years after the renewal of peace for the Piobaireachd Society to reinstate its South Uist tuition. The earliest mention in Society records of a Uist course post-Second World War comes from a General Meeting in January of 1950, at which was heard:

> [A] recommendation resolved upon by the Music Committee 'that the General Committee should authorise a subscription of £10 towards the expenses of a course of winter instruction in South Uist which is being arranged by the President.' Arising out of this recommendation, the President reported that by the gracious permission of HM the King, Pipe Major Nicol was meantime conducting classes in South Uist. The Committee accepted the recommendation and authorised a payment of £10 towards the expenses of the class.[84]

Robert Nicol was born in Durris, Aberdeenshire, in 1905, and by the age of nineteen was piper to King George V, a post he held jointly with another famous Aberdeenshire piper, Robert Brown, for many years. Together, Nicol and Brown were sent by the King to receive tuition in *ceòl mór* from John MacDonald, Inverness, on a yearly six-week basis from 1926 to 1939; it was during MacDonald's tutelage that Nicol took both the Oban and Inverness gold medals in 1930, and the Clasp in 1932. Just as MacDonald enjoyed a reputation for having received authentic MacCrimmon teaching, so Nicol and Brown, popularly known as the 'Bobs of Balmoral', enjoyed the same as a result of their time with MacDonald.

The 1950 course was well received and the same was arranged for the following year, with the Piobaireachd Society again contributing £10 toward the expenses. In 1952, it was agreed that 'the President be given authority to arrange for the continuation of instruction in South Uist and Inverness on the same terms as for the past year'.[85] and this set the paperwork for the South Uist course, under Pipe Major Nicol, to continue with a yearly grant of £10 until the winter of 1958. It may interest some to note that the Piobaireachd Society's financial contribution in 1958 was the same as it had been every year that classes were held since 1910. It doesn't seem like much when compared to the gift of Duncan MacLeod of Skeabost, Skye, an honoured visitor to the Uist Games of 1929 who addressed the committee at the evening's post-Games social:

> He thanked the people of Uist for their kindness to him on his first visit to the island, the pipers for their playing at the Gathering and that evening, and the Chairman for his kind attention to him at the Gathering. He asked the pipers to remember that in all things a piper is a man apart, a man with a message, a man above his fellows, and he should never forget it. At the close of an evening, perhaps in Uist, perhaps on the mainland, perhaps in the Colonies, the words would be said to him – 'Is math a fhuair thu, is math a rinn thu'. [Mr. MacLeod] learned with regret that there was now no tutor for the young pipers in Uist, and he would give £100 as a nucleus of a fund to engage a tutor.[86]

Compared with MacLeod's generosity, the Piobaireachd Society's pittance leaves the impression that their interest in the Hebridean quarter had waned since earlier days.

By Nicol's time, automobiles and adequate roads had long been the norm in South Uist, as opposed to the coaches and horses of John MacDonald's day. This didn't stop many from attending MacDonald's courses; such was their devotion to the man and his teachings that, it is said, the Uist pupils would come from twenty miles' distance – almost the entire length of the island.[87] Because of the improvement in transportation, Nicol's courses took on a wider scope in that he would hold classes in various parts of the island during the six-week period. Calum Beaton was a member of Nicol's class in the 1950s. He amassed his repertoire of *ceòl mór* mainly in this period, although, as Chapter 7 will show, he received occasional instruction for many years from other pipers in the community who were among John MacDonald's original Daliburgh pupils. His memories give valuable insight into Nicol's techniques of instruction and the general make-up of his class. He describes, for instance, where and when the classes were held and how many tended to participate:

> CB: *Thòisich [Nicol] air tighinn a dh' Uibhist is bhiodh clasaichean aige, o, mìos gu sia seachdainnean a h-uile geamhradh airson bliadhnachan . . . Thàinig e turas no dhà 's t-samhradh, cuideachd, ro na Games, mu sheachdainn ro na Games, airson gum [faicte] mar a bha sinn a' dèanamh, is bha e a' toirt dhuinn teagasg cuideachd. Bha e an Dalabrog, is Cill Donainn, is Beinn na Faola. Bha mi dol a Dhalabrog is Chill Donainn, is tha mi smaoineadh gu robh mi aig a h-uile clas a bh' aige . . .*
> JD: *Có bh' anns a' chlas sin?*
> CB: *Bha tòrr a' dol dhan chlas an uairsin. Bhiodh suas ri ceithir duine deug co-dhiùbh.*
> JD: *Dé an aois a bha thu aig an àm?*
> CB: *Bhithinn dìreach seach no ochd bliadhn' deug, tha mi smaointinn.*[88]
>
> CB: Nicol began coming to Uist and holding classes, oh, a month to six weeks every winter for years . . . He also came once or twice in the summer, about a week before the games, to see how we were getting on, and he gave us teaching then too. He was in Daliburgh, Kildonan, and Benbecula. I went to Daliburgh and Kildonan, and I believe I was in every class he gave . . .
> JD: Who were in that class?
> CB: There were loads attending at that point. There would have been at least fourteen.
> JD: How old were you at the time?
> CB: I would have been just seventeen or eighteen, I think.

Nicol's tenure in South Uist was unique among those sent by the Piobaireachd Society because he was the only one to have actually competed in the games at Askernish while an active instructor, thereby pitting his skills against those of his own pupils. This occurred in 1955, at which he took first place in the *ceòl mór*, and in 1956, where he took third.[89] These were probably the instances of summer tuition that Beaton mentioned above.

His teaching style in these courses largely reflected his own tuition under John MacDonald. Beaton said of Nicol:

> CB: *Bha e uamhasach crosda, e fhéin; leam-sa, co-dhiubh. Bha e a' gabhail duine mu seach, ach dh' fheumadh tu fuireach, 's ann 'sa sgoil a bha e, bha sinn 'nar suidhe ann a shin, agus ged a bhithinn-sa aige a' chiad duine, dh' fheumainn suidhe ann a shin ag éisdeachd ri càch. Bha e a' toirt difir port dhan a h-uile duine, is bha agad a h-uile port a dh'ionnsachadh.*
> JD: *Gheobheadh tu puirt aig daoine eile?*
> CB: *Gheobheadh, ag éisdeachd ris, dé bha e ag ionnsachadh an duine eile. Dh'fheumadh tu éisdeachd ris a'* whole lot.[90]

CB: He was a terrible curmudgeon; with me, anyway. He took people in turns, but you'd have to stay there, it was in the school, we'd be sitting there, and although I'd be the first one, I'd have to sit there listening to everyone else. He gave a different tune to every man, and you had to learn every tune.
JD: You would get the tunes of other people?
CB: Yes, listening to what he was teaching the next man. You would have to listen to the whole lot.

This account echoes that given by Robert Brown when speaking to researcher Robin Lorimer in 1953 of the tuition he and Nicol had received from MacDonald:

RL: You would both be listening to him teaching at the same time, I suppose?
RB: Yes, yes, I had all he taught Nicol, and Nicol had all he taught me. Our method was to take twenty or thirty tunes, different tunes; you heard all [the other's] faults and wee points, and of course you never had them yourself.[91]

Despite the stated aims of the Piobaireachd Society and the South Uist Piping Society during their long period of co-operation, the instructors were under considerable constraints as regards the transmission of *ceòl mór* on the island. This becomes apparent when comparing their teaching methods with their own experiences in receiving the music. The hallmark of John MacDonald's own education was the transmission of tunes by oral/aural means and a near-total avoidance of the written note: 'I received most of my tuition from Calum MacPherson of Catt Lodge, Badenoch,' he once wrote. 'Calum was easily the best player of Piobaireachd I have ever known. He would . . . sit down beside me, take away all books and pipe music, then sing in his own Canntaireachd the ground and different variations of the particular Piobaireachd he wished me to learn. It was from these early associations with Malcolm MacPherson that I realised that Piobaireachd must be transmitted by song from one piper to another in order to get the soul of it – the lights and shades. Most of the Piobaireachd players of the present day rely on the score, but you can not express in musical notation what you would like to. It is really impossible.'[92] *Canntaireachd* was his most valued tool of transmission and his reliance on it formed the basis of his reputation as a master of the perceived MacCrimmon tradition; a tradition which Ronald Morrison believed MacDonald 'passed on to his beloved South Uist pupils without the slightest deviation.'[93] He in turn taught Robert Nicol what he had learned with the same strict avoidance of the score. The fact remains, however, that one of the Uist Society's fundamental objectives was the introduction of literacy, and that MacDonald, Ross and Nicol were employed by the Piobaireachd Society and paid a yearly salary to teach their own specific settings – settings which many pipers, including MacDonald, personally loathed for deviating from accepted tradition as they had received it.[94]

That MacDonald taught *ceòl mór* in South Uist using the Piobaireachd Society's notated settings is beyond question. The Society's committee minutes, for instance, record an agreement to send two copies each of their publications with MacDonald for use in his 1933 course,[95] while more recently, the late Donald Morrison of Loch Eynort and Aberdeen, who attended his courses in the 1930s, recalled MacDonald teaching strictly 'what's printed in the book'[96] while contemporaneously teaching the King's pipers, Brown and Nicol, other versions. Furthermore, MacDonald's employment by the Society rested in the first place on his willingness to adopt their printed settings – something which another eminent competitor at the time, Pipe Major G.S. MacLennan, refused to do. When the Society was looking for someone to teach their Aberdeen course in 1913, John Campbell of Kilberry, one of the architects of the Society, stated on record that 'the Committee do not intend to recommend Pipe Major MacLennan except under condition that he gives up his traditional style'.[97] This of course was necessary in order to establish the credibility of their reformed competition system, but proscribing variability in favour of practicality still seems at odds with the Society's original purpose, for example 'the Preservation of Old Highland Piobaireachd and the diffusion of knowledge concerning them' as Campbell himself put it in 1902.[98]

MacDonald undoubtedly used *canntaireachd* when teaching in South Uist as a tool of expression, just as Nicol did after him, but both were obligated to base what they expressed, at least officially, on the Society's scores. On the other hand, they just as certainly turned to a pupil in Daliburgh's school hall now and then to offer him other ways of playing – a phrase of melody here or there, an alternative variation or adornment of grace notes passed down orally, outside the Society's sphere of control – with the proviso that 'they won't like this on the platform'. Calum Beaton, for instance, recalls Nicol showing him an alternative way of playing the *ùrlar* of the 'End of the Great Bridge' as he himself had got it from MacDonald, with the above advice.[99] Ross felt a similar obligation to adhere to Society settings, though he conceded to styles other than the Society's in certain circumstances. In the opinion of the late Colin Caird, a respected amateur player and a contemporary of Ross, 'much could be learned simply by listening to Willie Ross tuning his pipe, playing snatches of piobaireachd in the old style. His natural style was not that of the Piobaireachd Society's books, but as he was being paid his salary by the Society, he felt obliged to follow their way, except when he was tuning.'[100]

In the final analysis, the actions of the original South Uist Piping Society suggest what Gibson referred to as 'the superior stance of the inevitably modern and improved',[101] their appreciation of bagpipe music seemingly confined to the competition idiom. But they must have been intimately familiar with the ear-learned tradition of dance piping, as distinct from the literate technicalities of competition: before arriving in Lochboisdale, Simon MacKenzie had been manager of the Castlebay Hotel in Barra for many years, where piping was certainly of the aural idiom, and Fr MacDougall had been born in mid-nineteenth-century Morar, where Gaelic tradition was arguably still vibrant and relatively uninfluenced. Although they may have been motivated, in particular, by a dearth of *ceòl mór* on the island at the time, the signs of an active and thriving piping tradition in every other respect were in easy evidence. Instead of being unfamiliar with it, they likely saw it as antiquated, simple, behind the times. While this may have been true of most of the mainland where technical and competitive innovations had become the accepted standard, the sheer scale of *ceòl cluais* on the island relative to the rest of Scotland at the time suggests that it was perfectly in keeping with contemporary social life in South Uist. It was normal; it was common; it was how it had always been.

Enter the Juggernaut of the mainstream. Several writers have referred to the Piobaireachd Society's bestowing of a 'new tradition' in South Uist where formerly there was none, as if this sequestered bastion of old-world Gaelic culture were a desert made suddenly green with crops.[102] The corollary to this view is that, by the early twentieth century, the functions and aesthetics of piping in mainstream Scottish society – that is, outwith South Uist – had fundamentally changed. To be a 'good' piper no longer meant being able to perform an inexhaustible repertoire of reels for a Scots Foursome at the local wedding party, maintaining an impeccable dance-rhythm all the while, as it did in Nova Scotia until comparatively recent times; no longer were the subtleties and dynamics of melody resulting from aural transmission deemed worthy of an 'accomplished' piper's aspirations. In mainstream Scotland it had come to mean the technical mastery of a prescribed template of fingering in an environment where grace notes took precedence over dance-steps. The gentlemen who founded the South Uist Piping Society – a widely recognised hotelier, a respected priest, an estate factor and so on – were connected with and brought up in mainstream society and had learned piping within its modern literate idiom; they consequently saw the indigenous ceilidh piping which was still largely the norm in their corner of the world as little more than raw material for the improvements they felt obliged to introduce. The two societies' 'new tradition', in effect, saw the literate and the mainstream emerge as the measure of a piper's skill, and meant a gradual redressing of the community's view of their indigenous aural tradition as something inferior. Archie Beaton's words to his son in the 1940s say it all: '*Cha dearg mis' air sian a theagasg dhuit idir, cha do dh' ionnsaich mi fhéin a-riamh dòigheil*' he said. 'I cannot teach you a thing, I never learned properly.'

CHAPTER 7

SOUTH UIST, CLANRANALD AND *Ceòl Mór*

~ CONTINUITY OF TRADITION ~

According to living memory, very few individuals in South Uist displayed practical knowledge of *ceòl mór* in the years leading up to the twentieth century. It is commonly held by piping authorities that the classical form of piping completely died out in the Hebrides with the decline of musical patronage in the eighteenth to nineteenth century, and that it was reintroduced to the South Uist community with startling and long-lasting effect by the Piobaireachd Society from 1909. This is true to an extent, in that it was reintroduced from outside on a large-scale, organised basis, but the idea that *ceòl mór* had totally evaporated from the community by then is difficult to accept when considering that South Uist had been unanimously regarded for the previous fifty years as the last great storehouse of Gaelic tradition. There is evidence from oral and written sources that challenges the notion.

The written record is always scanty in this territory. Piping competitions had been a fixture of the annual Highland Games in South Uist ever since their inception on a cold Epiphany morning in January of 1898; but, as is detailed elsewhere, these competitions consisted merely of the march and the strathspey and reel. *Ceòl mór* did not enter the picture as a category of competition until a decade later, corresponding with the introduction of Piobaireachd Society tuition. If it were an isolated case, we might attribute it to any number of reasons that do not detract from the idea of a healthy classical tradition in Uist at the time, but games throughout the Hebrides appear to have fared the same. From Islay to

Colonsay to Lewis, local gatherings across the Hebridean seaboard at the dawn of the twentieth century were bereft of *ceòl mór* until the Piobaireachd Society began sponsoring courses. Naturally, this suggests the conventional wisdom – it can hardly be coincidental that conventional wisdom and the written, English-language record go hand-in-hand – that performance and staged competition of the big music was at a low ebb in the Isles, perhaps confined to those trained in the military, where *ceòl mór* was still possessed of practical function. In support of this one may point to the record of Neil MacInnes, a native of South Uist who enlisted in the Queen's Own Cameron Highlanders in 1889. Appointed Piper in the 1st Battalion in 1892, he took second place in *ceòl mór* at the regimental games in Malta in 1893 and first in 1896.[1]

One may comfortably speculate, however, that MacInnes had learned what *ceòl mór* he knew along traditional lines of transmission in South Uist rather than in the army, and that knowledge of the repertoire, and technical motifs such as the 'hiharin' and the echo beats, were kept alive among pipers in Uist and Benbecula up to the era of Piobaireachd Society instruction. For evidence suggesting this scenario, we must look to the oral record of living memory and personal memoirs, which even at this late date still gives some indication of a continuity of tradition between the end of chiefly patronage and the advent of mass literate tuition.

Local pipers remembered nowadays as having played *ceòl mór* before the arrival of the Piobaireachd Society include Lachlan MacCormick, Neil Campbell and William MacLean, the last having won the Inverness Gold Medal in 1901 and that of Oban in 1912. However, MacLean cannot rightly be considered as a bearer of any specific Uist tradition because he was an incomer from Mull and learned *ceòl mór* chiefly from Malcolm MacPherson, or Calum Piobair, in Badenoch; he was living in Benbecula by the time of his first medal, but by his second was residing in Glasgow. Neil Campbell – *Niall Chatrìona* of Frobost – does not appear to have possessed an extensive repertoire before taking part in John MacDonald's courses before the Great War, if modern reminiscences are to be relied upon. Calum Beaton once recalled him playing 'MacIntosh's Lament', but could not be sure that he had learned it before MacDonald's tuition, adding that he had played the tune in the typical mainstream style.[2] However, Campbell is reputed to have been taught to read music by a family of *ceòl mór*-playing MacGillivrays who leased land in Eoligarry, Barra, in the early 1880s, which suggests that he picked up a modest classical repertoire from them as well.[3] The case of MacCormick, on whom our most reliable source of information is the reminiscences of his former pupil, Willie MacDonald of Benbecula,[4] presents another difficulty. Although he was a very successful competitor in both *ceòl mór* and *ceòl beag* around the beginning of the century, we have already seen how *ceòl mór* was not apparently played in competition in South Uist prior to 1908; therefore, what is claimed in local tradition cannot be verified by written records. However, MacCormick was known to play settings of tunes in competition which conflicted with the Society's, and furthermore that he, like many other top-class pipers in Scotland at the time, held a very low opinion of the Society's settings; there is no reason to doubt that he learned his repertoire within the Uist community rather than, say, in the army where tuition was by Society instructors.

Lachlan MacCormick, or *Lachlainn Bàn*, 'Fair-haired Lachlan', was born in Creagorry, Benbecula, in 1859 and is regarded as the area's pre-eminent player in the days before the Piobaireachd Society era. He was partially blind and, like many Hebridean pipers historically, a left-handed player – that is, right hand top with the drone over the right shoulder. He was also a literate and prolific composer, his best known tunes being perhaps the strathspey 'The South Uist Golf Club' and the reel 'Creagorry Blend'. MacCormick remains somewhat legendary in piping circles, not only for his competitive success and technical fluency, but for maintaining an apparently inexhaustible supply of obscure tunes, marches and dance tunes in particular, absorbed by ear from the ceilidh houses of his home community. He is even said to have celebrated his 92nd birthday with a half-hour on the pipes, though it is unclear whether he played entirely his own compositions or simply settings of tunes that had not been heard in generations – both equally plausible.[5] Frederick Rea, the English Catholic master of Garrynamonie School from 1890 to 1913, was probably referring to *Lachlainn Bàn* when he opined on the big music in his memoirs, although, MacCormick having been an educated man, Rea's description of the unnamed piper as speaking no English is about the only aspect of the passage below that does not fit 'Fair-haired Lachlan':

> Much as I had enjoyed the sound of the pipes at times, I must confess that I was not able to appreciate the music of the pibroch. It was supposed to be a musical poem telling of the beauty of hill and dale, of gentle love, joys, war, of battles, victory, defeat, and sorrow... Among the pipers who played to Father Allan [McDonald, parish priest of Eriskay], there was one whom I saw only once or twice. He was a peculiar looking man with almost lint-white hair, smooth hairless face, was of squat figure, and spoke no English. There was no doubt about his ability as a piper. His speciality was the pibroch, and as he played the others seemed to listen to him in awe – I believe that he read and wrote music for the bagpipes and was himself a composer. I heard afterwards that he subsequently carried off many valuable prizes for pipe-playing at the various annual Highland gatherings held in many parts of Scotland.[6]

MacCormick disagreed with the Piobaireachd Society settings of *ceòl mór* in favour of settings which in comparison were melodically and, at times, technically anachronistic, begging the inference that the oral and manuscript tradition that characterised much *ceòl mór* transmission among the nineteenth-century performer community had included, to some extent, the remotest of the Western Isles. This was demonstrated when Archibald Campbell of Kilberry travelled to Uist to judge the piping events at the Askernish games in 1911. MacCormick entered the open *ceòl mór* event, playing 'The Battle of Waternish'. Kilberry awarded him second place, behind the Paisley Bard Donald MacIntyre's winning rendition of 'Black Donald's March', or '*Pìobaireachd Dhòmhnaill Duibh*'. Forty years later, however, when speaking with MacCormick's former pupil Willie MacDonald, an elderly Kilberry confessed that the setting of 'Waternish' he'd heard that day had been unfamiliar to him. MacDonald demonstrated a few bars of his old tutor's setting of this tune, and others, at the Piobaireachd Society conference of 1999;[7] from that it is evident that MacCormick's style, in comparison with the competitive standard at the time, was quick, rhythmic and anachronistic in the expression of technical motifs. He preceded the top-hand 'hedare' flourish with a short low A note, a motif that had faded from general use except where fossilised in the melody of a bare few tunes such as 'Lament for the Children', 'Lament for Donald Dougall MacKay' and 'I Got a Kiss of the King's Hand'. He preceded the E note which typically ends the leumluath movement with a low A grace note, a motif which by then was often seen as redundant. In 'Waternish', MacCormick discarded the first of the two taorluath movements in favour of a *fosgailte*, or open, tripling motif. He was also clearly conscious of a common stock between *ceòl mór* and Gaelic song: when discussing tunes with Willie MacDonald around 1950, just one or two years before his death, he claimed that 'MacLeod's Salute' – or 'Lament for Donald MacLeod of Grisornish', as he called the tune[8] – was based on an old Irish song.

These and other indications of his performance and lore give the impression that Lachlan MacCormick espoused a style of classical pipe music which even in the first decades of the twentieth century was considered archaic, and there is no reason to doubt that he learned it among the Hebridean Gaels of the late nineteenth century, at least two generations after the end of Clanranald patronage in South Uist. Allan MacDonald of Glenuig has suggested that MacCormick's repertoire represented a transitional stage in the evolution of *ceòl mór*'s performance style, from its roots in early Gaelic tradition to its competitive standard in the twentieth century.[9] This may indeed have been the case. Without doubt he bridged both the old world and the new – the aural tradition and the literate – in a seamless synthesis of music and culture, and accordingly should be considered a key figure in the history of Highland piping.

The experience of *Lachlainn Bàn* aside, possibly the most intriguing evidence of a historically unbroken tradition of *ceòl mór* performance in South Uist before the advent of the Piobaireachd Society comes from the experience of Calum Beaton, whose first lessons in classical piping were by a man from a neighbouring township in the 1940s:

> *Thuirt fear a bha agam a theagasg, Alasdair Peutan, nach b'aithnte dha airson [ceòl mór] a chluichd, agus dh'iarr e orm a dhol gu fear eile, John Archie MacLellan, a bha a' fuireach 'san ath-bhaile . . . Chaidh mi far a robh e is thuirt e nach cluicheadh e móran idir – dhà no trì a bha fhios aige. Thug e dhomh 'Cumha Màiri Nighean Alasdair Ruaidh', agus 'Cumha Phadruig Òig MacCruimein'. Bha e a' toirt dhomh difir dòigh . . . Bha mise smaoineadh gur ann mar sin a bha 'correct', is bha mi 'ga chluichd mar sin.*[10]

> The man who I had for teaching, Alasdair Beaton, said that he didn't know how to play *ceòl mór*, and he asked me to go to another man, John Archie MacLellan, who stayed in the next township . . . I went to him and he said that he didn't play much at all – he knew two or three. He gave me 'Lament for Mary MacLeod' and 'Lament for Patrick Òg MacCrimmon'. He gave me a different way . . . I thought that it was the correct way, and I played it like that.

John Archie MacLellan was taught by one of the Smiths of Howmore, who seems to have been the last family in Uist to maintain and pass on a distinctly nineteenth-century style of *ceòl mór* performance; speculating as to their sources leaves the impression of a vibrant classical tradition where there was formerly thought to be none. Sometime in the late 1800s, John Smith, crofter and piper, married Christina MacMillan in Howmore. Their three sons, Sandy, John and Neil, all became literate pipers of merit and played regularly for dances, soirées, and doubtless the odd *bàl suitheadh*, or blackhouse ball, at the turn of the century. On 10 February 1906, for example, the *Oban Times* reported a concert and dance at Howmore Public School, featuring selections on the bagpipe by 'Mr. Smith and Mr. Smith Junr', among other musical acts.[11] The Smith brothers were raised in Stoneybridge and Neil eventually moved back to Howmore, where he married Christina Gillies in 1905. At that time he was employed as a general labourer, but in later years he worked as a postman.

Neil and Christina had at least three sons who took up piping: Neil Jr. (b. 1906), John (b. 1908) and another named John (b. 1916), which in reality probably meant that one was named *Iain* and the other *Iagan* or *Seonaidh*, all of which correspond to 'John' in English. Neil and the elder John were quite successful for a time in local competition; both dominated the junior level March, Strathspey and Reel (MSR), for instance, during the years that Pipe Major Ross taught for the Piobaireachd Society in Daliburgh and Benbecula.[12] These two Smiths were Donald A. Morrison's first teachers.

According to Calum Beaton, Sandy and his brother John Smith (if not also Neil) attended MacDonald's Daliburgh courses in the pre-war era. If they had not already received literate tuition from their father, they certainly received it from Pipe Major MacDonald, along with a thorough grounding in the Piobaireachd Society's own settings of *ceòl mór*. Sandy, in turn, is reputed to have taught John Archie MacLellan.

In 'Mary MacLeod' and 'Patrick Og', MacLellan taught the young Beaton to play a technical and rhythmical motif very common in *ceòl mór* known as 'hiharin' (as it is called in the Campbell Canntaireachd), or the 'pibroch birl', in a very different way than was then, and is now, heard in mainstream competition performances. It in fact recalled an eighteenth- and early nineteenth-century style which appears to have gone largely out of fashion between the publication of MacKay's *Ancient Pìobaireachd* (1838) and the Piobaireachd Society's second series of collections which began in 1925. Contemporary notation suggests that in the former time period, 'hiharin' comprised a pulse on the low A note followed by a division of the A by two low G grace notes in quick succession; the whole of the movement making, apparently, two distinct beats. The A would invariably be introduced by a cadence of short G-E-D grace notes, such as in Donald MacDonald's setting of 'Patrick Òg' in his published collection, c. 1820. Shown below is the last bar of line 1 of the ground:

Figure 3. 'Lament for Patrick Òg MacCrimmon', Donald MacDonald (c. 1820)

MacKay's publication eighteen years later, however, represents the introductory E in general as having greater value. Whether MacKay's notation in this instance reflects a different style from MacDonald's, or simply a different way of depicting the same style, is uncertain; but in the case of the 'hiharin', one can clearly see that it absorbs some of the value of the themal A:

Figure 4. 'Lament for Patrick Òg MacCrimmon', Angus Mackay (1838)

Representations of the introductory E's value would become greater still in the early twentieth century under the editorship of the Piobaireachd Society, who based many of their settings on MacKay's. Their version of 'Patrick Òg' was published in Book 3 of their second series (1930); notice how the E of the 'hiharin' has become essentially equal in value to the themal A, taking up the whole of the first beat, while the A's division is compressed into a run of short grace notes as a result:

Figure 5. 'Lament for Patrick Og MacCrimmon', Archibald Campbell (1930)

I do not mean to suggest by these examples that the 'hiharin' motif's evolution over the course of a century was entirely linear and universal; only that, due to the priority given to MacKay's settings in competition and their later adoption by Society editors, by about the 1920s the motif as depicted in Figure 5 had become standard in mainstream performance. Other publications such as John MacLennan's *Piobaireachd as MacCrimmon Played It* (1907) and G.F. Ross's *Some Piobaireachd Studies* (1926) discuss styles of 'hiharin' whose emphasis, like Donald MacDonald's, favour the A; but these were written from the point of view of those marginalised by the predominance of the MacKay – Piobaireachd Society method.

Calum Beaton recorded for me on the practice chanter the 'hiharin' movement as he'd learned it from John Archie MacLellan.[13] In both 'Patrick Òg' and 'Mary MacLeod' the emphasis was firmly on the initial low A, with the introductory E receiving greater value than a grace note, but less than a full themal note; while the second of the divided As was played as quickly as a grace note:

Figure 6a. 'Lament for Patrick Og MacCrimmon' as taught to Calum Beaton, late 1940s

Figure 6b. 'Lament for Mary MacLeod' as taught to Calum Beaton, late 1940s

One can see from the above that in Beaton's playing the two beats of 'hiharin' are fulfilled by the themal A as in the manner depicted by Donald MacDonald in 1820 or, to take it further, by Joseph MacDonald in 1760.[14] Beaton believes that John Archie MacLellan learned this musical anachronism from Sandy Smith. He went on to theorise, after some investigation of his own among older relatives and neighbours, that Smith's first exposure to the big music came neither from his father nor from John MacDonald, but from either a family of Curries in Eochar or by Roderick MacDonald of Barra, a prominent local player in the Smiths' time.[15] This would have taken place probably near the turn of the twentieth century.

Beaton appears to be the last piper in South Uist to have played the 'hiharin' in the older manner, but he did not play it for long: after his time with MacLellan he went for lessons to Angus Campbell of Frobost, who had learned *ceòl mór* in the Piobaireachd Society's classes and who, throughout his life, remained the island's acknowledged authority. Campbell was curt in his appraisal:

> *Thòisich mi a' dol gu Aonghus Caimbeul à Frobost, fhios agad Aonghus Nill Chatrìona, is cho luath 's a dh' iarr e orm a chluichd, chluichd mi pìos do Mhàiri Nighean Alasdair, is 'O Dhia, chan ann mar siud a dh' fheumas tu 'ga chluichd idir,' thuirt e, 'tha siud ceàrr.*[16]

> I started going to Angus Campbell of Frobost, Angus son of Neil son of Katherine you know, and as soon as he asked me to play, I played a piece of 'Mary MacLeod', and 'Oh God, you mustn't play it like that at all,' he said, 'that's wrong.'

Campbell reportedly branded it *'seann dòigh an t-saoghail mhóir'* – 'the old-fashioned way of the world' – and promptly taught Beaton the Piobaireachd Society method. Beaton never played the older style in public again.

Shown in this context, such anachronisms as have been found in the southern Outer Hebridean tradition in the first half of the twentieth century suggest several things: first, that *ceòl mór* survived to an uncertain extent among South Uist pipers in the pre-Piobaireachd Society era; second, that at least some local pipers, Lachlan MacCormick among them, performed in an older style than that which was commonly played in mainstream circles; and third, that transmission of this style, or at least a remnant of it in the form of the 'hiharin' and other motifs as discussed above, continued among a few families or individuals until well after the piping community's initial exposure to mainstream influences. Of course, there is room for doubt. By Beaton's time, other styles of 'hiharin' had been in print for decades (such as in the works by MacLennan and Ross) and there is no way to know whether John Archie MacLellan, or the Smiths before him, had not come upon such publications themselves or been influenced by players outwith Uist who had. Indeed, the quick division of low A in the 'hiharin' as it appears in

MacLennan's *Piobaireachd as MacCrimmon Played It* (1907) is strikingly similar to Beaton's. But the idea that the South Uist community's conservative nature was tenacious enough to retain a fragment of old-world *ceòl mór* for so long, and under such pressure from conflicting influences, is a tempting one. It is surely possible that elements of the repertoire and style of Clanranald's MacIntyres, or even of the MacArthurs, were diffused among the rank-and-file of Uist's piping community long after the death of chiefly patronage; could this have been the origin of the 'hiharin' motif as Beaton first learned it? Or of MacCormick's settings? MacCormick was known to precede the echo beat on E with a poignant introductory F note in certain musical contexts, particularly in his setting of 'MacLeod of MacLeod's Lament', a motif characteristic of the MacArthur style.[17] True, he performed the 'hiharin' in the common modern 'pibroch birl' style, but in the light of Beaton's experience, this could very well suggest that various styles were performed contemporaneously within the community. They need not have been very different from each other. Like its bardic cousin, the instrumental tradition demonstrably gave way to a plethora of subtle melodic divergences, as dance tunes in the ceilidh were subject to continual recomposition and variation arising from the ephemeral nature of aural transmission. The same could very well have applied to *ceòl mór* in an environment such as Uist's.

If this scenario, based on available evidence and living memory, is correct, then we must see South Uist in the nineteenth century not as a place barren of the classical tradition, as Seumas MacNeill or Francis Collinson believed, but as a culturally self-supporting community in which various families from Barra to Benbecula maintained tradition in the face of change; a community in which, despite the lack of good roads or easy mobility, the transmission of music extended from township to township, region to region, and ultimately, island to island. I believe MacCormick's and Beaton's examples, combined with other indications presented above, make a strong case for it.

∾ TUNES ASSOCIATED WITH UIST AND CLANRANALD ∾

There are a handful of tunes in the extant *ceòl mór* repertoire whose associated folklore provides additional material to round out what has already been presented of South Uist and Clanranald's cultural and martial history. As often happens with *ceòl mór*, the tunes have multiple and at times inter-mixed titles – in both Gaelic and English – but this is not disadvantageous, as highlighting the phenomenon here will be of interest to scholars of Gaelic musical nomenclature.[18] The source material concerned includes early pibroch collections in which Gaelic titles were often given alongside English alternatives, from the Campbell Canntaireachd of 1797 to Thomason's *Ceol Mor* of 1900, as well as Highland Society of London programmes listing bilingual titles of pibrochs played in their competitions from 1781. This material forms a valuable vernacular Gaelic written record of the *ceòl mór* tradition of that age. As such it is also a relatively unbiased record, in terms of cultural perspective, since the titles were often supplied by the Gaelic-speaking performers themselves.

The tunes discussed below cover a range of categories, consisting of a battle, two gatherings, two salutes, a Jacobite event-commemoration and two that are more or less miscellaneous but whose surrounding origin tales survive in South Uist's oral tradition. The choice of tunes is based on the premise that the MacIntyres of Clanranald and those of Menzies were two distinct branches of a widely extended family, so tunes attributed to a MacIntyre tradition but less relevant to South Uist or Clanranald, such as 'The Battle of Sheriffmuir' and 'The Prince's Salute' (ascribed to John MacIntyre of Rannoch around 1715, the year of the battle) are not included here but are discussed elsewhere.[19]

'THE BATTLE OF WATERNISH'

This tune[20] commemorates a skirmish fought on the back of not inconsiderably acrimonious relations between the MacDonalds of Clanranald and the MacLeods of Dunvegan in the 1580s. Henry Whyte's account in his appendix to Glen's *Collection of Ancient Piobaireachd* finds the MacDonalds making a foray to Skye to attack the MacLeods in revenge for their defeat at what he called the Battle of *Milleadh Gàraidh*, where the MacLeods' Fairy Flag was said to have unfurled. Seeing them prepared and wary, however, the MacDonalds turned back, rustling cattle along the way. A party of MacLeods are said to have been alerted to the MacDonalds' movements and to have attacked them at Waternish as they moved back.[21] However, other accounts associated with the pibroch see the Battle of *Milleadh Gàraidh*, or the Spoilt Dyke, itself as the inspiration behind the tune. The MacDonalds in question are said to have set fire to a church in the Trumpan area of Skye as a number of MacLeods were at prayer within, Clanranald's piper playing as the church burned. According to Collinson's sources, the MacLeods of Dunvegan were alerted to this incident by a progenitor of the MacCrimmon piping dynasty, *Fionnlagh a' Bhreacain* ('Findlay of the Plaid'),[22] and in retaliation – in this respect echoing Whyte's account – they attacked the MacDonalds at Waternish as the latter were returning home. According to tradition, the dead were summarily buried on the field under an overturned drystone wall.[23]

Lachlan MacCormick, or *Lachlainn Bàn*, played 'Battle of Waternish' at the

South Uist Games of 1911 and was placed second by the judge, on that occasion, Archibald Campbell of Kilberry.

'Clanranald's Gathering Tunes'

There are two gathering tunes named for Clanranald. They are melodically distinct but share some technical motifs, in that both tunes employ a repetitive tripling motif on the bottom hand notes in the ground, or *ùrlar*, and are of the *fosgailte*, or 'open' idiom. One is found in Donald MacDonald's unpublished manuscript[24] and is entitled the 'Gathering of the MacDonalds of Clanranald' with a Gaelic title of '*Cnocan Ailein Mhic Iain*', or the 'Hillock of Allan Son of John'. '*Ailean Mhic Iain*' most likely refers to Allan, son of John Moidartach, who succeeded his father's place as chief of Clanranald in 1584. The other and better known of the two tunes is associated with the indecisive battle fought in Sheriffmuir in 1715, and its title differs according to the source: in Donald MacDonald's published *Collection* we find '*Cruinneachadh Chlaun Raonuill*, the Gathering of the MacDonalds of Clanranald to the Battle of Sheriffmuir in 1715 Where the Chief was Slain'; in Thomason's *Ceòl Mór* it is given as 'MacDonalds of Clanranald's Gathering to Sheriffmuir, *Cruinneachadh Cloinn Raonuill (Sliabh an t-Siorra)*'; and MacLennan's *Pìobaireachd as MacCrimmon Played It* gives it simply as 'Clanranald's Gathering'.[25] This tune is distinct from 'The Battle of Sheriffmuir' attributed to John MacIntyre of Rannoch, piper to Menzies, but is understandably confused at times with '*Cnocan Ailein Mhic Iain*'.

There is a tradition in South Uist that the body of Allan MacDonald of Clanranald, killed at the battle in question, was dragged off the field and carried ten miles to Inchaffray Church by a man, presumably of his own contingent and therefore from his own lands, named John MacIntyre.[26] If so, there is no suggestion that this was Menzies's piper. It could easily have been a piper in Clanranald's service, however. Certainly the presence of the chief's piper at the battle would account for the composition of a 'Sheriffmuir' gathering tune attributed to Clanranald. The Gaelic title of the first tune and the Sheriffmuir association of the second could suggest that '*Cnocan*' is an earlier composition and one on which 'Gathering to Sheriffmuir' was stylistically based by its composer – or re-composer, as the case may be.

'Boisdale's Salute'

'Boisdale's Salute' was played in the Highland Society of London competition of 1790 by 'John Cameron, a boy, Piper to John MacDonald of Lochgary'.[27] It is found in several sources.[28] We are again indebted to Donald MacDonald's *Collection* for his very descriptive titles, since with '*Fàilte Fir Bhoisdail*, A Salute to Allister More MacDonald First of Boisdale Upon his Taking Possession of the Estate'[29] we can safely deduce that the Boisdale in question was 'Big Alasdair' MacDonald who, in 1734, received the entire tack of South Uist from his half-brother the chief, Ranald elder – both being descendants of Donald MacDonald of Boisdale, Clanranald's brother. According to folklorist Henry Whyte, *Alasdair Mór* was by reputation the first to introduce kelp manufacture in South Uist and Benbecula in the 1730s,[30] a practice of which his family were to make much during the subsequent hundred years. He was succeeded by his son Colin – he of *Creideamh a' Bhata Bhuidhe*, the 'Religion of the Yellow Stick', who would famously attempt to proselytise his Catholic tenants by forceful means in 1770. Colin MacDonald of Boisdale is also associated with the pibroch 'The Finger Lock', which is discussed below.

With no written or oral evidence to go by, it must remain conjectural that 'Boisdale's Salute' was composed by a MacIntyre in South Uist.

'Clanranald's Salute'

This melodic and vigorous tune, although not often played in competition today, can be found in many nineteenth- and twentieth-century collections.[31] Like 'Boisdale's Salute', it is quite plausible that this tune was composed by a MacIntyre. It was played by, among others, 'Professor' John MacArthur, nephew of the famous Charles, as an exhibition piece at the Highland Society of London competition of 1785, held in Edinburgh. Years later, Donald MacKay of the Raasay MacKays, won the prize pipe with it while in service to Reginald George MacDonald of Clanranald, last to own South Uist, at the competition of 1822. It has gone by several titles in its time. Prior to 1823, it was recorded almost exclusively as 'Clanranald's March' at HSL competitions, and this is reflected by Gaelic cognates such as '*Siubhal*', '*Piobrachd*' and '*Spaidsearachd*' which were all used as titles in conjunction with '*Chlann Raghaill*' in late eighteenth- and early nineteenth-century records wherein Gaelic titles were printed along side English alternatives.[32] The tune was apparently well-known in the common repertoire of the late eighteenth century: in 1783, for instance, MacKay's *Collection* records that James Munro, Piper to the Canongate, played it in competition before being made, along with the eleven other competitors on that occasion, to cap the event's proceedings by playing it in unison while marching round St Andrew Square in Edinburgh. Perhaps not by coincidence, John MacDonald of Clanranald, Reginald's father, was acting as president of the HSL that year.[33]

'My King Has Landed in Moidart'

According to Jacobite lore, this tune, known widely in Gaelic as '*Thàinig Mo Rìgh air Tìr am Muideart*', was composed by a John MacIntyre to commemorate the landing of Prince Charles Edward Stuart on the mainland coast of Moidart in 1745. It is a tune in the *ceòl mór* repertoire whose association with Clanranald, as was discussed elsewhere, is ambiguous but arguable. Collinson identified this MacIntyre as he of the family in Rannoch, composer of 'Battle of Sheriffmuir' and 'The Prince's Salute' and piper to the chief of Clan Menzies.[34] In this he was both following, and propagating, conventional wisdom among the piping community whose roots lie with Angus MacKay's 1838 *Collection*. However, the historian Stewart put forward the much more likely case[35] that this John was of the Clanranald MacIntyres. He may or may not have been the same John who is said to have carried Clanranald's body off the field of Sheriffmuir in 1715 or who was among those extirpated for theft from Benbecula in 1738; indeed, he more than likely was not. Either way, if tradition asserts that the tune was extemporised by a MacIntyre piper contemporaneous with Prince Charles's landing in the Clanranald coastal territory of Moidart, then it is far more plausible that the MacIntyre in question was in Clanranald's service rather than in Menzies's, who were based in west Perthshire. This of course assumes that the tune was extemporised at the moment of the Young Pretender's landing, as lore would have it. If not – if it was composed at a later date, perhaps years later – it could indeed have been fashioned by a member of the Rannoch family. It could very well be that '*Thàinig Mo Rìgh air Tìr am Muideart*' refers to the first line of a song composed by a canny village eulogist at the time of the Forty-Five, on which John MacIntyre of Rannoch later arranged the famous pibroch. Composition and recomposition of this sort would have been quite normal among the musical and bardic class of Gaelic society in the eighteenth century.

'MacCrimmon's Sweetheart'

The pibroch 'MacCrimmon's Sweetheart' is generally acknowledged to be related to the Gaelic song '*Maol Donn*', by which the pibroch also is referred to in a Gaelic context. It translates roughly as 'brown hornless cow'. The derivation of the English title is unknown, but it undoubtedly stems from the post-Ossian fervour of the early nineteenth century, a time which did much to imbue Gaeldom, the Highland bagpipe and the MacCrimmon legacy with false romanticism in the popular mind. Be that as it may, the pibroch was (and remains) widely regarded as music of special significance in the South Uist piping community of the twentieth century, a favourite among many, often played in competition. It is certainly a catchy melody, as *ceòl mór* goes. Indeed, few tunes in the classical repertoire can match it for its arresting fluidity and its resonance through the variations.

General Thomason's unpublished work *Ceol Mor Legends* provides a traditional account of the tune's composition. In Benbecula, perhaps in the seventeenth or early eighteenth century, an old widow's cow wandered off and got lost in the marsh, and as livestock was the main source of income for West Highland farmers before the rise of the kelping industry, she was understandably distraught. The cow was never found, and only a year later was its skeleton discovered among the peat-bogs. According to the legend, the piper to Clanranald was among those in her community who had initially come out to help in the search; it is said that he composed the tune to commemorate the sad occasion, knowing the cow's importance to the old woman's livelihood. Peter Cooke's study of '*Maol Donn*' the pibroch compares the tune with its song variants[36] and quotes the lyrics, reputed to have been composed by the piper, as rendered by Kate MacDonald of Garryhellie:

> *Cha bu shealbhach dhomh t' fhaotainn, 's e mo ghaol am Maol Donn,*
> *Cha bu shealbhach dhomh t' fhaotainn, 's e mo ghaol am Maol Donn.*
> *Cha bu shealbhach dhomh t' fhaotainn, 's e mo ghaol am Maol Donn,*
> *'Gad iarraidh 's 'gad fhaotainn, 's 'gad shlaodadh à poll.*[37]

> I could not find you, my love is the brown cow,
> I could not find you, my love is the brown cow.
> I could not find you, my love is the brown cow,
> I couldn't get you, find you, nor pull you from the bog.

'THE FINGER LOCK'

Ronald MacDonald, prominent Morar tacksman, son of the fourth chief of Moidart and cousin to Clanranald, was known as *Raghnall mac Ailein Òig* ('Ronald son of Young Allan') and was a renowned piper and composer of the late eighteenth century. He was also evidently a Catholic of strong convictions. Henry Whyte, writing as 'Fionn' in Glen's *Collection of Ancient Piobaireachd*, gives an entertaining, if unlikely, account of Ronald's defence of the old faith in South Uist against the machinations of the infamous Colin MacDonald of Boisdale:

> It is said that when MacDonald, Boisdale, renounced the Catholic faith, he resolved to coerce his clansmen to follow his example. He fixed on a certain Sunday to carry out his purpose. When this came to the ears of Ronald, son of Allan Og, he resolved to frustrate the scheme. Taking with him a dozen of chosen

clansmen and a piper, he sailed for Uist early on the Sunday morning. He and a trusty henchman went ashore and called on the minister, who treated them hospitably – the 'shell' circulating freely. When Ronald saw the parson getting hearty, he suggested that he should accompany him to the birlinn, where he said he had a fine keg of brandy. The parson, nothing loath, accompanied Ronald. After sampling the brandy, the Laird of Morar, to gain time, suggested that they would sail a short distance from the shore, and that he would play his reverence his latest composition, '*An tarbh breàc* [sic] *dearg*' the brindled red bull. To this the parson was agreeable, and, while engaged in this performance, the minister forgot all about his duties to his congregation. They noticed Boisdale with a large congregation at the church. They immediately landed the parson, but the brandy had taken effect, and he walked with difficulty, and was in no mood for preaching. There was nothing for Boisdale but to return home. On Monday, Ronald of Morar went to Boisdale, and told him, if ever he heard of him trying the same trick again, he would double him up like an old pair of pipes. Boisdale desisted, and allowed his followers to follow their own convictions.[38]

Several tunes in the repertoire are ascribed to Ronald, including '*A' Ghlas Mheur*', or 'The Finger Lock', which is associated with the incident Whyte described above.[39] The tune is also enmeshed in Uist's local folklore. Piper and poet Donald Ruadh MacIntyre told a version of the *Pìobairean Smearclait* tale to collectors in 1952 which attributes to the pibroch a supernatural origin. The reader is by now familiar with the tale: the youngest son in a family of pipers in Smerclate, in Uist's south end, cannot play well but is given the power to do so by a fairy in a knoll. He returned home that night and prepared for bed, which he shared with his father:

> *N' air a chaidh 'ad dhan leabaidh, nis có bha cadal còmh ris a' bhodach, ach an gill' òg, am fear beag a b' òige. Agus bha 'm bodach a' dèanamh suas pìobaireachd 'na inntinn fhéin agus, fhios agad, rug e air a mhac 'na achlais a's a' leabaidh agus bha e 'g obair le chorragan; bha e dèanamh a' phuirt le chorragan a's a' leabaidh mar a sheinneadh e air a' phìob e. Ach 'tad thus' ort an làrna-mhaireach n' air a dh' éirich am bodach, gu dé 'n diabhol a chual' e ach an gille beag a' seinn air a' phìob am port a bha e fhéin a' cur air a chorragan an oidhche roimh'n a-sin. Cha chuala duine riamh leithid e. Dh' fhaighneachd e dhe'n ghille, 'Cà 'n cual' thu am port?' ars esan. 'Cha chuala mi riamh am port,' ars esan, 'gun cuala mi agad fhéin a-raoir e,' ars esan. 'Bha thu 'g obair le d' chorragan a-raoir air.' 'Well ma tà,' ars am bodach ris, 'sin agad,' ars esan, 'am port,' ars esan, 'ris an can mise 'A' Ghlas Mheur'. Agus 's iomadach meur air am bi e glaist' a bharrachd air a' mheur agad-sa,' ars esan.*[40]

When they went to bed, now who was sleeping with the old man but the little boy, the youngest one. And the old man was making up a tune in his mind and, you know, his hand rested under his son's arm in bed and he was working with his fingers, making the tune with his fingers in bed as he would play it on the pipes.

But wait – the next day, when the old man rose, what the devil did he hear but the little boy playing on the pipes the tune that he himself put on his fingers the night before. No one had heard anything like it before. He asked the boy, 'Where did you hear the tune?' he said. 'I never heard the tune,' he said, 'until I heard you last night,' he said. 'You were working it out with your fingers last night.' 'Well then,' said the old man to him, 'here you have the tune which I'll call "The Finger Lock". And many's the finger will it be locked on besides your own.'

CHAPTER 8

'You could catch it by the ear'
PIPERS AND THE PIPING FAMILY IN TWENTIETH-CENTURY
SOUTH UIST

What follows is an introduction to a few families and individuals who occupy an important place in the South Uist piping community in the twentieth century, whether from the point of view of the performer, the enthusiast or the scholar. It is by no means exhaustive, for one chapter has not the scope for such an undertaking, but even a limited survey yields insights into the nature of transmission and the legacy of mainstream influence this past century. The two are ultimately linked: the passing of music on to succeeding generations has been, above all, the jurisdiction of the family unit, and a father's example to his children has meant the survival of the aural idiom in some cases and the perpetuation of the literate in others. It is less often the mother's example; the instrumentalists in Gaelic tradition tend to be men, and the vocalists women.[1] While certainly not always the case, it was a striking enough commonality among piping families in South Uist whom I have encountered over the course of this study, but even so, the influence of women tradition-bearers is there: Alasdair Boyd first heard pipe music as a child in Eochar when his aunt, *Anna nighean a' Phìobaire*, rocked him to sleep with pibroch songs; and the MacDonald siblings in Garryhellie, profiled below, owe much of their repertoire of light music to their mother's *puirt-à-beul*. *Ceòl mór* too seems to have been maintained and transmitted by various families throughout Uist, possibly allowing an early and marginalised style of the big music to vie, however imperceptibly, against the mass acceptance of Piobaireachd Society tuition up to the 1940s. Transmission therefore began within the family, but ultimately extended between townships and across whole regions.

The profiles below are meant to add a biographical dimension to most of the tradition-bearers who have contributed to the present work, but they also call into sharper focus the communal network in which they live, or lived, and operated. The first three families discussed (the MacDonalds of Garryhellie and Daliburgh and the Campbells of Frobost) share close ties in blood and marriage, and among them piping can be observed as a living inheritance, transmitted vertically as well as horizontally within an extended family network. The next section is devoted mainly to Louis Morrison of the Loch Eynort area; he is the only member of his family still resident in South Uist, playing and teaching, and his reminiscences depict the literate tradition's typical progress from one generation to the next in the competitive era. Finally, we consider the backgrounds of Jessie MacAulay and Calum Beaton, whose value as informants on the nature of Hebridean tradition is unmatched.

It need hardly be said that these represent only the tip of the iceberg in a community such as Uist's in the past century. There are many families and individual pipers of renown who, for lack of space, cannot but be mentioned in passing throughout this and the next chapter: Catriona Garbutt of Benbecula and her brother, the late Calum Campbell, for instance, both cousins of Angus Campbell of Frobost, are respected as pipers throughout the Highlands; Duncan MacLellan, also of Benbecula, has taught pipe music locally for generations and in 2000 was awarded the Balvenie Medal for services to piping. Among his many ex-pupils is his nephew, Donald MacDonald (or *Dòmhnall Bàn*), formerly of the Queen's Own Highlanders, current Pipe Major of the South Uist Pipe Band and piping tutor to schools throughout South Uist and Benbecula. Of course, the island's reputation for piping would never have flourished were it not for local families such as the Walkers (Willie and Calum, or *Uilleam* and *Calum Dhòmhnaill 'ic Iain 'ic Ruairidh*) or the MacMillans of Daliburgh, the Morrisons (*Clann Sheonaidh Aonghuis Ruaidh*) of Gerinish, the MacIntyres of Boisdale or the Lindsays of Garryhellie – families whose prominence in the prize-lists testifies to their place in the twentieth-century competitive tradition. While those profiled below remain the most knowledgeable, experienced and articulate informants available today, no study would be complete without giving a nod to the many others who, in whole and in part, made South Uist truly the 'home of piping'.

~ THE MACDONALDS OF GARRYHELLIE ~

On 28 January 1967, at the annual Flora MacDonald Cup competition for local piping held in Daliburgh, Alasdair MacMillan of Alginates, Ltd took the floor to award one promising competitor the Finlay MacKenzie Memorial Pipes. He

Army piper at the Uist games in Askernish, probably local, c. 1930–31. Name unknown. (Courtesy of the late Dr Margaret Fay Shaw Campbell of Canna)

Pipe Major Neil MacLennan of Lochboisdale with his sisters Ina, left, and Mona, right, c. 1930. (Courtesy of the late Dr Margaret Fay Shaw Campbell of Canna)

TOP. The remains of the old MacMhuirich steading in Stilligarry, opposite Loch Skipport to the east. The MacMhuirichs were hereditary bards to Clanranald in South Uist from roughly the sixteenth to the early eighteenth century. (Photograph by the author)

ABOVE. The low hill in Smerclate is known locally as *An Claigeann*, or The Skull, upon which Clanranald's MacIntyre pipers are said to have resided. The family were known as *Pìobairean a' Chlaiginn*, or the Pipers of the Skull. (Photograph by the author)

ABOVE. Angus MacAulay (*Aonghus Sheòrais*) of Benbecula playing at the games on Askernish machair, c. 1931. The judges, from left, were John MacDonald of Inverness, Lord MacDonald of Sleat, Major Fincastle and Seton Gordon.
(Courtesy of the late Dr Margaret Fay Shaw Campbell of Canna)

OPPOSITE TOP. John MacDonald, Inverness at the Lochboisdale Hotel in South Uist, c. 1932. (Courtesy of the late Dr Margaret Fay Shaw Campbell of Canna)

OPPOSITE BELOW. John MacDonald, Inverness (far bottom left) and Seton Gordon (far right) travelling by ferry in the Hebrides, c. 1930s. The two could have been on their way to Uist to judge the piping at the Askernish games; the ferry would have been the mail boat *Loch Mor* and the top left man its skipper, Captain Donny Robertson.
(Courtesy of the College of Piping, Glasgow)

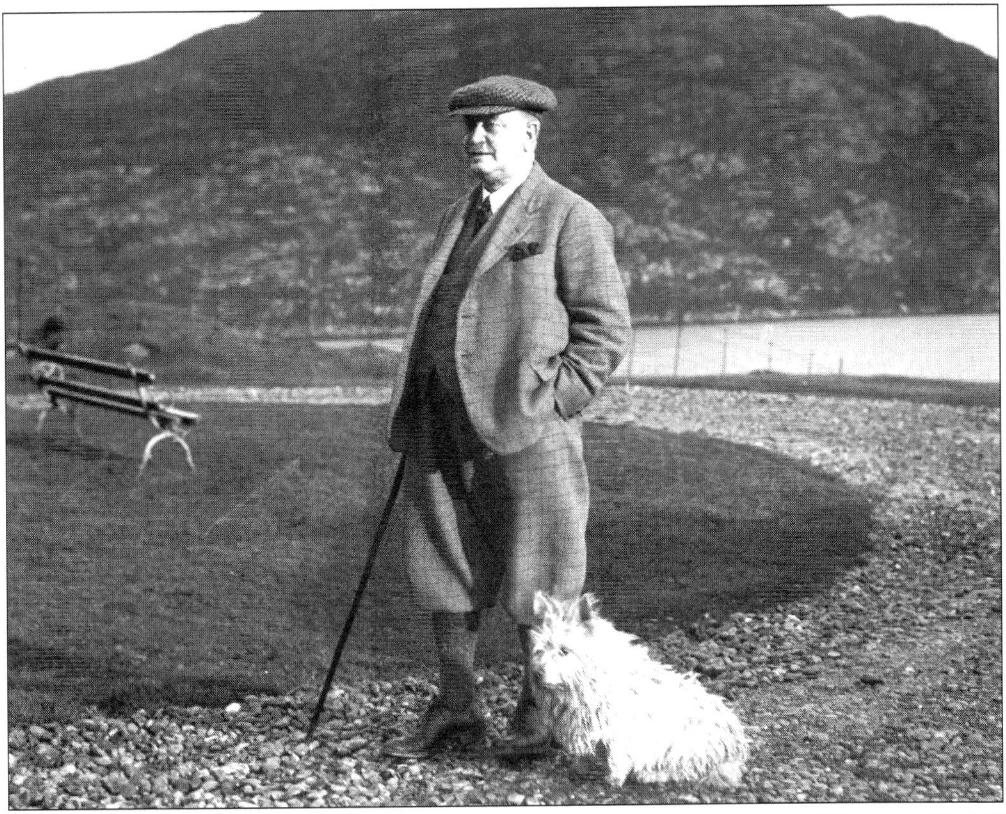

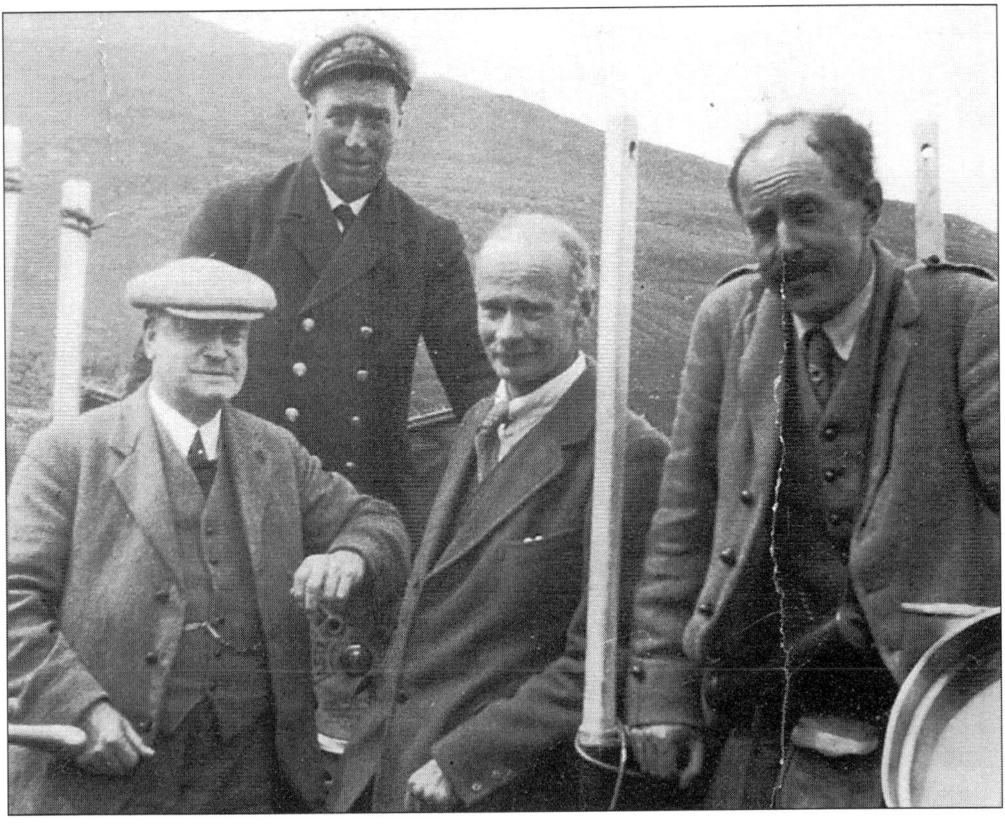

Rona MacDonad (Lightfoot), Garryhellie, on the pipes as her brother Neil helps tune her drones, early 1950s, Glasgow. Notice Rona plays left hand top, a common characteristic among Hebridean pipers; her brother Neil, however, played right hand top. (Courtesy of the College of Piping, Glasgow)

Rona MacDonald (Lightfoot) as a young girl on the practice chanter in Daliburgh, c. late 1940s. (Courtesy of the College of Piping, Glasgow)

Angus Campbell, Frobost, as a boy before the Great War, preparing to compete at the Askernish games. (Courtesy of the School of Scottish Studies, Edinburgh University)

Angus Campbell of Frobost, with pipes, in military dress and kilt. The photograph's origin is unknown; Campbell was not a military man, and the photograph's background is not the typical Uist landscape. It may be that it was taken on the occasion of Campbell's only trip to the mainland, the Argyllshire Gathering piping competitions in 1934, in which he was placed second in the Gold Medal. Although he typically wore plus-four trousers in competition at Askernish in his early years, as a competitor in Oban the judges would have required him to wear a kilt. (Courtesy of the School of Scottish Studies, Edinburgh University)

LEFT. Pipe Major John MacDonald, or *Seonaidh Roidein*, of Daliburgh and Glasgow, c. 1940s. (Courtesy of the College of Piping, Glasgow)

RIGHT. Roderick MacDonald, or *Ruairidh Roidein*, of Daliburgh and Glasgow, c. 1940s. (Courtesy of the College of Piping, Glasgow)

TOP. The late Seonaid 'Jessie' MacAulay, née MacIntyre, in Uist House, Daliburgh, 1998. (Photograph by the author)

ABOVE. Calum Beaton and his youngest son Calum Antony Beaton on the croft in Stoneybridge, with Beinn Mhór in the background, 1998. (Photograph by the author)

TOP. Unidentified piper competing at the South Uist games on Askernish machair, 1981. (Courtesy of the School of Scottish Studies, Edinburgh University)

ABOVE. Pipers and judges posing at the Askernish games, 1954.
Back row from left: competitors John Garroway, William M MacDonald, Neil Angus MacDonald of Barra, James MacGillivray, Donald MacLeod, Micky MacKay, Seumas MacNeill, Angus Campbell of Frobost, John Scott and Adam Scott of Lochboisdale.
Front row from left: Archie MacDonald of Garryhellie, John MacLennan, Rona MacDonald, Neil MacLennan of Lochboisdale, judges Campbell of Shirvan, Sheriff Grant of Rothiemurchas and Archibald Campbell of Kilberry, Archie MacNab, Dr George MacKinnon and John (*Seonaidh Roidein*) MacDonald.
(Courtesy of the College of Piping, Glasgow)

TOP. Pipes and drums of the 4th/5th Battalion Queen's Own Cameron Highlanders, taken in Aldershot, 1953. Nine of the 14 pipers seen above are from South Uist. *Top row*: second from left, piper MacDonald; second from right, piper Campbell; far right, piper MacKillop. *Middle row*: the first five from the left, pipers MacDonald, Angus Walker, Donald John Steele (son of John Steele), MacMillan and Calum Beaton. *Bottom row*: fourth from right, Pipe Major Donald MacIntyre, Boisdale. (Courtesy of Tim Atkinson)

ABOVE. The South End Piping Club practising in Daliburgh Drill Hall, April 1999. Calum Beaton appears second from the right, and the author appears at far left.
(Courtesy of Tim Atkinson)

A trio of pipers, South Uist, c. 1930–31. Pipe Major Neil MacLennan at left; Finlay Martin, also a native of Uist, at centre; and at right is John MacDonald of Inverness. (Courtesy of the late Dr Margaret Fay Shaw Campbell of Canna)

spoke of MacKenzie's abiding affection for the island and its music and of the Trust set up in his memory. He then referred to 'two families, especially, who supported these meetings and virtually carried it on their shoulders'. These were 'the MacDonalds of Clanranald Cottage and the Morrisons of Locheynort; all taught within their own family circles. Neil and Rona MacDonald were taught by their uncle Angus Campbell and cousin John MacDonald.' Neil and Rona were born in the township of Garryhellie, immediately north of Daliburgh, and raised in the house their father had called Clanranald Cottage. In 1967, Rona took home the Cup for the most points won; the MacKenzie Pipes, complete with case and silver plaque, went to Neil.[2]

Neil MacDonald, or *Niall Eairdsidh Raghnaill*, was born in 1934 and passed away in the spring of 2001. His sister Rona (now Lightfoot), or *Rona nighean Eairdsidh Raghnaill*, was born in 1936 and is the last of her immediate family to inherit a long tradition of piping. Rona has long since made Inverness her home. Neil, however, preferred to stay in Uist, running a bed-and-breakfast accommodation with his wife Angela in the house in Garryhellie, just across the road from their own childhood home, built near the site once occupied by the thatched home of their grandfather, Neil Campbell, *Niall Chatriona*, before he moved north to Frobost. It is called Clanranald House – indicative, perhaps, of a deliberate continuity with past traditions of which Neil was always immensely proud. They were taught most of what they know from their uncle and older cousin (both of whom represent distinct piping families in their own right, as will be discussed) but, as was characteristic of piping transmission among the island community, they were given the rudiments of the chanter by their father Archie.

Archie MacDonald, or *Eairdsidh Raghnaill* (1893–1973), was one of five sons of Ronald and Mary MacDonald, who had married in 1875. All five were involved in the military during wartime; four of them – Alex, Angus, Ronald and Archie himself – as pipers.[3] The latter two served in the Lovat Scouts during the Great War, while Angus was commissioned in the Middlesex Regiment and Alex enlisted in the Tyneside Scottish. Ronald Sr (1852–1921) and his two brothers, Donald and James, were well-known pipers, the latter at one time Piper to the Marquess of Bute. It remains uncertain whether or not their own father Roderick was a piper, but given the nature of the family unit in the transmission of piping in South Uist, we have no reason to doubt that he was.

Archie maintained a croft in Garryhellie throughout his adult life, though he supplemented this with occasional work as a gillie at Lochboisdale Hotel.[4] He was, by all reports, a most musical man, though it is safe to say that his piping abilities and/or style leaned toward the literate idiom more than the aural, judging by his military affiliation and that of his brothers. His history of competitive piping further suggests this. In conversation in 1998, Neil compared his father's skill to his own and his sister's:

> *Bha e glè mhath, ach cha robh e cho math 's a bha sinne nuair a dh'ionnsaich sinne suas. Bha e* compete-*adh ceart gu leòr, ach cha robh e faighinn gin de phrizichean 's a bha mi fhìn is Rona a' faighinn.*[5]
>
> He was quite good, but not as good as we were when we learned. He competed right enough, but he wasn't getting the prizes that Rona and I were getting.

Archie in fact took second place in the *ceòl mór* event confined to pupils of John MacDonald, Inverness, at the 1914 Games, the last before the outbreak of war, and took prizes in marches and strathspeys and reels on that and two other occasions.[6] We can discern from this that he was at least skilled enough in the competition idiom over a period of around ten years to compete successfully on a local level, and that he was a pupil of John MacDonald during the latter's 1909–14 courses in *ceòl mór*.

In 1925, he married Kate Campbell. Kate (1897–1977) was born into a similarly gifted family which represented a storehouse of Gaelic arts. Her father Neil was a well-known piper from the Frobost area north of Askernish, as was her brother Angus, while her mother Marion (*Mór*), née MacLellan, was a local authority on traditional Gaelic song. Kate's uncle, Angus MacLellan, was a published storyteller and a recipient of the MBE for the preservation of Gaelic oral tradition.[7] Kate, or *Bean Eairdsidh Raghnaill* ('Wife of Archie son of Ronald') as she became known throughout her married life, gathered a vast repertoire of songs while growing up amid these influences and eventually recorded nearly two hundred for the School of Scottish Studies.[8] Just as Archie MacDonald transmitted his piping to his children, so Kate passed on her vocal tradition in her own way: Rona, long retired from competition, is known today almost as well for her singing of *puirt-à-beul* and pibroch songs as she once was for her piping, and is in great demand for workshops, while Neil claimed to have inherited his memorisation skills, particularly with regard to *ceòl mór*, from his mother's ability to remember songs. More was at work in this family than the simple passing on of a craft or technique; musical ability, interpretation and retention – immaterial, enduring, larger than the performer himself – were considered inherited gifts.

Kate worked for two to three years as a domestic servant in the estate factor's residence in Askernish, and spent nearly a decade in the same capacity at Lochboisdale Hotel before settling down with Archie in Garryhellie. Together they had seven children, two of whom – Neil and Rona – took up piping seriously.

The two MacDonald siblings were competition pipers first and foremost.

This was a reflection of the times; like Calum Beaton, they came of age in the post-Second World War era when the best competitors from the mainland were flocking to Askernish for the annual Games and the reputation of Uist's home-grown talent, fostered by decades of Piobaireachd Society instruction, was at its zenith. But unlike Beaton, it had also to do with the dynamics of family tradition at Clanranald Cottage. Archie MacDonald was a literate-minded piper; their uncle Angus Campbell was a firmly-established local prize-winner and authority on John MacDonald's teachings. Their cousin John MacDonald of Daliburgh was famed throughout Scotland for his successes at the big meetings, both in solo piping and as Pipe Major of the Glasgow City Police band. Neil was also a student of Robert Nicol. Mainstream piping was therefore instilled in the MacDonald siblings from a very early age. In conversation, they each recalled how their father would have them compete with each other, and perhaps with other local children, for prize-money in the family's sitting room once a week. Rona described the parameters of the event:

> *Nuair bha mise 'nam chnapach, bhiodh co-fharpais bheag againn a h-uile oidhche h-Aoine, as deaghaidh na sgoile . . . Bha leithid do dhaoine is do ghillean òga an uairsin . . . 'S e leth-chrùn a bha thu a' faighinn . . . sin agad a' chiad duais, uill, sin an aon duais a bh'ann, cha robh ach an aon duais.*[9]

> When I was a young girl, we would have a small competition every Friday evening, after school . . . There were adults and youngsters [coming round] then . . . You'd get a half-crown . . . that was the first prize, well, that was the only prize there was, there was nothing but the one prize.

According to Neil, this weekly household contest was nothing more than an incentive to practise and to entertain visitors:

> *Cha robh ach gum biodh iad fhéin, mo phàrantan, 'na* judges – *chan ann ach dìreach spòrs, car, feuch an cluichdeamaid na b' fheàrr, is bhiodh na gillean anns a' bhaile a' tighinn a-nuas a' céilidh, is bhiodh sinn a' cluichd airson tasdan agus sia sgillin, air* first *a'* second. *Bhitheamaid a' sìor*-practice *gu faigheamaid an tasdan.*[10]

> It was only my parents themselves judging – it was really only for fun, to see if we could play better, and the boys from the township would come up for a visit, and they'd play for a shilling and sixpence for first and second. We were always practising so that we'd get the shilling.

Taking Neil's view into account, his family's custom – I have come across nothing similar in other South Uist piping families – gives the impression that aurally-learned piping had no place in the MacDonalds' home. We may look on their weekly contests as an incentive to hone skills and to entertain neighbours, but behind these functions it seems a product of the mainstream idiom cultivated in Uist since the beginning of the century, and I suggest that it would not have developed had they or their father acquired their piping in an age before the advent of the games or of Piobaireachd Society tuition. This is not to say that indigenous Gaelic tradition is inherently non-competitive; far from it. Keenly contested foot- and horse-racing, among other traditional sports, were a natural part of Hebridean life until the nineteenth century[11] and elements of these survived into the twentieth century as events in South Uist's Games. Local piping, also, was doubtless not above informal competition before the mainstream influences of the twentieth century came to bear. Around the turn of the century, for instance, Frederick Rea organised a school picnic along the machair at Kilbride and arranged for a piper to come along:

> The pipes were playing and many of the older children were dancing reels, the rest of them clapping hands and laughing – it was a happy scene! Afterwards the piper selected a few boys and girls who danced the 'Highland Fling', and I was surprised at the agility and lightness of foot they showed. Next I found that a number of boys had brought their 'chanters', and the piper held a competition to ascertain the best player. It was amazing to me to see and hear how well these lads played, and as I watched their easy but rapid fingering of the notes and listened to the variety of tunes I felt that they were natural players. The teachers seemed to take it as a matter of course, and when I expressed my surprise they told me that the families to which these boys belonged had been noted as great pipers for many generations; indeed, there was scarcely a house on the island where you would not get one or more pipers in the family.[12]

Rea does not intimate the details of the boys' contest, nor with what type of pipe music they competed – probably reels, if the coincident dancing of the day and his description of 'easy but rapid fingering' are anything to go by. But his account does suggest that competition among pipers was not entirely alien to indigenous tradition in South Uist before the era of what we call mainstream piping today. It lends support to Neil MacDonald's point of view that competition is a natural and intrinsic part of piping; it is important to keep in mind, however, that whereas the school-children's contest seemed impromptu and inspired by light dancing, Neil's perspective is based rather on the staged nature of piping in its modern idiom, divorced from any indigenous Gaelic context. The weekly contests in Clanranald Cottage were not of the old tradition, then, but of the new.[13]

Rona has been celebrated as the 'finest woman piper ever produced in Scotland'[14] but her record would be impressive regardless of gender: after competing successfully in practice-chanter competitions at the Uist games as a pre-teen in the late 1940s, she went on to take first prize in the junior pibroch, march strathspey and reel (MSR) and jig events in 1952.[15] She had great success at both the open South Uist games and the local Flora MacDonald Cup since then, and it was not long before she was recognised at the national level. Being a female piper in a predominantly male tradition has provided Rona with a valuable perspective into a side of the Hebridean tradition rarely discussed. Her reminiscences suggest what may have amounted to a double standard accorded to female piping depending on one's age:

> *Cha robh móran ann ach mi fhéin do bhoireannaich, do nigheannan . . . Nuair thòisich iad air ionnsachadh air a' phìobaireachd anns an sgoil, bha cuid a bharrachd nigheannan a' dol a-staigh airson a bhith a' cluichd na pìoba. Ach nuair a bha mi òg, a' dol suas anns na teens . . . uaireannan, gheobhadh tu faireachadh gu robh feadhainn ann ag ràdh gu robh e car fireann a bhith 'ga dhèanamh, nach robh e boireann a bhith 'ga dhèanamh. Ach cha do chuir sin dragh sam bith orm-sa. Bha e fad na bu duiliche dhomh a dhèanamh nuair a bha mi anns na teens, ach fhuair mi seachad air a sin.*[16]

There weren't many females, girls, around but myself . . . When they started teaching the pipes in school, most of those going in for the pipes were girls. But when I was young, reaching into the teens . . . sometimes, you would get the impression that there were those who said it was a masculine thing to do, that it wasn't feminine to do it. But that didn't bother me. It was far more difficult for me to do it when I was in my teens, but I got past that.

Rona's remarks support the impression that in South Uist up to the post-Second World War era, and by association in conservative Gaelic society, roles in the inheritance of traditional performing arts were broadly determined according to gender, but that such inheritance was less discriminate before adulthood. That is, younger children in the old Gaelic world may have been viewed as unofficial tradition-bearers – proto-bearers, in effect – to whom roles were not as stringently applied in the performing arts as they were in more material or pragmatic areas of tradition such as farming and keeping house; that gendered roles in the apprehension of music and song tended to come into effect only upon adulthood. Noting how successful Rona nonetheless became in a tradition dominated by men, it is difficult to determine how significant such a double standard may have been in the scheme of things. There are signs that even in the mid-twentieth century, the culture of the bagpipe in the southern Outer Hebrides did not lightly admit the conspicuous participation of women. Rona recalled that her mother Kate Campbell, or *Bean Eairdsidh Raghnaill*, could play well on the practice-chanter, if not also on the full pipes, but hid that fact from others and made her daughter promise to keep the secret for as long as she, Kate, were alive. Rona recalled that her mother had even taken up the chanter on one occasion, once the men had left the house, and corrected her daughter's fingering by performing a full competition march, strathspey and reel – to Rona's complete amazement. Kate's lifelong powers of silent observation in the presence of men such as her father, brother and husband must have been truly remarkable, to say nothing of the power of the social taboo which compelled her silence.

On the other hand, the success of Rona and others, like Catriona Garbutt of Benbecula and Jessie MacAulay, as public performers did not occur entirely in a vacuum. Although today, thanks to the general breakdown of gendered restrictions, one points easily to Anne Spalding, Margaret Houlihan and Sue MacIntyre as performers of note in Scotland, there are indications that women were involved in less conspicuous roles throughout the history of piping in the old Hebridean world – not so much in public performance, but in the process of transmission. *Bean Eairdsidh Raghnaill* was perhaps the last to fit this mould, though her example could hardly have been unique. By Rona's own reckoning, many women of her mother's generation in the Uist community must have known how to play, picking it up by ear as she herself did at first, but refraining from public performance. Before her, the wives and daughters of the MacCrimmon pipers are said anecdotally to have been just as good as the men and, in an uncanny prelude to Kate's practice, to have assumed the instruction of pupils when the men were absent.[17] Duncan Ross, a pupil of John MacKay of Raasay, told folklorist John Francis Campbell of Islay that when MacKay taught Ross's own teacher, John Ban MacKenzie, in the early nineteenth century, MacKay's sister was always at the fireside during lessons, chanting in *canntaireachd* along with her brother's playing.[18] And John Archie MacLellan, Calum Beaton's first pibroch tutor, notably learned a pipe reel from *Bean Aonghuis Ruaidh*, a widow living alone near Stoneybridge, who claimed she had received the tune in *canntaireachd* from the fairies. So the antecedents to public performance by women had always been there. Nowadays, any prejudice in South Uist against women playing the pipes has happily faded away, thanks in no small part to the post-war introduction of piping in the school curriculum and the example of performers like Rona Lightfoot.

∽ THE CAMPBELLS OF FROBOST ∽

In Frobost, a west-coast township situated between Askernish and Milton, Kate MacDonald, née Campbell, was born into a family rich in folklore and oral tradition. She, of course, sang; her mother Mór sang also; the writer Basil Davidson, visiting Uist over a period of months in 1954, described them both as representing the 'oldest living culture in Europe'.[19] Kate's paternal grandmother, Catrìona, was also known for her singing and her uncle Angus, as noted earlier, was a published storyteller. The instrumentalists in her family were her father Neil and brother Angus – both highly regarded pipers whose backgrounds encompass tradition and change in South Uist over a period of 140 years.

Neil Campbell was born in 1860, the son of Donald Campbell, a crofter, and Catherine (or Catrìona) MacMillan. Whether or not Catrìona was related to the MacMillans of Daliburgh or Benbecula, both piping families of repute, is uncertain; nor is it certain that Donald was a piper. In either case, Donald may not have been around to teach his son much of piping anyway because Neil's traditional name was matronymic – *Niall Chatrìona* – which in Gaelic society suggests that the father may have died young, leaving children to be raised by the widow. Neil is remembered as being musically literate, but there is no indication that he had been in the military. Rona Lightfoot could not account for it, but Ronald Morrison claims, on the basis of testimony by Neil's son Angus, that he was taught to read staff notation by the MacGillivrays of Barra in the 1880s.[20] This, coupled with the lack of information on his father, naturally suggests that he learned much of piping in general from the MacGillivrays and was therefore one of Uist's earliest exponents of the competitive idiom, to be grouped with such militia-trained pipers of that era as Lachlan MacCormick and Neil MacInnes. Also, his name appears in the prize-lists of the pibroch events at the South Uist Games confined to John MacDonald's pupils in 1909 and 1911,[21] so we know that he attended at least the pre-war courses of Piobaireachd Society tuition; although he was nearly fifty when MacDonald first arrived, this could only have added to his mainstream experience and his competitive repertoire. Calum Beaton could recall Neil playing only one *ceòl mór* tune, 'MacIntosh's Lament', and was not sure if he'd learned it during or before the Piobaireachd Society's courses. According to Morrison, the MacGillivrays were able masters of *ceòl mór*, so either case is plausible. Neil reportedly played it in the mainstream 'Kilberry' style, however, which suggests rather the Society's tuition. Neil's literate credentials should be tempered, however, by the era and culture into which he was born. *Niall Chatrìona* came of age in a crofting community in old-world South Uist in the 1860s and '70s, when the compilation of repertoire by manuscript and the strategic importance of the written stave were beginning to be established features of piping in all quarters save the grass-roots West Highlands and Islands; the cultural imperative simply did not exist in that region, in that world, outside military circles and the upper class. Neil's experience as a piper, therefore, like Lachlan MacCormick's, would have encompassed both the ceilidh and the platform; the dance and the competition; the aural and the literate.

Neil was quite a character in the local lore of turn-of-the-century Uist life. One can still hear the bagpipes referred to in Uist today as *na cnàmhan* – 'the bones' – due to his fabled and unfruitful efforts at that time to fashion drones out of the leg bones of wether sheep;[22] like the many pupils who turned up at John MacDonald's 1909 course barefoot, it is a telling reminder of the state of the island's economy. Another tale still in circulation is Neil's alleged encounter with a bull stuck in a bog: he and a fellow piper are said to have chanced upon the bull as it was helplessly sinking in the mire, and the two grabbed a horn each and began to pull. Neil is said to have suddenly begun fingering grace notes; he asked his companion, 'Is this the way to make the throw on D?', and performed the flourish on the bull's horn; with his grip loosened, the bull slipped from their hands and immediately sank.[23] No points awarded for believing it to be true, but the anecdote is noteworthy as it bears a certain relation to the legend of *Maol Donn*.

In 1896, he married Mór MacLellan and they had three children: Kate, Mary and Angus. The latter would carry on his father's piping tradition.

Angus Campbell was born in 1900 and lived most of his life in Frobost, but resided for the last years of his life in Uist House, a Daliburgh rest home. He died in July 2002, aged 102. Although arthritic hands had left him unable to play the pipes for many years, he remained to the end of his days the pre-eminent authority on *ceòl mór* and the teachings of John MacDonald in South Uist. He in turn taught many younger players who have since made names for themselves, either locally or nationally: Rona and Neil, of course, though the latter did not learn directly from Angus; of the two, Rona was always considered Angus's favoured pupil, and Neil just picked up from his sister what she had learned during her own lessons. Calum Beaton also received lessons occasionally, as did Angus's younger cousin Calum Campbell of Benbecula. Fred Morrison, Glasgow-born but rooted in the Morrison piping family *Clann Sheonaidh Aonghuis Ruaidh* ('children of John son of Red Angus') of Gerinish, also counts Angus as a major influence. The late Bell Morrison, Angus's wife, was his aunt. Angus's contemporaries included some of the finest competitive pipers of the modern age, such as John and Roderick MacDonald of the Glasgow Police (cousins of his through the MacDonalds of Garryhellie) and Angus MacAulay of Benbecula, who emigrated to New Zealand in 1952. Angus Campbell had a connection, through either blood or music, with nearly every piper in the tight-knit community that made up South Uist in the twentieth century.

Although his father reputedly taught him the 'basics' of notes and grace notes as a child, the training with which he was associated during his entire life began in 1909 with John MacDonald of Inverness. Angus was considered by many to have been MacDonald's star pupil in the local courses and, as Rona illustrates, he remained a lifelong devotee:

> *Teagasg a thug Seonaidh Dòmhnallach do dh' Aonghus Nìll . . . cha do chaill e riamh. Chan eil mi smaoineadh gun do dhì-chiumhnich Aonghus a-riamh* note *a fhuair e; cha do dhì-chuimhnich e rud sam bith a thuirt an duine. Cha do sgrìobh e sìan a-riamh sìos. Nuair bhithinn-sa faighinn* lesson *bhuaithe, chanadh e rium, 'Mar a thuirt an Dòmhnallach rium . . .'*[24]

> The teaching that John MacDonald gave to Angus (son of) Neil . . . he never lost. I don't think Angus ever forgot a note he received; he didn't forget anything the man said. He never wrote a thing down. When I would get a lesson from him, he would say to me, 'As MacDonald told me . . .'

MacDonald's tutelage served Angus well: out of twenty-seven years of competition at the local Games (that's 40 years minus wartime), he placed in the *ceòl mór* event no fewer than twenty-one times and won it outright on at least ten occasions. His presence on the competition platform at Askernish became an established fixture of the annual games, and his performances became the stuff of Hebridean legend. The late Duncan Johnstone of Glasgow, whose roots lay in Barra and Benbecula, reminisced on watching Angus compete in the late 1940s and '50s:

> He was some sight to see. He used to play in plus fours. He used to dander round the boards and come down on his knee when he was expressing a bit of the tune. He had a big Harris tweed bunnet. He never wore a kilt but that all changed when Sheriff Grant of Rothiemurchas started judging, you had to be properly dressed.[25]

The image of a young Angus Campbell treading the Askernish boards in the plus-fours style of trousers in the early decades of the twentieth century suggests something important about the old Hebridean view of mainstream competition. While men such as Lachlan MacCormick and the MacMillans were well acquainted with the convention of donning the kilt for piping due to long experience in the British army, the less worldly among Uist's pipers saw piping as a functional, everyday affair and saw no reason to dress differently for it. Rona Lightfoot still possesses a photograph of Angus playing the bagpipe at twelve years of age, taken the day before he competed at Askernish; he was barefoot and clad in plus-fours which his sister Kate, Rona's mother, had stitched for him specially to be worn for the games. He is not the only one on record in South Uist to have dissociated the pomp of the kilt from the act of piping before the forces of change pervaded Hebridean traditional life too greatly this past century. Archives at Kildonan Museum in South Uist contain a photograph of the late Adam Scott piping at Askernish in a full tweed suit around the 1940s. We are fortunate, so late in the day, to have even these fleeting glimpses – suggestions, rather – of how the aboriginal Gaelic piper perceived his craft. If the formidable Sheriff Grant, an amateur piper and irascible advocate of the kilt,[26] had begun judging the games in Uist earlier, such things might be outwith living memory.

Angus's only foray outside South Uist, to his own recollection, was the Argyllshire Gathering of 1934. The *ceòl mór* competitions at the Gathering included an open event as well as that of the gold medal, and he entered both. Unfortunately, he was given the same tune to play in both events – 'The Blue Ribbon' – and many pipers will agree that the sheer repetition involved in playing the same tune twice in one meeting, especially one as long and as taxing as the 'Ribbon', is off-putting. For this reason perhaps, despite a 'very musical performance', Angus took second place in the gold medal behind Pipe Major Charles D. Smith of the Black Watch.[27] Most would consider placing runner-up in the Gold on one's first and only attempt as a worthy feat in itself, but, as he told his story over sixty years later, his tone was still laced with invective.

Naturally enough, 'The Blue Ribbon' was not his favourite tune. His masterpiece, however – the tune with which he was most successful, and most remembered, in competition – was 'Patrick Og MacCrimmon's Lament'. He himself claimed that he won the local games so often with this tune in his prime that he was eventually asked not to submit 'Patrick Og' any more, and he is on record winning the John MacDonald Cup for local pibroch in the late 1940s playing this tune. Local reminiscences of Angus's playing usually include a reference to 'Patrick Og', such as Rona Lightfoot's:

> *Nuair a chluichd e Pàdruig Og, uill, mar a chanadh iad fhéin, cha do dhearg aig duine an duais a thoirt bhuaithe. 'S e a* favourite *a bh'ann. Bha e faighinn a' chiad duais leis a sin co-dhiubh, co-dhiubh. Bha e cinnteach as an rud, agus gu dearbh fhéin, bha e breagha bhith ag éisdeachd ris nuair a bha e cluichd.*[28]

> When he played Patrick Og, well, as they would say, no one could take the prize from him. It was his favourite. He'd get the first prize with that, no bother at all. He had the thing down pat, and it was indeed a pleasure to listen to him when he was playing.

Neil MacDonald commented on Angus's playing of this tune, and in his remarks we can see the survival of the concept of orality in musical transmission among South Uist's pipers in modern times:

> NM: *Chan eil mi smaointinn gu robh duine ann a-riamh a chluichdeadh ceòl mór coltach ris. Chanainn nach robh cho math ris . . . chuala mi air cantail nach gabh e sgrìobhadh, mar a Pàdraig Òg Mac Cruimein – sin agad am* favourite *a bh'aige – cha ghabh a sgrìobhadh mar a tha e air a chluichd ceart, agus 's iomadh duais a fhuair e leis.*
> JD: *Dé bha difireach mu dheidhinn a' chluichd aige?*

NM: *Dìreach an t-òran. Bha e fhéin a' dèanamh a-mach nach robh, 's ann glé bheag a bha an t-òran anns a phìobaireachd a bha sinneach. Is mar a tha mi fhìn a' dèanamh a-mach, gu bheil cuideachadh mór ann a bhith bruidhinn Gàidhlig leis a' phìob.*

JD: *An robh e a' leantail an òrain?*

NM: *Chanainn-sa gu robh, is tha mi cinnteach gun canadh gu leòr eile nach eil e dèanamh difir sam bith, ach tha mise smaointinn gun dèan e difir mór co-dhiubh.*[29]

NM: I don't think that there was ever anyone who could play pibroch like him. I would say there were none as good as he was . . . I've heard it said that it can't be written, 'Patrick Og MacCrimmon's Lament', that is – that was his favourite – it can't be written how it is played correctly, and it's many a prize he got with it.

JD: What was different about his playing?

NM: Just the song. He himself figured that it wasn't, that there was often very little of the song put into that pibroch. And as I myself see it, it's a big help to be speaking Gaelic with the pipes.

JD: Was he following the song?

NM: I would say so, and I'm sure that plenty of others would say it doesn't make any difference, but I think it makes a big difference anyway.

Angus was ninety-five years old when I first went to him in the summer of 1995 with tape recorder in hand, only to find that, first, he was past the point in life where a productive interview could be conducted, and second, he hated tape recorders. Over the course of my stay in Uist, I visited Angus several times and decided to approach each session as if it were a lesson – the objective being to grasp, by his comments and criticisms of my own playing, how he himself would have played before arthritis had set in about two decades earlier. I would play *ceòl mór* and the occasional competition march to him all afternoon while he and his wife Bell sat and listened. Though nearly deaf, he would sing the *canntaireachd* of the tunes – his singing of 'The Lament for Donald Dougal MacKay', for instance, was strained and pulse-laden; he often swung a knarled fist through the air for emphasis – in order to indicate where he believed I'd gone wrong in the score or on some point of ambiguous interpretation. However, I got the impression that the way Angus sang at this time was a mere approximation to how he'd played in his prime. He was strong for a man of his age, but the years had undeniably taken their toll. The BBC recorded Angus playing 'My King has Landed in Moidart' on a set of eighteenth-century pipes in 1938, the year he took second in the gold medal at Oban, but the recording is not of lasting quality. The recordings made by ethnomusicologist Peter Cooke for the School of Scottish Studies, who interviewed Angus in October and November of 1970, probably contain the best records of his playing while he was still able to do so: 'The Old

Woman's Lullaby' and 'I Got a Kiss of the King's Hand' were given a full airing on the pipes, while snatches of 'MacCrimmon's Sweetheart', 'My King has Landed in Moidart', 'MacIntosh's Lament' and the 'Earl of Seaforth's Salute' were played on the practice-chanter amid discussion of grace notes and cadences.[30] In these recordings, Angus's playing was slow and deliberate in the main melodic thread, but brisk in the transitional movements between phrases; a style reminiscent of John MacDonald himself and others taught by him, such as the 'Bobs of Balmoral' and Donald MacLeod of Lewis.

Angus encapsulated the best of both idioms. He was a literate player probably from the day he first picked up a practice-chanter; his father Neil, who taught him the rudiments, was literate, and John MacDonald's courses, in which Angus took part as a child prodigy, emphasised literate transmission. However, MacDonald's insistence on *canntaireachd* as the only authentic means of expression imparted to his pupils, including Angus, the idea of the 'song', or *òran*, inherent in *ceòl mór*. This reflected piping's roots in Gaelic oral tradition, and was in keeping with MacDonald's own education even if the settings he taught in Uist were not. Like many of MacDonald's better-known pupils on the mainland, Angus forever after emphasised the necessity of grasping the perceived *òran* that lay underneath the printed score in order to express it properly.

THE MACDONALDS OF DALIBURGH

This family is closely connected to the MacDonalds of Garryhellie through the paternal line. Donald MacDonald, or *Dòmhnall Bàn Roidein* ('Fair Donald of the Running Leap'[31]) as he was known, was the son of Roderick and Annabella MacDonald and the younger brother of Ronald, whose son Archie was the father of Neil and Rona. Pipe Major Neil MacLennan (1895–1985) was quoted in the *Piping Times* in 1966 as calling Donald one of 'only two pipers of note in this area' as far back as he could remember,[32] which, knowing MacLennan's sensibilities, indicates that he was thoroughly literate; the other piper he mentioned was Lachlan MacCormick. He went on to refer to both as being in the 'old Militia', which was of course latterly the Camerons, and all this information together puts Donald's heyday roundabout the 1890s. Although militia-trained, *Dòmhnall Bàn* was widely celebrated as a traditional dancer. In the 1920s, he danced and taught Ewan MacLachlan's pieces at the Askernish games, prompting some to say he'd learned from MacLachlan himself and others to say he was the 'local comedian' and had only picked up the steps long after MacLachlan's death.[33] He also taught formal Highland dancing (the Highland Fling, Gillie Calum, etc.) in the Daliburgh area during Frederick Rea's time.[34] Knowing Donald's penchant for both piping and dancing, he could well be the same 'D. MacDonald' who was praised in the *Oban Times* for his entertainment at a soirée in 1895:

> Dalibrog: The pupils attending the Evening Continuation School closed the session with a most enjoyable soiree and dance . . . Music was supplied by Mr. D. MacDonald, Dalibrog, on the bagpipes, while Mr. A. Morrison, joiner, Kilpheder, handled the bow with his usual good style and spirit . . . A feature of the evening was the fine step-dancing of D. MacDonald.[35]

Two of Donald's children (first cousins once removed to Neil and Rona) became celebrated mainstream competitive pipers. These were John MacDonald (1898–1988), or *Seonaidh Roidein*, and Roderick MacDonald (1900–81), or *Ruairidh Roidein*. To avoid confusion with his namesake from Inverness, this John MacDonald will henceforth be referred to by his Gaelic name, *Seonaidh*.

Both learned piping from before the age of ten from their father until their tuition, like Angus Campbell's, was taken over by John MacDonald, Inverness, in 1909. The earliest record of *Seonaidh* as a competitor is in 1913 when, at the age of fifteen, he won the first division of the junior level MSR at the local games – it says something about the breadth of piping in the community when the junior competitions had to be separated into three divisions just to accommodate the number of entrants.[36] He went on the following year to gain second place in both the marches and the open *ceòl mór*, and won the *ceòl mór* event confined to John MacDonald's pupils.[37] Roderick's first appearance on the prize-list was in 1922, the first meeting of the games since 1914, and he managed to win the marches and take second in the MSR.[38]

Seonaidh was involved in the military from a very early age. Whether influenced by his father's tenure in the militia or by John MacDonald, who had held the post of Pipe Major in the Camerons for twenty-four years, *Seonaidh* reputedly walked from Mallaig to Inverness in order to enlist in the 3rd Camerons at the outbreak of the Great War.[39] Although a year under age, he was aided by 'a muscular frame and a sympathetic recruiting sergeant'[40] and served thereafter with the 6th and 7th Battalions in France and Belgium.

Emerging from the war unscathed, he moved to Glasgow in 1920 to join the city's police force, and was swiftly drafted into their pipe band. His brother followed him into the Glasgow Police, and the band, in 1923. Thereafter followed many years of competitive success for both the *Roidein* brothers and the band; in 1926 *Seonaidh* set a record for winning the gold medal at both the Northern Meeting in Inverness and the Argyllshire Gathering in Oban, plus the march and the strathspey and reel events in Inverness, plus the open *ceòl mór*, the strathspey and reel, and second place in the MSR for former winners in Oban. Roderick also placed highly in these events throughout the 1920s and '30s. His successes perhaps had not quite the impact his older brother's had had in 1926, but it hardly mattered; after winning the gold medal in Oban in 1938 and in Inverness in 1946, playing 'Mary's Praise' at each, there was little need to prove himself further. The City of Glasgow Police were already famously successful during these years under Pipe Major William Gray, and their status as world champions only continued after he stepped down in 1932, leaving *Seonaidh* at the helm.

Although they spent their professional lives in Glasgow, they returned to Uist upon retirement and thereafter settled into the life of tradition-bearers, passing on, as did Angus Campbell, the music they'd made their own. *Seonaidh* gave lessons to Rona, Neil, Calum Beaton and any number of other young players, and played regularly for the dancers at the annual games. Of the two brothers, however, Roderick was universally considered the better teacher. This was particularly true of *ceòl mór*; he was responsible, for example, for teaching several past gold-medal winners, such as Iain MacFadyen, Kenneth MacDonald and Allan and Angus MacDonald of Glenuig. Neil Johnstone, a contemporary of Neil MacDonald and Rona Lightfoot, remarked on this perceived difference between the *Roidein* brothers:

> *Tha mi smaoineadh gun d'fhuair Seonaidh a h-uile* major award *a bha 'dol* over the years, *fhad 's a bha e 'na* Phipe Major. *Bhiodh a'* bhand *a' dol air feadh an t-saoghail... Bha Ruairidh, mar a chanadh iad, direach 'na* lone piper; *bhiodh e 'na* phrofessional *e fhéin, fhuair e móran de chupannan is do* mhajor prizes; *ach leis na bha do dh' eòlas agam air Ruairidh, chanainn gur e na b'fheàrr airson ionnsachadh na Seonaidh, a chionn bha Seonaidh cho fior dhomhainn air fad – tha mi cinnteach gu robh e gu math duilich dha tighinn a-nuas agus tòiseachadh air duine, duine aineolach ionnsachadh. Mar a bha Ruairidh, bha dòigh air choireigin aig Ruairidh.*[41]

> I think *Seonaidh* got every major award that was going over the years, while he was Pipe Major. The band would go all over the world... Roddy, as they used to say, was only a solo piper; he was a professional himself, he got many cups and major prizes; but from what I knew of Roddy, I would say that he was better at teaching than *Seonaidh*, because *Seonaidh* was so deep altogether – I'm sure it was quite difficult for him to come down to the level of tutoring a beginner. While Roddy, Roddy just had a certain way.

∼ THE MORRISONS OF LOCH EYNORT ∼

At the Flora MacDonald Cup in 1967, the master of ceremonies referred to the MacDonalds of Garryhellie and the Morrisons of Loch Eynort as two families who 'supported these meetings, and virtually carried it on their shoulders'.

'The Morrisons comprise four young men and one girl, all first-class pipers,' he went on. 'They were exclusively taught by their father, Donald John Morrison, a woodwork teacher in the South Uist Schools. The grandson is the kingpin of the lot.'[42] The grandson in question is William J. Morrison, born in 1948, a mainstream competitor of some renown who left Uist at twenty-two to work in Ayrshire and has resided in Glasgow for over twenty years. Willie was brought up in a particularly large family of pipers who can be confused at times with one or two other, though probably distantly related, piping families named Morrison in the same general area: Donald Andrew Morrison (1927–88), for instance, came from Loch Eynort. *Dòmhnall Anndra* was a highly successful competitor and composer[43] among mainland piping circles in the 1950s and '60s, having won the gold medal in Inverness in 1961 and numerous other awards at the premier gatherings; he won many of the light music events at the South Uist Games during the 1950s, both local and open, although his *ceòl mór* was at times overshadowed by mainland competitors and one or two other local exponents. After spending time in the Merchant Navy, he joined the Aberdeen City Police in 1952 and was Pipe Major of the Police band for many years. Another family of Morrisons, from Gerinish, were known locally as *Clann Sheonaidh Aonghuis Ruaidh* or 'the Children of John son of Red Angus'. They are most noted for two brothers, Alfred and Ronald (both now deceased), and Alfred's son Fred, who is considered one of Scotland's most gifted pipers in both competitive and non-competitive idioms. Fred was brought up in Bishopton but, in a conscious attempt to re-connect with his heritage, now lives in South Uist with his wife Deirdre. Bell Morrison, Angus Campbell's wife, also belonged to this family. Of Willie's family, only his uncle, Ludovic or 'Louis' Morrison, remains in South Uist today. He is among Uist's most prominent players and teachers.

Louis was one of eight sons and daughters of Donald John Morrison, or *Dòmhnall Iain*. Their mother was known as *Mairead Dhòmhnaill 'ic Dhòmhnaill Ruaidh*, or 'Margaret, daughter of Donald, son of Red Donald'; her father, a Gaelic bard, was noted for his composition *Fàgail Bhòirnis*.[44] Donald John was born in Lewis, raised in Strom, Benbecula, and spent some time in Glasgow before settling on a croft in Loch Eynort in 1933. During his childhood in Benbecula, he attended John MacDonald's courses in Daliburgh from 1909 to 1914; later in life, he was a technical teacher who travelled throughout South Uist and Benbecula teaching a joinery class with an unofficial half-hour chanter class alongside, spending two to three days each in Garrynamonie, Daliburgh, Loch Eynort, Gerinish, Eochar, Torlum and parts of North Uist.

According to Louis, his father's parents were not pipers. Nonetheless, he probably picked up the basics of the practice-chanter within the Strom community before taking classes with MacDonald, and probably carried on learning and playing among the Highland element of Glasgow before settling in Loch Eynort. As his mainstream education suggests, he was above all else a literate player who reputedly taught all eight of his children in the same spirit. Louis claims to have picked it up mostly by 'listening to the singing and playing'[45] of his father and older siblings – attesting, in itself, to the survival of aural transmission in South Uist – but this disregards his grounding in staff notation as a child at Donald John's knee. Although intimately familiar with the nuances of dance-music and its place in the local ceilidh tradition, Louis is, like Neil and Rona, a product of the mainstream era. As a competitor, he rose to prominence at the South Uist Games in the late 1970s and early '80s; he began figuring highly in *ceòl mór* in 1981 and won it outright in 1982 and 1986 against such formidable mainstream players as Roderick MacLeod and Norman Gillies.

Louis is a widely recognised tutor on the island, and is called upon regularly to teach chanter classes with Calum Beaton. He has taught his own children in Ormiclate, where his family have lived since 1993 after leaving the old croft in Loch Eynort. He is typical of today's piper of South Uist origins: raised on a diet of competition settings and staff notation, measured by the yardstick of the Games, yet sharing that foundation in the staff-notated idiom with the myriad folk melodies and nuances of *ceòl cluais* extant throughout his life. Reconciling this musically bilingual repertoire against the backdrop of the twentieth century is a matter for a later chapter, in which we again look to Louis' example.

∽ SEONAID 'JESSIE' MACAULAY (NÉE MACINTYRE) OF SMERCLATE ∽

Seonaid 'Jessie' MacIntyre was born c. 1913 – 'I'm eighty-five,' she told me proudly when I first met her in 1998 – in the township of Smerclate in Uist's south end, and passed away in March of 2002. She was a school-teacher by profession and resided in Uist House, the Daliburgh rest home, during her final years. When I met her in 1998, her grasp of piping and of pipe tunes was still sharp: on the occasion of our first meeting, I played several sets on the bagpipe for the home's residents, and Jessie intently followed along with her fingers on such competition-style tunes as 'Marchioness of Tullibardine' and 'Maggie Cameron'. However, due to her infirmity, she had not played for many years.

According to Jessie, her family had lived in Smerclate for approximately 150 years. One may be forgiven for thinking that her family were connected with *Pìobairean Smearclait*, so immortalised in folk memory, but she makes no claim to this. While most sources identify the Smerclate Pipers as MacIntyres, Jessie suggested the possibility that the quasi-mythical family were MacNeils who came over from Barra, and in any case were established in Smerclate long before her own family. When asked about her own *sloinneadh*, or direct ancestral line, she replied in English that her family did not go untouched by Cluny's Clearances in the nineteenth century:

> They were famous pipers in Skye, the MacIntyres. They came across the Minch to the back of Ben Mór, a place called Corodal. My great grandfather left Corodal in the 1840s; they were driven out, you see, with the sheep coming in. They lost the hill at Ben Mór, and they came to Smerclate. His wife was from Smerclate, so that's where they went. That's where we are today.[46]

Since losing the hill, her father and grandfather were each referred to by the appellative 'of Corodal', and for this reason, Jessie was known as *Seònaid Dhòmhnaill Chorodail* or 'Jessie, daughter of Donald of Corodal'. On another occasion she referred to her ancestors as having been pipers and archers to Clanranald upon arriving from Skye, which purports a connection not so much with the Pipers of Smerclate as with the historical character *Gille Phàdruig Duibh*, a Skye-born MacIntyre who resided in South Uist in the seventeenth century as Clanranald's personal archer. As noted elsewhere, a family in Cape Breton, descended from Donald MacIntyre, who left South Uist in 1826 and settled at French Road, made a similar claim; it is as yet uncertain if the families are related, but Jessie had mentioned having relations in Boisdale, Cape Breton, so it is entirely possible.

Jessie's perspective on South Uist's piping tradition this century was every bit as valuable as Calum Beaton's, not only for the corroboration they provide for each other's testimony, but for their individual, experiential differences as well. Jessie's perspective covered a greater period of time, for instance. Her memories of life in the 1920s portrayed a fundamentally musical community whose inventive creativity belied their lack of material wealth. For instance, she described pipers in the ceilidhs of her youth sitting on creels (presumably up-turned) as they played, passing round the pipes one after the other, while dancing continued till morning.[47] They likely sat because the blackhouse ceilings of the period were too low for the drones when a piper stood at full height. This custom became common among pipers in Gaelic emigrant communities in Nova Scotia, whether or not the pipes are being played under a ceiling of any height, and produced in that region an elaborate foot-tapping technique in which the piper accompanies his own playing by tapping out rhythms designed to mimic the steps of the dancers.[48] Although the cultural imperative of dance survived in Uist, Jessie could not recall pipers in her own locality practising the same elaborate tapping.

Ultimately, the development of the sitting and foot-tapping as an entrenched aspect of performance may rightly be considered an innovation peculiar to the Gaelic emigrant culture of Nova Scotia, rather than a true surviving remnant of pre-Culloden Highland piping. Jessie seemed to believe the habit of sitting in Smerclate went out of style due to military influence:

> JD: *Am biodh [pìobairean] 'nan suidhe a' cluichd anns na ceilidhean?*
> JM: *Cha robh mu dheireadh, ach bha an toiseach. Nuair bha mise òg, bha iad 'nan suidhe. Mo bhràthair fhéin, cha robh e 'na shuidhe uair sam bith a-nisd, ach bha e anns a'* regiment, *is* pipe band, *is rudan a bharrachd.*[49]

> JD: Would pipers sit while playing at ceilidhs?
> JM: Not lately, but at first. When I was young, they would sit. Now, my own brother never sat at any time, but he was in the regiment, and the pipe band, and so on.

Practice-chanters and reeds were prohibitively expensive for most crofting families in the early decades of the twentieth century, to say nothing of the full bagpipe. Jessie earlier noted how many young men in Uist, including her older brother Alasdair, joined the army just to get their hands on a set of pipes; as for chanters and reeds, they were not often imported from the mainland. Young pipers instead made do with instruments constructed locally from wood and barley:

> JM: *Cha robh feadain furasda fhaighinn. Bha feadan daor do dhaoine, agus bhiodh iadsan a' faighinn pìos fiodh a bha freagarrach agus dhèanadh iad tuill air. Bha an t-seann fheadhainn, na seann bhodaich, glé mhath air an dèanamh, bha iad na b' fheàrr na na gillean òga, fhios agaibh; bha an t-seann fheadhainn a' dèanamh feadain dhan fheadhainn òig.*
> JD: *An robh iad a' dèanamh reeds?*
> JM: *Seadh, yes, cha robh gleusan*[50] *againn idir. Bha sop eòrna againn, a' gearradh pìos dheth, am beulag air a' chéile, is bha e a' dèanamh ceòl math math bog, fhios agaibh. Cha robh e cruaidh idir mar a tha an gleus a tha 'san fheadan an-diugh. Dh' fhaodadh tu feadan a chluichd a-staigh leat fhéin agus daoine a bruidhinn, is cha robh e cur dragh sam bith orra. Ceòl bog bog.*[51]

> JM: It wasn't easy to get practice chanters. The chanter was expensive for people, and they would get a piece of wood that was suitable and would make holes in it. The old people, the old men, were very good at making them, they were better than the boys, you see; the old ones made chanters for the young ones.
> JD: They would make reeds?
> JM: Yes, we didn't have reeds at all. We would take a straw of barley, cut off a piece of it, bind them up against each other, and they would make very soft music, you see. It wasn't harsh like the reed in the chanter today. You could play a chanter indoors on your own, with people around talking, and it wouldn't bother them at all. Very soft music.

Although Jessie's reminiscences on piping in the 1920s and '30s are an important contribution to our knowledge of the area's material customs and folklore, her greatest value as an informant lay in her observations of an indigenous aural tradition set against encroaching mainstream influences. In this vein, she had much in common with Calum Beaton: her father, like Calum's, was a piper who had learned entirely by aural transmission in the *taigh-céilidh* in the nineteenth century; as a result she, like Calum, was unusually articulate among South Uist pipers about the effect of games and literate tuition on playing style in her community; and like Calum, her perception of what the local style used to be reflected her perceived cultural identity. Her piping tuition outside the environs of her immediate family was literate, having received lessons as a girl from Willie Ross in the 1920s and from John MacDonald of Inverness in the 1930s. In conversation, she implied that these lessons were irregular and informal, somewhat on the side of the proper courses, which may have had something to do with her gender but perhaps also, in the case of Ross, with her youth. Both had ramifications for her in open competition:

JM: *Cha robh e doirbh anns a'* chompetition *agam ... 's e nighean no aon bhoireannach a bh' ann ... agus ùine a' cluichd dhaibh, agus bhithinn a' faighinn* special prize.
JD: *Seach gu robh thu 'nad [bhana-]phìobaire a-mhàin?*
JM: *'S mi, seadh, 's mi gu dearbh.* Well, *chan e* 'competition' *a bh'ann ach bha iad sin a' toirt orm a dhol suas chun a'* phlatform *airson* selection *a thoirt seachad, is bhithinn a' faighinn* special prize.
JD: *Chluich thu* selection –
JM: March, strathspey *is* reel.[52]

JM: It wasn't difficult when I was in competition ... There was only a girl or one woman ... playing for them for a while, and I'd get a special prize.
JD: Because you were the only girl?
JM: That's right, I was. Well, it wasn't really a 'competition' but they were there, having me go up to the platform and give a selection, and I'd get a special prize.
JD: You'd play a selection –
JM: March, strathspey and reel.

Jessie's situation probably had less to do with being young (after all, the Games committee had already organised 'junior division' events by 1913) than with being a young girl. Her account is interesting compared to Rona Lightfoot's remarks on being a female piper in South Uist for the corroboration it gives of a double standard between male and female piping. Rona's testimony suggests that at the mid-point of this century, piping was discouraged among girls in their teen years as being un-feminine; Jessie's remarks imply that this was also true of an earlier date, and that unlike Rona, who managed to be taken quite seriously in competition, Jessie was relegated to the periphery of the competition proper. It's always possible that Jessie may have simply been a poor competition-style player – she is, after all, never mentioned in any Games prize list – but if so, there would not have been much reason for giving her a 'special prize'.

Despite her literate tuition with these giants of the competition world, she grew up in a household which, unlike Clanranald Cottage, resounded with the rhythms of *ceòl cluais*. She therefore grew to observe first-hand the difference in style which the influence of mainstream piping – whose functional context was radically different from the hitherto predominant ceilidh piping[53] – must necessarily have produced. In describing the difference, she contrasted her father's playing against her own and her brother's:

> *Tha mise a' smaoineadh gu robh an ceòl a bha m' athair a' toirt as an fheadan na b' fheàrr na 'n ceòl a bha mi 's mo bhràthair a' toirt as, 's an aon phuirt. Bha rudeiginn aige-san nach robh sinn a' glacadh idir, le bhith 'ga leughadh as an leabhar. Bha e toirt 'nam chuimhne-sa ceòl Éirinneach, an ceòl a bh' aige-san, nuair a chluichdeadh e. Bha rudeiginn ann a bha sinn a' call, le bhith 'ga thoirt as an leabhar. Mar gum biodh* 'abiding by the rules'; *cha robh esan idir . . . bha e car traditional.* You could catch it by your ear.[54]

> I think that the music my father got out of the chanter was better than the music my brother and I got out of it, and playing the same tunes. There was something he had that we weren't catching at all, reading it from the book. It reminded me of Irish music, the music he had, when he would play it. There was something there that we lost, reading from the book. It was 'abiding by the rules' in a sense; but he didn't . . . he was somewhat traditional. You could catch it by your ear.

The 'Irish' character of her father's displaced musical idiom was a theme she developed at length:

> JM: *Tha mi smaoineadh gun do dh' atharraich e, co-dhiubh.* The music. *'Nam dh' aois òig, seach mar a tha an-diugh . . . Tha mi smaoineadh gu robh na seann daoine, mar a bha m' athair fhéin, bha e a' cluichd leis a' chluas. Bha rudeiginn anns a' cheòl nach robh againne, a' toirt as an leabhar. Bha sinne 'ga cluichd* straight from the book, *mar gum biodh. Agus* music *coltach ri ceòl a bh' aig m' athair, 's e ceòl Éirinneach. Bha* lift *air choireiginn, fhios agad, nach robh againne idir.*
>
> JD: *Togail?*
>
> JM: *Seadh. Bha rudeiginn aotrom air choireiginn anns a' cheòl aige. 'S ann a chluinneadh sibh ceòl Éirinneach a' tighinn as an* radio; you know it, that's Irish music. What tells you it's Irish music, different from Scots music? It's

got a certain lift *air choireiginn nach eil ann an ceòl Albannach idir. Tha [ceòl Albannach] an-diugh gu tric as an leabhar, co-dhiubh. Tha* lift *air choireiginn anns an* Irish, *is bha sin aig m' athair, anns na puirt a bh' aige*.[55]

JM: I think it changed, anyway. The music. In my youth, compared to today . . . I think the old people, like my father, he played by ear. There was something in the music we didn't have, getting it from notation. We were playing it straight from the book. And music like my father played is Irish music. There was a kind of lift, you see, that we didn't have at all.

JD: A lift?

JM: Right. There was a kind of lightness in his music. It's like when you listen to Irish music on the radio; you know it, that's Irish music. What tells you it's Irish music, different from Scots music? It's got a certain kind of lift that Scottish music doesn't have at all. Scottish music today is often based on notation, anyway. There's a certain lift in Irish music, and that's what my father had, in the tunes he had.

Jessie clearly identified culturally with the dance music of her father's generation, as opposed to the competition music of her own. This in itself betrays an insider's point of view toward what may have been regarded as a foreign idiom. Yet she perceives the culture in question as Irish, which I found to be unique among informants. The fact that Jessie was alone in comparing the local ear-learned idiom to Irish music does not detract from its insightfulness; the anthropologist Edward Sapir recognised that an individual's divergence from the norm can be a fundamental property of any given culture, revealing truths that would otherwise remain unvoiced.[56] The truth in Jessie's perception recalls, on one hand, the traditional ties between South Uist and Gaelic Ireland, maintained for centuries through common politics, oral literature and Roman Catholicism; on the other hand it suggests the influence of Jessie's own ancestry. Her mother's family were O' Henleys, who were among the bridal entourage of Àine Ní Cathan of Keenaght, Co. Derry, who married Angus Òg MacDonald, Lord of the Isles, in South Uist in the thirteenth century. It is often said that the Gael's breadth of knowledge runs not horizontally, but vertically; in the case of the late Jessie MacAulay and her apprehension of the past, this is most certainly so.

～ CALUM BEATON OF STONEYBRIDGE ～

Calum Beaton, or *Calum Eairdsidh Choinnich* ('Calum, son of Archie son of Kenneth'), has been a valued source of information on local lore and oral tradition for many years, most notably in his collaborations with Peter Cooke for the School of Scottish Studies.[57] He is one of very few remaining in South Uist who can give an intimate account of local piping and its changing meanings through the course of the twentieth century. He was born in 1931, the son of a piper who learned exclusively by ear and who, as discussed elsewhere, subsequently refused to pass on to Calum the tradition as he'd received it. Times had changed since Archie Beaton first picked up tunes in the *taigh-cèilidh*: the Piobaireachd Society and the Piping Society of South Uist had spent the last generation introducing the values and mechanics of literacy to Uist's backwater dance-pipers; post-war depression had seen a decline in the local gatherings in which music was most often heard and enjoyed; the *Roidein* brothers from down the road were the toast of Glasgow; and the Games, which had been held on Askernish machair for over thirty years, were beginning to attract more and more professional mainland competitors on the summer circuit. Most young pipers by then aspired to the platform and the prize, the spectacle and the recognition, rather than to a style and social context that seemed comparatively bijou. By Calum's day, South Uist had come round to the modern age.

As discussed in an earlier chapter, Calum did not begin on the bagpipe himself until an older cousin of his, Alasdair Beaton, returned home from the Second World War and agreed to give him lessons. Even Alasdair was a reluctant teacher, though perhaps for different reasons than Archie:

> *Deagh phìobaire bha sin, gu h-àraid air ceòl aotrom; cha robh e suas ris a' cheòl mhór idir. Ach nuair a thàinig e dhachaidh, cha robh e deonach sam bith, ionnsachadh sam bith a thoirt dhomh. Bha e builteach air . . . obair deoch, is òl . . . bha e 'g ràdh mar gum biodh pìobairean, gum biodh an deoch daonnan . . . Ach co-dhiubh, bha mise gu math titheach airson tòiseachadh, agus thòisich e ionnsachadh dhomh an uairsin.*[58]

> He was a good piper, especially of light music; he wasn't up to the pibroch at all. But when he came home, he wasn't at all willing to teach me. He was inclined to the drink . . . he was talking as if pipers were always drinking. But no matter, I was very keen to start, and he began to teach me then.

Both Alasdair, born in 1901, and his brother Roderick, born in 1894, were literately-trained pipers whose skills were polished in the military. In addition, Roderick was a member of John MacDonald's initial courses in Daliburgh. Alasdair, on the other hand, was not a performer of *ceòl mór*, which was why he sent young Calum to John Archie MacLellan. Calum remembers his cousin as a great lover of the big music, however; Alasdair would often sit listening to his erstwhile pupil playing at home and, according to Calum, was always keen to hear tunes like 'Mary MacLeod' and 'Kiss of the King's Hand'.

In the early 1950s, Calum followed a path taken by many a Uist piper before him when he enlisted for a tour of duty with the Queen's Own Cameron Highlanders. He served in the 4th/5th (Territorial) Battalion under Pipe Major Robert MacKay – more popularly known as 'Mickey' MacKay – and fellow Uist man Pipe Major Donald MacIntyre of Boisdale. Pipe Major MacKay was a native of the Inverness area who was taught by John MacDonald in the latter's capacity as an army instructor. Calum in turn received a few lessons from MacKay while serving in the band, and it was under his tutelage that, between 1952 and 1953, Calum made two consecutive appearances at the gold medal competition at the Northern Meeting in Inverness. In his first appearance he was given 'Mary MacLeod', and as he remembers it, his chances were 'scuppered by nervousness' when his bottom hand slipped off the chanter. The pride of his battalion was saved, however, when Pipe Major MacKay took the Gold with, aptly enough, 'MacKay's Banner'. In his second appearance Calum played 'Beloved Scotland'.

Calum and Pipe Major MacIntyre were not the only *Uibhistich* among the ranks of the 4th/5th: out of fourteen pipers serving in the band in 1953, no fewer than nine hailed from South Uist, a measure of nothing so much as the vestigial force of the island's martial tradition in modern times. Calum even recalls that the 1953 contingent was actually a low ebb; in other years the number of Uist pipers in the band was significantly higher. Looking at a photograph of the band fifty years later, Calum could point out each of the other eight pipers by name, their pipes in hand.

In his competing days, Calum placed often in the South Uist games and the Flora MacDonald Cup. He won the jig event at Askernish in 1956, won the *ceòl mór* in 1968 and took third in the MSR in 1972.[59] He won the *ceòl mór* event at the Flora MacDonald Cup in 1966 with the 'Lament for Mary MacLeod',[60] but, like his performance at the Northern Meeting, it is doubtful that he performed it in the manner in which he had first learned it from MacLellan. The very fact that the judges in this local competition accepted his performance means, in itself, that he had by then adopted the mainstream Kilberry style as passed on to him through intermittent lessons under Angus Campbell, Calum Walker and the *Roideins*, in the Battalion under Mickey MacKay and in group classes under Bob Nicol. Today, like Louis Morrison, Calum is much in demand for dances, ceilidhs and lessons. He teaches a twice-weekly chanter class with Louis under the auspices of the South End Piping Club.

Despite his long association with the literate idiom through competition and his spell in the military, Calum has never forgotten his childhood days listening to *ceòl cluais* at his father's knee. Because of this, perhaps, he is particularly conscious and articulate about the stylistic implications of aural transmission and long-cherished dance customs to local piping. In his view, these influences led to a difference in playing style between pipers of the southern Outer Hebrides and those from the mainland up until the post-Second World War era. Since then, Calum perceives that all piping in Uist has come to reflect mainstream influence as literate transmission became the norm, but he looks back on local piping up to the post-war period as being literally a class apart:

CB: *Nuair a bha pìobaireachd a' dol gu làidir ann an Uibhist – a' dol fada roimhidh sin, ro'n chogadh mu dheireadh ach nuair thòisich mi fhìn air pìobadh, 's ann as deaghaidh an Darna Cogadh is thòisich na games as ùr ann an Uibhist – bha mòran phìobairean matha ann an Uibhist an uairsin. Bha an ceòl a bh' aca, chanainn-sa gu robh an ceòl aig muinntir Uibhist ann a sheo na bu chruaidhe, fhios agad; 's e daoine a bh' ann, bha iad ag obair daonnan air a' chruit is àiteachan eile, is bha na corragan aca na bu chruaidhe. Gheobhadh tu an ceòl aig an fheadhainn nach robh ag obair le 'n lamhan – ged a bha iad uamhasach fileanta, bha an ceòl aca car bog air choireiginn. Cha robh e tighinn suas idir ris a' cheòl chruaidh a chluinneadh tu [aig?] muinntir Uibhist. Tha mi cinnteach gum bi gu leòr nach aontaich ris a sin, ach sin mar a chuala mise iad co-dhiubh . . . Car bog anns a' chluichd aca. Bha gu leòr aig an àm co-dhiubh . . . bha na* doublings, *mar a chanas sinn, is na* gracenotes, *bha iad 'gan dèanamh na bu chruaidhe na chluinneas tu an-diugh iad . . . Bha a h-uile* gracenote *agus* doubling *cho soilleir is cho cruaidh 'gan dèanamh.*

JD: *Anns na farpaisean?*

CB: *Anns na farpaisean is 'gan cluichd ann an àite sam bith. Dannsa cuideachd.*

JD: *'S mar sin, bha difir dòigh aig muinntir Uibhist anns na seann laithean, an robh?*

CB: *Uill, cha robh difir sam bith anns na puirt, mar sin, ach chanadh tu anns a' cheòl, gu robh difir ann . . . A' chuid bu mhotha dhe na bha tighinn far tìr-mór, 's i an obair a bh' aca – feadhainn dhiubh dotairean, is tìdsearan, is maighstirean-sgoile, feadhainn ag obair ann an oifis. Cha robh iad ag obair le 'n lamhan, is corragan bog' orra. Cha b' ionnan iad 's mar a bha na corragan a bhios air duine a bha 'g obair le spaid is . . . na gnothaichean a bha sin idir; òrd mór is piocaid. Sin mar a bha a' chuid bu mhotha co-dhiubh do mhuinntir Uibhist. Bha corragan cruaidh orra is tha mi smaointinn air a thàilleabh sin gu robh an ceòl a bha iad a' toirt a-mach na bu chruaidhe is na bu shoilleire na'n ceòl grinn a bh' aig an fheadhainn a bha tighinn dhachaidh far tìr-mór. Sin am beachd agam-sa co-dhiubh.*[61]

CB: When piping was strong in Uist – since long before the last war but when I started piping myself, which was after the Second World War and the Uist games started anew – there were many good players in Uist then. I would say that the music that the Uist people had here was harder, you see; the people here, they were working on the croft and other places, and their fingers were harder. You would get the music of those who didn't work with their hands – although they were very skilled, their music was somewhat soft. It just wasn't up to the hard music that you would hear the Uist folk playing. I'm sure there are many who won't agree with that, but that's how *I* heard them, anyway... Their playing was a little soft. Often enough at the time... the doublings, as we call them, and the grace notes, they made them harder than you would hear them today... Every grace note and doubling was made so clear and so hard.

JD: In competitions?

CB: In competitions and played in any other place. Dances, too.

JD: So, the Uist people had a different way of playing in the old days, did they?

CB: Well, it wasn't any different in the tunes, as such, but you could say in the music, there was a difference... Most of those who came from the mainland, it was their work – some of them doctors, teachers, schoolmasters, those who work in an office. They didn't work on the land, and their fingers were soft. They weren't like the fingers of someone who worked with a spade and... that sort of thing; a sledge-hammer and pick. That's how most of the Uist people worked anyway. They had hard fingers, and I think that's why the music they made was harder and clearer than the delicate music of those who came home from the mainland. That's *my* opinion, anyway.

Although I translate the word *cruaidh* as 'hard' in the above extract of our conversation, it does not refer to difficulty. Calum was trying to convey the notion that Uist pipers (up until the present generation) tended to strike the chanter with their fingers more solidly and resoundingly than their mainland counterparts, producing a 'crack' in ornamentation that he did not hear in the playing of those with 'soft fingers' who spent their days 'in an office'. This may be Calum's own nostalgia coming across, but in his remarks we can see a perception of the local playing style as a symbol of identity and social boundary, where agriculture meets white-collar and island meets mainland. The difference lay not in 'the tunes', but in 'the music'. Music as an expression of identity along such lines has been the subject of study within many cultures,[62] and in the case of the Hebridean Gael, Calum's remarks suggest the point of view of a community on the periphery of the mainstream, where 'differentness' is cultural and social as well as geographical. It is the point of view of the insider looking out. It is this particular frame of mind, combined with his long inheritance of all the roles and repertoires of piping, which make Calum Beaton the ideal informant: a genuine tradition-bearer, a skilful performer and a sensitive observer of his own cultural heritage.

CHAPTER 9

'Nowhere in Scotland do the pipers come forward in such numbers'
THE HIGHLAND GAMES IN SOUTH UIST

Families such as the MacDonalds of Garryhellie and Daliburgh, and individual pipers such as Angus Campbell and Louis Morrison, measured their worth as exponents largely by the yardstick of the annual Highland Games held on Askernish machair. Because Games became in South Uist (as they did elsewhere in Scotland) the standard measure of a piper's skill, an overview is needed on the Games' history in Uist and to an extent the wider Hebrides in order to understand their role in the local tradition. To this end, contemporary reports from the *Oban Times* serve as an excellent source of information; correspondents in the early decades of the century often inundated the reader with what may at first seem like trivialities, listing the names of gentry, clergy and honoured visitors who came to watch the day's events, describing the performance of competitors under adverse weather conditions, and quoting nearly verbatim the toasts made at the post-Games ceilidh. But such trivialities will often elicit a vivid portrait of piping's golden days and the characters who lived them.

Pipe music has always been at the heart of the South Uist Games; it is the feature for which it has been most identified, by players and tourists alike, since its inception. 'The great attraction was the piping events,' reported the *Oban Times* of the Games in 1931, 'not to be wondered at when one knows South Uist to stand out predominantly as the home of piping.'[1] Indeed, it attracted such stiff competition by the post-Second World War era that Askernish was considered a qualifier, among several, for the premier contests at the Northern

Meeting (Inverness), the Argyllshire Gathering (Oban) and latterly the Bratach Gorm (London). This is not so often the case nowadays, but the memory of the Uist Games' status in the wider circuit of Highland gatherings is long lived. Rona Lightfoot competed successfully against the best the mainland community could offer during the 1950s, '60s and '70s and her remarks depict the passing of former glories:

> *Aig an àm ud, nuair a bha mi òg, bha móran, móran do dheagh phìobairean a' dol a-mach chun na* games *an Uibhist. Cha mhór nach robh na* games *Uibhist a' cheart cho cudthromach 'sa bha an* Northern Meeting *agus an t-Òban. Bha na pìobairean air fad a' dol a-mach . . . Bha na* MacFadyens *a' dol a-mach, is bha Dòmhnall MacLeòid a' dol a-mach, is bha* Seumas MacNeill, *is* Mickey *MacAoidh . . . fìor dheagh phìobairean . . . Tha cuimhn' am mo mhàthair a bhith ag ràdh nuair bha na* games *seachad, bha a' phìob 'na cluasan airson trì no ceithir a laithean as a dheaghaidh . . . Bha i laidir, laidir anns an eilean.*[2]

> At that time, when I was young, there were many, many good pipers going out to the Uist games. The Uist games were almost as important as the Northern Meeting and Oban. All the pipers were going out . . . The MacFadyens were going out, and Donald MacLeod was going out, and Seumas MacNeill and Mickey MacKay . . . really good players . . . I remember my mother saying that when the games were finished, the pipes were in her ears for three or four days afterwards. It was extremely strong on the island.

Rona was speaking in this instance primarily of mainland competitors journeying to South Uist while completing a summertime circuit around a host of Highland Games, and indeed this facet of the yearly competitions at Askernish has been an invariable fixture since the 1930s. But as is discussed below, local competition has always been steady and by no means scarce. Studying contemporary Games records in order to better understand this local/non-local ratio has made clear just how popular the Askernish Games became in the twentieth century among competitive pipers outwith the islands. It has also proven valuable for identifying those who were most prominent in the Uist piping community – at least as regards the competitive idiom.

Consulting the prize-lists and commentaries on the Uist Games from sources such as the *Oban Times* and the *Piping Times* is not without its drawbacks. Reports do not appear in some even-numbered years, such as 1908, 1910 and 1912. And they cannot, of course, tell us who may have excelled in traditional ear-learned dance-piping and for how long; as discussed in previous chapters, the Games carry literate connotations which necessarily preclude consideration of the aural idiom. However, verbal testimony tends to reveal in that regard what written records leave out (see, for instance, Chapter 10), and we will concern ourselves for now with the Games and their place in the community's mainstream tradition. I first discuss the circumstances around which the South Uist Games began in relation to other Hebridean areas. I then highlight the conservation of tradition – whether genuine or perceived – within the surrounding artificiality of the Games, using sporting events and traditional dance as examples. Finally, I review successive generations of South Uist pipers on the competition platform and the more outstanding characters among them, showing, at the same time, how mainland competitors have increasingly saturated the prize-lists through the century.

∾ BEGINNINGS ∾

Organised Highland gatherings as we know them today, complete with competitions among athletes, dancers and pipers, are a product of the 'Celtic twilight' made popular by King George IV and Queen Victoria in the nineteenth century. Admittedly, the spirit of post-Jacobite romanticism had permeated high society with the image of the Gael as 'noble savage' and inspired notions of cultural preservation since earlier times – MacPherson's *Ossian*, Johnson and Boswell's travels and the establishment of the Highland Society of London are just a few examples – but these developments merely paved the way for the occasion of George IV's visit to Edinburgh in 1822, the preparations for which were spearheaded by Sir Walter Scott. The caricatured pageantry which adorned those proceedings, and George's espousal of it, heralded a national infatuation with all things perceived to be Highland. Games developed in the years that followed as the popular, if flawed, image of traditional Gaelic pastimes, and these benefited in time by Queen Victoria's patronage from her vantage point in Balmoral. One of the earliest Games established was at the Northern Meeting in Inverness in 1837, and as transportation and mobility between rural and urban areas improved in the 1860s, Games cropped up all over the country.[3] Oban saw its first Argyllshire Gathering in 1871.

Although Highland Games, as a cultural phenomenon, gained popularity incrementally and were known to find a solid footing in the west only in the twentieth century,[4] there are a number of Hebridean islands which had organised annual Games, including piping events, prior to the turn of the century. Islay, for instance, held 'Highland Sports' and piping competitions in Bridgend in 1895, reportedly 'revived after several years' lapse'. In the same year, a regatta was held in Colonsay which ended with entertainment put on by the MacNeills of Oronsay, and which included 'bagpipe competitions among the native youths'.[5] Annual gatherings for sport and music were held in Lewis and Skye by this time as well.[6] So while the sub-culture of Highland Games was far from intrinsic to the whole of Scotland's western seaboard before 1900, the process was well under way.

South Uist, too, saw its first mainstream Highland gathering prior to the turn of the century, though at the unlikeliest of times and places. Games were held at Ardvachar machair, on Uist's extreme north-west coast, on 6 January 1898. The gentlemen who organised and funded it came mainly from the immediate surrounding area – Ardvachar township, Eochar, Liniquie, Ardkenneth, a man from Aird, Benbecula and another from further south in Drimsdale – which probably explains why the games took place at Ardvachar as opposed to the more populous south end. 'These are the first Highland games that have ever been held in South Uist,' wrote the *Oban Times* correspondent. 'The day was rather showery in the morning, but it turned out very favourable and the afternoon was beautiful. There was a large turnout of spectators and competitors, there being over three hundred in all.'[7]

Events included throwing the hammer, putting the ball and tossing the caber (although where they obtained a caber in the Outer Hebrides is anyone's guess); several types of jumps and races, including a race especially for boys under sixteen; a tug-of-war between married men and bachelors; two dances, the Highland Fling and the Sword Dance; and two light music competitions for the bagpipe – one for marches, and another for strathspeys and reels. The lack of *ceòl mór* was a common feature of piping contests in the fledgling years of Hebridean Games: while *ceòl mór* competition had long been an institution on the mainland, *ceòl beag* remained the only music played in piping events in many gatherings in the Hebrides until John MacDonald, Inverness, first made his rounds for the Piobaireachd Society in 1909. As discussed elsewhere, this is a strong indication that performance, if not knowledge, of the *ceòl mór* repertoire was at too low an ebb in these areas to provide for varied competition until the Society's tuition was introduced. Six gentlemen of local standing judged the day's events, including Revs Angus MacRae of Ardkenneth and Alexander MacDougall of Benbecula – the same Fr MacDougall who would later co-found the South Uist Piping Society in Daliburgh. The piping was judged by Lachlan (*Lachlainn Bàn*) MacCormick of Benbecula, the well-known militia piper,[8] and the winner of both events, John MacLellan, was an Eochar man who went on to take prizes in subsequent Games such as in 1905, 1906 and 1907.

The *Oban Times* report, being the only existing record of the Ardvachar Games, gives no explanation as to why the committee chose to hold what has come to be regarded as traditionally a summer-time event in early January, nor does it give any clue as to what prompted the establishment of Games in the first place. We can reasonably suppose, however, that the holy Epiphany had something to do with both. Epiphany was by custom a day of festivity and sport in Catholic Highland communities, as was New Year's Day and Michaelmas,[9] and the Ardvachar Games' falling on 6 January seems too much of a coincidence not to be related. Furthermore, that the Games' committee members came mainly from the immediate surrounding area suggests that its timing and location was their decision, not the proprietor's, as was often the case in the late nineteenth century.[10] In effect, we are left with the impression that this was a gathering by and for the folk of Uist; a product of the people, not the gentry; and that its establishment accordingly contained elements of traditionalism not often seen in Games across the mainland. Considering the overall Victorian context of a 'Highland gathering', however, complete with a caber toss, hammer throw and tug-of-war, the committee members probably had some connection with mainstream Scottish society and were not typical of the grass-roots Uist crofting community at the turn of the century. The same applies to the founders of the South Uist Piping Society, as was discussed elsewhere. South Uist's introduction to the modern age, therefore, can be traced back to these men.

According to the Ardvachar Games report, the committee intended to hold subsequent Games in the month of August, and to hold the next Games at either Drimore or Grogarry machair. However, it appears that the whole matter was dropped, for no record exists of any Games in South Uist for another four years.

The year 1902 marked the establishment of games on several Hebridean islands, such as Tiree, Coll and Gigha. Reasons for their inception varied. In Tiree, for instance, the advent of Games came apparently with the desire to cater to the rising influx of tourists during the months of July and August. An *Oban Times* correspondent in Coll remarked in July of that year:

> Our islands always look their best this month, and may be said to have put on their annual new suit for the visitors. The only drawback is that a social gathering of the inhabitants . . . is not arranged to meet the visitors . . . We understand the people of Tiree are alive to this want, and have arranged games and athletic sports to be held on the 22nd inst.[11]

The number in attendance at this first Tiree gathering was estimated at 2,000, and the events included piping competitions for marches and for strathspeys and reels.[12] The year 1902 also marked the first Games in South Uist since January 1898, but for reasons other than tourism. As the coronation of King Edward VII approached in July of that year, the communities of many islands arranged to celebrate the occasion with a day of sporting events. A 'Coronation gala' was held in Coll, where pipers played but apparently did not compete; and in South

Uist and Benbecula combined, no fewer than three such gatherings – at Nunton, Howmore and Daliburgh – took place in one day. No piping competitions were held in the latter two, though bagpipes were indeed played; in Howmore, for example, after an inter-school shinty match, 'the children were reformed into procession, and headed by the pipers, they were conducted to a beautiful hollow on the opposite slopes of which the children sat down to the number of 200'.[13]

On Nunton Farm, matters differed:

> In anticipation of the King's Coronation . . . the Committee wisely arranged that a public holiday would be held . . . and athletic sports would be open to all competitors. The judges were, for bagpipe playing: Messrs. MacLean, Creagorry Hotel; MacDonald, Moss Cottage; ex-Sergt. Piper MacCormick, Creagorry; and D.L. MacLennan, Sorrell Lodge. Rev. Father A. MacDougall acted as secretary.[14]

The first judge mentioned was undoubtedly William MacLean, gold medallist and Pipe Major of the 4th and 5th Cameron Highlanders during the Great War, and Lachlan MacCormick again took to the bench, as he had in 1898. The other two, MacDonald of Moss Cottage and MacLennan of Sorrell Lodge, may have been landed gentlemen on holiday, flattered by the Games committee's offer to adjudicate the strains of the national music but knowing little of real piping; it was this sort of thing which prompted the establishment of the Piobaireachd Society in Edinburgh in December of that year. Events for marches and for strathspeys and reels were held, both for adults and for boys aged seventeen and under, but unfortunately there was no mention of the prize-winners.

Fr Alexander MacDougall appears to have had a leading hand in the proceedings which were to make the Games in South Uist an annual event. He was a financial backer of the Ardvachar Games in 1898; he also acted as captain of the bachelors' tug-of-war team that year (while Fr MacRae of Ardkenneth, dubiously, led the married men's team). He was then made secretary of the committee for the 1902 Games and was frequently involved at some level with the committees of subsequent years. He was certainly recognised later in life as having spearheaded their inception, for in 1925, by-then Canon MacDougall (who was at that point a resident of the Castlebay parish) was mentioned as having 'founded the Uist Games in Benbecula 23 years ago', a clear reference to the Nunton Farm coronation festivities.[15] Perhaps by 1925, the Ardvachar games had been forgotten. Fr MacDougall's name appears in 1903 in connection with establishing the permanence of what was deemed a successful day of sport:

> We had our Coronation Sports . . . last year, and they were such a decided success and so much interested the spectators that the Committee in charge arranged to have them annually. The Committee would feel grateful to any native or friend

of Benbecula who would contribute towards the prize fund. Contributions may be sent to Rev. Father MacDougall, Benbecula, and they will be publicly acknowledged.[16]

The Games continued to be held on Nunton Farm until 1906, in which year they were held on Askernish machair, just north of Garryhellie; Simon MacKenzie of the Lochboisdale Hotel acted as President of the Gathering.[17] Events then reverted to Nunton until 1909, at which point Askernish became the Games' permanent home. As Askernish was that time included among the holdings of the Lochboisdale Hotel, Simon MacKenzie's role in the newly formed South Uist Piping Society was probably a deciding factor in the Games' placement.

⁓ SPORTS AND DANCING AS ELEMENTS OF CONSERVATISM ⁓

Although Highland gatherings in the Hebrides are largely an invention of the past hundred years, sporting activities, both organised and spontaneous, have been central to the character of traditional Hebridean life since far earlier times. Stone-throwing, wrestling, jumping, shinty and all manner of races were typical athletic pastimes in west-coast and island communities of the eighteenth and nineteenth centuries. Shinty in particular, in Gaelic *camanachd* or *ioman*, boasts of a connection to Irish Gaelic tradition going back to *Cù Chulainn* and the Ulster Cycle.[18] The sports played at coronation celebrations and gatherings throughout the Hebrides in 1902 reflected these pastimes in many ways. At the coronation gala in Coll, for instance, 'putting the stone, throwing the hammer, jumping, running, etc., brought out a large number of competitors'. For the first official gathering in Tiree, athletic events included races, putting a sixteen-pound stone, a long jump, a running high jump, throwing a hammer and a football match. And in the celebration at Howmore, South Uist, there occurred a curious mix of the indigenous and the alien when 'the proceedings opened with a shinty match, the teams being Howmore v. Stoneybridge Schools . . . The winning team were awarded a large Union Jack, the gift of Mr. Guthrie, Grogarry, the captain of the team being directed to keep said flag for the use of the school'. The day went on to include events for jumping and separate races for 'young men', 'young women' and 'married men'.[19]

Since then, 'Highland sports' have indeed been imported to the Uist Games, some becoming established and others fading away: the caber, for one, was tossed in 1898 and again between 1922 and 1925, but thereafter only rarely; vaulting and hammer-throwing, by contrast, have enjoyed a long life. Despite these mainstream elements, the gamut of athletics at Askernish has stayed remarkably true to traditional pastimes involving running and feats of strength in Gaelic folklife. Wrestling, jumping and stone-throwing (albeit with regulated poundages) have remained the cornerstone events, as has a huge variety of races over the years: take the 'married men's race' which occurred in 1902, or the 'old men's race' in 1924; Finlay MacKenzie won a bare-back pony race along the seashore in 1922, and again in 1928; a motorcycle race was introduced in 1925; and so forth in like manner to modern times.[20] These events echo the Hebridean *oda*, or annual horse-race, last enacted in South Uist in 1820, and recall the more unusual races observed at games throughout the greater Highlands in the late nineteenth century. In Kintyre, for instance, the Athletic Sports of 1878 included a 'blindfold wheelbarrow race', and the Castleacres Games of 1883 included a 'hurdle sack race . . . a race for ploughmen over half a mile, and a fisherman's donkey race'.[21] To some extent, the racing tradition in South Uist survives today, albeit along more standard lines. Flat races of 100 yards, 220 yards, 440 yards, 880 yards and a full mile still occur, as does a race from Askernish machair to the summit of Ben Kenneth and back again on the day of each annual Games. In modern times, then, we find in South Uist the essentials of traditional rural Gaelic sports surviving in what is outwardly the manifestation of nineteenth-century 'Celtic twilight'.

The Gaels' love of racing is matched only by their love of dancing. Highland Games from the beginning included dance among the competitions, incorporating well-known traditional pieces such as the Highland Fling, Seann Trubhais and the sword dance Gillie Calum into an increasingly smoothed-out and standardised framework from the nineteenth century to the twentieth – like piping, the scope for free and dramatic interpretation diminished under the constraints of adjudication. These dances, performed solo and to pipe music, were never peculiar to South Uist, nor indeed to the Hebrides as a whole; they rather evolved within a Highland-wide tradition of Pyrrhic, pantomimic and social dancing with analogies across medieval Europe.[22] The South Uist Games have included events for the Highland Fling and Gillie Calum every year since its inception in 1898 and, unusually, for the foursome Scotch Reel since at least 1909. The foursome Reel is considered to have been the 'supreme social dance of Scotland', both Highland and Lowland, in the eighteenth century and is not ordinarily subject to competition; that it has been included in the South Uist Games for nigh on a century suggests, along with the races, the kind of traditionalism preserved at Askernish within the surrounding artificiality of the 'Highland Gathering' phenomenon. The Scotch Reel was not, however, the only element of dancing at the Games to suggest this, as events in 1923 were to show all of Scotland.

The Games had only just been re-established the previous July after eight long years of war and recovery. Roderick MacDonald, Angus Campbell, Archie

MacDonald of Garryhellie and 17-year-old Neil Smith of Howmore were out in competitive force in the summer of 1923, and the whole day was handsomely patronised by – among others – the British Chemical Co. of Glasgow, Lady Gordon Cathcart, the 4th Cameron Highlanders, the Lovat Scouts and one or two of the leading piping authorities of the day: John MacDonald of Inverness, Willie Ross and the well-known naturalist and piping judge Seton Gordon. Piping and athletic events carried on as they had in years past, but the line-up of dances included something new or, rather, something old:

> A novel feature was a competitive exhibition of old Highland dances which are remembered in South Uist and Barra, but which are almost entirely forgotten in other parts of the Highlands. There were two competitors, Mr. Archd. MacPherson, Eochdar, South Uist, who is over 75 years of age, and Mr. Donald MacDonald, Daliburgh. This event was much appreciated by the judges and spectators, and will be suitably developed at future gatherings.[23]

The three dances exhibited – The First of August, Over the Water to Charlie and Scotch Blue Bonnets Over the Border – were stepped solo and to pipe music like the formal competitive pieces, but clearly they were of a peculiar enough character to impress the onlookers. The judges may not have fully appreciated what they saw that day, for they came primarily for the piping and had no special expertise in dancing that I am aware of.[24] But the community appreciated it. These dances were the legacy of Ewan MacLachlan, an itinerant dance-master from Moidart who lived and taught in South Uist from the 1840s until his death in Loch Eynort in approximately 1880, and as the *Oban Times* report suggests, by the early 1920s his dances were considered peculiarly Hebridean rather than universally Highland like the Fling or the Reel. Archie MacPherson of Eochar had learned them, and others, from MacLachlan as a boy of ten or eleven years; Donald MacDonald of Daliburgh was in fact *Dòmhnall Bàn*, 'renowned piper and exponent of Highland dancing' as he was regarded in his own locale,[25] and father of the celebrated *Roidein* brothers. His tutelage under MacLachlan is less certain than Archie's, but he could have easily learned the steps second-hand. Over the next decade, these two men became the lynchpin in the dances' survival into modern times.

From 1924 to 1931, more of MacLachlan's solo step-dances – such as Miss Forbes, Scotchmakers, Flowers of Edinburgh, Tullochgorm, Scotch Measure and Highland Laddie – were included in the Games' competitions, until MacPherson and MacDonald began taking on pupils in order to pass the dances on. Prizes were soon offered to the best learners under the age of thirty.[26] They began to attract the patronage of prominent gentlemen like Duncan MacLeod of Skeabost, Skye, and William Donald of Glasgow, and even the Celtic Society of Edinburgh took notice enough to donate prize money. Headlines in the *Oban Times* reading

'Revival of Ancient Celtic Dancing' and 'Interesting Exhibition of Old Highland Dances'[27] attracted the attention of D.G. MacLennan, an authority on dance in his day and a cousin of Pipe Major George S. MacLennan, who was then one of Scotland's outstanding competitive pipers. Soon D.G. was a regular visitor to Askernish. He went on to author *Traditional and Highland Dances of Scotland* (Edinburgh, 1950), considered a seminal work at the time, based in part on his own interpretations of Archie MacPherson's steps at the Askernish exhibitions. Soon he too was a regular visitor to Askernish in these years. After 1931, however, interest seemed to slacken. The dances began to appear far less frequently in the record of events, and of them all, only Over the Water to Charlie and Highland Laddie have featured more or less continuously since. Clearly a feeling of great traditionalism and revival pervaded the South Uist Games during the 1920s on account of these dances; but the question remains: how authentically Hebridean were they?

It is said that MacLachlan studied for the priesthood in France as a young man, but that an illness which left an arm deformed caused him to give it up.[28] It is generally accepted that he either learned the dances there or composed them himself after settling in South Uist in the 1840s. Emmerson, however, noted that a dance called Highland Laddie was extant in Scotland from at least the 1830s and that MacLachlan's studies and continental influences had probably led him to come up with his own version of it, which he later taught only in South Uist and Barra.[29] The same can likely be said of the rest of his surviving repertoire – that he either composed them himself or arranged them based, like Highland Laddie, on pre-existing dances he had learned in his travels prior to 1840. Undoubtedly it was a bit of both. In this sense, the dances seen at Askernish during the 1920s were indeed peculiar to the Hebrides, and we are left with the impression that the South Uist community considered their local games a venue for exhibiting – that is, preserving – what they perceived as a genuinely Hebridean style of dance. At the same time, the Games authorities and the press applied the stamp of romantic caricature to these dances by presenting them as 'ancient', 'Celtic' and as 'old-world Hebridean dances . . . rescued from oblivion'; it bespeaks an invention of tradition, deliberate or otherwise, in the spirit of the Games phenomenon itself.[30]

∼ PIPING AT THE GAMES: LOCAL V. MAINLAND ∼

For practicality's sake, I have separated the years since 1898 into four eras: 1898 to 1914, 1922 to 1939, 1946 to 1979 and 1980 to the present.

Sectioning off the years in this manner is meant to reflect times of interruption caused by the two world wars, as well as the length of time which any one generation has maintained prominence on the boards before giving way to the younger, up-and-coming body of competitors. As we look at each of these eras in turn through the prize-lists and occasional eloquent correspondences found in the *Oban Times*, we see not just changes in the 'who' and 'when' of local piping, but the increasing influx of mainland competitors and how this eventually necessitated a separation of events between local and non-local. Readers will find the appended chart (see Appendix) a useful reference, as mainland competitors' names have been highlighted to show more clearly the proportional dichotomy over time. Competitors from Barra and North Uist, for the purposes of the chart, are considered local.

When trying to convey the fluctuations of entire generations of local competitive pipers over a century-long period, there is a strong temptation not to leave any one piper out of the picture in the belief that every individual has been an important part of the whole and worthy of mention. There is, in effect, a fear of casting too bright a light on one while passing it entirely by another; the inevitable result is a running-on of names and competition details which may be peripheral to, or too large a scope for, the point of the present work. Accordingly, I must remind the reader that this work can only be qualitative, not quantitative. I discuss only enough names, dates and competition details as are necessary to illustrate adequately the generation in question. The bulk of statistical data remains in the appended chart.

1898–1914

Piping events during these fledgling years of the Games consisted entirely of *ceòl beag* until 1908, the year before John MacDonald of Inverness began his annual tuition. But unfortunately no record exists of the prize-winners. Until then, events for marches and for strathspeys and reels were held with separate divisions for boys (aged eighteen or under) and men. This was taken a step further in 1906, when a separate full MSR (march, strathspey and reel) event was held for 'old men' in which Ronald MacDonald of Garryhellie, Neil and Rona's grandfather, took second.[31] First in the MSR for boys that year went to John Smith of Howmore. Available records show that in 1909, 1911 and 1914, when the Society's tuition was under way, *ceòl mór* was played under two categories: one confined to those who took Pipe Major MacDonald's course the previous spring, and one open to all.

This was the era of Neil Campbell and Archie MacDonald, and the coming-of-age of *Seonaidh Roidein* as a competitor; and yet John MacLellan of Eochar, altogether less well remembered, was the first big name at the Games, having taken the overall award at the inaugural events of 1898 and several other top places in the years following. He appears last in 1907, having placed third in the strathspey and reel contest.[32] These pipers' successes notwithstanding, the man universally remembered as South Uist's pre-eminent player before the days of Piobaireachd Society tuition was Lachlan MacCormick of the 'old Militia' and Lovat Scouts. On Askernish machair, he won the march events in 1905, 1907 and 1909, won the strathspeys and reels in 1907 and placed second in the open *ceòl mór* competitions of 1909 and 1911, among various other top placings.[33] He does not seem to have attended John MacDonald's courses in the years leading up to the Great War – or at least that is the impression gained, since his name does not appear on the prize-lists for the class-confined *ceòl mór* event. Naturally, however, it may just mean that he competed in the event but did not place. He died in 1951 aged 92, a legend in his own time.

Two other pipers of merit from this era were the brothers Angus MacIntyre (b. 1893) and Donald MacIntyre (b. 1890). Both received tuition in the Piobaireachd Society courses. It seems that Angus was a *ceòl mór* player first and foremost, having won both the class-confined and open *ceòl mór* events in 1909. He went on to take second place in the open event of 1913 before emigrating to Ontario some time later. He returned to Scotland, however, and by the 1960s was living out his days in Glasgow.[34] Donald MacIntyre, or *Dòmhnall Ruadh* ('Red-haired Donald') as he was known, stood out in his hey-day for his ability not just as a literate piper, but also as a competitive Highland dancer. In 1911 he pipped Lachlan MacCormick to first in the open *ceòl mór* playing 'Black Donald's March', came second in the event confined to MacDonald's pupils and third in the strathspey and reel; he then won all three of the dancing events – the Highland Fling, the Scotch Reel, and Gillie Calum.[35] Few have since attained such a record in one meeting. Donald's talents extended beyond music and dance, however, and he is remembered today mainly for his poetry.[36] Although born in the township of Snishival between Stoneybridge and Howbeg, he spent the better part of his postwar years in Paisley; hence his nickname in literary circles, the Paisley Bard.

His biographer and editor, Somerled MacMillan, believed, as Gaels often do, that Donald's piping talent was a blood inheritance, the gift of ancestors.[37] In this respect he credited the bard's mother, Kate MacLean, and her forebears with the transmission of his literary and musical abilities rather than his father's side, whom he dismissed as a somewhat prosaic people. To Kate he attributed a prodigious memory for words and music, particularly *canntaireachd* and pibroch songs, Gaelic proverbs and prayers; her father, Angus MacLean, was known as *Am Pìobaire Bàn* ('the Fair-haired Piper') and had been a regimental pipe major and piper to MacNeil of Barra before the latter emigrated to America in the early nineteenth century. Donald himself, meanwhile, was not quite so dismissive of his MacIntyre roots. He was of the opinion that his father's people came originally from Skye and had served as archers to Clanranald, a claim made also by piper Jessie MacAulay, née MacIntyre, and by the descendents of a piping MacIntyre family who emigrated to Cape Breton from Uist in the 1820s.[38] MacMillan acknowledged that several MacIntyre families arrived in Uist from Skye in the seventeenth and eighteenth centuries and that one branch in particular were noted archers as well as pipers;[39] indeed, of their musical prowess MacMillan repeated the traditional phrase *bha am foghlum os cionn Mhic Cruimen*, 'their education was over and above that of the MacCrimmons', something Calum Beaton said of the MacIntyres of Smerclate. *Dòmhnall Ruadh* clearly identified with this branch of MacIntyre ancestry and credited his own skill, on the bagpipe at least, very much to their influence. By explicitly dissociating Donald's abilities from his MacIntyre forebears in favour of the MacLeans, however, MacMillan showed that he regarded Donald's link, whether real or perceived, with the MacIntyre pipers of old as of no importance – something I believe the bard himself would have hotly disputed.

Donald served as piper to Cameron of Lochiel before and during the 1914–18 War. His contemporary, the Pininerine-born bard and ethnologist Donald John MacDonald (*Dòmhnall Iain Dhonnchaidh*) has left us probably the most fitting tribute to MacIntyre's musical abilities, revealing the importance of dance piping in South Uist even in the age of mainstream competition:

Ann an ceòl 's ann an dannsa
Measg do sheòrsa 's gach àm bhiodh tu 'm bàrr ann.
Meur a b' fhinealt air sionnsar
'S a chuireadh òigridh gu ùrlar le àbhachd.[40]

In music and in dance
Among your kind, at all times, you were supreme.
Fingers most fine on the chanter
That would send the young ones merrily to the floor.

It wasn't just the pipers who made this era a colourful one. Archibald Campbell of Kilberry, co-founder of the Piobaireachd Society, travelled to Uist to judge the piping events in 1911, and it is said that he hitched a ride from Lochboisdale to Askernish machair with Simon MacKenzie in his coach and horses – this being in the days before paved roads and motor vehicles were the norm. MacKenzie's expertise at the reins was well known, and he apparently drove the horses at such breakneck speed that Kilberry, at the end of the day, preferred to walk the five miles back.[41]

1922–1939

We come now to the era framed between two World Wars. The Great War had ended in 1918, but so severe and debilitating was the depression it caused, and so many were the casualties, that it took another four years for the pace and character of Hebridean life to recover sufficiently for a return to the Games. The day in July 1922 opened with considerable fanfare and optimism: 'On July 18th, upon the "machair" at Askernish, near Lochboisdale,' wrote the *Oban Times* correspondent,

> this Highland meeting was revived. For the island, the event was a great one, for the games have not been held since 1914. As is only natural for an island noted for its pipers, the piping events were the most important ones of the meeting, and the prizes for these events were handsome . . . Before the games commenced pipers were tuning their pipes along the seashore, with a foreground of many-coloured flowers on the machair, and in the background the misty slopes of Hecla and Beinn Mhor, while across the machair spectators walked in crowds from every part of the island. The attendance was unusually large'.[42]

The piping events began before noon and continued till seven that evening; it was close to nine before the Games ended entirely.

The format of the piping events was changing with the times: a full, open MSR event was added, at least for a time, to the existing format of separate march and strathspey and reel events, and a jig event was introduced in 1923. The jigs were absent again from the programme until 1927, from which point it has remained standard.[43] *Ceòl mór* was reduced now to a single, open event except on rare occasions when two patrons would each sponsor their own, as was the case in 1931 – the prize for one contest given by the President of the Gathering, and the prize for another given by Colonel John Grant of Rothiemurchus, one of the judges. Rothiemurchus – known in South Uist as *Cnamhan*, 'Bones', due to his famously slim build – was a former officer of the Lovat Scouts and thereafter a sheriff of Inverness. He was also an amateur piper and stalwart of the Piobaireachd Society, and is remembered among mainstream piping circles today as one of the century's great authorities; he also remains the longest-serving judge in the history of the games in South Uist. He first appeared in 1931 and judged the piping, along with various other leading figures, every year until 1960.[44]

Several of the century's most prominent local players emerge in these years. Angus Campbell, Roderick MacDonald and Angus MacQuarrie all make a name for themselves, as do Archie Lindsay, Finlay Martin and Pipe Major John Steele of Lochboisdale, all veterans of the Great War. Steele (1889–1961) had enlisted as a piper in the 3rd Battalion of the Queen's Own Cameron Highlanders in 1906, and received some lessons from John MacDonald while stationed in Inverness in 1908; he could thereafter be found taking many of the top places at army gatherings at home and abroad until the outbreak of war, and it was not until about 1920 that he was able to return to Uist. Like the celebrated John MacColl of Oban, Steele excelled in the piping events but was also a gifted athlete: in 1922, for instance, he took first place in the MSR and *ceòl mór* and third in the march, then proceeded to win the hammer throw and the caber toss, in addition to tying for first in the stone throw and second in the long jump.[45] He continued to compete with some success until 1937. In 1962, a year after his death at the age of seventy-one, a new open event was inaugurated at the Games in his memory: each competitor played a march, strathspey and reel taken from set lists of Steele's favourite tunes, the winner receiving the John Steele Cup.[46]

Calum Johnston of Barra, or *Calum Aonghuis Chaluim* ('Calum, son of Angus son of Calum'), was another prominent name in this era. He made his mark locally by winning the *ceòl mór* event in 1924 and went on in later years to place highly, and often, at the Argyllshire Gathering's gold medal competition. In addition to his piping, Johnston was a valued informant of Barra traditions for the School of Scottish Studies.[47]

When speaking to Uist pipers today, one still hears constant references to Angus MacAulay of Benbecula (1902–95), or *Aonghus Sheòrais* ('Angus son of George'), one of the most consistently successful competitors, local or otherwise, in the history of the Uist games. He had received a grounding in tuition from his father and from Pipe Major Willie Lawrie during the latter's Piobaireachd Society course in Ballivanich in 1913. His name was never absent from the prize-lists at Askernish between 1923 and 1952, and in 1947 he had the singular distinction of taking all four events – the *ceòl mór*, the march, the strathspey and reel and the jig – in the same meeting. He was also a prolific prize-winner at the Skye Gathering, the Bratach Gorm, the Northern Meeting and the Argyllshire Gathering, having won the first jig competition ever held at the Northern Meeting (1938) and taken the Bratach in London twice in succession (1948–9). For all his competitive successes, however, he is still acknowledged today by those who remember his playing as an extraordinarily gifted and rhythmic dance piper. He was for some years resident in London as a Highland outfitter, and in 1952 he emigrated to New Zealand when offered the position of Pipe Major in the Whangarei Pipe Band. In 1993, he was awarded the MBE for services to piping in that country.[48]

These were the men to whom the Uist Games belonged in the era between the two world wars – infringed upon only slightly by an influx of competitors from the mainland and other islands which began in 1933 and gradually increased in the years following. The reason for their appearance in the lists at that particular time is unclear, since the practice of travelling around the nation-wide Games circuit by seasoned competitors was nothing new, then as now. Perhaps the answer lies in transportation improvements. An *Oban Times* correspondent had remarked three years earlier how the mail boats *Lochmor* and *Lochearn* were filled to capacity with travellers on their way to Lochboisdale the night before the Games,[49] so it is not hard to imagine that professional pipers on the circuit would soon take advantage of the service just as John MacDonald of Inverness, Campbell of Kilberry and other piping authorities had done in years past. Whatever the reason, the gathering in South Uist was soon removed from the peripheral aspect it had hitherto enjoyed and into a position ever closer to the popular and the mainstream. In 1922, the *Oban Times* correspondent had commented:

> It is safe to say that nowhere in Scotland do the pipers come forward in such numbers, and it is all the more remarkable because of the fact that it is all local talent. At Oban, Inverness, or Braemar, the prizes are usually carried off by those world-famous pipers who travel to most Highland meetings to compete, but South Uist is too remote for them to appear at these games.[50]

In 1933, things changed. Owen MacNiven of Paisley came to compete at Askernish that year, and took second place in the strathspey and reel and the jig events. In 1935, Corporal Bain of the Scots Guards and Hugh Kennedy, a native of Tiree, were present and took third and fourth place respectively in the *ceòl mór*. MacNiven appeared as well, and placed highly in the march and the strathspey and reel. In 1936, double gold medallist and clasp winner John Wilson of Edinburgh made an appearance and placed second in the *ceòl mór* behind local exponent Calum Walker, *Calum Dhòmhnaill 'ic Iain 'ic Ruairidh*, of Garryhellie. Wilson also placed second in the jigs behind Angus MacDonald of Milton, *Aonghus Beag mac Dhòmhnaill 'ic Fhearguis*, who by then had won the jigs for the fifth consecutive time; and placed first in the march and the strathspey and reel. By the eve of the Second World War, despite the formidable presence of men like Angus Campbell, Angus MacAulay, Calum Walker and others, both the big and the light music events were dominated by competitors from the mainland, with Wilson, MacNiven and Archie MacNab of the Glasgow Police taking the lion's share.[51]

These numbers would only increase in the post-war years.

1946–1979

After the Second World War, it seems as if word had spread in mainland Scotland of the standard of local piping found at the South Uist Games, for by 1950 the number of visiting competitors had swelled quite beyond those of the mid- to late '30s. In that year, Donald A. (*Dòmhnall Anndra*) Morrison of Loch Eynort, Angus Campbell and the Morrison brothers from Gerinish, Ronald and Alfred, managed to secure places in the *ceòl mór*, but all prizes in the light music events (save one in the strathspey and reel and the jig) were won by prominent competitors from the mainland:

> Piobaireachd – 1, J. Garroway; 2, **Alfred Morrison**; 3, **Ronald Morrison**; 4, **D.A. Morrison**; 5, Pipe Major Donald Maclean; 6, **Angus Campbell**.
>
> Marches – 1, Pipe-Major Donald MacLeod; 2, Pipe-Major Donald Maclean; 3, Pipe-Major Ramsay; 4, John Garroway; 5, Duncan Johnstone; 6, D. Lawrie, Oban.
>
> Jigs – 1, Pipe Major Donald MacLeod; 2, Pipe-Major Ramsay; 3, Pipe-Major D. Maclean; 4, **Donald A. Morrison (Locheynort)**.
>
> Strathspeys and Reels – 1, Pipe-Major Ramsay; 2, Pipe-Major D. MacLeod; 3, Pipe-Major D. MacLean; 4, John Garroway; 5, Duncan Johnstone; 6, **D.A. Morrison**.[52]

Practically overnight, it seems, the piping community in South Uist found themselves facing the best competitors in mainstream Scotland, from Pipe Major Donald MacLeod of the Seaforth Highlanders to John D. Burgess of the Camerons and Duncan Johnstone of Glasgow – these were just a few of the men who characterised piping in the post-war years at the national level. Paradoxically perhaps, this was also the time Calum Beaton remembers local piping being at its strongest, at least in the competitive sense. It was the season, after all, of the Morrison brothers of Gerinish, and of Willie Morrison from Loch Eynort; of Angus Campbell's cousin Calum from Benbecula, and of Beaton himself, all of whom held their own in open competition; it was the season in which Rona *nighean Eairdsidh Raghnaill* was introduced to the national stage under headlines such as 'Garryhaillie Girl Takes the Trophies' and 'Woman Piper Wins 5 Cups at Uist Gathering'.[53] Another local phenomenon to have emerged in those years was William MacDonald of Benbecula, formerly of the Highland Light Infantry and the Cameron Highlanders and now living, like Rona Lightfoot, in Inverness. Willie first appeared in local prize lists in the mid-1950s and thereafter took the gold medals at Inverness and Oban in 1965 and 1967, respectively. He was taught in his early years by Lachlan MacCormick.

The first indication that local pipers were being purposefully separated from non-locals at the Games comes from the prize-list of 1949, when a quaich named after John MacDonald of Inverness was awarded to Angus Campbell who, having performed his masterpiece 'Patrick Og MacCrimmon's Lament' for fourth place, was the highest-placed local player in open competition.[54] This was only a precursor to entirely separate events. It would appear that the sheer number of top-level mainland pipers at Askernish had grown high enough that the Games committee had to address it in no uncertain terms; consequently, in 1953, we find one group of judges overseeing the open events and another group entirely judging events confined to local players.[55] As the chart shows, the open events were dominated entirely by visiting competitors while the local *ceòl mór* went to Rona MacDonald (Lightfoot) and the local MSR to North Uist man Norman MacLean. This move toward a local/visitor separation culminated in the establishment of the Flora MacDonald Cup in the late 1950s, a competition for *ceòl mór*, MSRs and jigs, confined strictly to locals and held each spring in Daliburgh School.

1980– THE PRESENT

With regard to the mainland contingent, the last twenty years have seen a saturation point at the Games. Few local competitors of late have taken places in the open competitions, and a look at the appended chart shows that of these, the most consistently successful have been Calum Campbell, Louis Morrison, Donald John MacIntyre (son of Pipe Major Donald MacIntyre of Boisdale of the 4th/5th Cameron Highlanders, and now a Pipe Major himself in the amalgamated Queen's Own Highlanders) and Donald MacDonald of Kyles Flodda, Benbecula, Pipe Major of the South Uist Pipe Band and piping instructor for the Uist and Benbecula schools.

Because of the Uist Games' popularity in the mainstream circuit, they are no longer really considered the primary measure of the local community's standard. Satellite competitions like the Flora MacDonald Cup have since made up for the Games in that respect and are eagerly anticipated every year. On the whole, though, the Games still matter a great deal to the South Uist community – aside from being just a good reason for neighbours to gather in fellowship and rivalry, they represent a channel to the establishment and the means by which this peripheral community transformed itself, in the world of competitive piping, from backwater to mainstream. Piping in South Uist today is far removed, after all, from what it was in the eighteenth and nineteenth centuries, when *ceòl mór* was primarily the jurisdiction of the Clanranald MacIntyres and *ceòl beag* echoed the song and dance tradition stylistically, learned by ear and played for a variety of functions – in particular, group labour and dancing. As discussed elsewhere, military duty was likely the only avenue to musical literacy as the nineteenth century progressed. There is no record of organised, regular competition among the island's piping community until the dawn of the twentieth century, though if it did take place before then, it probably would have been either among military pipers or of an informal nature, such as during Frederick Rea's picnic outing in the 1890s or the household contests at Clanranald Cottage during the middle years of this century.

Several elements were to bring changes in the status quo. Literacy on the mainland became more widespread in keeping with the rising influence of the competition system in the 1800s, and by the turn of the twentieth century the South Uist Piping Society were keen to encourage this state-of-the-art idiom among what they must have considered their rustic piping community. Accordingly, the arrival of the Piobaireachd Society tutors heralded a new age wherein literacy and competition-style settings became not just the business of the Lovat Scouts or the Militia, but standard among most South Uist pipers, and the competitive climate of the modern era has since maintained that standard.

So while dance piping stylistically reminiscent of *ceòl cluais* may still be heard and practised in the odd South Uist ceilidh, the competition system – as represented by the games, the Flora MacDonald Cup, and so forth – has ensured that the literate idiom has become just as much 'tradition' in modern South Uist as was the aural in the previous century.

CHAPTER 10

'A credit to the Hebrides, which has given of its best sons'
SOUTH UIST PIPING AND THE GREAT WAR

Military service has played an ever-present role in the cultivation of literate, competitive piping in South Uist. This work's Appendix offers name after name of prominent local players, from the last decades of the nineteenth century to the present day, who have spent time in the army: Lachlan MacCormick, Angus MacLellan, John Steele, John (*Seonaidh Roidein*) MacDonald, Neil MacLennan, Archie MacDonald, William MacDonald, Calum Beaton, Donald John MacIntyre; these are but a latter-day few who have followed in the tradition of Clanranald's patronised pipers from the Covenanters' War to Sheriffmuir to the Heights of Abraham. Indeed, the military can justifiably be considered piping's modern-day patron. Jessie MacAulay earlier attested to this regarding the early decades of the twentieth century: a Uist man too poor to own a set of pipes (and these were many) had but to enlist and he was furnished with all he needed. To an extent this form of patronage continues to the present day, and can be interpreted as having effectively replaced the patronage of clan chiefs in the eighteenth century and of Highland gentry in the nineteenth. On the whole, Uist's affinity for military service, since the late nineteenth century at least, may arguably be put down to a genuine scarcity of employment options;[1] but, as the above suggests, the vestigial force of a deeply rooted Highland martial tradition cannot be entirely ruled out.

Highlighting the role of South Uist's pipers in the First World War, and that conflict's effect on traditional life at home, serves to illuminate the particulars of a significant aspect to the twentieth-century tradition – military service – while also addressing the changes in Hebridean life which came as a result of post-war depression. While the 1939–45 War had a comparably disastrous impact throughout Scotland, the transition from an old-world way of life in South Uist to a more mainstream social culture had been long under way thanks to the events of 1914–18. Traditional ceilidh customs and local dances of great antiquity began to fade slowly from the scene around this time,[2] and the radio was introduced soon after. Competitive piping lost, at least temporarily, a certain vibrancy as so few were left to play it. As the present work aims fundamentally to portray this transition and its effects on local piping, emphasis is given accordingly to the Great War.

The Queen's Own Cameron Highlanders, and latterly the Lovat Scouts, have been the main recruiters in South Uist ever since the Inverness-shire militia were incorporated into the regular army in 1881. Uist men probably felt at home among the Camerons, not only for the regiment's association with famous pipers[3] but also for their long-established Gaelic leanings: when first inspected at Stirling in January, 1794 and its strength raised to a thousand men, the regiment's patron and commander, Alan Cameron of Erracht, made sure that all recruits were Gaelic-speaking. 'Erracht was so determined to have his regiment not merely nominally but really a Highland corps,' writes Adam,[4] 'that he enlisted none but Gaelic speakers, so that the 79th was long familiarly known as the *Cia mar thas*!' ('*Ciamar a tha thu*'s, meaning the 'How are you's.)

The seeds were sown. Over a hundred years later, the 3rd (Militia) Battalion Camerons contained so many monoglot Gaels from the Western Isles that its drill instructors were ordered to attend Gaelic language classes so as to better acquaint themselves with, and relate to, the men serving under them.[5] At the outbreak of the Great War, two-thirds of officers and men in the 1/4th (Territorial Force – formerly Militia) Battalion, which drew primarily from Skye and the Outer Hebrides, were Gaelic-speaking.[6]

The Lovat Scouts, though not principally associated with the Western Isles, would have contained many Gaelic speakers as well. Simon Fraser, 16th Lord Lovat, had raised the regiment for the purposes of reconnaissance in the Boer War in 1900. Alasdair, Lovat's younger brother, was made a lieutenant. As their second contingent left for war in June 1901, Lindley records[7] that Alasdair was studying Gaelic; one could reasonably infer that he was doing so to cope with the number of Gaelic speakers under his command. Soldiers and pipers from South Uist may have been drawn to the Scouts for this reason, but they may also have been attracted by the regiment's Catholic leanings.[8] In any case, by 1908 there were enough Uist-born soldiers in the Scouts to warrant large-scale training at home. The *Oban Times* records wargames and firing exercises being held by the regiment's 2nd Squadron in Eochar on 13 July of that year;[9] every name on the published score-lists except a very few were typical of South Uist and Benbecula. Only one piper was listed among them, a James MacDonald, but there were undoubtedly others who played outwith an official capacity.

In addition to home exercises in these years, the men of each militia battalion were required to meet at their regimental headquarters annually for a month's training. Those of the Camerons met in Inverness every summer, during which time communities in South Uist could feel particularly empty, especially considering that summer was the season when young men were most needed at the peats and on the croft. The Eochar correspondent to the *Oban Times* called attention to the annual event in 1908, but could not refrain from hinting at the irony of native patriotism in the face of governmental neglect of the region's economic problems:

> Off To Camp – This district at present is almost entirely denuded of its young men, who are all either in the militia or the Lovat Scouts. The militiamen went for their annual training two weeks ago, and the Scouts on Tuesday morning last week. They assembled at midnight at the Gerinish crossroads and rode to Loch Skipport to await the arrival of the s.s. Dunara Castle . . . The military spirit is very strong among the hardy and stalwart Hebrideans, and the Government can render no greater service to the country at large than by making it possible for these brave and capable men to earn a living at home.[10]

Hebridean 'military spirit' would hold dire consequences for South Uist's militia and Lovat pipers in the years that followed.

The Great War of 1914–18 caused an upheaval in the daily routine of Highland life. During this period, the *Oban Times* frequently ran short biographic pieces on absent soldiers in order to cheer the hearts and fortify the morale of Highland communities emptied of their fighting-age men; it was a welcome distraction from the obituaries. On 5 February 1916, they published a photographic spread of five brothers posed in Highland and regimental dress under the title:

A GALLANT UIST FAMILY

———

FIVE SONS WITH THE COLOURS

These were the MacDonalds of Garryhellie, sons of Ronald and Mary MacDonald, four of whom – Alexander, Archibald, Ronald and Angus – were pipers like their father before them. The war saw them scattered over the theatres in various regiments: Angus held a commission in the South African Forces; Alexander served with the Tyneside Scottish; the non-piper, John, was decorated for gallant conduct in France while serving with the 1st Canadian Contingent; Ronald also fought in France; and Archibald, or Archie (*Eairdsidh Raghnaill*), went to the Dardanelles with the Lovat Scouts. All but Angus survived the war. Archie would later have seven children, one of whom, Ronald, who died a young man, was a piper in the army while two others, Neil and Rona, are well known to the reader by now as pipers of note. 'There are few families who can show such a fine record,' wrote the *Oban Times* in 1916, 'and they are a credit to the Hebrides, which has patriotically given of its best sons for King and Country'.[11]

The Hebrides indeed gave its best during those four years, and as a result the daily flow of traditional life in South Uist was severed. The ceilidh, Gaelic tradition's primary social context at the time, became less common due to the gloom cast over communities by casualty reports and news from the front;[12] dancing a reel or telling a tale simply held no joy any more. As storyteller Donald Alasdair Johnson of Loch Carnan told collectors of oral tradition in the early 1970s:

> *Faigheadh tu rudeiginn air bàsachadh air falbh a choreiginn seach mar a b'àbh . . . . nach fhaigheadh tu an toil-inntinn 's an gnothach cho* lively *'s a bha e idir roimh'n a' chogadh. Chan fhaigheadh tu na daoine cho cridheil 's cho sunndach idir. Well, bha gu leòr dhe sinneach a thaobh feadhainn a chaill daoine sa' chogadh . . . Bha gu leòr dhiubh a thaobh an dòigh sin.*[13]

> You would find that something had sort of died away compared to what used to be . . . that you wouldn't find the pleasures and what have you at all so lively as they were before the war. You wouldn't find the people as hearty or joyful at all. Well, that was often enough the case for those who had lost people in the war . . . and there were plenty in that way.

Indeed there were, as the statistics bear out. Out of over 5,500 officers and men of the Cameron Highlanders killed or mortally wounded in the Great War, 186 were from Barra, the Uists, Benbecula and Harris; of these, at least 88 were from South Uist and Benbecula.[14] The number recorded is undoubtedly conservative and does not even take into account the casualties of other regiments.[15] Looking over the Camerons' Roll of Honour at the National War Memorial, it seems as if almost every township had cause to grieve: from Smerclate, Lochboisdale, Daliburgh and Askernish in the south, to Bornish, Stoneybridge and Stilligarry, to Eochar, Creagorry and others towards the north – all had 'given of their best sons', often more than one, to King and Country.

Pipers were naturally the most conspicuous targets for enemy fire, so one's prospects for survival in a battalion band were not great. The statistics for the Cameron Highlanders tell a grim tale: of the 155 pipers who made up the battalions' bands, 69 were either killed or wounded. Of the 34 pipers in the 2nd Battalion alone, among whom were South Uist's John Steele and 17-year-old Archie Lindsay, 21 were killed or wounded, and this in addition to illness having 'caused the disappearance of the band' as it entered Bulgaria;[16] Steele himself was wounded in February 1915, but recovered. The 5th Battalion, probably containing the most South Uist pipers of any battalion in the war, lost 14 out of 43 and invalided six more.[17] They were hit particularly hard, as were the other battalions, at the Battle of Loos in September of 1915, in which 'practically all the pipers became casualties'.[18] The 5th Battalion's pipe band was led at the time by Pipe Major William MacLean, one-time resident of Creagorry, Benbecula, who had been promoted and transferred from the 4th Battalion's band.

We are fortunate to have been left a glimpse of life among the Uist pipers of the 5th through the poetry of Snishival-born Donald MacIntyre, or *Dòmhnall Ruadh*, otherwise known as the Paisley Bard. Piper, poet, and myriad other professions, Donald had completed a tour of duty in the 3rd Battalion Camerons some time before the war, serving as personal piper to Donald Walter Cameron of Lochiel, but upon the outbreak of war and formation of the 5th he again enlisted and was appointed once more as Lochiel's piper.[19] In his song *Pìobairean Camshronach anns an Ruaig Mhór (1918)* or 'The Cameron Pipers in the Great Retreat (1918)', he conveyed the action his battalion faced when falling back from the German army's final offensive along the front lines in France:[20]

Bu sgairteil am feachd air an t-sliabh ud,	Frantic the fighting on that hill,
'Gam faicinn 's Lochial air an ceann, –	Seeing them and Lochiel at their head, –
A' gluasad gu cruachanach, calpach,	Moving with heavy legs
Is suaicheantas Albann ri crann.[21]	And the standard of Scotland above us.

MacIntyre was able to convey the terrors he and other pipers faced with a poignant and wry humour:

Nuair thàinig na Gearmailtich tarsuinn,	When the Germans came across,
'S chuir iad an gas *oirnn a nall, –*	And sent the gas upon us, –
Chuir sinn ar n-aghaidh air Calais	We about-faced toward Calais
Is thug sinn ar casan leinn ann;	And hoofed it without delay;
Chaidh sinn a-stigh a dh' Estaminet	We made it to Estaminet
Is cheannaich sinn galan de'n dram,	And bought a gallon of drams,
'S bha mise 's am Bòideach is Lachlann	And the *Bòideach* and *Lachlann* and I
S am pige ma seach air ar ceann.	Took turns up-ending the pitcher.
O, 's ann againn bha 'n dram, –	Oh, indeed we had the drams, –
Cha robh e 's an fhasan bhith gann;	It wouldn't do to hold back;
Bu sud againn buideal is pige	The cask and the pitcher were ours,
Agus botul-ar-fhichead Vin Blanc.[22]	As were twenty-one bottles of *Vin Blanc*.

'The *Bòideach*' and '*Lachlann*' referred to were fellow South Uist pipers Alasdair Boyd of Eochar and Lachlan MacLean of Creagorry. Boyd lived latterly in Oban and gave much valuable information on local oral tradition and *puirt-à-beul* to the School of Scottish Studies, as was noted in earlier chapters; MacLean competed in the South Uist games before the war and placed third in the strathspey and reel in 1906. MacIntyre described other pipers whom we would have known otherwise only by their competition records:

Fionnla' Martainn is Tormad MacFhilip	*Fionnla' Martainn* and *Tormad MacFhilip*
Na sùilean gun sheas iad 'nan ceann,	Their eyes stood in their heads,
Nuair thàinig iad goirid dha 'n station,	When they approached the station and found
Gun sgial air an tréan 's i air chall.	No word on the train, as it was lost.
O, chan urrainn sinn ann,	Oh, we can't get there,
Ciamar is urrainn sinn ann;	How can we get there,
Chan urrainn sinn coiseachd nas fhaide,	We can walk no farther
'S an t-acras 'gar dalladh 's sinn fann.[23]	Being faint and blinded by hunger.

MacIntyre refers in this stanza to Finlay Martin of Daliburgh and Norman MacKillop, a piper from Harris. Martin had attended the Piobaireachd Society courses under John MacDonald, Inverness. He must have been a very young soldier in the 5th Battalion, perhaps just seventeen like his contemporaries Archie Lindsay in the 2nd and *Seonaidh Roidein* in the 7th, since he placed second in a march, strathspey and reel event for juniors at Askernish in 1913. He went on to place highly at the games in the post-war years.

Piping in South Uist at this time would have been affected as much as any other cultural institution on the island. Literate, competitive piping probably suffered more than ear-learned dance piping in these years, since many who could read staff notation had either learned in the Piobaireachd Society courses or as members of the militia battalions, or both; hence, when the battalions were called out, there were simply few pipers left in wartime South Uist who could read music. The situation would have been parallel to that of the 1939–45 War, which caused a similar haemorrhage. Calum Beaton recalled:

Bha an fheadhainn a' dèanadh pìobaireachd ceart, bha iad sa' Chogadh. Cha robh air fhàgail a seo ach seann daoine . . . Mar sin, cha do rinn mi móran gus an tig [sic] *caraid, a thill dhachaidh as a' Chogadh – Alasdair Peutan . . . 'S e a thug dhomh a' chiad tòiseachadh air an fheadan.*[24]

Those who could play correctly, they were in the War. There was nobody left here but old people . . . So, I didn't do much until a relative returned from the War – Alasdair Beaton . . . It was he who first started me on the chanter.

Though literate pipers like Donald MacIntyre and those to whom he referred in his song survived the war and returned home, there were many who did not. Pipers who lived on only as names on the granite memorial south of Bornish: Neil Wilson, Donald MacPhee, Alex MacEachan, and so on.[25] In addition, Pipe Major William Lawrie of the 8th Argyll and Sutherland Highlanders, who had been brought in by the South Uist Piping Society in 1913 to teach its course in Balivanich, was wounded two years later and soon after died of illness. It comes as no surprise, then, that eight years elapsed from the outbreak of war before the Games at Askernish began again, which says as much for the organisational depression of the time as it does for a decline, albeit temporary, in the mainstream idiom's vitality.

We can reasonably infer that the situation for *ceòl cluais* in these years was broadly parallel to that of storytelling, which shared the same cultural context in South Uist. As has been discussed earlier, both would have suffered as a consequence of the decline of the traditional ceilidh. Donald Alasdair Johnson described the striking change to collector Donald Archie MacDonald:

DAM: 'S bha gnothach nan sgeulachdan, cha mhór nach do sguir e leis a' chogadh fhéin.
DAJ: O cha mhór gu dearbh. Cha chualas móran dhe as deaghaidh a' Chogaidh Mhóir. Cha chualas móran de sgeulachdan 'gan gabhail air feadh thaighean.
DAM: Aye. Mun do dh' fhalbh sibh bha iad 'gan gabhail.
DAJ: O bha iad 'gan gabhail. 'S e an aon chluichd a bha 'dol a' cur seachad na h-oidhcheadh a's a' gheamhradh, eadar cairtean is sgeulachdan.[26]

DAM: And the practice of storytelling, it was nearly stopped by the war itself.
DAJ: Nearly indeed. Not much of it was heard after the Great War. Not many tales were heard being told throughout the houses.
DAM: Aye. Before you went away [to war] they were being told.
DAJ: Oh yes they were being told. It was the only thing going around to pass the evening in the winter, between cards and tales.

The depression caused by the Great War was not itself responsible for the demise of the aural transmission of piping associated with traditional dance in South Uist. Rather, this was the long-term effect of the Piobaireachd Society courses, the Highland games and the growing overall importance of staged competition and literacy that these forces represented. However, the War's effect on tradition in Highland communities did signal the beginning of the end for the old-world ceilidh in the twentieth century, such as in the manner described by Johnson; and being Gaelic musical tradition's primary social institution, this could not have but facilitated the decline of *ceòl cluais* in South Uist.

CHAPTER 11

'B' fheàrr leotha fear a bha cluichd leis a' chluas'
AESTHETICS AND TRANSMISSION IN SOUTH UIST PIPING

The above title translates as 'They preferred someone who played by ear' – something Jessie MacAulay remarked of dancers in the ceilidhs of bygone days. As it suggests, aural transmission of music is closely associated with dance in the traditional Gaelic world.[1] The reasons underlying the association, at least in the Hebridean quarter, are largely cultural and functional: the aural idiom comprised music picked up by ear within the surroundings of the ceilidhs and played specifically to provide rhythm for dancing; it flourished, therefore, within the social setting of the old-world Gael. The literate idiom instead comprises staged competition, playing music learned from staff notation in a setting divorced from traditional dance and the associated milieu of ceilidh customs. Thus in South Uist, aurally-learned piping was associated with local dance while literately-learned piping implied, in its transmission and performance, a wholly distinct cultural and functional environ. That *ceòl cluais* survived as long as it did alongside the mainstream tradition in South Uist is testimony in itself to the community's conservative nature, and has undoubtedly had a bearing on how local pipers perceive, apprehend and evaluate their own music.

There are no genuine exponents of the ear-learned dance-piping tradition left in South Uist. The closest we have to a recording of genuine aurally-learned piping, to my knowledge, is an interview with Kenneth Morrison by ethnomusicologist Dr Peter Cooke during a research tour of the Hebrides in 1970.[2] Morrison had learned to play by ear from about the age of ten. However, the recording is not truly representative of the *ceòl cluais* idiom as observed in the ceilidh setting. To be sure, one can clearly hear false fingering – from the literate player's point of view, at least (one wonders if Mr Morrison himself considered his fingering false; it is quite possible that he did, considering Archie Beaton's precedent in the 1940s). However, in the interview Kenneth Morrison played tunes associated with the competitive, literate repertoire such as the 2/4 march 'John MacFadyen of Melfort' and the strathspey 'Maggie Cameron'; tunes composed or arranged with complex grace-noting in tempos too deliberate and measured for traditional dance. It says something about the influence of mainstream piping that Morrison probably believed (as nearly all pipers now do, in the Hebrides as elsewhere) that to play by staff notation is to be a better piper, and may have simply played what he thought would impress the researcher.

Mainstream Games culture and the decline of the traditional ceilidh (occasioned by war and television[3]) may have undermined the social and functional value of *ceòl cluais*, but a collective memory still exists among informants of a certain age. What follows, therefore, is devoted to the local ear-learned idiom, its association with dance, its relationship to the literate idiom and how it has influenced local aesthetic perspectives. I give a brief background to traditional dance in South Uist in order to provide some functional context; I then argue that both the ear-learned and the notation-learned (or note-learned) idioms are bound by a local aesthetic sensitive to the context of associated traditions, whether it be in the ceilidh or on the platform. I also address the aesthetic paradox encountered when informants evaluated music of different idioms based on different functional standards. I then refer to the 'voiced' and 'unvoiced' aesthetics of musical terminology in Gaelic tradition and review their use among South Uist pipers. Finally, I call attention to the dual existence of aurally-learned and literately-learned tunes in local pipers' repertoires, explore their distinctions and postulate some reasons behind the balance with which they are maintained. Following convention,[4] I distinguish the dance known as a 'Reel' from the tune 'reel' by the use of the capital R throughout the following text.

∼ TRADITIONAL DANCE ∼

The character of dance itself in South Uist has changed over the course of the twentieth century. Modern Scottish country dances such as the Quadrilles, imported from Paris after the Napoleonic Wars, are often danced in local town halls today but were virtually unknown in Hebridean communities before the late nineteenth century. The Fletts, for instance, were told by an informant on traditional dance customs that in Eriskay, in 1895, 'they were not keen on Country Dances at all. Give them the Scotch Reel and the Highland Schottische all the time'.[5] The Schottische appeared in the Hebrides in about 1855 and has since been used as a step in a variety of Reels. The four-hand Scotch Reel is indeed considered to have been the supreme social dance of Scotland in the eighteenth and nineteenth centuries, as much in South Uist as anywhere else. The Fletts further observed:

> Throughout the mainland of Scotland and in the Western Isles, the commonest Reel within living memory was the Scotch (Foursome) Reel. Indeed, up to about 1880–90 this dance was so popular among the ordinary working people of the Central and West Highlands and the Western Isles that in these regions it was almost the only dance in the local repertoire.[6]

This is supported by Frederick Rea's memoirs of time spent in South Uist between 1890 and 1913, in which he occasionally comments on local dance. On a day out to the seaside with 150 schoolchildren in tow, 'pipes were playing and many of the older children were dancing reels'. He later observed the Scotch Reel at an evening dance for the young men and women in his charge. 'The dance went on into early morning, reel succeeding reel as though there were no other dance, and I strongly suspected this to be the only dance they knew.'[7] Reels were almost always danced to common-time strathspeys and reels, the only exception being a number of pantomimic dances collected by researchers in South Uist and Barra such as '*Cath nan Coileach*', or 'The Combat of the Cocks', and '*Cailleach an Dùdain*', or 'The Old Wife of the Mill-dust', which were performed to compound-time jigs until around the turn of the century. Alexander Carmichael witnessed many such dances in South Uist in the late nineteenth century, some on the occasion of Michaelmas: 'The song and the dance, the mirth and the merriment, are continued all night, many curious scenes being acted, and many curious dances being performed, some of them in character.' Of *Cailleach an Dùdain*, he observed: 'The tune varies with the varying phases of the dance. It is played by a piper or a fiddler, or sung as a 'port-a-bial', mouth tune, by a looker-on, or by the performers themselves.'[8]

The tradition of singing to provide a rhythm, as opposed to playing an instrument – such as the *port-à-beul* tradition – is of great antiquity across the West Highland seaboard, as has been discussed elsewhere. *Port-à-beul* survived in South Uist well into the twentieth century, which says much for the conservative nature of Uist's Gaelic social culture, but even before the turn of the century, imported Scottish Country dances were gaining an appreciable foothold. This appears to have been due to class differences and social changes as much as to the whims of national popularity. For example, in stark contrast to seaside Reeling, kitchen foursomes, blackhouse balls and the enacting of *Cailleach an Dùdain* among the common folk, a dance was held at Lochboisdale Hotel sometime after 1890, to which Frederick Rea was invited. A lavish drawing-room set the scene for thirty to forty of Uist's 'high society' – the proprietor, the clergymen, the banker, the factor, the doctor, several tenants of the largest farms, the accountant, the estate office clerk, a 'gallant captain of the Camerons and one of the heroes of Dargai', etc. The music was supplied solely by a piano – 'several ladies willingly presiding there in turn' – and a few 'Scottish songs' were sung. Rea himself recited Shakespeare. The dances reflected contemporary British rather than traditional Gaelic tastes: 'I was happy to dance again the polka, the waltz, the quadrille, and the lancers,' writes Rea, 'which were the dances in vogue when I had first left my native city to come to the Hebrides.'[9]

The nature of the professions listed gives the impression that like Rea, who hailed from Birmingham, many of the guests were not native to the Hebrides. This, as much as their place on Uist's social ladder, may explain the evening's lack of indigenous Gaelic flavour; no pipe or fiddle played for a Foursome Reel at this party. However, the late nineteenth century would see the spread of Country dances beyond the confines of the Hebridean upper class, due in great part to the visits of itinerant professional dance masters. In Rea's time alone, at least two such masters visited South Uist among their rounds, teaching the fashionable Country dances as well as more traditional social dances and those solo dances introduced to South Uist earlier in the century by Ewan MacLachlan.[10] According to contemporary observers, for instance, a woman from Perth retained her own fiddler and taught in Uist during the winter months and a man named MacDougall taught occasionally on the island from 1890 to 1912.[11] By the mid-point of the twentieth century, Country dances were a common fixture in the local repertoire. Calum Beaton illustrates this during a discussion on the kinds of tunes played for dancing in the ceilidhs of the 1950s:

> JD: *Dé seòrsa puirt a bha sibh a' cluichd?*
> CB: *Bha sinn a' cluichd* marches *gu leòr airson danns' a bha gu math bitheanta aig an àm,* Canadian Barn Dance . . . *'S e 2/4* marches *a bha thu cluichd an àm sin, ged a chluichd thu na bu luaidhe na chluichdeas tu aig farpaisean. Agus bha ruidhlidhean gu math tric, airson* eightsome reels, jigs *airson* quadrilles, *6/8s a bha sin. Gu leòr dhiubh co-dhiubh, 's e ceòl cluais . . . Bha feadhainn dhiubh as an leabhar, ach bha e cho furasda dhuinn na puirt a thogail mar sin.*[12]

> JD: What sort of tunes were you playing?
> CB: We were playing many marches for a dance that was quite popular at that

time, the Canadian Barn Dance... It's 2/4 marches you'd play then, though you'd play faster than you would at competitions. And there were reels very often, for eightsome reels, jigs for quadrilles, those were 6/8s. Enough of them anyway, it's ear-music... A few of them were from the book, but it was so easy for us to pick them up that way.

Both Beaton's comments and MacAulay's before him testify to the association of dance with aural transmission of music among South Uist pipers, independent of the dance's character – whether it be a Foursome Reel or the Military Two-Step. This is a fundamental property of local aesthetics in South Uist, and one which sets the theme for the rest of the chapter.

∽ TOWARD A LOCAL AESTHETIC ∽

For our purposes, we may define musical aesthetics as a society's evaluation of their own music, culturally embedded and expressed in a variety of ways both verbal and behavioural. Merriam[13] has listed the six factors which he feels characterise the nature of the voiced and analytical aesthetic commonly found in Western or other urban, literate societies: the presence of psychic distance (to be explained below); manipulation of form for its own sake – like composition, it presupposes a knowledge of such elements as rhythm, pitch and melody and a cultural imperative to manipulate them; emotion-producing qualities attributed to music conceived strictly as sound; attribution of beauty to the piece and/or the process; a purposeful intent to create something 'aesthetic'; and last, the presence of a philosophy of an aesthetic. In considering their relevance to non-Western or traditional societies, Merriam writes:

> It seems impossible to determine which of these is the most important, if any one of them is, or whether the absence of one, two, three or more indicates a lack of an aesthetic. If, however, the six factors are correctly adduced, their limited attribution or their absence in another society would seem to indicate serious question as to the presence of an aesthetic, defined always in Western terms.[14]

Thus if a society's aesthetic lacks one or more of the above criteria, then their aesthetic cannot, by Merriam's definition, be typically Western. Pipers in South Uist display a few characteristics reflecting this model: like Highland pipers elsewhere, they can manipulate the form of existing tunes and at times compose new ones; they are capable of attributing beauty to a piece or performance; and they engage in critical discussion of piping, though, as will be discussed in the following section, this last implies influence outwith native Gaelic tradition. One may conclude, therefore, that South Uist piping today possesses an aesthetic that is recognisably 'Western' when viewed from certain angles. But the Uist pipers' sensitivity to context when evaluating their music is, by its sheer acuity, outwith Merriam's model. A piper playing a competition-idiom reel for a Scotch Foursome in an old-world ceilidh, for example, would receive quizzical looks from the dancers because the tempo and melodic nuance would be regarded as unsuitable; and a piper playing instrumental *puirt-à-beul* on the platform at the Askernish games would receive equally short shrift for much the same reason. While this particular aesthetic quality can be attributed to all Highland piping in Scotland, it nonetheless illustrates in practical terms the relevance of functional context in South Uist.

This leads us to focus for a moment on one particular element in Merriam's list – psychic distance – which, despite his reservations about placing more or less relevance on any single point, can indeed hinge on the difference between the aesthetic of analytical discourse and the aesthetic of contextual and unvoiced functional preference. The term implies a sense of objectivity; that an observer within a society can stand back and analyse that society's music, or a performance of it, with a detached awareness of the sum of its parts. It has been observed in the past[15] that this can occur in our urban civilisation whenever we turn on a radio and listen to a song or melody unfamiliar to us, not knowing who composed it, when or why. Still, we evaluate it and find it pleasing or dis-pleasing depending on our personal tastes, and often express such tastes verbally. The absence of psychic distance, on the other hand, leaves an aesthetic based not only on the sheer artistry or beauty of the music concerned, but on the social and functional values associated with it. This is the type of aesthetic observed among many peoples who lack an extensive musical vocabulary or maintain a non-literate tradition.[16] McAllester, for instance, wrote of the Western Apache:

> There is little esthetic discussion in our sense. Appreciation of a song is nearly always phrased in terms of understanding it – of knowing what it is for. One or two informants did speak of preferring songs with long choruses and short verses since these are easier to learn, but the usual preference was for the important healing songs or the sacred songs in the puberty ceremony. This 'functional esthetic' is found very widely among preliterate peoples.[17]

Merriam has problems accepting McAllester's use of the phrase 'functional esthetic', as he figures that music evaluated largely by its function could not foster an aesthetic in his defined terms – i.e. one without overt context. However, more recent ethnographic studies show that a folk society can find its music pleasing (or displeasing) and can verbalise its appreciation (or criticism) *because* of the music's context as much as a literate society can in the absence of it. Of the Bulgarian bagpipe tradition, for example, Rice observed that playing the *gaida* well, in the opinion of native players, entails 'good ornamental technique and a strong sense of rhythm' because the greatest priority lies on dance music, wedding dances in particular and the ability to play 'lightly'.[18] One can see how playing lightly (the ability to make rapid, easy finger-movements) facilitates both ornamental technique and good rhythm, which in turn makes for better dancing. The functional context, therefore, guides the evaluation. This is also true of the Cape Breton fiddling tradition in that bowing techniques and intra-rhythmic expression are based fundamentally on step-dance accompaniment.[19] Furthermore, Cooke found that to the Shetland fiddler, rhythm is all-important so that particular steps could be established when his music is danced to.[20] Of course, rhythmic function is not the only factor in a positively valued musical performance for any of these examples. In South Uist particularly, the manipulation of musical form, the feedback that occurs between instrumentalist and dancer and the music's conformity to surrounding custom can all have a direct bearing. Nevertheless, a performance's evaluation is influenced largely by its contextual value. The following will show that the South Uist piping tradition is a similar example of a context-sensitive aesthetic in that the surrounding function, be it for ceilidh-dancing or for competition, plays a prominent role in one's evaluative criteria.

In South Uist, literate transmission is fundamentally associated with competition and technique, while the process of learning tunes aurally and the performance of ear-learned tunes – *ceòl cluais* – comprise an idiom fundamentally associated with dance and, by extension, timing. Therein lie both its functional value and the reason for its survival in the local tradition. Jessie MacAulay hinted at one point about the functionality of ear-music in the context of dancing and its place in the Uist aesthetic in the early decades of the twentieth century:

JD: *Am biodh tu a' cluichd airson dannsa anns na seann laithean?*
JM: *Bhiodh. Bhithinn a' cluichd* the Military Two-Step, Scotch Reels; *cha robh me a' cluichd airson* Eightsome Reels *no* Quadrilles, *bha iad cho fada.*
JD: *... An robh daoine an uairsin ag ionnsachadh le cluas?*
JM: *Bha, bha gu dearbh – cha robh cothrom aca co-dhiubh air leabhar a dh' ionnsachadh ... Bha feadhainn dhiubh math math, gu h-àraid air ceòl dannsa; b' fheàrr leotha fear a bha a' cluichd leis a' chluas air ceòl dannsa, na fear a bha mach as a' leabhar air ceòl dannsa.*[21]

JD: Would you be playing for dances in the old days?
JM: Yes. I'd be playing for the Military Two-Step, Scotch Reels; I wasn't playing for Eightsome Reels or Quadrilles, they were so long.
JD: ... Were people at that time learning by ear?

JM: Yes indeed – they had no opportunity anyway to learn from a book. Some of them were very good, especially with dance-music; they preferred one who played dance-music by ear to one who played dance-music out of a book.

She reiterated this in a later interview:

JM: *B' fheàrr leotha, na dannsairean, b' fheàrr leotha fear a bha cluichd leis a' chluais na fear a bha . . . as a' mhusic.*
JD: *. . . Carson a tha siud?*
JM: *Bha barrachd* lightness *air choireigin ann ... Bha* rhythm *air choireigin aige, fhios agaibh. Cha robh e* cut-and-dry. *Bha* lilt *air choireigin anns a' cheòl chluais nach robh anns a' cheòl eile.*[22]

JM: They preferred, the dancers, they preferred someone playing by ear to someone playing by the staff notation.
JD: . . . Why is that?
JM: It had more lightness . . . It had some kind of rhythm, you see. It wasn't cut-and-dry. There was a kind of lilt in the ear-music that wasn't in the other music.

MacAulay's use of the word 'lilt' calls to mind its use by Shetland fiddlers. Cooke found that it 'pertains to the rhythmic flow of the melody' and is used by Shetlanders to describe the dynamic accents made with the bow by ear-learned players so that notes equally valued on the stave become unequal and given to lights and shades in practice. It is what Dunlay and Greenberg refer to as the 'subtle inequality of note-lengths' that characterises the style of traditional Cape Breton fiddling; it adds bounce to a tune which, Cooke contends, makes Shetlanders 'feel like dancing'.[23] This recalls MacAulay's memories of dance-piping in South Uist exactly. It seems therefore that the community of MacAulay's youth preferred ear-learned music to note-learned music when dancing because its rhythms were perceived to facilitate more naturally the steps involved – something that Calum Beaton confirmed when explaining what, in his experience, makes a good performance for dance-piping:

JD: *Nuair a bhios tu cluichd airson banais no céilidh no rud sam bith, am bi* preference *agad dé chluicheas tu?*
CB: *Tha mi smaoineadh a h-uile pìobaire, bidh puirt aige fhéin, tha e smaointinn co-dhiubh, a tha freagairt air dannsa na's fheàrr na port air choireigin eile. Feadhainn de phuirt, tha iad trom – car doirbh a chluichd – is bidh e feuchainn ri port car simplidh, mar sin. 'S e an* time-eadh *aig an danns' a tha cunntais . . . Nam fàgadh tu as* gracenote *thall 's a bhos, chan eil duine dol a ghearain mu dheidhinn sin fhad 's a tha deagh* time-eadh *agad.*[24]
JD: When you are playing for a wedding or a ceilidh, etc., do you have a preference as to what you play?

CB: I think that every piper, he has tunes, he believes so anyway, that better suit dancing than some other tune. Some tunes are heavy – quite difficult to play – and therefore he'll try a relatively simple tune. It's the timing of the dance that counts . . . If you leave out a gracenote here and there, no one will complain about that while you have good timing.

'Timing', then, or rhythm and tempo, is the most important factor of good dance piping in Beaton's experience, just as it was in MacAulay's. Local dancing may have changed somewhat in character and form since the nineteenth century, but these findings suggest that music learned aurally is perceived by the South Uist community to make for better dancing in any case – whether it be Reeling to instrumental *puirt-à-beul* or the latest continental waltz. One finds the same principle in the traditions of Shetland and Bulgaria; in Orkney, too, the Fletts encountered this with regard to fiddling. 'The essence of good dance-fiddling,' they wrote, 'was once very succinctly stated by an old Orkney fiddler, Danny Rosie. At a dance on the island of Flotta about 1920, a young fiddler playing with Danny Rosie stumbled over a difficult part of the music and fell out of time with the dancers.' Afterwards, Danny Rosie commented on this and 'told the young player "never lose time by trying to get in a note – the dancers won't notice if you leave it out. There are only three things which are important when you are playing for dancing, time, sound, and dird."'[25] One can hear Beaton's words echoed in this account. 'Dird', according to the Fletts, was to Orkney what 'lilt' was to Shetland and, as we've seen, to Jessie MacAulay.

If the community in MacAulay's day preferred *ceòl cluais* to staff-notated music when dancing, the difference in timing must necessarily have been the reason why. Aurally-learned piping was perceived to provide more suitable rhythms for the stepping and travelling of the Reels than literately-learned piping because a tune picked up by ear implied that it had been learned in the ceilidh – i.e. in the same social setting as the Reel itself. Naturally, the timing of the tune would fit the Reel steps as the dancers were accustomed to performing them. A tune learned by the book, however, implied music heard on the competition platform, with grace-noting too cumbersome and a tempo too plodding for the Reels as they were locally danced. The whole environment of transmission, essentially, was different. One need only recall MacAulay – saying that dance-tunes in the ceilidhs of her youth, when the Scotch Reel was still supreme, were basically instrumental versions of *puirt-à-beul* – to see the intuitive connection dancers must have felt with the music of ear-learned local pipers, and how the timing of the tunes would have encouraged their dancing – that is, facilitated their steps – far more than would tunes learned in written measures with a comparatively dragging tempo and no basis for improvisation. Tunes that were in effect 'cut-and-dry', as she put it. From this point of view, the difference between aurally-learned and literately-learned piping within the South Uist tradition emerges as cultural as well as musicological, perceived as well as real. Aurality implied one culture, literacy another.

If we accept that timing was and remains the most important factor in good dance-piping in South Uist, it follows that *ceòl cluais*, as an idiom of performance, requires competition-idiom technique less so; this is what Calum Beaton had in mind when commenting below that the ear-learned piper would not succeed in competition, where technique is king. Conversely, he feels that modern competition piping dismisses over-much the 'natural' timing for which his long familiarity with the *ceòl cluais* idiom has bred great appreciation:

CB: *Bha feadhainn dhe na chluichdeadh an ceòl cluais a bha sin, 's e an fheadhainn a bha, a dh' ionnsaich na* scale, *is rudan mar sin, b' fheàrr leam-sa bhith 'g éisdeachd riubha a chionn 's gu robh* timing *aca cho nàdurra. Pìobairean matha an-diugh, tha iad a' cluichd airson a bhith cho buileach ceart, is tha iad a' call pàirt dhen cheòl nàdurra a bh' aig na seann daoine a bha dol an uair ud.*

JD: *Chan fhaigheadh iad duais ann an co-fharpais ach* . . .

CB: *O chan fhaigheadh iad duais sian air farpais gu dearbh!*

JD: . . . *ach math airson éisdeachd?*

CB: *Bha iad math, ag éisdeachd riu', is nuair bha thu a' dannsa riu'; cus na b' fheàrr na bhith a' danns ri cuideiginn a bha uamhasach math gu bhith 'gléidheadh duais air na farpaisean. An-diugh, feumaidh a h-uile sian a bhith cho ceart. Tha iad a' call air an* timing *nàdurra.*

JD: *Siud a tha air chall an-diugh?*

CB: *Well 'nam bheachd-sa, tha, co-dhiubh.*[26]

CB: Of those who used to play the ear-music, I preferred listening to those who learned the scale and so forth, because they had such natural timing. Good pipers today, they play so entirely correctly that they lose something of the natural music that the old people had at that time.

JD: They wouldn't win a prize at a competition but...

CB: Oh, of course they wouldn't win a thing in competition!

JD: . . . but good to listen to?

CB: They were good, listening to them, and when you were dancing to them; much better than dancing to someone who was awfully good at gaining prizes in competition. Today, everything must be so correct. They lose the natural timing.

JD: That's what's lost today?

CB: Well, in my opinion at least, yes.

Beaton is clearly influenced enough by his literate training to require accurate fingering technique in the appraisal of a performance, but likewise appreciates the timing that the elderly ear-pipers in his youth displayed in the *taigh-ceilidh*. This seems to form a personal aesthetic which combines the two idioms – finding most pleasing the ear-music of 'those who learned the scale', i.e. those who learned the technical rudiments. It would be premature and unrealistic to suggest that this aesthetic sense reflects that of all other pipers in South Uist, both past and present, but it is significant that of those pipers interviewed, only one explicitly rejected one idiom in favour of the other.[27]

Ceòl cluais, then, in accordance with its function in the Uist community, emphasises timing just as staff notation emphasises technique. Through the course of interviewing, I was struck by the impression that this leads to an aesthetic paradox of sorts: pipers tended to contrast what they termed 'correct' playing, i.e. playing by staff notation, and playing by ear – the implication being that *ceòl cluais* is inherently incorrect – while praising each for its respective function. Put another way, those spoken of as exceptional dance-pipers were in the same breath dismissed as being 'not good' – implying that they did not possess the mechanically precise fingerwork needed to succeed in competition. The frequency with which I encountered this perception gives a clear impression of how far mainstream influence has penetrated local tradition since the nineteenth century, when literate competitive piping was uncommon in Uist, likely the domain of the volunteer battalions, and most piping was performed for ceilidh dancing. It is this paradox, this emic evaluation of different idioms based on different functional standards, which first suggested to me the idea of an aesthetic based overall on function and context in South Uist. It is this paradox which allowed Louis Morrison to speak of a neighbouring piper as having been 'never very good' but who 'played dance music well',[28] and which prompted Rona Lightfoot to remark in 1996:

> *Nis, Niallaidh Scott, cha robh e dol a-staigh airson co-fharpais idir, ach cha chual' thu riamh cho math 'sa chluich e airson dannsa.*[29]
>
> Now, Neillie Scott, he was never one for competing at all, but you never heard such good dance-piping.

This was also the case for Calum Beaton when speaking of his father, his township and the older generation of pipers who resided there. One can see how he distinguishes between 'correct' piping (i.e. competition-idiom) and ear-piping (i.e. *ceòl cluais*) while evaluating both positively. I have emboldened particularly relevant text:

> CB: *Ged a chluichdeadh m'athair, cha b'e pìobaire math a bh' ann. Ach an aon rud a bha math mun deidhinn . . . na seann daoine bha sin a bha cluichd, bha* time-*eadh, mar a chanas iad, aca bha air leth math. A chionn bha iad*

JD: *eòlach air a bhith a' cluichd do dhannsairean. 'S toigh leam a' smaoineadh gun do thog mi pàirt dhe sin, a chionn bhìte 'gam iarraidh gu math tric, no co-dhiubh roimhidh seo, airson cluichd do dhannsairean is games is céilidhean is rudan mar sin.*

JD: *. . . A bheil Staoineabrog ainmeil idir airson pìobaireachd air an eilean?*

CB: *Well 's e na Smithich a bha sin, is Alasdair Peutan, is Ruairidh; bha móran do phìobairean, mar a bha mi 'g ràdh riut, a chluichdeadh ceòl cluaiseadh; 's e a chanainn e.* Playing by ear.

JD: *Sin an dòigh a bh' aig Alasdair is Ruairidh Peutan?*

CB: *O chan eil – bha iad-san suas ris. Leughadh iad an ceòl. Fhuair iad, dh' ionnsaich iad ceart e. Ach a' chuid as motha dhe na seann daoine bh' ann . . . Bha an fheadhainn a dhèanadh pìobaireachd ceart, bha iad sa' Chogadh. Cha robh air fhàgail a seo ach seann daoine. Gu leòr dhiubh sin anns a' bhaile seo, a chluichdeadh air feadan is a' phìob cuideachd, ach **cha robh iad math idir**. Bha timing aca bha air leth math, co-dhiubh na's fheàrr na chluinneas tu an-diugh, ach . . . Bha tòrr dhiubh, ach bhàsaich iad. Bha Ailean Còcair'; chluichdeadh fear dhe na gillean aige cuideachd, ach cha robh e ro mhath. Bha Ailean Dòmhnallach, Ailean Dhòmhnaill Ruaidh a chanadh iad ris – uill, sin an aon fheadhainn a chuala mise cluichd. Niall Steele – bha am fear sin na b' fheàrr na càch air ceòl cluais.* **Bha e cluichd glé mhath,** *am fear sin.*

JD: *A bheil e ann fhathast?*

CB: *O, chan eil . . . Chan eil duine aca beò an-diugh.*[30]

CB: Although my father would play, **he wasn't a good piper. But the one thing that was good about them** . . . the old people who played, their timing, as they say, was excellent. Because they were accustomed to playing for dancers. I like to think that I picked up part of that, because I'm called on quite often, up to now anyway, to play for dancers, games, ceilidhs and so on.

JD: . . . Is Stoneybridge known at all for piping on the island?

CB: Well there were those Smiths, and Alasdair Beaton, and Roderick; there were many pipers, as I told you, who played ear-music; that's what I'd call it. Playing by ear.

JD: Was that the way Alasdair and Roderick Beaton played?

CB: Oh, no – they were up to it. They could read the music. They received and learned it correctly. But most of the old people around . . . Those who played correctly, they were in the War. There was nobody left here but old people. Enough of those in this township would play the chanter and the pipes as well, but **they weren't good at all.** They had extremely good timing, better anyway than what you hear today, but . . . There were many, but they've died. There was Alan Cook; one of his boys played as well, but he wasn't too good. There was Allan MacDonald, Allan son of Red-haired Donald they'd call him – well, that's the bunch I heard playing. Neil Steele – that one was better than the rest with ear-music. **He was playing very well,** that one.

JD: Is he around still?

CB: Oh, no . . . Not one of them is alive today.

Alasdair and Roderick Beaton, being 'up to it', learned and played correctly while Neil Steele did not; Calum praised them all, however, according to their respective functions. The key here is that Beaton evaluated his relatives and Steele by different standards – the literately- and the aurally-learned – and recognised skill in each.

It bears reminding that the aesthetic of differing standards is not universal to pipers in South Uist. Not every piper shares the same views, just as not every piper shares the same particular background and experience; however, I encountered this view often enough to warrant the generalisation that addressing a 'functional aesthetic' implies. Whether indeed there has ever been a completely homogenous aesthetic among Uist pipers is doubtful – one need only think of *Lachlainn Bàn* or *Dòmhnall Roidein* in the otherwise aural climate of the 1890s. To demonstrate the difference of opinion within the tradition and among its bearers in more recent times, however, it may be useful to contrast Calum Beaton's views with those of Neil MacDonald. Although much of my contact with MacDonald went unrecorded, I was able to grasp his point of view by assuming the role of pupil whenever it suited him to give a lesson, a method I also adopted with his uncle, Angus Campbell.

While Beaton acknowledges the importance of ear-piping, recognises that a degree of it is quite universal to pipers' repertoires in Uist and appreciates their musicality and function, he stresses also the importance of clean fingerwork. This reflects his early exposure to *ceòl cluais* in the family and his subsequent literate training by his cousins and in the army. MacDonald, like Beaton, was a competition piper, but unlike Beaton, he evaluated piping by no other criteria. He tended to marginalise ear-piping and the playing of *puirt-à-beul* as 'for entertainment only' and not serious piping by any means. In this way, he was undoubtedly influenced by his personal background just as Beaton is influenced by his own: as one sees in an earlier chapter, MacDonald's family, going back at least two generations, were scions of the competition platform and the military regiment. Thus in his childhood home, *ceòl cluais* was frowned upon. However even here we see an element of the functional creeping into MacDonald's aesthetic: he recognised that *ceòl cluais*, though marginalised, occupies a definite place in the social and functional context of the Uist tradition – i.e. as 'entertainment'. Furthermore, he always evaluated a performance of mine in terms of prize-winning: 'That would never get a prize' or 'Now that would get a first'. Here too, the function is the guide. The perceptions of Beaton and MacDonald reflect both the competitive and the non-competitive natures of the South Uist piping tradition and were doubtless shared in varying proportions by the pipers who have come and gone before them in the twentieth century, as well as by those few who remain.

∽ THE VOICED AND THE UNVOICED ∽

Music in the *Gàidhealtachd* was transmitted through the voice and the ear before the drive for preservation through literacy took root in the nineteenth century. One unsung leader in this drive was Angus Fraser, son of Captain Simon Fraser of Knockie, who compiled a list of over two thousand musical terms in Gaelic around the year 1855.[31] It is not a comprehensive glossary of established literate terms used throughout Gaelic society; rather, it is an illustration of just how expressive the Gaelic language can be, in the hands of its song-makers, about the qualitative character of musical or otherwise artistic phenomena. Hence we find *breabadaich-mheòir*, literally 'a kicking of the fingers', for playing lightly and nimbly, in the sense of rapid finger movement, and *mil-cheòl*, 'honey-music', for melody, or 'the rhythmical descent which accompanied . . . hymns and chants'. Many of Fraser's piping and harping terms (for indeed, their shared nomenclature in his and others' work testifies to a common musical stock) possess an equally technical character, such as *barr-lu* [sic], 'top movement', which refers to a pibroch variation and grace note flourish involving much top-hand activity, sadly no longer extant in modern piping; and the perhaps somewhat spurious *cath-lu* [sic], 'battle movement', referring to the last pibroch variation played, according to Fraser, 'in the heat of battle' and synonymous with the modern-day *crunluath*. The terms were all drawn from forty-four works of poetry, songs, hymnals and dictionaries extant at the time, ranging from 1770 to 1848, which he listed at the beginning of the manuscript and quoted from in support of many terms entered thereafter. The work was never published, however. Even if it had been, it might have come too late, for a comprehensive musical vocabulary has not survived in modern Gaelic as much as it has in, say, English, Italian or Chinese, whose literate traditions have preserved a wealth of technical terms and fostered an aesthetic based on critical discourse, notational analysis and philosophical reflection; an aesthetic conforming for all appearances to Merriam's Western criteria.

Fraser's is not the only evidence we have that suggests Gaels enjoyed an extensive vocabulary in the past. Bunting's *Ancient Music of Ireland* (1840), a treatise on the Irish harp tradition of the late eighteenth century, is not listed among Fraser's sources but it is clear nonetheless that he consulted it. Bunting offers many technical terms which he had collected from elderly Irish Gaelic harpers at a great gathering in Belfast in 1792, each quite as descriptive and qualitative as the terms in Fraser's work. Hence we find the Irish harpers used the phrase *sruth mór*, 'a big stream', for an ascending or descending line of notes along the entire range of the scale; *bualadh suas no suaserigh* [sic], 'a striking up or rising up', for an upward succession of triplets; and *leith leagadh*, 'a half-falling', for the gracing of a main note from one half-note's distance above.[32] The now-extinct *barrludh* variation in piping (*barr-lu* in the Fraser MS) is found in Bunting's work as a harping term. Joseph MacDonald's treatise on the Highland pipes (c. 1760) also gives *barrludh* and other terms of the same character pertaining to pipe-music. And eighteenth-century poets such as Duncan Bàn MacIntyre and Alasdair MacMhaighstir Alasdair referred to various piping terms as well. We are left with the impression that a considerable vocabulary and aptitude for discourse – a 'voiced' aesthetic – existed among learned Gaels at a time when the language and the socio-musical institutions were held at a higher premium in Highland society than they are today.

There is also a case to be made for a predominant 'unvoiced' aesthetic among the Gaelic grass-roots, both historically and currently. A process of selection takes place, for instance, between a composer of songs and his or her audience. A song deemed 'good' was one which survived in the repertoires of the wider community, whether because the song was easy to memorise, had particularly catchy verses, was contemporarily topical, or any other reason. McKean had this in mind when commenting on the popularity of Duncan Bàn MacIntyre's songs in the eighteenth century.[33] A related criterion would have been the size and diversity of one's repertoire which, in the Irish folk tradition at least, was the source of keen rivalry among musicians. Memorisation and the 'singability' of songs, as McKean put it, are paramount aesthetic criteria. A music producer for a Belfast television station specifically contrasted this type of aesthetic against more literate verbal analysis during a conference in 1991:

> There is no language of criticism in traditional music . . . there are no established aesthetics for the music, no uniform way of judging it: tradition itself only seems to give you one way of judging, if you go by the tales that are told about musicians, and that is that the person who plays the most tunes or sings the most songs is regarded as the best. There are innumerable stories about pipers who have it out all night, one tune after the other, and the guy who wins is the guy who goes out for a break, hears the lark singing outside and bases the tune on it,[34] comes in, and the other fellow doesn't have it; therefore he wins. Thirty miles away from here in Teelin in County Donegal, Conal O' Cuinneagain, a local singer, won the competition with a neighbouring townland by running away to his own townland and waking up a woman in the middle of the night to learn a song from her, so that he could run back to the competition and sing it, and no one else would have it! That seems to me to be the only evidence of an aesthetic we have in the tradition itself. There are no words about value and judgement in performance common to everyone.[35]

There is little basis for verbal critical analysis among the Gaelic folk because, as in the Donegal tradition described above, the musical information conveyed by an evaluative vocabulary – words like 'rhythm', 'pitch', 'grace note' and 'quaver' – are assumed in the aural transmission of the music, making their verbalisation in many cases redundant. Naturally this means that such terms in modern Gaelic are quite rare. Shaw[36] has noted their scarcity in the Gaelic of the Cape Breton fiddling community, and I have observed a similar situation among pipers in South Uist. The 'unvoiced' nature of the Gaelic folk aesthetic has been classified by Merriam as distinctly non-western, but that is not to say that the 'voiced' aesthetic is confined to the West; certain Asian societies, for instance, possess a comparably sophisticated aesthetic, and Feld's study of the Kaluli singers in Papua New Guinea revealed a tremendous capacity for verbal discourse and enquiry.[37] At the same time, other 'unvoiced' aesthetics besides the Hebridean pipers' exist in Europe – albeit eastern Europe – as Rice showed when he undertook lessons in Bulgarian piping from a native master who could not verbalise the difference between melody and grace notes.[38] As was stated earlier, pipers in South Uist engage in critical discussion of piping; they can all state the difference between melody and grace notes. It is a sign of the mainstream community's influence, however, that whenever they do so, they state it in English.

Calum Beaton once remarked on the playing style of most mainstream pipers today:

> **Too clinical**; *leis an leabhar, mar gum biodh tu dìreach a' tomhas a h-uile* **crotchet** *is* **quaver** *is* **semi-quaver**. *Uill tha mis' a' smaointinn nach toireadh ceòl sam bith . . .* **expression**, *ma tha thu 'falbh* exactly *mar a tha sgrìobhte, co-dhiubh air ceòl beag no ceòl mór . . . Bidh iad* **overstressing**, *mar a chanas iad. Bidh iad a'* **stretch**-*eadh tuilleadh 's a' chòrr feadhainn dhe na* **notes**.[39]

> Too clinical; by the book, as if you were exactly measuring every crotchet and quaver and semi-quaver. I think that no music would give . . . expression, if you're going exactly as is written, either with the light music or the pibroch . . . They're overstressing, as they say. They stretch out too much some of the notes.

Again in a later interview, he remarks on the playing style of local Uist pipers around the mid-century post-war era as he at least remembers it:

> *Bha na* **doublings**, *mar a chanas sinn, is na* **grace notes**, *bha iad 'gan dèanamh na bu chruaidh' na chluinneas tu an-diugh iad . . . Bha a h-uile* **gracenote** *agus* **doubling** *cho soilleir is cho cruaidh 'gan dèanamh.*[40]

> The doublings, as we say, and the grace notes, they made them harder than you hear them nowadays. Every grace note and doubling was made so clear and hard.

Beaton casually refers to 'expression', 'crotchets', 'grace notes', 'timing', etc., and we have already read Jessie MacAulay's references to 'rhythm', 'lightness' and 'lilt'. Rona Lightfoot similarly spoke of '*Ceòl dannsa – 's e* **art** *tha sin, a bhith a' cluichd aig a'* **speed** *ceart*' ('Dance music – it's an art, to play at the right speed').[41] The phenomenon is by no means confined to South Uist piping; that the borrowing of English terms when verbalising a musical aesthetic is found in other areas of modern Gaelic society is suggested by McKean's study of the Skye song-maker Iain MacNeacail, who tried to explain how he chose melodies for his songs:

> *Cha robh* **music** *a'masa dhaibh gad [a bha mi] gan chur ri chéile. Bha mi coma fhad 's a bha... ad a' dol ann an* **rhythm***. O cha robh* **music** *agam... idir... Chuirinn na faclan ri chéile ceart gu leòr air bha ad* **correspond***-adh... facal air an fhacal eile... ach a chur ann am* **music***, bhiodh e eadar-dhealaichte, mar a tha fhios agaibh fhéin... Cha robh mi ach dìreach a' smaoineachadh... a bha ad a'* **rhyme***-adh... bha na faclan a'* **rhyme***-adh, bha mi ga chur air a'* **rhythm** *a bha sin. Cha robh fonn agam dha na càil... mu facal tighinn ann a'* **rhythm***, fhios agaibh, go* **sound***-adh ad mar sin.*

> I didn't have music for them, although I was putting them together. I was happy as long as they were going in rhythm. Oh I didn't have music at all. I would put the words together right enough till they were corresponding, one word with another, but to put them to music, it's different, as you know yourself... I was only just thinking that they were rhyming, the words were rhyming, I was putting it to the rhythm there. I did not have a tune for it at all... [I think] about words coming in rhythm, you know, till they would sound like that.[42]

The use of English loan-words in each of these cases represents a native Gael's attempt to articulate critical evaluations of his or her own music, and in so doing, they automatically turn to English-language cultural conventions with which they associate the very idea of a verbal discourse on music. Articulate analysis does not often occur in Gaelic aural tradition because the information conveyed in such words as 'doubling' and 'timing' is inherent in the transmissive process. This is precisely why in 1880, when the eminent folklorist John Francis Campbell of Islay asked Duncan Ross, Gaelic-speaking piper to the Duke of Argyll, to explain the written *canntaireachd* 'hiririn', the man could only play the movement on the chanter over and over, unable to describe the movement in any other way.[43] It is also why Angus Campbell of Frobost, when asked by Peter Cooke in 1970 to explain the theory behind cadences in *ceòl mór*, found himself similarly lost for words:

> PC: What is a cadence?
> AC: [silence]...
> PC: This is one thing in piping I don't understand.

AC: The cadence, you see – you get more song out of the tune; it's more or less written like that as a guide. It's a join, a join between the notes. [Plays examples on the chanter, then sings the *canntaireachd* of a cadence on C, then on B, then plays the second bar of line 2 of the 'Old Woman's Lullaby'.] I can't explain more.[44]

A final insight into how the traditionally raised Gaelic piper associates aural transmission with Gaelic and literate transmission with English, and its aesthetic implications, is Jessie MacAulay's earlier testimony that dancers in her youth preferred ear-learned piping to note-learned. Read again how she put it:

B' fheàrr leotha, na dannsairean, b' fheàrr leotha fear a bha cluichd leis a' chluais na fear a bha . . . as a' **mhusic** *. . . Bha* **lilt** *air choireigin anns a' cheòl chluais nach robh anns a' cheòl eile.*

They preferred, the dancers, they preferred someone playing by ear to someone playing by the staff notation . . . There was some kind of lilt in the ear-music that wasn't in the other music.

'*Ceòl*' is Gaelic for 'music'; while she uses the Gaelic word when describing ear-learned piping, she uses the English for staff notation: *fear leis a'* mhusic.[45] Undoubtedly a degree of idiom was involved, as many English-speaking pipers (and other musicians) will say 'music' when meaning 'notation'; but in this instance a difference was clearly meant, consciously or otherwise, between '*ceòl*' and 'music'. I would speculate that Iain MacNeacail of Skye was using the word 'music' in the same way during his interview with McKean, but the context leaves it open to interpretation. For now, we can only observe the mainstream's linguistic legacy and say that in South Uist, a 'voiced' aesthetic – that is, one conforming to Merriam's West and Feld's Kaluli – exists predominantly within the cultural conventions of English, and that MacAulay's unconscious word-association represents the surviving emic aesthetic of the old-world Gael.

Despite the 'unvoiced' nature of the Gaelic folk aesthetic, a limited vocabulary of technical terms survives – especially, as was mentioned earlier, where piping is concerned, and in particular *ceòl mór*. This we may attribute to its status as art music relative to the lighter and more immediately functional *ceòl beag*, as well as to the terms' preservation in written collections over the past 250 years; supported, one should add, by the explosion of interest in piping around the globe over the last several decades. The literate idiom, therefore, has preserved for widespread use what the aural idiom, in this case, could not: pipers the world over (whether or not they have Gaelic) refer casually to the *ùrlar, siubhal, dithis, taorluath* and *crunluath* – the ground and variations of a pibroch.

In 1999, Willie MacDonald of Benbecula spoke to the Piobaireachd Society of his early days of piping in his native island and recalled that the technical term *calpa*, literally a pillar or the calf of a leg, was used in his home community to denote the ground of a pibroch, in contrast to the far more widespread term *ùrlar*. This appears to have been an interesting survival of nomenclature perhaps once widespread, but fallen from general use: the only known reference to *calpa* as a technical term for Highland piping is found in Joseph MacDonald's treatise of 1760.[46] *Calpa* is no longer commonly heard in the Uist area. The more widespread terms as listed above, however, are indeed heard today, albeit with a subtle but significant difference. In Uist I often heard pipers of the elder generation refer not to *taorluath* and *crunluath*, but to *taorludh* and *crùnludh*, which recalls the terms as noted by, among others, Joseph MacDonald in 1760, Donald MacDonald in c. 1820 and Angus Fraser in 1855. Joseph referred to *tuludh* and *creanludh*, Donald to *turludh*, *taorluidh* and *creanluidh* and Fraser to *crùn-lu*; the connection being the suffix *ludh* or *lùth*, a word which used to mean, among pipers, the activity or movement of the fingers to produce certain grace note groups or variations.[47] The modern mainstream use of the suffix *luath*, meaning 'quick', is a latter-day misconception occasioned by the shift in piping's setting from mainly Gaelic in the eighteenth century to mainly English in the twentieth, and the survival of *ludh* in South Uist pipers' unwritten terminology underlines their conservative nature despite the English setting's influence.

I have recorded several other terms in South Uist which are largely descriptive and subjective. The reader is already familiar with the term *ceòl cluais*, 'ear-music', which I have heard being used nowhere else but among the Gaelic-speaking pipers of South Uist. It may be that this term was more widespread in the past, and used differently: Angus Fraser listed '*ceòl cluaise*' among his compilation of terms as joyful music, 'music of ecstasy and rapture', as if happiness were somehow connected to aurality in Gaelic music. He gives ten examples of this use from published Gaelic poetry. Surprisingly, he went on to define a related term, *ceòl cluais'-aire*, as 'Competition music, – or that which is performed before an audience and is addressed solely to the ear, as at competitions and concerts, without any intention on the part of the performers to move the passions or create emotions, – but to delight and gain approbation by their several performances.'[48] This appears a somewhat affected description and may have involved more than a little personal interpretation on Fraser's part, but if the term *ceòl cluais* was indeed used to denote music played in competition more commonly in traditional Gaelic society in the late eighteenth to early nineteenth century – the period encompassed by Fraser's listed source material – then its use in South Uist today reflects an opposite and more literal meaning. One may with reason surmise that today's meaning came about in response to the introduction of literacy among Uist's pipers from the nineteenth to the early twentieth century, and the consequent shift in musical aesthetics.

In his Cape Breton study, Shaw gives us words such as *blas*, 'flavour', meaning in the musical sense a 'stylistic sound' and in the linguistic sense an 'accent'. His informant would say of fiddle performances lacking the traditional local style: '*Chan eil am blas aca*', 'They don't have the sound'[49] – implying of course that they lacked the 'true' or 'correct' sound from his traditionalist point of view, i.e. the sound, or style, associated with the local language rhythms. Coming from the same cultural source and serving the same social function, traditional Cape Breton fiddling and *ceòl cluais* piping in South Uist are basically the same music played on different instruments. Accordingly, South Uist's Neil MacDonald and Angus Campbell used *blas* as a similarly technical term regarding the performance styles of Gaelic-speaking and non-Gaelic-speaking pipers. In addition, Calum Beaton often refers to the timing of the ear-pipers of his youth as *nàdurra*, 'natural', compared to that of pipers entirely note-learned, which bespeaks the outside influence with which written music is associated there. *Slaodach*, 'dragging', is a word MacDonald would use to describe my phrasing in *ceòl mór* if it was too slow and needed brisker treatment. Calum Beaton used *grinn*, 'handsome' or 'neat', to describe what he perceived as the 'delicate' fingerwork of mainland pipers as opposed to that of locals. All these terms illustrate the survival of a voiced aesthetic among Gaelic-speaking South Uist pipers. They are of course subjective; *blas* and *nàdurra* in the uses described reflect a traditionalist nature while *grinn*, in Beaton's case, reflects his own perceptions of cultural identity as well as the influence of the competition idiom.

An indication of how deeply this competition influence has pervaded the South Uist aesthetic compared to that of Cape Breton fiddling is the use of a term common to both – *ceòl ceart*, or 'genuine, correct or proper music'. Another subjective expression, it is used by Cape Breton fiddlers to describe the older, traditional style which, as Shaw's informant reveals, they clearly differentiate from the modern style resulting from non-Gaelic influences:

> *Chan eil fhios a'm gu dé an diofar a th' ann. Tha mi smaointinn gu robh an seann cheòl a bh' ac' an uair ud na b' fheàrr na'n ceòl a th' ac' an dràs . . . .'S e an* **ceòl ceart** *a bh' aca an uair sin.*

> I don't know what the difference is. I think the old music they had back then was better than what they have now . . . they had the genuine music then.[50]

If the reader casts an eye back to Calum Beaton's comments earlier in this chapter, one sees the fork in the road: his idea of *ceart* is mainstream, not traditional piping:

JD: *Bha* timing *math aig na seann daoine a bha cluichd, nach robh?*
CB: *O, 's e* timing *a b' fheàrr a chual' mise riamh, co-dhiubh. Ach cha robh iad a' cluichd ceart idir. Bha* false fingering *a' dol.*[51]

JD: The old people who played had good timing, did they not?
CB: Oh, they had the best timing that I ever heard, anyway. But they didn't play correctly at all. There was a lot of false fingering going on.

Beaton's use of the term reflects the widely held perception in modern Uist that 'correct' or 'proper' piping is the competitive and note-learned style; in this sense South Uist is no different from mainland Scotland. That *ceòl ceart* is still used at times in Cape Breton to describe a *ceòl cluais* style of fiddling means that, until relatively recently, that area has been far less subject to mainstream influence than has South Uist.

∼ BY THE EAR V. BY THE BOOK: ATTITUDES AND REPERTOIRES ∼

Earlier in the present work, Calum Beaton related how his ear-learned father refused to teach him piping because he felt that he himself played *gu mì-dhòigheil* – ineptly, i.e. by the ear. Beaton had to wait until after the war for his older cousin Alasdair to return in order to get 'proper' lessons, i.e. by the book. Beaton's father was self-deprecating due to the prevailing local aesthetic in Uist at that time and, it must be said, since: that ear-piping was backward and mechanically incorrect and that to be notation-learned is to be a better piper. Neil Johnstone told a similar story regarding his own tuition as a boy in the 1950s. His lessons with his first teacher depict the same aesthetic sense in favour of literate transmission:

JD: *Bha thu ag ràdh rium air* Pipe Major Neil MacLennan, *gu robh e fiadhaich air ceòl cluais – nach robh ùine aige idir air ceòl cluais.*
NJ: *O cha robh, cha robh e airson 'na dhèanadh duine le cluas, cha robh e airson a-muigh no a-mach idir . . . bidh tu a' leughadh is a' sgrìobhadh, 'ga chluichd mar a bha 'san leabhar. Cha robh e airson duine sam bith a bha ri obair le cluaiseadh.*
JD: *Cha robh e a' leigeadh –*
NJ: *Cha leigeadh e leat idir a chluichd mura biodh e dìreach* note perfect. *Cha robh e air a shon. Ged a thachair gu leòr a bhith 'nan deagh phìobairean cluaiseadh. Bha daoine gu math ainmeil 'nam pìobairean cluais; le ciùil eile cuideachd, mar a tha feadhainn dhiubh air bocsaichean is gnothaichean. Bha iad 'ga thogail dìreach, is bha iad gu math ainmeil, feadhainn dhiubh sinneach . . . Tha mi a' smaoineadh, duine mar Neil MacLennan a bha sin, 's ann anns an Arm a dh' ionnsaich e fhéin, far an do chuir iad* polish *air an*

> *teagasg a fhuair e 'na òige. Cha robh e idir idir a-muigh no a-mach airson sian ach an rud ceart.*

JD: *An esan a' chiad tìdsear a bh' agad air a' phìob?*

NJ: Neil MacLennan, *'s e. Agus bha* William Walker *an uairsin ann. Bha e fhéin math math.* Pipe Major Nicol, *bha e ag ionnsachadh ceòl mór dhuinn...* 'Mary MacLeod', *'Cumha Chatrìona,'* 'Kiss of the King's Hand', *feadhainn mar sinneach.*[52]

JD: You were telling me about Pipe Major Neil MacLennan, that he was incensed about ear-music – that he had no time for ear-music at all.

NJ: Oh no, he didn't want to produce anyone by ear, he wouldn't have anything to do with it at all ... You read and write and play it as it was in the book. He didn't like anyone who was working by ear.

JD: He didn't let –

NJ: He wouldn't let you play if it were not absolutely note perfect. He wasn't for it. Although there did happen to be many good ear-pipers about. There were quite popular ear-pipers; with other music too, like some of them on the box and that sort of thing. They would just pick it up, and they were quite popular, some of them there ... I think that a man like Neil MacLennan, it was in the Army that he himself learned, where they put the polish on the tuition he got in his youth. He wasn't at all for anything except the correct thing.

JD: Was he your first teacher on the pipes?

NJ: Neil MacLennan, yes. And then there was William Walker. He himself was very good. Pipe Major Nicol, he taught us *ceòl mór* ... 'Mary MacLeod', 'Catherine's Lament', 'Kiss of the King's Hand', some like that.

The prevalent aesthetic sense in South Uist cannot always have been one in favour of literate piping, since musical literacy itself has become prevalent in South Uist only within the past century. Evidence has been presented in the present work to suggest how this came about; evidence that in effect points toward significant change in the performance and transmission of local piping from the nineteenth century to the twentieth. This suggests a change in local aesthetics as well.

Today, preferences among my informants generally steer toward the competitive repertoire of marches, strathspeys and reels, *ceòl mór* and jigs. That many note-learned pipers have excelled in the playing of jigs reflects the deeply-rooted function of dance music in South Uist and its survival amid mainstream literacy. John Steele, for instance, was noted for it by Alex MacAulay. 'At a ceilidh in Uist about the mid-twenties,' wrote MacAulay in Steele's obituary in 1961,

> there were present among an enthusiastic audience some very famous players. John Steele, in good form, gave an excellent selection of Marches, Strathspeys and Reels. John MacDonald, Inverness, also present, gave a rousing applause and requested an encore. Steele lifted his pipes, tuned them, and played one tune, a jig,

'Shaggy Grey Buck', with a flow and expression of musical simplicity that I never heard before nor since.[53]

Jessie MacAulay spoke of another piper from the pre-war era named Angus MacDonald: '*Aonghus Beag* (Little Angus) . . . He specialised in jigs; no one could touch him, he always got the first wherever he played. *Cha chluicheadh duine* jigs *coltach ris* (No one could play jigs quite like him).'[54] Angus MacDonald, or *Aonghus Beag mac Dhòmhnaill 'ic Fheargius* to give him his local *sloinneadh* ('Little Angus son of Donald son of Fergus'), was brought up in Milton, north of Frobost, and was a lifelong friend of Angus Campbell; the two would walk to Daliburgh together in order to attend John MacDonald's Piobaireachd Society courses. Little Angus won the Fincastle Star for jigs at Askernish consecutively from 1931 to 1936, and was noted in particular, like John Steele, for his often extemporaneous rendering of the jig 'The Shaggy Grey Buck' on the boards. According to local reminiscences, Angus would add new, extemporised ornamental flourishes to the tune every year, and the Games' judges would travel to Askernish every summer during the 1930s merely to catch this gifted player's latest interpretation.

The jig tradition continued. The first jig competition ever held at the Northern Meeting, in Inverness, was won by Angus MacAulay of Benbecula on the eve of the Second World War and William Morrison of Loch Eynort and Glasgow, still competing today, has won too many jig competitions in both South Uist and mainland Scotland to note here. Such an abundance of strong jig-players in Uist echoes the days when *ceòl cluais* prevailed. Even so, the overall preference for competition MSRs and mainstream *ceòl mór* in today's community confirms that the improver mentality, which developed at the turn of the century, has stood the test of time.

Despite a prevalent attitude in favour of the literate idiom, all my sources indicate that their repertoires include at least some tunes, invariably dance tunes, learned by ear. For example, Louis Morrison's musical education was typical of twentieth-century Uist in that it was influenced primarily by literate transmission – his father's first task in teaching his son the pipes was to mark out the scale and progressive grace note groups, etc. on the stave – and Louis has since amassed a repertoire made up of competition MSRs, jigs and *ceòl mór*. However, even while growing up in an era when skill is measured by the yardstick of the Games, the island's surviving oral tradition ensured that he became familiar with the melodies and nuances of *puirt-à-beul*. As a result, his knowledge of their instrumental versions in the form of short strathspeys and reels is exhaustive. An indicator of his functional aesthetic is that although he practises competition tunes on a daily basis, he considers the 'local tunes', as MacAulay called them, being dance-music, too simple to require regular practice. Speaking as a piper, however, I can understand if this does not reflect purely evaluative feelings, but is rather to maintain the dextrous fingering that competition demands. Even here, though, the function remains the guide.

Jessie MacAulay's repertoire was similar in that she was, in her playing days, an able exponent of both *puirt-à-beul* music and the more technically precise competitive standard. Notice how she distinguished the process of ear-learning from the performance of MSRs and *ceòl mór*, a sign of the functional aesthetic that automatically associates ear-learned music with dance and note-learned music with competition:

JD: *Nuair a bha thus' a' cluichd air a' phìob, bha puirt agad a fhuair thu le cluas, an robh?*
JM: *O bha, puirt mar gum biodh* 'local tunes', you know.
JD: *A bharrachd air* march, strathspey and reels?
JM: *Seadh, tha.*
JD: . . . *An toigh leat ceòl cluais a bharrachd air ceòl leughte?*
JM: *O, 's toigh leam ceòl cluais . . . Uill, 's toigh leam deagh cheòl sam bith; 's toigh leam* march, strathspey and reel, *no* jigs; *pìobaireachd cuideachd, ceòl mór.*[55]

JD: When you were playing on the pipes, did you have tunes you'd got by ear?
JM: Oh yes, 'local tunes', you know.
JD: Apart from march, strathspey and reels?
JM: Yes, that's right.
JD: . . . Do you enjoy ear-music in addition to notated music?
JM: Oh I like ear-music . . . Well, I like any good music; I like march, strathspey and reel, or jigs; pibroch as well, *ceòl mór.*

Neil Johnstone's story is similar again, as he depicts ear-learning as preceding his literate tuition:

JD: *Nuair a bha thu ag ionnsachadh na pìoba an toiseach, agus b' fheudar dhuit an ceòl fhaighinn as an leabhar, an robh ceòl cluais idir agad?*
NJ: *Cha robh, cha robh. Well, dh' fhaoidte gu robh ann an toiseach tòiseachaidh, direach mun deach gu dh' ionnsachadh no sian, bhithinn a' togail is bhithinn a' feadarachd; bhiodh sinn a' cluichd, mar a tha mi 'g ràdh, bho* jew's harp is mouth organ, *na tionndaidhean tha sin, bhiodh sinn 'gan togail leis a' chluas. Ach nuair a thòisich mi air ionnsachadh, cha do ghabh mi turas ri ceòl cluaiseadh tuilleadh. Bha* [MacLennan] *a' ràdh rium, 'Uill ma tha thu dol a dh' ionnsachadh rud, ionnsaich ceart e.' Sin agad an gnothach.*[56]

JD: When you were first learning the pipes, and you had to get the music from the book, did you have any ear-music at all?

NJ: No, no. Well, it could be that in the beginning of the beginning, just before learning anything, I would pick up things and I would whistle; we would be playing, as I say, from a jew's harp and mouth organ, those turns, we'd be picking them up by the ear. But when I started to learn, I no longer had the chance for ear-music. MacLennan said to me, 'Well, if you are going to learn a thing, learn it correctly.' That was the way it was.

Just as formal lessons with literate tutors, regimental pipe band involvement, Piobaireachd Society involvement and the increasing availability of sheet music all provided a setting for the literate transmission of piping in South Uist, so too was aural transmission perpetuated within its context. The dance-gathering was its prime setting, whether the ceilidh in MacAulay's time or the *bàl*, or town ball, in Beaton's. We have already seen in an earlier chapter how, according to MacAulay, winter-time ceilidhs were often the natural place for a learner to 'pick up' melodies and rhythms, coming not just from other pipers, but from the singing of *puirt-à-beul* when pipes were not at hand. Beaton too observed this setting of transmission within his own generation, albeit lacking the vocal resource of *puirt-à-beul* singers and relying instead on the playing of older pipers. By Beaton's time the transition between a predominantly aural tradition and a predominantly literate one was long under way, and young pipers invariably had a grounding in staff-notated movements – the doublings, the *taorluath*, etc. – while still 'picking up' tunes by ear at local ceilidhs and balls. The era produced in South Uist what Gibson referred to as 'the musically literate traditional Gaelic piper':[57]

JD: *A thaobh ceòl cluais, tha cuid ceòl cluais agad-sa, a bheil? Puirt a fhuair thu le cluas?*

CB: *O thogainn gu leòr dhe na puirt, mar bu tric air na bàltaichean a bha sin. Cha robh leabhraichean ach gann aig an àm. Bha iad gann an uair ud; chan eil an-diugh. An uair ud, mar bu trice bha thu faighinn leabhraichean* Willie Ross; *bha còig leabhraichean ann,* book one *gu* five; *ach cha robh móran airgead a' dol. Bha* Logan's Tutor *is* Robertson's Tutor, *ach ma bha, cha robh fhios againn-e mun deidhinn! Mar sin, tha thu a' togail gu leòr dhe na puirt – uill, bha fhios agad, bha sinn air ionnsachadh mar a bha na* doublings *is na* gracenotes, *is bha thu a' tuigsinn far a robh còir agad na* doublings *a chur; is* taorluath,[58] *is rudan mar sin, as na leabhraichean. Ach bha sinn a' togail gu leòr dhe na puirt air na bàltaichean – gu h-àraid ruidhlidhean,* strathspeys, *is rudan mar sin . . . Bha sinn fileanta gu leòr air an ceòl a leughadh nam biodh leabhraichean gu leòr againn.*[59]

JD: Regarding ear-music, you have some yourself, do you? Tunes you've got by ear?

CB: Oh I used to pick up many tunes, most often at the balls. Books were scarce at that time. They were scarce then; no longer. At that point, most often you'd get Willie Ross's books; there were five of them, book one to five; but there wasn't much money going around. There were Logan's Tutor and Robertson's Tutor, but if there were, we didn't know about them! So, you pick up many of the tunes – well, you knew, we had learned the doublings and the grace notes, and you understood where you should put the doublings, and the *taorluath*, and so on, from the books. But we'd pick up many of the tunes at the balls – especially reels, strathspeys, etc . . . We could read music fluently enough if we had enough books.

Calum Beaton's reminiscences of acquiring the local piping tradition through both aural and written means call to mind Fr (now Canon) John Angus MacDonald's analysis of the life and work of Donald Allan MacDonald, or *Dòmhnall Ailean Dhòmhnaill na Bàn-fhighich'* (1906–92), the late Uist bard.[60] Canon MacDonald's is a singularly important contribution to our understanding of the shifting aesthetics of traditional performance in the Hebridean community in the twentieth century. In observing the 'making' of Donald Allan as a bard in the local tradition, he proposed that a certain schema of skill and repertoire development was in evidence which one could, with profit, apply to Beaton's experience as a piper in order to suggest consistencies between the transmission of sibling traditions.

In particular, Canon MacDonald proposed a three-tiered schema representing the main phases of skill and repertoire development which went into Donald Allan's apprehension of the bardic tradition as practised in his home community. The first was a phase of absorption and assimilation, in which Donald Allan, as a youth, acquired a great deal of local oral tradition within his family and his wider network of neighbours. He also familiarised himself with Gaelic vernacular poetry in general through the study of published written sources available to him. By the bard's own recollection, '*Bha mi ag èisdeachd is bha mi ag èisdeachd is bha mi a' leughadh seann leabhraichean . . .* (I was listening, and listening still more, and reading old books . . .'[61] The second phase comprised the application of his knowledge and creativity through the composition of new songs, involving private practice and the making of songs first for small occasions and family members, and for increasingly larger audiences in tandem with the growth of his reputation. The third and final main phase in Donald Allan's development, as articulated by Canon MacDonald, was the transmission of his songs at ceilidhs, pub sessions and formal concerts – wherever songs would normally be sung – which established his stature as a bard and allowed many of his songs to be adopted orally, so to speak, into the wider communal repertoire.[62]

Based on Canon MacDonald's schema of Donald Allan's development, it seems evident that in the traditional Gaelic world, the life and training of a village bard, composing in the vernacular speech for the appreciation of his community, unofficial and unpatronised, was a far cry from the rigorous literary apprenticeships of his professional counterparts. Though vernacular composition and professional *bàrdachd* are thought to have been practised concurrently in Gaelic society since before the sixteenth century, oral accounts within living memory, like Donald Allan's, suggest that the priorities and training of the one differed markedly from the other.[63] When comparing Donald Allan's development with Calum Beaton's experience as a piper, it seems also evident that the transmission of sibling traditions in South Uist in the twentieth century shared certain factors in common. Beaton, like Donald Allan, underwent an initial period of absorption and assimilation of the piping tradition of his family and neighbours; his father Archie's *ceòl cluais* was of course an important influence, as was the piping of his cousin Alasdair and his neighbour John Archie MacLellan in later years, amongst others. His assimilation of traditional style and repertoire by aural means was a fundamental feature of his development, as he himself remarked on the influence of older pipers and his imitation of their timing and rhythms:

> *Cha bhithinn a' bodrachadh ris an fheadhainn a bhiodh a' dannsa 'sna bàltaichean [ach] ag èisdeachd ri có bha pìobadh, agus bha thu a' togail, a' togail an time, mar a bha iad-san a' cluichd. Bha beagan do dhifir seach mar a chluinneadh tu gu leòr ann an Glaschu . . . 's ann mar a bha e tighinn nàdar riut fhéin, mar a bha thu a' cluintinn nan seann phìobairean eile, na bu shine na bha thu fhéin, a chluichdeas mar a bha iad an uair ud airson dannsaichean no bàltaichean.*[64]

> I wouldn't bother with those who danced at the balls, [but would be] listening to who was piping, and you would pick up, pick up the time, like the way they were playing. It was a little different from what you'd hear often in Glasgow . . . It was as if it came natural to you, like you would hear the old pipers, older than yourself, who would play as they did then for dances or balls.

However, like Donald Allan, Beaton's assimilation of tradition also involved recourse to literacy and the study of available published sources. Just as Donald Allan spoke of 'listening, listening still more and reading old books . . .', Beaton reminisced on his lessons with his cousin:

> *Alasdair Peutan – 's e a thug dhomh a' chiad tòiseachadh air an fheadan, is fhuair mi leabhraichean* – Robertson's Tutor, Logan's Tutor. *Bha mi fhìn a' togail gu leòr dheth cuideachd agus cha robh e uamhasach fada gus an rachadh agam air an ceòl a leughadh gu math fileanta.*[65]

> Alasdair Beaton – it was he who first started me on the chanter, and I got books – Robertson's Tutor, and Logan's Tutor. I picked up quite a bit too, and it wasn't long before I was able to read music quite fluently.

Beaton also underwent, as all pipers and other musicians do, a period of private practice just as bards such as Donald Allan spent considerable time composing and rehearsing their craft in solitude. Finally, akin to Canon MacDonald's third main phase of vernacular bardic development, Beaton eventually established his stature as a piper in his home community by playing at appropriate events, such as ceilidhs, weddings and balls, and competitions such as the games at Askernish and the Flora MacDonald Cup. Just as many of Donald Allan's compositions were eventually adopted orally into the local repertoire of songs through this kind of transmission, Beaton too has observed a few of his own settings of instrumental reels being played by others, just as he at times performs other pipers' settings. Such comparisons suggest that the aesthetics of traditional performance in the Gaelic-speaking community of the twentieth century, whether vocal or instrumental, were to a large extent consistent from discipline to discipline. Both bards and pipers seem to have felt, in equal measure, the impact of literacy competing with – or complementing? – aural acquisition and the shifting of attitudes to the mainstream. Clearly, there is much more to this subject worth exploring.

In the final analysis, we see a musical bi-lingualism emerging in the nineteenth- to twentieth-century Uist piping tradition as learning by the book slowly made its inroads. MacAulay received tuition in competition *ceòl beag* from both John MacDonald of Inverness and Willie Ross during their courses, but, like Beaton, grew up in an ear-learned piping family which provided a foundation of 'local' melodies and dance-based rhythms on which to build the technical, literate repertoire of later years. Morrison and Johnstone were likewise exposed to *ceòl cluais* despite the discouragement of their literate tutors, and their repertoires reflect it. This musical balance between ear-learned dance tunes and note-learned competition tunes in the repertoire of a single piper was made possible because, as we have seen, ear-piping retained an inherent social and functional value in the tradition and in the wider community, ensuring its survival against the juggernaut of 'improvement'.

The contexts of *ceòl cluais* dictated the setting and method of its survival. That is, ear-piping survived in South Uist because it was fundamentally associated with dancing, something not even the Protestant Reformation could stamp out there, much less the Piobaireachd Society. The social context of the ceilidh or the ball and the functional context of dancing ensured ear-piping's retention because the dancers and the community at large preferred it to literate piping, as MacAulay mentioned, for what they perceived as its rhythmical benefits. It had 'lightness' and 'lilt'. Just as in the Shetland fiddling tradition, where rhythm is perceived as the most important feature of performance so that particular dance-steps could be established, so too the South Uist community believes that music learned aurally makes for better dancing – whether it be the Foursome Reel or the Quadrille. In either case, though the character of the dances may be different, my studies suggest that the perception is the same.

CHAPTER 12

CONCLUSION

South Uist has seen many changes since the days when the MacIntyre pipers received patronage from Ormiclate and Nunton, or when MacArthur pipers may have been busy transporting cattle between Gerinish and Hunglater; a great many changes, even, since John MacDonald first stepped onto Lochboisdale pier in 1909, bringing with him all the institutions that had developed in mainstream piping over the previous century and that would influence its character in Uist over the course of the next. Throughout the present work I have discussed these institutions – the Piobaireachd Society, the Highland games, the standards of literacy and competition – and the changes associated with them. I have also discussed aspects of old-world culture and function in the southern Outer Hebrides to have transcended these developments, such as the intuitive importance attached to aurality, transmission within the family, the importance attached to dance-music and the complementarity between piping and other Gaelic arts. Despite their survival, however, piping in Uist is very much the mainstream compared to a century ago. Let us review the main points put forward in previous chapters illustrating this transition from a predominantly aural tradition in the nineteenth century to a predominantly literate one in the twentieth.

The community's martial history and the development of militia and territorial battalion pipe bands have encouraged literate transmission since at least the late nineteenth century. John Steele, *Dòmhnall Bàn Roidein*, Lachlan MacCormick, Neil MacLennan, Jessie MacAulay's brother Alasdair and doubtless many others were influenced in this manner by their military service. In addition, the overall climate of piping competition in Scotland contributed to the formation of the South Uist Piping Society, the involvement of the Piobaireachd Society and the general preference for literate piping in Uist that they and military service fostered. Staged competition was encouraged in the nineteenth century by the rise of Highland Games, and it caught up with the Outer Hebrides, on the periphery, by the twentieth. Changes also took place in the local *ceòl mór* tradition, however tenuous its existence at the time, on account of the Piobaireachd Society's involvement. This is indicated by Calum Beaton's testimony of a nineteenth-century performance style remnant practised by at least one man in Uist by the 1940s who was himself taught by a respected local piping family. The style was seen as an anachronism and rejected by Beaton's second tutor, Angus Campbell, as old-fashioned.

Our most compelling indication must be the testimony of local sources that the elderly, ear-learned generation of pipers in Uist from the 1920s to the 1940s played in a markedly different style from that of the younger, literately-learned generation, who saw it as backward. This argues strongly that great changes took place from the nineteenth to the twentieth century in local piping and that internal perceptions changed with it; enough so that *ceòl cluais* went from being the normal idiom to something seen as old-fashioned and out-dated. Although pipers still recognised its social and functional value in the local tradition, that did not make it any less technically 'incorrect' in the new era of musical literacy and standardised fingerwork.

Today, piping is not as universal a part of daily life in the southern Outer Hebrides as it was in previous generations, but this is not the fault of the literate and competitive era. Such influence may have altered the character of local piping, but could not have actively diminished it. From the point of view of local sources, the real reason is that young learners nowadays tend to lose interest in the pipes once they reach the age of between fourteen and sixteen; other instruments, such as the keyboard or the accordion, and other activities, such as football and computer games, grab their attention and most begin at that point to view piping as too time-consuming or parochial a discipline. Of course this isn't the only factor involved in the tradition's decreasing breadth. When searching for answers, one cannot ignore the inexorable pull of mainland work opportunities over the years, and how rarely those who leave ever return for more than a holiday. The *Roidein* brothers left for Glasgow, as did Fred and Ronald Morrison; Donald Morrison found work with the Aberdeen Police; Willie Morrison left for Ayrshire at the age of twenty-two and has since lived in Glasgow for many years; the list goes on. But moving to the mainland in search of work has always been an aspect of life in Uist, as has the pull of the army and the attraction of opportunities overseas, as in the case of the Empire Settlement Act in the 1920s or Angus MacAulay's move to New Zealand in 1953. Local piping was still considered to be in its golden age at that time. The real difference between then and now, I believe, is what local sources have been saying all along: that other activities now vie for young people's attention to a greater extent than ever before. There were no televisions, playstations or discos, for example, in 1953. Pastimes still mainly centred round the ceilidh – old-world foundation for music in the community and source of the Gaelic arts' seamless complementarity.

But despite its relatively diminished state, piping is still promoted within the community at various levels. The Local Education Authority added piping to school curricula after the Second World War and from the early 1970s the late Roderick Gillies, a native of Uist and formerly serving in the army, taught pupils from Eriskay to Eochar until his retirement in 1984. Gillies's work was taken over by Calum Campbell of Benbecula until Calum's own retirement only a few years ago. He in turn has been succeeded by Donald MacDonald of Kyles Flodda, Benbecula, Pipe Major of the South Uist Pipe Band. Two local societies, the South End Piping Club (SEPC) and *Comann Phìobaireachd Uibhist agus Bharraigh*, or the Uist and Barra Piping Society, also help carry the torch. The former was founded in 1989 by a committee whose first members included Fr Roderick MacAulay, parish priest of Daliburgh at the time, and the Rev Elliot of the Church of Scotland. At last glance, the Club organised classes twice a week, one in the Highlanders' Regiment drill hall in Daliburgh – source of local piping tuition and performance for geneations – and another in the community hall in Stoneybridge. They are taught by Calum Beaton and Louis Morrison and are open to all. The latter society tends to complement the SEPC's work by bringing well-known players to Uist for recitals. They also organise the prestigious Young Piper of the Year competition, an annual event which usually coincides with the Askernish games in late July and which is open to pipers under the age of thirty. The Flora MacDonald Cup, the annual locals-only competition for light music and *ceòl mór*, continues as ever.

Lest we forget present initiatives stemming from outwith Uist, the annual *Ceòlas* festival is held throughout the south end of Uist every summer, combining tuition in various Gaelic performing arts so as to promote local talent and emphasise a spirit of seamlessness. Lessons in *ceòl mór* can be complemented with lessons in pibroch songs, for example, so as to bring the music's Gaelic roots to the foreground in the learner's consciousness and thereby broaden his or her options as regards performance style; an important goal, considering that all young pipers in Uist today learn within the mainstream Kilberry idiom. The workshop was conceived in the mid-1990s by piper and pipemaker Hamish Moore of Birnam, Perthshire, who has advocated traditional Gaelic step-dance style piping in Scotland ever since encountering vestiges of it in Nova Scotia. He saw the potential in re-introducing piping's cultural and functional roots in Scotland as a counter-balance to its modern, regimented idiom, and recognised South Uist as the natural backdrop for such an exploration. *Ceòlas* now attracts students from home and abroad, though it has yet to be seen whether the festival will make any real difference in the number of players locally, or the style in which they play. The community have embraced it, however, for its economic benefits as well as its recognition of Uist's profound contribution to the panoply of Scottish music.

All in all, one hopes that the present work will be seen as a useful addition to past scholarship on the internal Gaelic perspective toward folk culture and music in Scotland, and no less as a foundation for research yet to be made; particularly in piping. The influence of competition on the aesthetics of Highland piping beyond the *Gàidhealtachd*, for instance, is open to further enquiry by ethnomusicologists or anthropologists of music. The particulars of change in other Gaelic-speaking areas could provide further insight into cultural conservation, transition and adaptation over the past century. And this record of piping in South Uist is by no means complete, as it does not delve as intimately into the details of many family histories as it could have. A greater and more detailed portrait of the communal give-and-take of musical transmision could have been construed, had greater co-operation from suviving members of some important families been forthcoming; but perhaps another day. Further research could also be done on the extemporaneous transmission of the Hebridean instrumental dance-music tradition, both historically and currently, and the ephemeral nature of the settings produced, using established sound archives and modern performances. Titles and settings of tunes specific to the southern Outer Hebridean community, if collected, could go some way toward refining our appreciation of the region's human and cultural geography: 'The Cameronian Rant', for instance, widely known nowadays as a competition strathspey, was once commonly played in Uist and Benbecula as a simple two-part reel called *'Cailleach a' Ghlinn Dorcha'*, or 'The Old Woman of the Dark Glen', the Dark Glen being a ridge under the shadow of Uist's largest hill, Beinn Mhór. Back in 1843, Angus MacKay included a similar variant of the tune in his 'Piper's Assistant' manuscript under the title *Tha 'Thu Mar a Tha Thu, a Bhodaich*' ('You Are the Way You Are, Old Man'), possibly indicating regional differences. One no longer often hears of such context to the music these days. An adequate treatment of this and other topics depends entirely on seeking out the elder Gaelic-speaking generation and utilising what they have to offer, as younger pipers, Gaelic-speaking or not, will have little knowledge of such bygone ways. Calum Beaton, Rona Lightfoot, William MacDonald of Benbecula and others are custodians of a perspective that will not long be in evidence, and only by considering them a bonafide resource for ethnographic or historical work will our knowledge – of piping and of all else concerning tradition and change in Scotland – find balance.

NOTES

See Bibliography for full references to titles

CHAPTER 1

1. MacInnes, 'Highland Societies'; Donaldson, *Highland Pipe*.
2. Collinson, *Bagpipe*; MacNeill and Richardson, *Piobaireachd and its Interpretation*; for a response to this attitude, see Cheape, Review.
3. Cooke, 'Problems'; Cannon, *Joseph MacDonald's Compleat Theory*; MacDonald, 'Relationship between Pibroch and Gaelic Song'.
4. Shaw, 'Language, Music'; Gibson, *Traditional Gaelic Bagpiping* and *Old and New World*.
5. Campbell, *Highland Songs of the Forty-Five*: xviii.
6. Matheson, Acc 9711, box 13/13: 9–11 (NAS).
7. Rice, *May It Fill Your Soul*.
8. See Blacking, 'Deep and Surface Structures'; Nattiez, *Music and Discourse*.
9. For more on these opposing methods, see Hammersley and Atkinson, *Ethnography*: 1–22.
10. See Collinson, *Bagpipe*; MacNeill and Richardson, *Piobaireachd and its Interpretation*; Cannon, *Highland Bagpipe*; Cheape, *Book of the Bagpipe*; and Donaldson, *Highland Pipe*.
11. Dr John Shaw, Senior Lecturer in Celtic and Scottish Studies, University of Edinburgh, has suggested in conversation that *puirt-à-beul* may not really be classified as 'songs' under the traditional Gaelic point of view; that a 'song', in Gaelic culture, is meant primarily to perform narrative – to tell a story – whereas *puirt-à-beul* are sung to provide music for step-dancing and thus any narrative component is minimal. For the sake of economy, however, I have opted for the English-speaker's point of view of a 'song' in the description above.

CHAPTER 2

1. Both songs can be found on record in the Sound Archive of the School of Scottish Studies under Kate MacDonald, SA 1965/88. *Latha dhan Fhinn* was recorded from other singers besides MacDonald in the late 1960s, as is noted in the Sound Archive catalogue.
2. MacDonald, *Òrain Dhòmhnaill Ailein*: 108.

3 MacGhilleain, *Ris a' Bhruthaich*: 106.
4 See Thomas McKean's treatment of bard Iain MacNeacail of Skye in *Hebridean Song-Maker*: 118 and Timothy Neat's profile of fourteen modern-day bards and their song-poetry in Neat and MacInnes, *Voice of the Bard*: ix.
5 Shaw, 'Gaelic Folksongs': 421.
6 Merriam, *Anthropology of Music*: 273. He referred here to 'arts' as music, literature, drama, etc., with all categories or classifications aside; presumably allowing scope for the reader to apply his or her own scholarly direction, whether 'high culture art' or 'folk art'. 'Literature', for instance, could be approached here as either oral or written, and 'drama' could as easily apply to the old Hebridean pantomimic dances as it could to Wagnerian opera.
7 Shaw, 'Language, Music': 39.
8 Gibson, *Traditional Gaelic Bagpiping*: 110. Joseph MacDonald died in India not long after composing his manuscript, and it remained lost in Bengal for forty years before being found by Sir John MacGregor Murray, a leading Highland aristocrat, and subsequently published by MacDonald's brother Patrick in 1803. For greater analyses on MacDonald's 1760 treatise see MacInnes, 'Highland Societies'; Cannon, *Joseph MacDonald's Compleat Theory*; Gibson, op. cit. and Donaldson, *Highland Pipe*.
9 Martin, *Description*: 240–1.
10 Ibid.: 154.
11 Martin, himself a Skye-born and Edinburgh-educated doctor, remarked: 'Fergus Beaton hath the following ancient Irish manuscripts in the Irish character; to wit, Avicenna, Averroes, Joannes de Vigo, Bernardus Gordanus, and several volumes of Hippocrates' (1994: 155). The Beaton family was widespread; a contemporary though apparently non-literate relation of his, Neil Beaton of Skye, was considered such a successful practitioner of herbal remedies that several islanders, according to Martin, thought he'd been in league with the Devil (*Description*: 238–40). Fergus Beaton's Gaelic medical library is discussed by Thomson ('Gaelic Learned Orders': 62) and by Stewart ('Clan Ranald'). See also John Bannerman's *The Beatons: A Medical Kindred in the Classical Gaelic Tradition*, Edinburgh: John Donald, 1998.
12 See Cameron, *Reliquiae Celticae*: 139.
13 Campbell, 'A slight sketch': 47–9.
14 MacLellan, *Stories from South Uist*: 83.
15 Campbell, *Popular Tales*, vol. 1: 17.
16 Carmichael, *Carmina Gadelica*, vol. 1: xxiv.
17 Rea, *A School*: xiii.
18 Logan, *Scottish Gaël*: 275.
19 Campbell, 'A slight sketch': 35–6.
20 John Shaw's study of aesthetics in the Cape Breton fiddle tradition ('Language, Music') discusses these rhythmic elements in depth, as does Chambers' Ph.D. thesis ('Non-lexical Vocables') on non-lexical vocables in Scottish music.
21 MacAulay, SA 1998.71.
22 See the Sound Archives of Edinburgh University's Dept of Celtic and Scottish Studies, section R1 for recorded examples from these and other local tradition-bearers of *puirt-à-beul*.

23 See Peter Cooke's study of the relationship between the pibroch song *Maol Donn* and recorded versions of its *ceòl mór* counterpart, also known as 'MacCrimmon's Sweetheart' ('Problems of Notating Pibroch': 41–59); and V.S. Blankenhorn's look at the Victorian-era song 'MacCrimmon Will Never Return', which was based on the pibroch song *Cha Till MacCruimein*, which in turn has its *ceòl mór* counterpart ('Traditional and Bogus Elements': 45–67). Both songs were recorded for the School of Scottish Studies by Kate MacDonald (SA 1970/309) and the classical pipe versions will be found in Campbell, *Kilberry Book*). Allan MacDonald used pibroch songs as the basis for reconstructing eighteenth-century *ceòl mór* performance styles in his M.Litt. thesis at Edinburgh University ('Relationship between Pibroch and Gaelic Song').
24 MacDonald, 'Relationship between Pibroch and Gaelic Song': 39–40.
25 MacAulay, SA 1998.68.
26 Shaw, *Folksongs and Folklore*: 130–2.
27 D.J. MacDonald MSS, Book 7: 594–5.
28 See, for example, Shaw's seminal article on Gaelic language and music aesthetics ('Language, Music') in which he describes several anecdotal references to bagpipe music conveying words. They refer to occurences in Scotland but were told by informants in Cape Breton, prompting speculation that the anecdotes themselves stemmed from before the era of emigration.
29 See Sound Archives, Celtic and Scottish Studies, section R1; and *Tocher*, vol. 1: 84–7.
30 *Tocher*, vol. 1, nos. 1–8: 86. See also Angus MacKay's setting of the 'Earl of Seaforth's Salute' (*A Collection*: 116), for which he includes Gaelic song lyrics beginning '*Slàn gu'n till fear chinn duibh* . . .' ('May the black-haired one return safely . . .'). The melody is entirely unrelated to *Fhir a' Chinn Duibh* as sung by Alasdair Boyd, but the common reference is indicative of Gaelic oral tradition.
31 Quoted in Shaw, 'Language, Music': 40 from Kathleen Lambert, *The Spoken Web: An Ethnography of Storytelling in Rannafast, Ireland*, Ph.D. thesis, Boston University, 1985: 112.
32 Use of the term *blas* ('accent' or 'flavour'), when used to describe musical style, has been recorded among the Gaelic community of Cape Breton; see Shaw, 'Language, Music'. For further discussion on this term and others, see Chapter 11.
33 Neil MacDonald, SA 1998.69.
34 Lightfoot, SC 2001.024.
35 D.J. MacDonald MSS, book 48: 4509–51.
36 Compare this tale with 'The Kintalen Changeling' in Rev. James MacDougall's *Highland Fairy Legends*: 8–10) which was originally published in 1910 as *Folktales and Fairy Lore in Gaelic and English*. The story is almost identical in the order of events – even the phrasing at times, and in translation – to MacInnes's version. It is also worth looking at a tale taken down in Kirkcudbright for J.F. Campbell and published in vol. 1 of his *Popular Tales* (426–7) which is similar, though by no means identical, to MacInnes's. The motif of the fairy playing the pipes in a cradle is the same, though the tailor is not at all threatening and the fairy leaves of his own accord upon hearing through the window 'his folk wanting him'.
37 The late Calum Johnston of Barra told a tale in which he imitated a piper's playing

38 E.C. Carmichael ('Never was piping so sad': 76–82) gives two examples of MacCrimmon musical origin tales, which follow along the same basic framework as the *Pìobairean Smearclait* tales (with the exception, as will be seen below, of the 'test'); other examples can be found in Robertson's *Selected Highland Folktales* (5–7) and MacLeod's *Tales of Dunvegan* (18–23), both of which depict a fairy woman bestowing the gift of music to MacCrimmon in the form of a silver chanter.

at a funeral, and what he sang corresponds with traditional *caoineadh* vocal chanting, which in turn is said by some to derive from birdsong (see Scottish Tradition Casssette Series, vol. 13: *Calum and Annie Johnston: Songs, Stories and Piping from Barra*; and Purser, *Scotland's Music*: 24–30).

39 Beaton, SA 2001.056. He played about ten tunes in all on the practice chanter using circular breathing. The widow *Bean Aonghuis Ruaidh* can probably be identified as Mrs Angus Campbell, who was photographed by Margaret Fay Shaw most likely in the early 1930s. These photographs appear in the 1999 Birlinn edition of her seminal work, *Folksongs and Folklore of South Uist* (1955).

40 Bowie, SA 1953.36.A1.

41 Duncan MacDonald, SA 1953.274.B9. The most notable of this family, George Johnstone, was a Pipe Major in the 1st Battalion Queen's Own Cameron Highlanders in the post-Second World War period and composed the popular competition jig 'Donella Beaton' (see *Cabar Feidh*: 216).

42 The name *Pìobairean a' Chlaiginn* has been encountered before by collectors for the School of Scottish Studies; see SA 1960/24/A7 for a version of the tale using this name, told by Donald MacDonald, South Uist.

43 MacAulay, SA 1998.68.

44 Rea, *A School*: 94.

45 See, for example, Fr Allan McDonald's notes in the Carmichael-Watson MS (58[A]57); E.C. Carmichael, 'Never was piping so sad': 83; F.G. Rea's memoirs, *A School*: 94; and interview with Calum Beaton, SA 1998.70.

46 See Chapter 5 for more discussion on the MacIntyres as pipers to Clanranald.

47 MacMillan, *Sporan Dhòmhnaill*: xvii. Calum Beaton offered this evidently quite traditional phrase in relation to the MacIntyres during an unrecorded conversation on 30 August 1995. Jessie MacAulay also asserted that her ancestors were 'pipers and archers to the MacDonalds of Clanranald', as is discussed in later chapters.

48 I use nine different versions from nine different sources in illustrating the *Smearclait* tales: two living tradition-bearers, Jessie MacAulay of Smerclate and Calum Beaton of Stoneybridge; five from the School of Scottish Studies archives (Archie MacDonald – Neil and Rhona's father – of Garryhellie, Duncan MacDonald of Pininerine, the 'Paisley Bard' Donald Ruadh MacIntyre, John Campbell and Roderick Bowie); E.C. Carmichael in the *Celtic Review*; and the collected notes of Fr Allan McDonald of Eriskay in the Carmichael-Watson MS.

49 Carmichael, 'Never was piping so sad': 82–4.

50 Archie MacDonald, SA 1953.36.B1.

51 Campbell, SA 1960.8.9.

52 MacIntyre, SA 1952.146.A/2.

53 The *deiseal*, or the encircling of something in a clockwise or sunward direction, was

a well-known superstitious ritual in the Highlands before it was stamped out in most Protestant areas; predominantly Catholic areas however, such as South Uist and Eigg, retained the custom to a considerable extent until modern times. See Chapter 3.

54 MacIntyre, SA 1952.146.A/2.
55 In Archie MacDonald's account the old man laid a bone across the boy's fingers before touching the boy's tongue with his own (SA 1953.36.B1); according to Roderick Bowie the old man instructed the boy to put his fingers on his fingers and to put his tongue on his tongue (SA 1953.36.A1); Fr Allan McDonald wrote that the boy encountered the *Sithean Ruadh*, or Red Fairy Hill, between Poll a' Chara and Smerclate, saw the hill, and propped open the door with a knife instead of a needle (Carmichael-Watson MS, 58[A]57); and in John Campbell's version, when asked what he wished for, the boy replies in a chant of sorts, '*ealdhain is rath, ealdhain is rath*' ('art and good fortune, art and good fortune') and is told to lay his fingers on those of the old man (SA 1960.8.9); the variations continue along these lines.
56 E.C. Carmichael ('Never was piping so sad': 78–9) wrote in a latter-day Victorian style that as a result of the fairy's gift: 'MacCrimmon could make his pipe move the hearts of his hearers so that they had no will but as it impelled them. Did he play "Geantraighe" they danced and sang for joy and pure happiness of mind and body. Did he play "Suaintraighe" they slumbered peacefully and with a happy smile dreamt of their dear ones and of pleasant days with their comrades. Did he play "Gultraighe" a wild pasionate longing and a great sorrowful lamenting came into every heart . . . MacCrimmon's music played with their souls as the north wind plays with the leaves of the birch tree on the brown mountain side.' The Gaelic terms used correspond to the technical vocabulary of eighteenth-century Irish harpers as recorded by Bunting (*Ancient Music of Ireland*) and reflect the connection between Irish and Scottish Gaelic musical traditions; Ralls-MacLeod (*Music and the Celtic Otherworld*: 81–6) discusses the terms' use in early Irish Gaelic literature.
57 Carmichael-Watson MS, 58(A)57. Fr Allan noted the tale in English except for the brother's exclamation, and its translation is my own.
58 Beaton, SA 1998.70.
59 The kelping industry in the Outer Hebrides had its beginnings in the 1730s but it was not truly remunerative in South Uist, and therefore relied on as the main source of income, until the late 1700s–early 1800s; see Chapter 4 for more detail and references on this subject. The mention of kelping in some variants does not mean that the tale itself is entirely derived from this period; one variant at least describes *Piobairean Smearclait* in the time of the Age of Forays (see Chapter 5) so the body of tales as a whole probably goes back to at least the seventeenth century. Clanranald is known to have patronised pipers as early as 1636.
60 *Seinn* has come in modern times to mean 'sing', so at first glance such a construction in the Uist dialect as *seinn na piobadh* is often interpreted as 'singing the pipes' and regarded as an allusion to the Gaelic speech/music affinity. However, the verb's original sense was of performing music on an instrument, and its use as such in the South Uist community today underlines the conservative nature of their oral tradition.
61 Bowie, SA 1953.36.A1.
62 Archie MacDonald, SA 1953.36.B1.

63 SA 1975.32.A1, told by D.S. Stewart to collector Donald Archie MacDonald.
64 Jessie MacAulay recalled ceilidhs in her youth in Smerclate lasting typically until five in the morning due to the dancing (to pipe music) of prolonged Scotch Reels.
65 MacDonald, *Òrain Dhòmhnaill Ailein*: 257.
66 Campbell, *Popular Tales*, vol. 3: 158–9.
67 Camichael, *Carmina Gadelica*, vol. 1: xxii–xxiii.
68 Bennett, *Last Stronghold*: 55.
69 MacNeil and Shaw, *Sgeul gu Latha*: 25–33.
70 MacDhòmnaill, *Uibhist a Deas*: 30.
71 MacAulay, SA 1998.71.
72 Shaw, 'Language, Music': 44.
73 Bennett, *Last Stronghold*: 80.
74 MacAulay, SA 1998.71.
75 See Flett and Flett, *Traditional Dancing* and Emmerson, *Social History*.
76 Beaton, SA 1998.70.

CHAPTER 3

1 Johnson and Boswell, *Journey*: 115.
2 Rea, *A School*: xiii.
3 GD 95/11/5/19 (2), National Archives of Scotland (NAS).
4 *New Stat Acc*: 195–6.
5 *Third Stat Acc*: 619.
6 Stewart, 'Clan Ranald': 338.
7 MacDonald, *Moidart*: 4.
8 See Stewart, 'Clan Ranald': 349–55 for more information on Bishop James Gordon's missions through the West Highlands and Hebrides, including South Uist, in 1707 and 1711. Details of the Irish Franciscans and other itinerant priests in South Uist will be elaborated upon below.
9 Stevenson, *Alasdair MacColla*: 22; Stewart, 'Clan Ranald': 76; MacLeod, *Sar Òrain*: 116. The MacDonells of Antrim were descended from *Iain Mór* MacDonald of Dunyveg and Islay, who married into a prominent Antrim family in the early fifteenth century and acquired lands there known as the Glens.
10 MacDonald, A. and A., *Clan Donald*, vol. 1: 100; see also Thomson's *Companion to Gaelic Scotland*: 3–4. Interview with Jessie MacAulay in Daliburgh, 1998.
11 See Cameron, *Reliquiae Celticae*. Many elegies contained in the Red Book show rich allusion to Catholic symbolism and to Irish Gaelic mythical sagas and descent, such as on the death of the chief Allan (c. 1510), who was 'dexterous like Cuchulainn' (p. 225), and his namesake who fell at Sheriffmuir in 1715, referred to as 'the leader of the army of the race of Fergus' (p. 249), i.e. Clan Donald.
12 Giblin, *Irish Franciscan*: vii; Mathew, *Scotland Under Charles I*: 194; Campbell, 'MacNeills of Barra': 34, quoting from W.C. MacKenzie's *History of the Western Isles* (1903): 184.
13 Stevenson, *Alasdair MacColla*: 257.

14 Thomson, *Alasdair MacMhaighstir Alasdair*: 132–65; MacLeod, *Sar Òrain*: 23–129.
15 This traditional verse ('*Urnaigh Mara Chlann Raghnaill*' in MacDonald, *MacDonald Collection*: 25) is similar to a prayer written down by Martin Martin c. 1695 (*A Description*: 187) most likely in Skye, which invokes the Holy Trinity. By all accounts, a prayer before sailing was a common thing, as it remains today.
16 The late sixteenth and seventeenth centuries were a time of alternating church government – between episcopacy and the presbytery – while the unity of the national Church as a whole remained intact; only when worship procedures were meddled with, such as the Five Articles of Perth and King Charles's introduction of the Book of Prayer in 1637, did matters affect the common people enough to lead to civil war in the 1640s. Presbyterian administration finally won out over episcopal bishoprics and ties to the crown in 1690 and was established into law. For a wider exposition see Donaldson, *Scotland: Church and Nation*: 70–9; *Scottish Church History*: 204–11).
17 Giblin, *Irish Franciscan*: xii. The missionaries claimed in all to have converted or reconciled 6,627 and baptised 3,010 in the west Highlands and Hebrides by 1633; the number was so unexpectedly high that their superiors in Rome for a time refused to pay the priests' meagre salaries until the figure could be verified.
18 Giblin, *Irish Franciscan*: 53.
19 Stevenson, *Alasdair MacColla*: 54; Stewart, 'Clan Ranald': 73–6.
20 Donaldson, *Scotland: Church and Nation*: 47.
21 Catholic incorporation of pagan superstitions in the Hebrides around this time was a standard tool for mass conversions and will be elaborated upon below.
22 MacPherson, 'Notes on Antiquities'. See also Robertson, 'Topography and Traditions': 194.
23 For records of the instances of veneration described above, see Giblin, *Irish Franciscan*: 63, 68, 73; Dressler, *Eigg*: 23; Campbell, *Canna*: 1.
24 Giblin, *Irish Franciscan*: 68.
25 Ibid.: 69, 73.
26 Stevenson, *Alasdair MacColla*: 54; Black, 'Colla Ciotach': 220–1; Mathew, *Scotland Under Charles I*: 194. Despite converting almost the entire population of Colonsay in 1625, the bishop was active there at the time and Ward was compelled to leave for his own safety.
27 Giblin, *Irish Franciscan*: 72; MacDonald, A. and A., *Clan Donald*: 347; Anson, *Underground Catholicism*: 38; Black, 'Colla Ciotach': 223. Hegarty withdrew from the field the following year due to this sort of persecution, but he thereafter directed the mission from its headquarters in Bonamargy, Co. Antrim until the mid-1640s.
28 Mention of these instances is contained in a discussion of Clanranald's religious observances during the period in question in James Stewart's unpublished Ph.D. thesis, 'Clan Ranald': 339, 346, 352–3, 355.
29 D.J. MacDonald MSS, book 3: 229. See also Stewart, 'Clan Ranald': 344 for further information on Fr Devoyer.
30 This tale was collected and written down by D.J. MacDonald and can be found in his MSS, book 3: 231–3.
31 Kirk, 'The Jacobean Church': 32–5.
32 Giblin, *Irish Franciscan*: 76, 144; Rea, *A School*: viii. Ward's report from this time

reveals that MacDonald first applied to the Scots college at Douai in France, but was refused admission on the basis of his Calvinist background, and that three English-speaking students were admitted in preference to him despite a letter of commendation from the nuncio in Belgium. Ward complained to Rome about the institutional neglect of Gaelic-speaking students.

33 (NAS) GD 95, SSPCK Minutes of General Meetings, vol. 1: 31.
34 (NAS) GD 95, SSPCK Minutes of General Meetings, vol. 2 (3 March 1727); Rea, *A School*: xvii.
35 (NAS) GD 95, vol. 2: 366.
36 (NAS) GD 95, vol. 2: 195.
37 Stewart, 'Clan Ranald': 340.
38 (NAS) GD 95, vol. 2: 342.
39 (NAS) GD 95, vol. 2: 349.
40 The Reformation was recognised by the Scottish Parliament but their acts were not established into law until 1690, at which time Parliament made official the intentions of the Church articulated at their first General Assembly on 20 December 1560 – e.g. 'to petition parliament to inflict punishment upon idolaters, and maintainers of idolatry, and those who say mass, or cause mass to be said, or are present thereat.' (See *An Abridgement of the Acts of the General Assembly of the Church of Scotland*, Edinburgh, 1831.) Westminster finally passed laws to protect Catholics in Scotland in 1829.
41 Campbell, *Father Allan McDonald*: 10; Rea, *A School*: xiv–xix.
42 Estimated by the Rev. Lawson, Daliburgh, during an informal conversation in April 1999.
43 *OT*, 26 February 1898: 6.
44 Martin, *Description*: 153.
45 Campbell, *Very Civil People*: 13.
46 Martin, *Description*: 303. The pagan rituality behind wells, springs, cairns and the *deiseal* among Gaels has been documented elsewhere and is widely accepted. Ross (*Pagan Celtic Britain*: 48–56) refers to the cult and sacredness of wells and springs in pagan tradition among the Celts of Gaul, Ireland and Britain; the Reeses (*Celtic Heritage*: 161) refer to the Irish tradition of a well of 'knowledge and inspiration' from which flow the Boyne, the Shannon and Ireland's 'seven chief rivers'. Donald John MacDonald of South Uist (MSS book 66: 6168), collector and tradition-bearer, remarks in a treatise on local traditions that a funeral party would circle the deceased person's house *deiseal*, or sunwise, before continuing on to the grave site, a custom which survived until about the turn of the twentieth century; and MEM Donaldson claimed that as late as 1920, 'throughout the Highlands the natives, wholly irrespective of the religion they profess, are not without relics of pagan superstition, being careful, for instance, to go *deiseal*, or sunwise, in leaving the house or in walking round anything. In this practice can be traced the remains of sun-worship' (*Wanderings*: 90).
47 Dressler, *Eigg*: 23.
48 MacBain, 'Gaelic Incantations': 230.
49 D.J. MacDonald MSS, book 3: 196. Carmichael (*Ortha nan Gaidheal*, vol. 1:

234–41) gives several variants of this smooring incantation, which is likely indicative of regional variations; they are all generally alike in theme and formula but differ in references to names of saints, such as John, Peter, Paul and so on. MacBain ('Gaelic Incantations': 232) gives one version, based on Carmichael's collected material, which invokes saints Peter and Paul.

50 Campbell, 'MacNeills of Barra': 33. This sort of superstitious custom deriving from Catholic veneration is echoed by Fr Allan McDonald of Eriskay's ritual blessing of the island's fishing fleet every May (perhaps in some connection to Beltane) for three years before his death in 1905: 'The fishermen at his request thoroughly cleansed out their boats and gave them the names of saints. He then gathered them together and blessed them. They cast lots to decide on what boat Mass would be celebrated. An altar with a canopy overhead was erected on the lucky boat, and the others gathered in a circle round it, all gaily festooned and decorated with flags and banners' (Campbell, *Father Allan McDonald*: 20–1). The sprinkling of dust from St Barr's grave and the celebrating of mass on the Eriskay fleet 300 years later both smack of pagan luck-belief incorporated into a Catholic framework.

51 Cambell, 'MacNeills of Barra': 83–4.

52 Fr Allan's high regard for folklore in Uist and Eriskay included the belief in second sight, information on which he collected on behalf of the American researcher Ada Goodrich-Freer (Campbell, *Father Allan McDonald*; see also Campbell and Hall, *Strange Things*).

53 Ward recounts that a member of the South Uist gentry took some holy water up to North Uist, where a woman apparently found that it multiplied food by a third when sprinkled on it (Giblin, *Irish Franciscan*: 87). It need hardly be said that a rumour that holy water multiplies food, in a place like the Outer Isles in the seventeenth century, would doubtless attract many to the faith. Baptism was also regarded by the people of South Uist as a way of ridding houses of spirit-pests, the ghosts of the recently deceased, and so on (Ibid.: 88).

54 Giblin, *Irish Franciscan*: 88.

55 'Spiritual independence' (Thomson, *Companion*: 86), or the separation of church and state, was the issue at the heart of the Disruption. Lairds and other dignitaries could place ministers of their own choosing in charge of congregations with no need of the congregations' approval. This system had its roots in the reign of James III, who in 1473 overrode the election of an abbot by a Dunfermline monastery and placed in his stead James's own nominee (Mathieson, *Politics and Religion*: 26). It was neither the first nor the last abuse of crown power in the Scottish Church, but it did set a precedent for the system prevailing over 300 years later. See also Drummond and Bulloch, *Scottish Church*: 58–9.

56 Ansdell, *People*: 98.

57 MacDonald, *Lewis*: 115.

58 MacAulay, *Nua-Bhàrdachd Ghàidhlig*: 165.

59 Carmichael, *Carmina Gadelica*: xxix.

60 Cheape, 'Get them off his fingers', 2005.

61 Kuyper, *Lectures on Calvinism*: 168.

62 Kuyper's comment recalls a debate at a folk music conference in Belfast in 1991. In

it the well-known Gaelic singer Mary Jane Campbell remarked on the legacy of the Free Church in Lewis: 'So, there was a great flood of new writing because of the destruction of the old songs. I think that in an island like Barra there is not the same need to produce new material. I was at a little session with an old man, and he sang a song. Somebody said, "Where did you get that?", and he said, "Oh, that's an old song. That was composed about 1920." Well now, if you said that to someone in Barra, they would say, "That was composed about 1620," or earlier' (McNamee, *Traditional Music*: 25). 'Destruction' in this case may have referred to folk songs 'purified and baptised' by the local ministry, altered beyond recognition for the sanctity of the church service; it gives perspective to Derick Thomson's 'Scarecrow', who 'took the goodness out of the music'.

63   Carmichael, *Carmina Gadelica*: xxv.
64   Meek, *Scottish Highlands*: 45.
65   Fotheringham, *Sinclair Thomson*: 5.
66   Kennedy, *Apostle*: 535.
67   Meek, *Scottish Highlands*: 45.
68   MacLeod, 'Calvinism': 46.
69   Carmichael, *Carmina Gadelica*: 198.
70   Blundell, *Catholic Highlands*: 52.
71   Campbell and Collinson, *Hebridean Folksongs*, vol. 1: 139, 146.
72   Calum Maclean interviewing Peggy MacDonald, SA 1959/58/A2.
73   Information on Mary of Guise from Donaldson, *Scotland: Church and Nation*: 65. Emmerson (*Social History*: 224) and the Fletts (*Traditional Dancing*: 271) mention one instance at least of the Eightsome Reel being proscribed and fiddles being destroyed by priests in Cape Breton, and there are old anecdotes and jokes in Ireland about priests banning traditional music and dancing (McNamee, *Traditional Music*: 65), but these all centre around Sabbath temperance rather than a general doctrinal intolerance.
74   Meek, *Scottish Highlands*: 38.
75   Johnstone, SA 1998.71.
76   Kennedy, *Apostle*: 338.
77   As a side note to priests' involvement in local piping, the dean of Daliburgh in the 1930s, Fr A.F. Gillies, was often chairman of the South Uist Games Committee and a keen supporter of the piping competitions throughout his residency. At a ceilidh in Lochboisdale after the games of 1932, the pipers, judges, committee members and others all gathered to toast the day's events and each other's contributions: 'in proposing the health of Dean Gillies,' wrote the *Oban Times* correspondent, 'Mr. Seton Gordon (a piping judge) said how fortunate South Uist was, when the Church entered into the festivities of the island and, as it were, gave them her blessing. He said that when Pipe Major John MacDonald or when any other master piper played a piobaireachd, it was an uplifting experience, and it was only right that the fine music of the pipes should be encouraged in every way possible' (*OT*, 13 August 1932: 2).
78   McDonald, *Gaelic Words*: 9.
79   Rea, *A School*: 86.
80   Watson, *Bàrdachd Ghàidhlig*: 3.

CHAPTER 4

1. J.L. Campbell listed these as the three options available to the typical young man in South Uist during storyteller Angus MacLellan's day in the 1880s; see MacLellan, *Furrow*: xiii.
2. When the famine hit, 'men came in significant numbers from the Outer Hebrides to work at the railways and in the farms of the central Lowlands. At least 107 natives of Barra, South Uist and North Uist were labouring as railway navvies in the summer of 1847' (Devine, *Great Highland Famine*: 157).
3. Devine speaks of the 'social disorientation' that lairds' changing economic priorities introduced in the post-Forty-Five era ('Landlordism': 93); MacKay refers to tacksmen 'taking offence at the policies of the post-Culloden lairds' as the first sign of the old economy being 'swept away' ('Glenaladale's Settlement': 16); traditional agricultural practices, according to Bumsted, began to change in the 1760s in the wake of the clan system's obsolescence (*People's Clearance*: 4, 32); and in western Inverness-shire, among the first signs of commercialisation was MacDonell of Glengarry's sale of Abertarff and North Morar to the Duke of Gordon in 1769 in order to repay debts (McLean, *People of Glengarry*: 17).
4. *Stat Acc*: 128; Gray, *Highland Economy*: 126.
5. McLean, *People of Glengarry*: 20.
6. *Stat Acc*: 128.
7. Gray, *Highland Economy*: 76–7; Bumsted, *People's Clearance*: 4, 38.
8. *New Stat Acc*: 190–3; Gray, *Highland Economy*: 81.
9. For protest against improvement measures in South and North Uist, see Bumsted, *People's Clearance*: 85–6; 'Ideas of improvement are seen with aversion', wrote MacDonell of Barisdale to the Board of Annexed Estates in 1763 (McLean, *People of Glengarry*: 24); Gray discusses rent raises across the Highlands from the mid-eighteenth century as reflecting 'progress and attention to the land' (*Highland Economy*: 146); and of the 1773–5 emigrations, which were unusually well recorded, most Highlanders professed to be emigrating because of high rents (Bailyn, *Voyagers*: 191, 198).
10. 'To a great extent the ordinary needs of life were met within the Highland farm, by work in the cottage, or by direct local exchange. Yet the self-sufficiency was never complete and there was always, everywhere, a margin of essential needs that could only be satisfied by imports from outside' (Gray, *Highland Economy*: 41). See also Devine, *Great Highland Famine*: 161; Bumsted, *People's Clearance*: 4.
11. Bumsted, *People's Clearance*: 14; McLean, *People of Glengarry*: 82.
12. See Vance, 'Politics of Emigration': 51 and Bumsted, *People's Clearance*: 4. In Gibson, *Traditional Gaelic Bagpiping*: 273, app. 3, piper William MacKenzie writes home in 1778: 'If it had not been for the war this is the Best Country in the World'; see also Hornsby, 'Scottish Emigration and Settlement': 63, which discusses letters praising the emigrants' situation, such as this man writing to a relative in Lewis in 1830: 'I go out and in [my house] at my pleasure, no soul living forces me to do a turn against my will, no laird, no factor, having no rent, nor any toilsome work but I do myself.' Some letters were rather warnings than encouragements, however – advocating

caution in the face of unscrupulous promoters and an uncertain future; see Bailyn, *Voyagers*: 37.

13 Vance, 'Politics of Emigration': 39; Devine, 'Landlordism': 91; Gray, *Highland Economy*: 64 and 'Course of Scottish Emigration': 33.
14 Bailyn, *Voyagers*: 58; Devine, 'Landlordism': 91.
15 Bailyn, *Voyagers*: 56.
16 Bumsted, *People's Clearance*: 132.
17 The lowering of import duties and the abolition of the salt tax in 1825 contributed to the decline in price for Highland kelp, as did advances in the chemical industry in mass-producing soda. Kelp declined from about £20 per ton in 1811 to about £3–5 in 1834, effectively ruining all viability. See Gray, *Highland Economy*: 156–7; Stewart, 'Clan Ranald': 568; Bumsted, *People's Clearance*: 42; *New Stat Acc*: 194.
18 1,872 tenants were still engaged in kelp manufacture in South Uist in 1837 (see Gray, *Highland Economy*: 158 and Devine, *The Great Highland Famine*: 25, 147). *New Stat Acc* (p. 194) reveals that 'the wages of the kelp-makers have been ... reduced, and indeed, the manufacture would not be continued at all, but to enable the tenants to pay their rents'.
19 Gray, *Highland Economy*: 33; McLean, *People of Glengarry*: 151; see also Vance, 'Politics of Emigration': 40, 41, 50 on the social and economic problems faced particularly in the Western Isles, the western Lowland districts such as Lanarkshire, and the central Highlands around Loch Tay.
20 The main analyses are MacKay, 'Glenaladale's Settlement'; Bumsted, 'Highland Emigration' and *People's Clearance*; Bailyn, *Voyagers*; Lawson, 'Passengers on the Alexander'; Adams and Somerville, *Cargoes*.
21 Memorial by Bishop Hay circulated in London, dated 27 November 1771 (Blundell, *Catholic Highlands*: 33).
22 These letters are held in the Scottish Catholic Archives as the 'Blair Letters' and are the primary source for much of what has been written about this emigration so far. Bumsted ('Highland Emigration') and Adams and Somerville (*Cargoes*) make the most in-depth analysis based on the Blair Letters, while Lawson ('Passengers on the Alexander') goes a step further and consults the Public Archives of Prince Edward Island to determine the numbers involved.
23 MacKay, 'Glenaladale's Settlement': 17. A slightly different version of this anecdote was recorded in 1965 for the School of Scottish Studies from Calum MacRae, South Uist (SA 1965/115/B3). *Creideamh a' Bhata Bhuidhe* is a legend known in Coll and Rum as well as Uist (*OT*, 12 March 1898: 3; Johnson and Boswell, *Journey*: 115), so it is difficult to pin down where the event that inspired the legend actually took place.
24 MacKay, 'Glenaladale's Settlement': 18–20.
25 Adams and Somerville, *Cargoes*: 64; Bumsted, *People's Clearance*: 58; Bailyn, *Voyagers*: 399.
26 There is some confusion regarding the number of passengers among the available analyses. Most writers quote 100 as the number which left Uist, out of a total of 210 (Bumsted, 'Highland Emigration' and *People's Clearance*; Bailyn, *Voyagers*; Adams and Somerville, *Cargoes*). Lawson, however, consulted the PEI Archives and refers to Bishop MacDonald's letter to Bishop Hay dated 14 February 1772 (Blair

Letters, Scottish Catholic Archives) and Glenaladale's letter to his cousin (MacKay, 'Glenaladale's Settlement': 19) to indicate that the 11 Uist families could only have amounted to about 55 individuals, while another 13 families from Barra and Eigg made up the rest of the 100 thought previously to have originated only in Uist. See Lawson, 'Passengers on the Alexander': 34–39.

27 Bumsted, 'Highland Emigration': 525; Adams and Somerville, *Cargoes*: 71.
28 Data extrapolated from Bumsted, *People's Clearance*: 225–6, app. A, table 1. Adams and Somerville (*Cargoes*: 212) give 200 people emigrating from both North and South Uist in 1802; in this year, they were likely to have gone to Cape Breton, and so may reasonably have been aboard the *Northern Friends*, which carried 340 to that island from Greenock in that year (Ibid.: 221). The failed harvest of 1802, in response to which Clanranald loaned 1,200 bolls of meal and sixty tons of seed potatoes to his tenants in South Uist and Benbecula, suggests itself as a catalyst for the emigrations (Bumsted, *People's Clearance*: 140).
29 Devine, *Great Highland Famine*: 301–2, app. 2.
30 AD 58/86 (NAS), Anon. to Sheriff of Inverness, 5 January 1847; F. Skene to Lord Advocate, same date; Sheriff of Inverness to Lord Advocate, 15 February 1847; and the Lord Advocate wrote to Coffin, 5 January 1847, '. . . It grieves me to the heart to think that destitution should have made a progress so stern and alarming on a property belonging to one of the most wealthy proprietors in this country. But there is no present help. I have little hope of assistance from him.' See also MacKenzie, *Highland Clearances* and Stewart, 'Clan Ranald'.
31 Treasury to Lord Advocate's Office, 30 June 1847: '. . . although Col. Gordon may have done his share with a bad grace, it is undeniable that he had performed it more fully than the proprietors of either North Uist or Harris' (AD 58/86, NAS). See also Devine, *Great Highland Famine*: 90–4.
32 AD 58/86 (NAS), Anon. to Sheriff of Inverness, 5 January 1847.
33 HD 20/183 (NAS), Account of Sales by Captain Pole, 18 January 1847.
34 *New Stat Acc* (p. 187) observed, 'The most important and useful shellfish on the shores of this parish, is the cockle . . . Great crowds of people, with horses and baskets or creels, are seen every summer, but especially in years of scarcity, picking up this shellfish, as a most useful article of food, upon which, with a little milk, and sometimes without that addition, the poor people, in years of scarcity, principally subsist for two months.'
35 AD 58/86 (NAS), 30 June 1847. For further testimony along the same lines involving South Uist and other Hebridean areas, see AD 58/86, W. Shaw to Lord Advocate, 12 April 1847.
36 AD 58/86 (NAS), 20 June 1949.
37 See Devine, *Great Highland Famine*, app. 10: 325–6; *Third Stat Acc*: 614–15.
38 Devine, *Great Highland Famine*: 200; MacKenzie, *Highland Clearances*: 259.
39 Donovan, 'Cape Breton Culture': 20; Devine, *Great Highland Famine*: 208; see also Hornsby, 'Scottish Emigration': 50,56.
40 MacKenzie, *Highland Clearances*: 250–61; Carmichael, *Carmina Gadelica*, vol. 3: 351; Stewart, 'Clan Ranald': 593–5.
41 See Maclean, Irish Folklore Commission, MS 1031: 421–6, 20 August 1947.

42 Extrapolated from Devine, *Great Highland Famine*: 206.
43 'The Cathcart Settlers', T.60.02: 6–9 (NAS).
44 See Harper, 'Crofter Colonists': 69–108.
45 D.J. MacDonald MSS book 52: 4886–7, January 1956. For further reminiscences by Duncan MacDonald along these lines, see D.J. MacDonald MSS, book 64: 5983–95.
46 See MacInnes, 'Highland Societies'; Gibson, *Traditional Gaelic Bagpiping*: 98, 192–3. Donald Ruadh eventually settled in mainland Glenelg, where he taught into old age, and died penniless in London in 1822.
47 Gibson, *Traditional Gaelic Bagpiping*: 174. See also MacKay, *Collection*.
48 MacKenzie, *Highland Clearances*: 390–1. For fuller accounts of the *Hector* voyage, see Bumsted, *People's Clearance*: 62 and Adams and Somerville, *Cargoes*: 71–6.
49 Adams and Somerville, *Cargoes*: 122–3. Cf. Bailyn, *Voyagers*: 191,198.
50 Collinson, *Bagpipe*: 133; Stewart, 'Clan Ranald': 311; James MacGregor Collection, GD 50/225/5 (NAS). For further discussion of the MacIntyres and the Robert MacIntyre emigration legend, see Chapter 5.
51 'People come together, though the world does not.' Carmichael-Watson MS 58 (A) 57, EUML Special Collections.
52 For the French Road MacIntyres, see Shears, *Gathering of the Clans*: 12 and MacEachen, 'The MacIntyre Pipers': 11. For the Boisdale MacIntyres see Shears (Ibid.) and MacMillan, *Hill of Boisdale*: 262–70.
53 MacAulay, SA 1998.68.
54 Gibson, *Traditional Gaelic Bagpiping*: 240.
55 'The Carthcart Settlers', T.60.02 (NAS): 18.
56 'The Cathcart Settlers', T.60.02 (NAS): 6, 11, 13, 17.
57 See Bumsted, *People's Clearance*: 65 and Devine, 'Paradox': 9.
58 *OT*, 8 June 1907: 5. Such assertions include a descendant of Donald MacIntyre of French Road recalling that 'very many of the violin players around at that time (early this century) could play the pipes' (MacEachen, 'The MacIntyre Pipers': 11); Gibson, too, points out that '[most] of those old pipers over here could [play] on two instruments – the fiddle as well as the pipes' (Anon., 'Bagpiping Revelations': 7).
59 Harper, 'Crofter Colonists': 80, quoting from the *Montreal Gazette*, 30 April 1923.
60 See Shears, *Gathering of the Clans*, vols 1 and 2, including photographs of considerable ethnographic value, historical notes, commentary and transcribed notation of traditional aurally-learned dance tunes from Nova Scotia.
61 An example in this regard is *Na Tri Seudan*, or 'The Three Treasures', an ensemble band organised by Moore which attempts to interlace the piping, dancing and singing traditions of the Gaelic community into seamless performance pieces. While the group ostensibly, and successfully, attempts to reintroduce the eighteenth-century Gaelic dance-piping context to a modern audience, the end product cannot help but be influenced by, for instance, elements of the modern pipe band tradition and the personal interpretation of its mainly non-Gael pipe corps. See 'Old Tunes Swing to a Rhythmic Revival' in *Piping Today* 3, 2003: 26–7. See also Rosenberg, *Transforming Tradition* for a wider discussion of the aesthetics of tradition in a revivalist context. For more recent thoughts in this regard in the context of piping, see Donaldson, *Highland Pipe*; West, 'Land and Lyrics'.

62 See *Am Bràighe* (Autumn 1998) for an interview with John Gibson involving broad stylistic questions; 'With Piper Alex Currie, Frenchvale' in *Cape Breton's Magazine* (no. 73, June 1998) on the playing and foot-tapping techniques of Alex Currie; MacEachen, 'The MacIntyre Pipers': 11 on stylistic elements of Joe Hughie MacIntyre's piping; and Flett and Flett (*Traditional Dancing*) on Nova Scotia piping's dance-stepping customs.

CHAPTER 5

1 MacDonald, *Highland*: 15.
2 Alexander Campbell's *Albyn's Anthology* and Capt. Simon Fraser's *Airs and Melodies*.
3 MacDonald, *Highland*: 14–15.
4 See Donaldson, *Highland Pipe*; MacInnes, 'Highland Societies'. Gibson (*Traditional Gaelic Bagpiping*) argues cogently that although the decline in the social stratum inhabited by chiefly pipers proved detrimental to the classical idiom, piping for dance and labour accompaniment carried on unaffected by the aforementioned conditions; this will be discussed below. See also Cannon, *Highland Bagpipe*: 73.
5 Dalyell, *Musical Memoirs*: 9; see also Donaldson, *Highland Pipe*: 64–5.
6 The Highland Society of Scotland was established in 1783 to officiate the contests due to accusations of bias among the HSL's judging panel that year. See MacInnes, 'Highland Societies'.
7 MacKay, *Collection*: 11.
8 See Cannon, *Highland Bagpipe*: 79–94; Gibson, *Traditional Gaelic Bagpiping*: 173–6; it was a symptom, essentially, of what Ramsay had referred to as 'the new model' of urban British values, among which literacy was foremost.
9 Matheson, *Songs of John MacCodrum*: 62.
10 Although contemporary documentary evidence and surviving Gaelic oral tradition (MacCodrum's *Diomoladh Pìob*, for instance; see also examples of traditional narrative in Chapter 2) suggest that the MacCrimmons were respected in their own hey-day and received pupils from throughout the Highlands to be schooled at their steading in Borreraig, much of modern-day sentiment toward the MacCrimmon dynasty is founded on a single published source – Angus MacKay's *Collection of Ancient Piobaireachd* of 1838 – and MacKay's reliability concerning Highland tradition has been questioned (see Campsie, *MacCrimmon Legend*). Samuel Johnson, during his visit to Dunvegan in 1773, famously referred to the MacCrimmon school as having closed a year earlier (see Johnson and Boswell, *Journey*).
11 MacDonald, A. and A., *Clan Donald*: 127. See also Sanger, 'The MacArthurs: Evidence': 13–17.
12 Pennant, *A Tour*, vol.2: 347.
13 Johnson and Boswell, *Journey*: 116.
14 Matheson, *Songs of John MacCodrum*: 252.
15 MacKay, *Collection*: 7.
16 As printed in Thomson, 'Niall Mór MacMhuirich': 21–2, omiting the final four stanzas.

17 Thomson, 'Niall Mór MacMhuirich': 18.
18 Collinson, *The Bagpipe*: 187.
19 MacDonald, 'Further Reminiscences'.
20 Ibid.
21 MacKenzie, *Sàr-Obair*: 67. Calum Beaton related a version of this anecdote to me in conversation on 30 August 1995.
22 Morrison, 'Clan Ranald Influence': 20.
23 Matheson, *Songs of John MacCodrum*: 253. At the risk of straining what may at first appear a pedantic point, one must temper Matheson's claim that Donald MacArthur drowned while ferrying cattle '*from* Uist *to* Skye' with a consideration of his sources and their veracity. He does not name them. Logan's historical notes in Angus MacKay's *Collection* of 1838 refer to the drowning, but he was cautious enough to say only '*between* Uist *and* Skye', which would indicate a degree of personal interpretation on Matheson's part if Logan was indeed his only source. Surviving oral tradition no doubt played a role, however. In either case, Matheson (or indeed Logan) may have been referring to North Uist.
24 GD 248/105/6/4; GD 248/105/6/5 (NAS), muniments of the Grant family, detailing accounts of deburgement for John Cumming, piper to the Laird of Grant, as prentice to Donald MacArthur of Skye from 1770 to 1774. Accounts show that Cumming boarded in MacArthur's house for fifteen months from 1773 to 1774. MacArthur gave Cumming a cassock in June of 1771. The middleman who brokered the apprenticeship appears to have been Dr John MacLean, MacDonald of Sleat's famous physician, who in a letter to Grant dated 18 July 1770 describes how MacArthur was MacLean's own recommendation as master for the fledgling piper. He goes on to detail his acquaintance with the 'Gerloch Pipers': 'the Grandfather of the present Generation has been a good Player and Composer But there has been a great Degeneracy Since his time' (GD 248/350/9/7).
25 MacDonald, *Clan Donald*: 127.
26 Buisman, *MacArthur–MacGregor Manuscript*: xxv.
27 Gray, 'The MacArthurs': 34.
28 Buisman, *MacArthur–MacGregor Manuscript*: xxii.
29 In the early 1950s, collector and tradition-bearer D.J. MacDonald of Pininerine, South Uist recorded his father, the late storyteller Duncan MacDonald, singing several examples of bardic verse with references to Clanranald's patronage; see D.J. MacDonald MSS, book 1: 62–3, and book 62: 5,862. See also Thomson, 'Poetry of Niall MacMhuirich': 289 and Cameron's *Reliquiae Celticae*: 252–3, for Niall Og MacMhuirich's references to the patronage of Allan MacDonald.
30 D.J. MacDonald MSS, book 45: 4,180.
31 D.J. MacDonald MSS, book 8: 676.
32 MacDonald, *MacDonald Collection*: 28; see also Thomson, 'Gaelic Learned Orders': 71 and Stewart, 'Clan Ranald': 307.
33 'MacDonald, John. Piper to the Captain of Clanranald. Was on 12 July, 1636, complained against along with others for seizing and plundering the ship *Susanna* which had been wrecked in the Western Isles – "striking and stripping the Marines of their clothes and leaving them nude and destitute", in December, 1634.' (Notices

of Pipers, *PT*, vol. 23, no. 4, 1971) See also MacKenzie, *History of the Outer Hebrides*: 289.
34 See, for example, MacGregor Collection, GD 50/225/5/27; MacDonald Papers, GD 221/118 pp 23 and 99, GD 221/114/1 (I); Breadalbane Papers, GD 112/29/51/6, GD 112/39/198/6; Logan, writing in MacKay, *Collection*; MacDonald, A. and A., *Clan Donald*: 125–7; and secondary sources such as Sanger, 'The MacArthurs: Evidence': 13–17; MacInnes, 'Highland Societies': 10. These references are not exhaustive. For discussion of the MacIntyres' service to Clanranald and MacNeil of Barra, see main text below. See Gibson, *Old and New World* for a thorough overview of the primary evidence linking MacIntyre pipers to all these families and regions. Dr Gibson does not go so far as to make conclusions on the inter-relatedness of the wider MacIntyre kindred, but allows the references to stand on their own.
35 Stewart, 'Highland Kindred': 307.
36 MacInnes, 'Highland Societies': 10.
37 MacKay, *Collection*: 10.
38 Morrison, 'Clan Ranald Influence': 21.
39 The single exception being the variant of the tale set in Bornish, noted above.
40 For the French Road MacIntyres, see Shears, *Gathering of the Clans*: 12 and MacEachen, 'The MacIntyre Pipers': 11. For the Boisdale MacIntyres see Shears (Ibid.) and MacMillan, *Hill of Boisdale*: 262–70.
41 MacAulay, SA 1998.68. Her reference to Skye origins may mean that she is descended from either of three incomers from that area who came to Uist in the eighteenth century: *Niall Sgiathanach*, *Dòmhnall Ruadh*, or *Ruairidh* MacIntyre (Maclean, *TGSI*: 500–1). In addition, MacAulay's reference to her ancestors as archers as well as pipers may represent a tradition in South Uist that surrounds a MacIntyre called *Gille Phàdruig Duibh*, Skye-born, who was in Uist about the mid-seventeenth century and who is remembered for his skills with the bow (Maclean, op. cit.: 500; Bruford and MacDonald, *Scottish Traditional Tales*: 417). *Gille Phàdruig Duibh* was not known for piping, however. MacAulay's reminiscences on her paternal genealogy may in effect represent two distinct Hebridean traditions.
42 Carmichael-Watson MS 58 (A) 57, Edinburgh University Special Collections. See Chapter 4.
43 Carmichael, 'Never was piping so sad': 79. Stewart ('Clan Ranald': 310) perpetuated the notion that one or more of Clanranald's MacIntyre pipers were among the last pupils to be schooled by the MacCrimmons in Borreraig, and his source was an article in the *Oban Times* published in 1930 by the naturalist and piping judge Seton Gordon (MacGregor Collection, GD 50/225/5/27); Gordon in turn may have read of this tradition in E.C. Carmichael's piece in the *Celtic Review*.
44 Breadalbane papers, GD 112/29/51/6.
45 Grant muniments, GD 248/105/6/4 and 248/105/6/5. See discussion on Donald MacArthur above.
46 See Stewart, 'Highland Kindred': 308–12.
47 GD 201/1/351/4 (NAS).
48 GD 201/5/102 (2 October 1759) and GD 201/5/1148 (23 November 1767).
49 MacDonald, *Uist Collection*: 173–8.

50 'A Circumstantial Account...' in MacKay, *Collection*: 10 (see also MacInnes, 'Highland Societies': 315).
51 Ibid.: 8.
52 MacInnes, 'Highland Societies': 315.
53 Stewart, 'Clan Ranald': 312.
54 Shears, 'The Fate of Clanranald Piper Robert MacIntyre'.
55 The MacGregor Collection, GD 50/225/5/27.
56 Campbell, 'A slight sketch': 58.
57 Eyre-Todd, *Highland Clans*: 247. See also Cameron's translation of MacMhuirich's original Gaelic record of the battle in *Reliquiae Celticae*: 170–1 (piping is not mentioned).
58 Carmichael-Watson MS, 58[A] 57, Edinburgh University Special Collections.
59 Although the war was fought over religious and political differences from the point of view of Montrose and Argyll, the Highland clans involved saw it as an opportunity to prosecute long unresolved feuds stemming from *Linn nan Creach*; see Stevenson, *Alasdair MacColla*; Cameron, *Reliquiae Celticae*; Ó Baoill and Bateman, *Gàir nan Clarsach*.
60 'Do thionail fecht Uibhisd, & Eige, mhuideord & arasaig' (Cameron, *Reliquiae Celticae*: 179; see also Stevenson, *Alasdair MacColla*: 140).
61 'Reimh runbhuiribh ro chalma reachtaigentaigh raghnallaigh' (Cameron, *Reliquiae Celticae*: 191).
62 'Mór-dhragh na falachd', from *Òran air Latha Blàir Inbhir Lochaidh eadar Clann Dòmhnaill agus na Caimbeulaich* by *Iain Lom*, in Ó Baoill and Bateman, *Gàir nan Clarsach*: 106.
63 Cameron, *Reliquiae Celticae*: 205; Stevenson, *Alasdair MacColla*: 257. For references to the battles cited above see Stevenson, op. cit.: 142, 156, 199, 201.
64 Gibson, *Traditional Gaelic Bagpiping*: 70, citing Buchan, John, *Montrose*, London: 1928: 120.
65 MacKenzie, *Sar-Obair*: 66. The translation is mine. Ranald was Allan's brother, who took over the leadership of the clan after Allan's death; the 'king doing well' is a reference to the Jacobite army affecting a stalemate with the Hanoverians at Sheriffmuir. See other examples of Niall Òg MacMhuirich's elegies in Thomson, 'Gaelic Learned Orders': 289–293.
66 Carswell, '"The Most Dispicable Enemy"': 29.
67 MacDonald, *Clan Donald*: 352. As opposed to 250 men, Eyre-Todd claimed that 'Clanranald could at that time put between 700 and 800 men into the field' (*Highland Clans*: 245).
68 Campbell, *Highland Songs*: 149. The translation is Campbell's. Alasdair Mac Mhaighstir Alasdair was born in the late seventeenth century of South Uist parentage and spent his life 'intertwined with the Clanranald and MacDonald clans, and with their territories' (Thomson, *Alasdair Mac Mhaighstir*: 5). Though he probably maintained a sporadic connection to South Uist throughout his life, he spent most of it in or around the mainland Clanranald territories of Moidart and Ardnamurchan. His involvement in the 1715 rising is inferential but his participation in the Forty-Five is well known.

69 Roseneath, 12 August 1745, to be found in RH 2/4/342/217 (NAS).
70 GD 50/229/3 (NAS), from the *Oban Times*, 24 December 1904. The historian Stewart ('Clan Ranald': 425, 434) believes that these men were transported to augment the Jacobite army at Falkirk. The letter's having neither address nor signature may cast some doubt on its quality as a source of evidence, but it is worth mentioning for its suggestion of South Uist's martial contributions.
71 RH 2/4/342/217 (NAS).
72 Letter from Roderick MacLeod of MacLeod congratulating Clanranald on his sons' commissions, 27 January 1757 (GD 201/4/81).
73 Letter, Clanranald to MacLeod: 'You need not doubt of my using all possible means to assist Donald in his recruiting, though I cannot help blaming him for promising more than he can expect reasonably to [perform?] in that way' (GD 201/4/85 [NAS]). *Dr. Walker's Report on the Hebrides*, compiled after 1771, estimated that seventy-two men from South Uist served in the Seven Years War (Adam and Somerville, *Cargoes*: 144). The practice of a chief recruiting men from his own holdings for military purposes at this time was undoubtably a remnant of clan-based society which had been dying out in previous decades.
74 Letter from MacLeod to Clanranald, 24 August 1758: 'I hope that your Stout son is by this time on his way home as his long stay in the country is truly of no advantage to him in many respects' (GD 201/4/86 [NAS]).
75 Gibson, *Traditional Gaelic Bagpiping*: 85, quoting from the diary of Sergeant Thompson of Capt. Donald MacDonald's grenadier company in Harper, J.R., *The Fraser Highlanders*, Montreal, 1979: 90.
76 See MacInnes, 'Highland Societies': 26; Dalyell, *Musical Memoirs*: 25. Pipers nonetheless remained unofficial in the British army until 1854 when a Piper Major and five pipers were allotted to several Highland regiments (see Henderson, *Highland Soldier*: 246 and Murray, *Music of the Scottish Regiments*: 113).
77 Knox, *Tour*: 136.
78 Burt, *Letters from a Gentleman*: 129–30.
79 D.J. MacDonald MSS, book 66: 6,169: '*Anns na seann laithean, bha e na chleachdadh aig daoine pìobaire a bhi air an tòrradh. Bhiodh am pìobaire a' falbh air thòiseach air na daoine uile gu léir agus e a' cluichd "port na marbh" air a' phìob.*' ('In the old days, it was customary for a piper to be at the burial. The piper would go at the head of all the people playing a "death-tune" on the pipes.') The translation is mine.
80 Campbell and Collinson, *Hebridean Folksongs*, vol. 2: 152. The translation is mine.
81 Campbell and Collinson, *Hebridean Folksongs*: 116. The translation is mine.
82 Campbell and Collinson, *Hebridean Folksongs*: 126. The translation is mine.
83 Campbell and Collinson, *Hebridean Folksongs*, vol. 2: 128: '*Chìteadh 'nad thalla muirn is macnas / Mairtfheòil 'ga bruich, crodh 'gam feannadh / Gachdan air òl, sùrd air dannsa, / Pìob is fiodhall 'dol 'gan deannruith / 'S cruit nan teudan 'cur ris an annsgair.*' ('Merriment and sport would be seen in your hall / Beef being cooked, cattle being skinned / Strong drink, furious dancing, / Pipes and fiddles run tightly together / And stringed harps joining in the ruckus.') The translation is mine.
84 '*Pìob bheag*' may not refer to what we know as the Lowland Scottish small pipes, but to a miniature set of Highland pipes which some say were used specially for dance-

music; in either case, any tradition of piping other than that of the full Highland bagpipe in South Uist has long been forgotten. It is not impossible that bellows-blown pipes were typically played in Uist at one point; Alexander Carmichael referred to 'bellow-pipes' as among the instruments played in the township of Ness in Lewis before the Free Presbyterian Church gained ascendancy there in the post-Disruption era (Carmichael, *Carmina Gadelica*, vol. 1: xxx).

85 Campbell and Collinson, *Hebridean Folksongs*: 68.
86 Gibson, *Traditional Gaelic Bagpiping*: 148.
87 *New Stat Acc*: 209.
88 Rea, *A School*: 132.
89 Rea, *A School*: 133.
90 D.J. MacDonald MSS, book 63: 5,948–58.
91 MacAulay, SA 1998.68.

CHAPTER 6

1 Rea, *A School*: xiv.
2 ED 7/1/80/3 (NAS).
3 *Third Stat Acc*: 614.
4 AF 39/16/3–5 (NAS).
5 MacAulay, 'The MacKenzies': 7.
6 *OT*, 26 March 1910: 2.
7 SA 1998.68.
8 SA 1998.69.
9 When discussing ceilidhs in her youth, MacAulay referred to the introduction of accordions in South Uist (as opposed to melodeons) for dance-accompaniment at around the post-Second World War period (SA 1998.71). Of other references to non-piping instrumental music in Uist around the turn of the century, the reader may recall in Chapter 4 a reference to the emigration in 1907 of E.C. MacRury, whom the *Oban Times* reported could play 'the violin and the bagpipe with grace and taste'; Chapter 8 below refers to *Domhnall Bàn Roidein*, a turn-of-the-century militia piper who may have been the 'D. MacDonald' who step-danced to fiddle music at a Daliburgh ball in 1895. References to the playing of clarsachs, jews' harps, fiddles and even small pipes ('*pìob bheag*') are plentiful in waulking songs ascribed to late medieval Uist, as was discussed in Chapter 5. See below for instances of melodeon music in ceilidhs and balls around that time.
10 Gibson, *Traditional Gaelic Bagpiping*: 181.
11 Dick Crawford's as yet unpublished compilation ('Queen's Own') of pipers' records from the Cameron Highlanders, 1854–1902, gives the names and brief details of seven South Uist pipers who joined the regiment in the nineteenth century. Two of them, Neil MacInnes and Lachlan MacCormick, were undoubtedly literate for having been successful competitors; the case of the others is less certain because they had no competitive record. These were, in order of enlistment: John Munro MacInnes, born c. 1868 and who took part in the Soudan campaign in 1884–5; James MacDonald of

Daliburgh, who enlisted in 1886 at the age of 23 having worked previously as a farm servant; Donald Morrison, who joined in 1887 and served at home stations as a piper in the 1st Battalion; Kenneth MacIntyre, who enlisted about 1889 and was for some time in the early 1890s stationed in Inverness as the Depot Piper; and John McLellan, whose term of service is uncertain. He died in Eochar in 1907.

12 Crawford, 'Queen's Own': 175.
13 *OT*, 15 January 1898: 6. See Chapter 9 for more discussion on this and subsequent Games in South Uist. A more in-depth look at Lachlan MacCormick's competitive record at the games is made then.
14 Gibson, *Old and New World*: 28.
15 The Societies had made plans to set up a school of piping specifically for army recruits, plans which dragged on from 1783 to c. 1816 and never actually bore fruit (MacInnes, 'Highland Societies': 117–23); plans which coincided with cash being awarded by the HSL for music written on the stave, such as in 1806, with the expectation that such material would herald a more 'scientific' and 'improved' method of teaching. In addition, one of the earliest publications of a staff-notated tutor to be sponsored by the HSL. was *The Bagpipe Preceptor* by Capt. Robert Menzies (1818), which first regaled the reader with anecdotes on the piping of the Fraser Highlanders at Quebec in 1760 and the 92nd Highlanders in the Peninsular War, then endorsed the military life in unsubtle terms: 'Many a Piper have I seen in the service, who would not take the best farm in the Highlands in exchange for his honourable post in the army, where they are courted and caressed by every body, especially the Ladies' (Menzies, *Bagpipe Preceptor*: 17). MacInnes ('Highland Societies': 123–6) comments on the *Preceptor* in more detail.
16 'As early as 1900 some Scottish regiments issued privately printed manuals of duty tunes for pipers' (Cannon, *Highland Bagpipe*: 49). Seton and Grant similarly asserted that during the First World War, 'every battalion has its own setting for every tune played in the band', and called for an army-wide standardisation of tunes (*Pipes*: 68). Regimental pipers were (and still are) required to play specific tunes in specific settings in the execution of their duties, which staff notation facilitates; this is even more pertinent for the pipe band since each member must play the same exact notes and grace notes of the tune in as synchronous a manner as possible. See Murray (*Music*: 209–24) for more on the various regimental duties and specific tunes of the military piper, and see also the various regimental collections of pipe music in required settings, such as the Gordons, Seaforths, and Scots Guards.
17 Fairrie, *Cabar Feidh*: 280.
18 Mackenzie, *Piping Traditions*: 113.
19 See Chapter 11 for Johnstone's and others' testimony in this regard.
20 SA 1998.68.
21 Sometimes there didn't need to be military piping at an evening's entertainment for the army's influence to be felt. At a soirée at the public school on Eriskay in 1908, for example, a young woman sang 'The March of the Cameron Men' to a 'crowded and happy assembly' (*OT*, 8 February 1908: 7.)
22 *OT*, 30 March 1895: 4.
23 *OT*, 5 March 1898: 6.

24 Ibid.
25 *OT,* 28 April 1906: 5.
26 *OT,* 3 March 1906: 4.
27 *OT,* 5 August 1922: 2; 4 August 1923: 7.
28 Crawford, 'Queen's Own': 187.
29 SA 1998.68.
30 Dalyell, *Musical Memoirs*: 9.
31 Gibson, *Traditional Gaelic Bagpiping*: 181.
32 SA 1998.68.
33 SA 1998.70.
34 *WHFP,* 6 December 1996: 21, in an interview with fellow piper Robert Wallace.
35 SA 1998.70.
36 Campbell, *Kilberry Book*: 8.
37 *OT,* 19 September 1903: 3.
38 This is the over-arching thesis of Donaldson's *Highland Pipe*; see also Cannon, *Highland Bagpipe*: 82; Gibson, *Traditional Gaelic Bagpiping*; and MacInnes, 'Highland Societies' for discussion of this and other problems besetting late nineteenth-century piobaireachd arising from a less than ideal competition system.
39 Industrialism, progress and missionary work by the Free Church all came together in the Victorian era to the degree that 'the qualities demanded in the Christian life had come to be regarded as a good foundation for success in commerce and industry' (Drummond and Bulloch, *Scottish Church*: 267); the new economic reasoning gave ground to the principle of competition as the best means of cultural preservation where piping was concerned (see Donaldson, *Highland Pipe*: 67).
40 Campbell (*Hebridean Folksongs*: 30) and Cannon (*Highland Bagpipe*: 90) at one time believed it was Archibald Campbell of Kilberry, scion of the Society and author of the *Kilberry Book of Ceòl Mór*, but Donaldson (*Highland Pipe*: 281) has presented a strong argument that it was in fact Archibald's brother Angus, also a founder member of the Society.
41 Piobaireachd Society Papers, Acc 9103/1 (NLS).
42 Ibid., 19 January 1903. The Society's summary opinion on the problems inherent in long tunes would have received short shrift from professional players such as John MacDonald, Inverness and his contemporary Malcolm MacPherson, grandson of MacDonald's foremost tutor Calum Piobair – for both of whom 'Donald Ban MacCrimmon's Lament' was a favourite.
43 The Society's most notorious shortcoming in its early years was the internal politicking which led non-players to take over most of the decision-making, in protest of which most of the real players resigned around 1905. Competitions accordingly continued to be judged, by and large, by well-meaning but ignorant aristocrats. Matters eventually improved, but enough damage was done to dog the Society's reputation more or less every since. See Campbell, *Hebridean Folksongs*; Cannon, *Highland Bagpipe*: 91 and Donaldson, *Highland Pipe*: 282–316.
44 Shaw, *Folksongs and Folklore*: 16.
45 Rea, *A School*: 46.
46 MacAulay, 'The MacKenzies'.

47 Fr MacIntosh was one of nine members of the South Uist Games Committee listed in the *Oban Times* of 8 September 1913: 2. Simon MacKenzie, Fr MacDougall and the factor MacDonald were also listed. The impetus behind the establishment of Highland Games being largely akin to that behind the South Uist Piping Sociey's formation, MacIntosh and MacDonald could have conceivably supported both groups; see Chapter 9.

48 The *Oban Times* of 6 June 1908 reported that 'Mr. Simon MacKenzie, lessee of the Castlebay Hotel, is leaving Barra. During his tenancy of the hotel, which dates from 1881, Mr. MacKenzie, by his genial and kindly nature has endeared himself to many ... When an epidemic of measles was rampant on the island in 1886, Mr. MacKenzie's beneficence was readily obtained, and no applicant for help went away empty-handed. The fishermen of Barra will ever remember his generous action in lending them money to buy boats, when the Normal Company became insolvent.' His tenancy of the Lochboisdale Hotel must have occurred some time before 1897, because in that year the *Oban Times* mentioned his name twice in that regard (30 January and 16 October).

49 See Anon., 'Major Finlay MacKenzie' in *PT*, January 1964: 6 and *OT*, 9 August 1924: 5 for mention of Finlay's position in the Society.

50 A extract dated 23 January 1923 from a collection of loose Piobaireachd Society Papers housed in the College of Piping, Glasgow. Norman MacKillop of Harris had served during the Great War in the 5th Battalion Camerons' pipe band along with many South Uist pipers. The Paisley Bard, Donald Ruadh MacIntyre, mentions MacKillop in his poem on the Germans' final offensive in 1918 (MacMillan, *Sporan Dhòmhnaill*: 41, 347; see Chapter 10).

51 SC 2001.024.

52 This incident is mentioned in MacKenzie's obituary in the *Piping Times* of January 1964: 6; it was written anonymously, but bears the tell-tale familiarity and style of Alex MacAulay.

53 Johnson, *Scottish Catholic Secular Clergy*: 127.

54 *Glasgow Catholic Directory*: 226.

55 Campbell, *Father Allan McDonald*.

56 MacAulay, 'The MacKenzies': 6.

57 *OT*, 6 August 1906: 6.

58 SC 2001.024.

59 Piobaireachd Society Papers, Acc 9103/1 (NLS), 15 December 1903.

60 Ibid., 19 January 1903.

61 Acc 9103/2 (NLS), 'Revised Rules of the Piobaireachd Society', 1912.

62 Acc 9103/1 (NLS), 20 September 1907. The committee minutes record: 'Three instructors were appointed this year to teach young pipers and a large number of applications were received – twelve of the most promising were selected and put through a course and their success at the various meetings this season shows the benefit they have derived.'

63 Acc 9103/1 (NLS), 6 July 1908: '... with reference to classes for the tuition of pipers *in the Society's tunes* [my emphasis] it was resolved to resume these classes during the Autumn and Winter of 1908 at Glasgow (to include pupils from Edinburgh),

Oban, Inverness and Aberfeldy, and the Secretary was instructed to make the necessary arrangements with the respective teachers at those centres, viz. MacDougall Gillies, MacColl, John MacDonald and Gavin MacDougall for twelve lessons each being given to four pupils at each centre.' For information on the MacDougalls as competitors and pipemakers, see MacAulay, 'MacDougalls of Aberfeldy'.

64 Piob. Soc. Papers, Acc 9103/1 (NLS), 5 July 1909.
65 SA 1952/119. Information derived from Calum Piobair's son Angus MacPherson (1877–1976), who was interviewed for the School of Scottish Studies by Calum Maclean in 1952.
66 Information on these piping genealogies can be found in numerous published works, including Campbell, *Kilberry Book*; MacNeill and Richardson, *Piobaireachd and its Interpretation*; Cannon, *Highland Bagpipe*; and Donaldson, *Highland Pipe*.
67 Crawford, 'Queen's Own': 192.
68 MacAulay, 'The MacKenzies': 7.
69 Morrison, 'Clan Ranald Influence': 21.
70 Anon., 'The Flora MacDonald Cup' in *PT*, March 1966: 8. Jessie MacAulay remarks on the making of practice chanters in the early years of the century in Chapter 8.
71 Piob. Soc. Papers, Acc 9103/1 (NLS); *OT*, 4 September 1909: 7.
72 Piob. Soc. Papers, Acc 9103/1 (NLS).
73 *OT*, 26 March 1910: 2.
74 Piob. Soc. Papers, Acc 9103/2 (NLS), 11 September 1913: 8.
75 Mackenzie, *Piping Traditions*: 6. MacDonald held this post until the outbreak of the Great War, when he was deemed unfit and invalided out from active service; see *Historical Records of the Cameron Highlanders*, vol. 3: 423.
76 See Piob. Soc. loose committee minutes, 11 September 1934 and 5 September 1936, held at the College of Piping; the committee discussed schemes by which MacDonald would be able to teach piobaireachd around his work commitments and his ill health; it was agreed that he be paid a salary of £100 a year and Col. Grant of Rothiemurchas agreed to approach MacDonald's firm (he worked for a distillery) to ask for two periods of two months' leave per year for this purpose.
77 Piob. Soc. Papers, Acc 9103/2 (NLS), 20 September 1912.
78 Piob. Soc. loose committee minutes, 5 January and 4 February 1913, College of Piping.
79 *OT*, 1 August 1914: 2.
80 *OT*, 5 August 1922: 2; see also Chapter 9.
81 Ross, *Collection*, vols 1–5, 1923–50; see also Donaldson, *Highland Pipe*: 371–4.
82 *OT*, 16 June 1923: 3.
83 *OT*, 4 August 1928: 7.
84 Piob. Soc. committee minutes, 20 January 1950, College of Piping.
85 Ibid., 19 January 1951 and 18 January 1952.
86 *OT*, 3 August 1929: 3.
87 The Piobaireachd Society's committee minutes of March 1920 record a discussion on classes to be held that year in the Highlands and Islands; Sir Colin MacRae pressed strongly for a renewed course in South Uist, claiming that 'we have had as many as sixty men and boys come distances of twenty miles to attend the course of instruction'

(Acc 9103/2, 4 March 1920: 15–16). He was also in favour of John MacDonald's re-appointment, but it fell to Willie Ross three years later.
88 Beaton, SA 1998.70.
89 *OT*, 20 August 1955: 10; 1 September 1956: 8.
90 Beaton, SA 1998.70.
91 SA 1953/256.
92 MacPherson, *Highlander Looks Back*: 66.
93 Morrison, 'Clan Ranald Influence': 22.
94 The Piobaireachd Society's music committee, which was responsible for arranging and publishing tune settings, fell into the hands of non-players in its early years and although they claimed to take the advice of expert pipers into consideration, what they eventually put out was largely criticised as unsatisfactory and at odds with conventional wisdom. Even when Archibald Campbell of Kilberry took over the editorship of an entirely new series and, later, produced his own collection entitled the *Kilberry Book*, John MacDonald in particular found his work sorely lacking. Many other pipers chose not to compete if it meant playing the Society's flawed texts. See Donaldson, *Highland Pipe*; Cannon, *Highland Bagpipe*: 89; Moss, *Pibroch*; Murray, 'The Maverick'; Ross, *Some Piobaireachd Studies*.
95 Piob. Soc. committee minutes, 20 January 1933, College of Piping.
96 Campbell, 'History of the Piobaireachd Society': 44.
97 Piob. Soc. Papers, Acc 9103/2 (NLS), 11 September 1913.
98 Ibid., Acc 9103/1, frontispiece.
99 From an unrecorded conversation with the writer in 1998. Nicol also taught the alternative setting to Norman Mathieson of Aberdeenshire in the 1970s, and a recording of it can be found in volume ii of the 'Masters of Piobaireachd' CD series, Greentrax, 1999.
100 Mackenzie, *Piping Traditions*: 113.
101 Gibson, *Traditional Gaelic Bagpiping*: 252.
102 This view has been stated most often with reference to *ceòl mór* performance. Francis Collinson noted of one celebrated Uist piper, the late Adam Scott: 'He studied under the late Pipe Major John MacDonald of Inverness, for long the doyen of pibroch players, who by his teaching has bequeathed to the island of South Uist a great piping tradition' (n.d.: 2). Seumas MacNeill similarly wrote that 'probably the place where [John MacDonald, Inverness] had the greatest impact was in the island of South Uist. When he first went there *piobaireachd* playing was practically non-existent, but soon this island became one of the most famous piping centres in the country' (*Piobaireachd*: 58); a comment which Hugh Cheape criticised for its lack of qualification (Review: 204). Peter Cooke was ultimately correct when he suggested that 'there is no present-day pibroch playing in the islands that does not stem from the teaching of visiting instructors sent by the Piobaireachd Society earlier this century' ('Problems of Notating Pibroch': 53) but this is not to say that nineteenth-century *ceòl mór* phrasing had entirely died out by then, as is discussed in greater depth in Chapter 7.

CHAPTER 7

1 Crawford, 'Queen's Own': 175.
2 Beaton in conversation with the author, 30 August 1995.
3 Morrison, Clan Ranald Influence: 22.
4 See MacDonald, 'Further Reminiscences': 1–13.
5 See Crawford, 'Queen's Own' and MacDonald, 'Further Reminiscences'.
6 Rea, A School: 86.
7 MacDonald, 'Further Reminiscences'.
8 Interestingly, the somewhat eccentric piper Simon Fraser of Australia, taught by one of the Bruces of Glenelg and whose repertoire was compiled and published by Barry MacLachlan-Orme (*Piobaireachd of Simon Fraser*), also claimed 'Lament for Donald MacLeod of Grisornish' to be the correct title of the tune more commonly known as 'MacLeod's Salute' or 'The Rowing Piobaireachd'. To my knowledge, however, he did not claim that the tune was derived from an Irish song.
9 In conversation with the author, 11 April 2003.
10 Beaton, SA 1998.70. Beaton discussed his first lessons with John Archie MacLellan with ethnomusicologist Dr Peter Cooke in 1970. See his article 'Changing Styles in Pibroch Playing, Part 2' in *The International Piper* 1, part 3, 1978: 12.
11 *OT*, 10 February 1906: 4.
12 *OT*, 4 August 1923: 7; 9 August 1924: 5; 15 August 1925: 7.
13 Beaton, SA 1998.70.
14 See Cannon, *Joseph MacDonald's Compleat Theory*: 27.
15 Interview with Calum Beaton on 30 August 1995 and also recorded in SA 1998.70. Roderick MacDonald of Barra was the father of Neil Angus MacDonald (1910–94), a piper who worked as a headmaster in Inverness for most of his life and who compiled a book of tunes (*New Bagpipe Collection*), based on his father's playing style. Roderick would have been extant as a piper and tutor in the Smiths' time, so Beaton's postulation is reasonable. The possibility of tuition from the Curries is also intriguing. The late Duncan Currie of that family, who had a keen knowledge of piping himself, maintained that his family were descended from the MacMhuirichs of Stilligarry, Clanranald's dynastic bards, which suggests a lateral shift of professional skill from *bàrdachd* to *pìobaireachd* among the family, possibly in the post-Jacobite era.
16 Beaton, SA 1998.70.
17 See Buisman, *MacArthur–MacGregor Manuscript* and MacDonald, 'Further Reminiscences': 8.
18 MacInnes ('Highland Societies': 151–94) discusses the ambiguity of tune titles in the *ceòl mór* repertoire during the 1781–1844 period. See also Cannon, 'Gaelic Names of Pibrochs'.
19 These tunes and others are commented on by the late Ronald Morrison of South Uist and Glasgow in an article for the journal *An t-Uibhisteach* (1999: 21), though, since he made no distinction between the MacIntyres to Clanranald and Menzies, the tunes are listed under '*pìobaireachd* compositions associated with South Uist'. One other tune begs mention which may be relevant but could not be properly included among the examples of *ceòl mór*. Adam (1960: 549), in a list of titles associated with

Clanranald, gave '*Cumha Mhic 'ic Ailein*' or 'Clanranald's Lament', which does not appear in any collection and, judging by the context of the passage, would seem to have been listed on the basis of oral tradition rather than documentary research. However, in Patrick MacDonald's *Collection of Highland Vocal Airs* of 1784, there appears a jig entitled '*Bhliadhna Dh' éirich an Iomart* – Lament for Clan Ronald' (p. 14). The Gaelic title is literally translated as 'The Year the Endeavour Arose' and may refer to the 1745 Jacobite rising, known traditionally as *Bliadhna Theàrlaich* or 'Charlie's Year'. The similarity of the English titles is probably coincidental.

20 The tune is found in the Piobaireachd Society's series Book 2 (p. 48) and Archibald Campbell's *Kilberry Book of Ceòl Mór* (p. 83).
21 Whyte, 'Historical, Biographic and Legendary Notes'. Henry Whyte customarily went by the non-de-plume of 'Fionn'.
22 Collinson, *Bagpipe*: 154; Poulter and Fisher, *MacCrimmon Family*: 8. The lore surrounding *Fionnladh a' Bhreacain* would be an interesting connection between MacCrimmon piping and Clanranald piping. The only other known references to contact between the two are the wealth of *Smearclait* tales depicting MacCrimmon pipers journeying to South Uist to test the Smerclate pipers' skill and the legend that one or more MacIntyre pipers received tuition at the MacCrimmon school in Boreraig. Collinson (op. cit.: 147) reports a tradition that *Fionnlagh a' Bhreacain* composed 'Waternish'.
23 Collinson, *Bagpipe*: 147.
24 MacDonald, unpublished MS, 1826: 13.
25 MacDonald, *Collection*: 68; Thomason, *Ceol Mor*: 16; MacLennan, *Piobaireachd*,: 2.
26 MacLean, 'Notes on South Uist Families': 500. See also Eyre-Todd, *Highland Clans*: 300.
27 MacKay, *Collection*: 10.
28 The tune appears as 'Boisdale's March' in the Campbell Canntaireachd (vol. 2: 28); it is also found in Thomason (*Ceòl Mór*: 25), who lifted it from Donald MacDonald's *Collection*; Lt MacLennan (*As MacCrimmon Played*: 5) gives the tune in his family's style, and another *canntaireachd* setting was written out by the Australian authority Simon Fraser (MacLachlan-Orme, *Piobaireachd of Simon Fraser*: 282).
29 MacDonald, *A Collection*: 56.
30 Whyte, 'Historical, Biographic and Legendary Notes'.
31 See MacLachlan-Orme, *Piobaireachd of Simon Fraser*: 157); Campbell (*Kilberry Book*: 85); Piobaireachd Society series Book 7 (p. 213); Thomason (*Ceòl Mór*: 249) and Reid (MS, 1826: 19).
32 See MacInnes, 'Highland Societies': 177. As a matter of interest, Daniel Dow recorded '*Piobrach Chlann Raonailt* or Clanranald's March to Edinburgh' in his fiddle tune collection of c. 1783 (Cannon, *Bibliography*: 18), so we know that the tune, like many others, transcended the bagpipe.
33 See MacKay, *Collection*: 10 and MacInnes, 'Highland Societies': 178.
34 Collinson, *Bagpipe*: 167.
35 Stewart, 'Clan Ranald': 308–12.
36 Cooke, 'Problems': 41–59.
37 MacDonald, SA 1970/309/7.

38 Whyte, 'Historical, Biographic and Legendary Notes'.
39 This tune will be found in the Piobaireachd Society's series Book 1 (pp. 8–10).
40 MacIntyre, SA 1952/146.A/2.

CHAPTER 8

1 This can also be seen in the Bulgarian tradition, where the *gaida* players are often men and the singers women (Rice, *May It Fill Your Soul*: 43).
2 *PT*, vol. 19, no. 6 (March 1967): 10–11.
3 MacAulay, 'Alex. MacDonald', in *PT*, vol. 22, no. 10 (July 1970): 8–9.
4 *Tocher*, iv: 131; Strand, *Tir a' Mhurain*: 50.
5 MacDonald, SA 1998.69.
6 *OT*, 1 August 1914: 2; 9 August 1913: 2; 4 August 1923: 9.
7 Angus MacLellan's biography and repertoire of tales were edited and published by the late folklorist John Lorne Campbell – see *Stories*; *Furrow*; and *Tocher*, iv, 1977–8: 130.
8 See Sound Archive recordings, section R1, in the department of Celtic and Scottish Studies, University of Edinburgh.
9 Lightfoot, SC 2001.024.
10 MacDonald, SA 1998.69.
11 One great competitive tradition in the Hebrides was the *oda*, a race-meeting which Carmichael described as accompanying festivities on St Michael's Day and consisting of 'the athletics of the men and the racing of horses' (*Carmina Gadelica*, vol. 1: 198). The last such meeting in South Uist took place, according to Dwelly, in 1820 (*Gaelic to English Dictionary*: 703; see also Gibson, *Traditional Gaelic Bagpiping*: 225).
12 Rea, *A School*: 82.
13 Competitive piping in and of itself was never entirely alien to old-world Hebridean tradition. A sizeable body of folklore on the MacCrimmons of Skye refers to competition among chiefs' pipers for the sake of clan pride (see MacLeod, *Tales of Dunvegan*: 18–23; Carmichael, 'Never was piping so sad': 80–2), and the *Piobairean Smearclait* tales in South Uist, which depict MacCrimmon pipers coming to test the MacIntyres' ability, imply a competitive spirit. However, these examples had their place firmly within the surroundings of traditional Gaelic social culture, while the 'staged' nature of modern-day competition is rooted in the philosophies of nineteenth-century mainstream Britain.
14 *Tocher*, iv: 132.
15 *OT*, 23 August 1952: 8.
16 Lightfoot, SC 2001.024.
17 See the anecdotal reference to 'Bess' MacCrimmon by John Johnston of Coll published in *OT*, 12 September 1896, and quoted in Donaldson, *Highland Pipe*: 212. Calum Beaton, in conversation in August 1995, referred to the local legend that Iain Dubh MacCrimmon (d. 1825) married a MacAskill woman from Skye and had eight daughters, two of whom married Uistmen – Effie to a *Geirinis* tacksman and Flora to a MacDonald man from *Peighinn nan Aoirean* – and brought MacCrimmon secrets with them to Uist.

18 Campbell, *Canntaireachd*: 33.
19 Strand, *Tir a' Mhurain*: 53.
20 Morrison, 'Clan Ranald Influence': 21. More on the MacGillivrays elsewhere.
21 *OT*, 4 September 1909: 7; 12 August 1911: 5.
22 In conversation with Calum Beaton, 30 August 1995.
23 Beaton, 30 August 1995. This particular interview was conducted in English and was not tape-recorded, so I have phrased Neil's 'D throw' question according to my notes. The late Ronald Morrison of Gerinish gave this anecdote in an interview with the BBC (date unknown) and to my recollection he quoted a different grace note technique in his version. Other versions of this short and whimsical legend doubtless exist among the elder generation in the Uist area.
24 Lightfoot, SC 2001.024.
25 *WHFP*, 6 December 1996: 21.
26 See General Frank Richardson's reminiscences of Sheriff Grant as a judge of piping in the 1930s and '40s in MacNeill and Richardson, *Piobaireachd and its Interpretation*. See also the *West Highland Free Press* interview with the late Duncan Johnstone (6 December 1996) cited above.
27 Angus was identified in the *Oban Times* review of the Gathering as one of John MacDonald's Daliburgh pupils, and he was not the only one to compete that day. Other pipers of South Uist origin played for the Gold Medal but did not place, and significantly, they were all pipers in the Lovat Scouts: 'A notable new competitor at Oban was Piper Malcolm [i.e. Calum] Walker, Lovat Scouts, another of Pipe Major John MacDonald's South Uist pupils. He played the "Bells of Perth" but unfortunately lost the thread of his tune and broke down. He is, however, a very promising player and with more experience should come well to the front. Pipe Major Angus MacAulay, Lovat Scouts, rendered the "Finger Lock". Through an oversight he omitted to play the first half of the second bar of the ground, rather an unusual occurrence for an experienced player. Apart from this lapse he might have been in the prize list ... Piper Angus MacQuarrie, Lovat Scouts, another member of the South Uist piping school, was handicapped by a very much over-used set of reeds. His tune was "Patrick Og MacCrimmon's Lament". He was apt to drag out the piece, but otherwise he gave a very good performance, which was full of expression' (*OT*, 15 September 1934: 2). These pipers receive some mention in Chapter 8, and their record in South Uist's Games can be found in the appended chart. Campbell also spoke of his experience at the Argyllshire Gathering with collector Jenny Fulton in 1987 (SC 87.07.B).
28 Lightfoot, SC 2001.024.
29 MacDonald, SA 1998.69.
30 Campbell, SA 1970/5, /6 and /309.
31 Dwelly (*Gaelic to English Dictionary*) defines *roidean* as the run-up or bounce before a great leap, but it may possess some other meaning in South Uist; perhaps Donald MacDonald was the athletic type. The nickname naturally fell to his sons in the course of time, as is standard practice in Gaelic society.
32 *PT*, vol. 18, no. 6 (March 1966): 7–9.
33 Flett and Flett, *Traditional Dancing*.
34 Rea, *A School*: vi.

35 *OT*, 2 March 1895: 5.
36 *OT*, 9 August 1913: 2.
37 *OT*, 1 August 1914: 2.
38 *OT*, 5 August 1922: 2.
39 Fairrie, *Cabar Feidh*: 280.
40 *PT*, vol. 40, no. 10 (July 1988): 35.
41 Johnstone, SA 1998.71.
42 *PT*, vol. 19, no. 6 (March 1967): 10–11.
43 Donald A. Morrison famously composed the 9/8 jig 'Donald, Willie and his Dog', which he composed after a trip up Ben Mór with fellow Loch Eynort piper, the William J. Morrison in question.
44 In conversation with Louis Morrison, 22 April 1999. Louis's sister Peggy MacDonald (née Morrison) sang *Fagail Bhòirnis* for the School of Scottish Studies Archives in 1957 (SA 1957/100, item 4).
45 In conversation with Louis Morrison, 3 September 1995.
46 MacAulay, SA 1998.71.
47 MacAulay, SA 1998.68.
48 See Anon., 'With Piper Alex Currie'.
49 MacAulay, SA 1998.68.
50 Jessie's use of the word *gleus* for 'reed' seems to be unique to South Uist; Fr Allan McDonald of Eriskay noted it (*Gaelic Words*: 141).
51 MacAulay, SA 1998.68. Donald John MacDonald, collector and tradition-bearer from Pininerine, South Uist, described a similar process of constructing chanters and reeds in his youth (MacDhòmhnuill, *Uibhist a Deas*: 30).
52 MacAulay, SA 1998.68.
53 See Chapter 10 for an expanded discussion on the difference in functional contexts between local and mainstream piping.
54 MacAulay, SA 1998.68.
55 MacAulay, SA 1998.68.
56 Moore, *Visions*: 92–4.
57 Calum Beaton was just one of many performers of song, story and music in South Uist whom Peter Cooke and Morag MacLeod, both researchers for the School of Scottish Studies, interviewed in the autumn of 1970. They recorded Calum discussing *ceòl mór* such as the 'Prince's Salute' with examples on the practice chanter, and singing its cognate pibroch song *Isbeal Nic Aoidh* (SA 1970/122/5 and /6); they also recorded the goings-on at a ceilidh in which Calum plays for an extended Eightsome Reel (SA 1970/145/2 and /3). He also discusses with Cooke how the local style of playing cadences altered with the advent of the Piobaireachd Society courses (SA 1970/2 and /133).
58 Beaton, SA 1998.70.
59 *OT*, 1 August 1956: 8; 15 August 1968: 7; 10 August 1972: 5.
60 *PT*, vol. 18, no. 6 (March 1966): 7–9.
61 Beaton, SC 2001.025.
62 England (1967), Blacking (1971) and Magowan (1994) present indigenous African and Australian examples of music symbolising identity, whether social or geographical.

While they are concerned more with structure and organisation than style, they show the capacity that musical expression allows on that front and the emphasis which scholars have lent this subject in the past. Examples from other South Uist pipers can either support or conflict with Calum's point of view. Angus Campbell once commented on when, as a young man, he would work as a labourer on the roads all day before competing at the Games in the afternoon, his hands 'all corns' (SC 1987.07.B), while Neil MacDonald has claimed that Willie Morrison's grandfather and piping tutor, Donald John, wouldn't allow him to work on the land as a boy, saying it would have spoiled his fingers for piping (informal conversation, August 1995).

CHAPTER 9

1 *OT,* 15 August 1931: 7.
2 Lightfoot, SC 2001.024.
3 See Donaldson, *Highland Pipe*: 197–203.
4 See Gibson, *Traditional Gaelic Bagpiping*: 223.
5 *OT,* 17 August 1895: 2; 3 August 1895: 2.
6 *OT,* 5 September 1896: 2; 4 September 1897: 2.
7 *OT,* 15 January 1898: 6. The correspondent remarked: 'Great praise is due to the committee that arranged the sports, viz: Messrs. D.J. MacDonald, Iochdar; Donald Morrison, Aird; Ranald MacEachen, Liniquie; Ewen MacDonald, Drimisdale; Norman MacPhee, president; Norman MacLeod, treasurer; Roderick MacKay, secretary; John MacEachen, assistant secretary.' All these names, with the possible exception of MacLeod and MacKay, suggest that they were native to South Uist. See Alasdair Maclean's lecture 'Notes on South Uist Families' in *TGSI*, vol. 53: 491–518.
8 That MacCormick, as a professional-level piper, was chosen to judge the piping events at the Ardvachar Games is surprising, since the major competitions throughout the nineteenth century were often marked by non-playing, unknowledgeable judges whose only claim to the bench was social superiority. It could be that this was the case only with the major Highland Society of London competitions in Edinburgh and latterly in Inverness and Oban, and that minor, peripheral Games actually fared better in that regard.
9 New Year's Day and Epiphany were traditionally celebrated with village-wide shinty matches throughout the Highlands and Islands in the nineteenth century, which MacLennan (1999: 83–99) interprets as a remnant of an ancient Irish Gaelic celebration; St Michael's Day was also celebrated with sport in South Uist.
10 Hamish Telfer ('Play, Customs': 117) remarks that 'events such as Highland Gatherings were often subject to the patronage and control of the local landlord or landlady. The timing of events, for example, often suited the social calendar of the patron more than the working pattern of the estate workers and other factions of the working class.' The Ardvachar games of 1898 probably had nothing to do with Uist's proprietor at the time, Lady Emily Gordon Cathcart, since she seldom visited the island and took little interest in her tenants' affairs. Funds for it came from the tenants themselves and the Catholic clergy.

11 *OT*, 26 July 1902: 6.
12 *OT*, 2 August 1902: 2.
13 *OT*, 12 July 1902: 2.
14 Ibid.
15 *OT*, 15 August 1925: 7.
16 *OT*, 18 July 1903: 6.
17 *OT*, 8 September 1906: 2.
18 MacLennan, 'Shinty': 83–99. See also Gibson, *Traditional Gaelic Bagpiping*: 225–6. According to Telfer ('Play, Customs': 113–24), villages in Skye commonly gathered for stone-throwing and shinty matches up to the 1850s, and similar activities constituted a typical Saturday evening in Lochgilphead in the 1860s and '70s; wrestling and leaping games were also indulged in by people throughout the west coast and islands, presumably to pass the time, when watching over a body the night before a burial.
19 For the Coll games, see *OT*, 12 July 1902: 2; for Tiree, see *OT*, 2 August 1902: 2; for the Howmore games in Uist, see *OT*, 12 July 1902: 2.
20 *OT*, 12 July 1902: 2; 9 August 1924: 5; 5 August 1922: 2; 4 August 1928: 7; 15 August 1925: 7.
21 Telfer, 'Play, Customs': 121.
22 See Emmerson, *Rantin' Pipe*: 7–26, 181–92. 'Pyrrhic' dances involved weapons and were meant for military drilling and exercise, such as the Dirk Dance, Gillie Calum and Argyll Broadswords.
23 *OT*, 4 August 1923: 7.
24 The piping and dancing that year were judged by Brigadier-General Cheape, John MacDonald of Inverness and Sir John Bartholomew of Glenorchard. Little is known of General Cheape's knowledge of dancing; MacDonald would have certainly been familiar with Highland dancing, but I doubt he was really qualified to judge it; and Bartholomew's tenure as a judge of piping at Askernish was quite long – from 1913 to 1927 – but there is no indication that he was a dancing expert. Bartholomew was a steadfast member of the Piobaireachd Society and its Music Committee (Campbell, 'History': 41) and over the course of years was considered 'a staunch friend to South Uist' (*OT*, 15 August 1931: 7) for his judging at the Games.
25 Rea, *A School*: vi.
26 See *OT*, 9 August 1924: 5; 15 August 1925: 7; 20 August 1927: 2.
27 The headlines appeared in *OT*, 9 August 1924: 5 and 13 August 1927: 2; see also 15 August 1925: 7.
28 Còmhlan Dannsa nan Eileanach (1995) *Hebridean Dance*: 14–15.
29 Emmerson, *Rantin' Pipe*: 162.
30 *OT*, 14 August 1926: 2. See Trevor-Roper, 'Invention of Tradition' for a discussion of Highland customs in the light of the 'invention of tradition'.
31 *OT*, 8 September 1906: 2.
32 *OT*, 7 September 1907: 2. It remains uncertain if this was the same John McLellan who served with the Queen's Own Cameron Highlanders and died in Eochar on 20 December 1907, as noted in Crawford, 'Queen's Own'.
33 *OT*, 12 August 1905: 2; 7 September 1907: 2; 4 September 1909: 7; 12 August 1911: 5.
34 *OT*, 4 September 1909: 7; 9 August 1913: 2.

35 *OT*, 12 August 1911: 5.
36 See MacMillan, *Sporan Dhòmhnaill*. For poetry concerning Uist pipers in the Great War, see Chapter 9; for an example of his storytelling, see his rendition of *Piobairean Smearclait* in Chapter 2.
37 Alex MacAulay (d. 1984), piper of Uist roots and correspondent for the *Piping Times* in the 1960s, wrote quite genuinely that 'if it was in you to be a piper, you would be a piper' (1961 source). This feeling has endured the era of systemic notation and organised instruction with surprising resilience. During one afternoon with Angus Campbell in 1995, he and his wife Bell listened as I played the ground of 'The Lament for the Children' in their sitting-room. They thought it a good performance. 'There must be something in you,' mused Bell, knowing that I was not Scottish and had come to the bagpipe from well outside the tradition as she knew it. 'My father used to play,' I offered. 'Ah,' she said, as Angus nodded, 'that explains it.'
38 See Chapter 5 under the subheading 'Patronage' and Jessie MacAulay's profile in Chapter 7.
39 See Alasdair Maclean's lecture 'Notes on South Uist Families' in *TGSI*, vol. 53: 491–518.
40 'Marbhrann do Dhomhnall Ruadh Mac an t-Saoir', in MacDhòmhnuill, *Sguaban Eòrna*: 64.
41 MacAulay, 'The MacKenzies'.
42 *OT*, 5 August 1922: 2.
43 *OT*, 4 August 1923: 7; 13 August 1927: 2.
44 *OT*, 15 August 1931: 7. For detailed reminiscences of Rothiemurchus as a judge and Highland gentleman, see MacNeill and Richardson, *Piobaireachd and its Interpretation*: 108–22.
45 *OT*, 5 August 1922: 2.
46 Anon., 'John Steele Contest' in *PT*, vol. 16, no. 11 (August 1964).
47 *OT*, 9 August 1924: 5. See the School of Scottish Studies' 'Scottish Tradition' cassette series, vol. 13: *Songs, Stories and Piping from Barra*, featuring Calum and his sister Annie.
48 *OT*, 16 August 1947: 7. The best published source for information on Angus MacAulay's life is his obituary by Anne Picketts in *PT*, vol. 48, no. 2 (November 1995). Anecdotes about his prowess still circulate in South Uist: Calum Beaton has referred to his composing of a competition 2/4 march known only as *Port Aonghuis Sheòrais*, or 'Angus MacAulay's Tune', which reportedly has been written down only in an unpublished collection compiled by Catriona Garbutt of Benbecula; and Rona Lightfoot described MacAulay as an extremely gifted player of dance-music as well as of the standard competition tunes (SC 2001.024), reflecting the innate survival of the dance function in the Uist musical tradition this century.
49 *OT*, 9 August 1930: 2.
50 *OT*, 5 August 1922: 2.
51 *OT*, 5 August 1933: 7; 31 August 1935: 8; 15 August 1936: 7; 12 August 1939: 3.
52 *OT*, 19 August 1950: 8.
53 *OT*, 30 July 1970: 2; 19 August 1971: 3.
54 *OT*, 20 August 1949: 3.

CHAPTER 10

1. When the late Gaelic storyteller Angus MacLellan was coming of age in Loch Eynort, South Uist in the 1880s, he found that he had three choices, as J.L. Campbell explained in *The Furrow Behind Me* (p. xiii): 'Escape from these conditions was only to be made by seeking employment elsewhere. For an islander this usually meant the armed forces or the merchant marine, where one could get by with a minimum of English; a job on a mainland farm where Gaelic was spoken; or emigration to Canada.' MacLellan enlisted in the militia in 1889.
2. The Fletts (*Traditional Dancing*) discuss the disappearance of old dances like *Cailleach an Dùdain* and the Threesome Reel in the Hebrides around the time of the Great War, to be replaced often by the Quadrilles and Lancers of mainstream influence; see Chapter 10 for further detail on the aesthetic implications of these developments.
3. The Cameron Highlanders were well known for their pipers since the Napoleonic Wars. Kenneth MacKay is famously credited with playing the pibroch '*Cogadh no Sìth*', 'War or Peace', around the square his battalion had formed in preparation for the Battle of Waterloo (Malcolm, *The Piper*: 159), for which he received the Victoria Cross; another Cameron piper, Donald Stewart, took second place at the Highland Society of London competition for *ceòl mór* in 1824 and first in 1825 (MacKay, *Collection*: 13). John MacDonald, Inverness was for years a Pipe Major in the Cameron's Volunteer and Territorial Battalions. To date, forty-four of the winners of the HSL gold medal, from Donald MacRae in 1791 to Alasdair Gillies in 1989, have served with the Cameron (or the amalgamated Queen's Own) Highlanders (see *Cabar Feidh*: 282–92, and Argyllshire Gathering prize-lists).
4. Adam, *Clans, Septs*: 468–9.
5. 'Recruiting from the Highlands' in *OT*, 7 May 1898: 3. The order was given by a General Chapman, commanding Scottish forces, upon inspection of the battalion's drill instructors in Inverness. Classes were immediately started under a 'Sergt-Piper Cameron'.
6. *Historical Records of the Cameron Highlanders*, vol. 3: 422.
7. Lindley, *Lord Lovat*: 96.
8. The Frasers of Lovat were traditionally Catholic; the 15th Lord in fact built a church at Eskadale and donated land in Fort William for a Benedictine monastery (Lindley, *Lord Lovat*: 24). Mass was even performed at the South African front for Lovat's troops (see photograph, Ibid.: 92).
9. *OT*, 25 July 1908: 7.
10. *OT*, 27 June 1908: 5.
11. *OT*, 5 February 1916: 2.
12. Over a thousand pipers are estimated to have been killed or wounded in the first World War; Bruce Seton remarked in his preface to *The Pipes of War* that 'with over 500 pipers killed and 600 wounded, something must be done to raise a new generation of players'(Seton and Grant, *Pipes*); see also Donaldson, *Highland Pipe*: 318–19.
13. Johnson, SA 1970.206.A2.
14. See *Historical Records*, vol. 4: 515, app. D. Cf. the Cameron Highlanders' Roll

of Honour at the National War Memorial, Edinburgh Castle, for the number of casualties specifically from South Uist and Benbecula.

15 There was some overlapping among regiments that makes definite casualty figures elusive. The Lovat Scouts, for instance, second only to the Camerons in recruiting from the South Uist area, consisted of two battalions that were amalgamated into the 10th (Reserve) Battalion of the Camerons in 1916 in order to build up infantry strength. Some South Uist men killed or wounded who enlisted initially in the Lovat Scouts were therefore named in the casualty lists of both regiments. See *Historical Records*, vol. 4: 389; Malcolm, *The Piper*: 190–1; Rolls of Honour, National War Memorial, Edinburgh Castle.

16 Seton and Grant, *Pipes*: 131.

17 Breaking the figures down, the 1st Battalion lost 9 out of 17 pipers; the 2nd, 21 out of 34; the 4th Battalion (presumably the 3rd fed reserves to the others) lost 8 out of 15; the 5th Battalion lost 14 out of 43, by far the largest band with most of its pipers coming from the Western Isles; 6 out of 18 were killed or wounded in the 6th Battalion; and the 7th, in which sixteen-year-old *Seonaidh Roidein* served, lost 11 out of 28. Data extrapolated from Seton and Grant, *Pipes*: 130–5.

18 Seton and Grant, *Pipes*: 132.

19 MacMillan, *Sporan Dhòmhnaill*: xviii–xix.

20 The German offensive lasted from March of 1918 to late summer, by which time the British (mainly Scottish) contingents were able to respond and end the war; the Camerons, led by Pipe Major William MacLean of the 5th Battalion band, were the first to cross the Rhine into Germany. See *Historical Records*, vol. 4: 118–23.

21 MacMillan, *Sporan Dhòmhnaill*: 40–2.

22 Ibid.

23 Ibid.

24 Beaton, SA 1998.70.

25 Cf. Seton and Grant, *Pipes*: 131–5 with the Camerons' Roll of Honour.

26 Johnson, SA 1971.43.A2.

CHAPTER 11

1 This is supported by existing scholarship on the Scottish Gaelic aesthetics of instrumental music. Shaw ('Language, Music') gave an unprecedented account of the internal perceptions of Cape Breton Gaelic fiddlers by essentially treating his subjects as non-western; Gibson (*Traditional Gaelic Bagpiping* and *Old and New World*) describes in broad scope the association of ear-learning and dance-accompaniment among Gaelic pipers in Scotland and Nova Scotia up to the Second World War era.

2 Morrison, SA 1970/334.

3 For a commentary on the eroding influence of television and like media on Gaelic tradition, see Bruford and MacDonald, *Scottish Traditional Tales*: 8.

4 See Flett and Flett, *Traditional Dancing* and Gibson, *Traditional Gaelic Bagpiping*.

5 See Flett and Flett, *Traditional Dancing*, 1964: 3–4; Emmerson, *Social History*: 143, 152. According to Gibson, 'even in Britain, where Highland society was affected by

the vast social changes of the 19th century, pockets of proud conservatism remained in the Hebrides and on the mainland where outside cultural influences, such as quadrille dancing, were powerfully resented and effectively resisted' (*Traditional Gaelic Bagpiping*: 4).

6   Flett and Flett, *Traditional Dancing*: 2. The Foursome Reel was undoubtedly a variant of the Four-handed Reel found in Nova Scotia, known as the *Ruidhleadh Cheathrair*, which the Fletts (op. cit.: 278–9) in turn associate with the dance found in South Uist and Barra, *Ruidhleadh nan Coileach Dhubha*, or the Reel of the Blackcocks.

7   Rea, *A School*: 82, 134.

8   Flett and Flett, *Traditional Dancing*: 87,167; Emmerson, *Social History*: 225, 231, 239; Carmichael, *Carmina Gadelica*, vol. 1: 206–7.

9   Rea, *A School*: 149–50.

10 MacLachlan taught solo dancing in South Uist from 1840 until his death in c. 1880. At least two of his pupils, John MacMillan and Archie MacPherson, taught locally after MacLachlan's death. See Chapter 8.

11 Rea, *A School*: vi and Flett and Flett, *Traditional Dancing*: 22.

12 Beaton, SC 2001.025.

13 Merriam, *Anthropology of Music*: 261–9.

14 Ibid.: 261.

15 Stokes, *Ethnicity, Identity*: 2–3.

16 Merriam names several studies up to 1964, including his own among the Basongye and Flathead (*Anthropology of Music*: 261–72). Finnegan (*Oral Traditions*: 131) refers to many more in recent times. Other studies of 'ethno-aesthetics' more relevant to this chapter are mentioned in the main text.

17 McAllester, 'Music in Western Apache Culture': 471–2.

18 Rice, *May It Fill Your Soul*: 48.

19 See, for instance, Dunlay and Greenberg, *Traditional Celtic*: 4, 12–14.

20 Cooke, *Shetland Fiddle*: 98.

21 MacAulay, SA 1998.68.

22 MacAulay, SA 1998.71.

23 Cooke, *Shetland Fiddle*: 98; Dunlay and Greenberg, *Traditional Celtic*: 13.

24 Beaton, SC 2001.025.

25 Flett and Flett, *Traditional Dancing*, 1964: 47.

26 Beaton, SC 2001.025.

27 Neil MacDonald of Garryhellie, as is described below, considered *ceòl cluais* to be mainly frivolous and not worthy of discussion. This was the strongest aesthetic rejection of ear-piping I had met with among local sources, since other pipers, even if literately trained, would at least concede to the rhythmic skill of ear-learned dance-pipers, if not their technique. MacDonald's feelings probably stemmed from the strong competitive piping tradition within his own family's history, as is discussed in the main text.

28 In conversation with the author, 22 April 1999.

29 Lightfoot, SC 2001.024.

30 Beaton, SA 1998.70.

31 Fraser, 'A Glossary', Adv 73.1.5–6 (NLS).

32 Bunting, *Ancient Music of Ireland*: 18–36.
33 McKean, *Hebridean Song-Maker*, 1997: 158.
34 Birdsong as the origin of pipe music is a concept firmly enmeshed in Gaelic musical folklore. See Chapter 2.
35 McNamee, *Traditional Music*: 57.
36 Shaw, 'Language, Music': 40–3.
37 Feld, *Sound and Sentiment*: 231.
38 Rice, *May It Fill Your Soul*, 1994.
39 Beaton, SA 1998.70.
40 Beaton, SC 2001.025.
41 Lightfoot, SC 2001.024.
42 McKean, *Hebridean Song-Maker*: 118–19.
43 Campbell, *Canntaireachd*: 11–12; see also Donaldson, *Highland Pipe*. The musicologist Jean-Jacques Nattiez discusses the lack of a Western-like musical vocabulary among indigenous peoples and the assumptions some ethnomusicologists make because of it during interviews with informants (*Music and Discourse*: 188–9). The movement 'hiririn' was a long A pibroch birl as discussed in an earlier chapter, though apparently lacking the introductory E note contained in the 'hiharin' of today.
44 Campbell, SA 1970/5.
45 Sharon MacDonald discusses the shifting of cultural classifications with regard to language use in her article 'A bheil am feur gorm fhathast?'(pp.186–97). Her concern is primarily the growing tendency of English labelling over traditional Gaelic concepts which may not be exactly equivalent, and the problems in translation which ensue as a result.
46 MacDonald, 'Further Reminiscences': 4; Cannon, *Joseph MacDonald's Compleat Theory*. MacDonald also referred to a man he had known in his youth as a *puiseartach*, a term which has eluded the compilers of dictionaries but, according to Dr Roderick Cannon, who raised the issue with MacDonald after his Piobaireachd Society presentation, was a local name for an inept piper. It remains unclear whether *puiseartach* hinged on transmission; that is, referring to someone poorly taught, and therefore playing badly, or to someone who played by ear – many of whom in South Uist and Benbecula were regarded as excellent dance pipers. My thanks go to Dr Cannon for his correspondence concerning Willie MacDonald's remarks.
47 Cannon, *Joseph MacDonald's Compleat Theory*: 106; MacDonald, *A Collection*: 4; Fraser, 'A Glossary', Adv 73.1.5 (NLS). Cannon (op. cit.: 105) and more extensively Ó Baoill ('Gaelic Musical Circles') discuss the various forms and uses of the *ludh* or *lùth* term in Gaelic music.
48 Fraser, 'A Glossary', Adv 73.1.5 (NLS).
49 Shaw, 'Language, Music': 41.
50 Ibid.: 42.
51 Beaton, SC 2001.025.
52 Johnstone, SA 1998.71.
53 MacAulay, 'Pipe Major John Steele': 21. 'The Shaggy Grey Buck', it should be noted, is the English title for '*Bochd Liath nan Gobhar*', a traditional jig used in Barra until the late nineteenth century to accompany the dance '*Cath nan Coileach*', or the 'Combat

of the Cocks' (Flett and Flett, *Traditional Dancing*: 169; see also Emmerson, *Social History*: 225–6).

54 MacAulay, SA 1998.68.
55 MacAulay, SA 1998.71.
56 Johnstone, SA 1998.71.
57 Gibson, *Traditional Gaelic Bagpiping*: 246.
58 Although Beaton in this instance says *taorluath* rather than *taorludh* – which, as I indicated earlier, was what I had heard most often from Uist pipers of the older generation – the reader should keep in mind that he was speaking within the context of literate piping and had just mentioned terms like 'doubling' and 'gracenote'; conceivably this could have influenced his use of *taorluath* in the spirit of a Freudian slip. It relates to MacAulay's use of '*ceòl*' for music and 'music' for staff notation.
59 Beaton, SC 2001.025.
60 MacDonald, *Òrain Dhòmhnaill Ailein Dhòmhnaill*.
61 Ibid.: 60.
62 Ibid.: 60, 255.
63 For an overview of what is known of the training of the professional bards of old, see MacInnes, 'The Bard Through History' in Neat and MacInnes, *Voice of the Bard*.
64 Beaton, SA 1998.70.
65 Ibid.

APPENDIX

SOUTH UIST GAMES' PIPING RESULTS, 1898–1999

The following chart details the piping events' prize-winners at the Games in Askernish from their inception to nearly the close of the twentieth century, excluding years for which records are unavailable or inconclusive. For space and formatting reasons, the chart is in two parts, each listing a different range of events: the first part covers the open pibroch (shown here as 'piob.'), open march, open strathspey and reel, open jig, local pibroch, local jig, local march, strathspey and reel (MSR) and junior grade march; the second part covers the pibroch confined to the Piobaireachd Society courses, the junior pibroch, open MSR, junior MSR and three separate practice-chanter events for children of various ages.

Ostensibly, the chart best illustrates the growing proportion of non-local competitors at the Askernish Games over the years compared to that of the local contingent, and names of non-locals have been shaded so that they may more clearly be distinguished. The chart has other uses, however. It measures generations of local pipers during the competitive era and how long each lasted at the top of the field before giving way to a younger crowd. It records many local families who have competed successfully but who have not been mentioned specifically in the present work. It traces the progress of individuals from practice-chanter competitions to the open level. And of course, it reveals the types of events put forward over the years. In the end, the chart is simply raw data, a century-long record of the competitive piping tradition of the southern Outer Hebrides; as such its uses are only limited by the purposes of those studying it.

I have of course attempted to be as accurate as possible in the detailing of names and placings, and any remaining inaccuracies in the chart are entirely of my own making.

	Piob. (open)	March (open)	S/R (open)	Jig (open)	Piob. (local)	March (junior)	Jig (local)	MSR (local)
1898 1st		MacLellan, John	MacLellan, John					
2nd		MacDonald, Allan	MacPhee, Norman					
3rd		MacDonald, Angus	MacDonald, Angus					
1905 1st		MacCormick, Lachlan	MacLellan, John					
1906 1st		MacLellan, John	MacLellan, A.J.					
2nd		MacLellan, A.J.	MacLellan, John					
3rd		MacIntyre, Kenneth	MacLean, Lachlan					
1907 1st		MacCormick, Lachlan	MacCormick, Lachlan					
2nd		MacPherson, Alex	MacLellan, A.J.					
3rd		MacLellan, Angus John	MacLellan, John					
1909 1st	MacIntyre, Angus	MacCormick, Lachlan	MacLellan, Gilbert					
2nd	MacCormick, Lachlan	MacLellan, Gilbert	MacCormick, Lachlan					
3rd	MacMillan, Donald	MacIntyre, Angus	MacDonald, Ronald & MacMillan, Donald					
1911 1st	MacIntyre, Donald	MacMillan, Donald	MacMillan, Donald					
2nd	MacCormick, Lachlan	MacLellan, Gilbert	MacCormick, Lachlan					
3rd	MacMillan, Donald	MacCormick, Lachlan	MacIntyre, Donald					
1913 1st	MacMillan, John	MacMillan, John	MacMillan, John					
2nd	MacIntyre, Angus	MacDonald, Archibald	MacIntyre, Angus					
3rd	MacIntyre, Donald	MacIntyre, Donald	MacLellan, Gilbert					
1914 1st	MacMillan, Donald	MacMillan, Donald	MacDonald, John					
2nd	MacDonald, John	MacDonald, John	MacMillan, George					
3rd	MacMillan, George	MacLennan, Neil	MacDonald, Archibald					
1922 1st	Steele, John & MacKinnon, George	MacDonald, Roderick	MacMillan, George					
2nd		MacKinnon, George	Currie, Donald					
3rd	MacIntyre, Donald	Steele, John	MacCormick, Lachlan					

Appendix

	Piob. (open)	March (open)	S/R (open)	Jig (open)	Piob. (local)	March (junior)	Jig (local)	MSR (local)
1923 1st	MacMillan, George	Steele, John	Lindsay, Archibald	Steele, John				
2nd	MacDonald, Roderick	MacAulay, Angus	Currie, Donald	MacMillan, George				
3rd	Steele, John	Martin, Finlay	MacDonald, Archibald	Lindsay, Archibald				
4th	Campbell, Angus	MacDonald, Roderick	MacAulay, Roderick					
1924 1st	Johnstone, Malcolm	MacAulay, Angus						
2nd	Campbell, Angus	Martin, Finlay						
3rd	Steele, John	MacKinnon, George						
4th	MacAulay, Angus & Lindsay, Archibald	MacMillan, George						
5th		Steele, Malcolm & Beaton, Alex.						
1925 1st	MacDonald, Roderick	Campbell, Angus						
2nd	Campbell, Angus	Steele, John						
3rd	Johnstone, Malcolm	MacAulay, Angus						
4th	MacMillan, George	Martin, Finlay						
1927 1st	MacDonald, Roderick	Steele, John		MacAulay, Angus				
2nd	Campbell, Angus	MacAulay, Angus		Steele, John				
3rd	MacAulay, Angus	Campbell, Angus		MacLennan, Neil				
4th	Martin, Finlay	Martin, Finlay						
1928 1st	Campbell, Angus	Steele, John		Currie, Allan				
2nd	MacAulay, Angus	MacAulay, Angus		MacAulay, Angus				
3rd	Lindsay, Archibald	MacQuarrie, Angus		MacDonald, Angus				
4th	MacLennan, Neil	Walker, William						
1929 1st	Johnstone, Lachlan	MacAulay, Angus	MacAulay, Angus	MacAulay, Angus				
2nd	MacAulay, Angus	Campbell, Angus	MacDonald, Angus & Campell, Angus	MacDonald, Angus				
3rd	Lindsay, Archibald	MacQuarrie, Angus		MacQuarrie, Angus				
4th	Campbell, Angus & MacLennan, N.	Walker, William	MacQuarrie, Angus	MacLennan, Neil				

	Piob. (open)	March (open)	S/R (open)	Jig (open)	Piob. (local)	March (junior)	Jig (local)	MSR (local)
1930 1st	Campbell, Angus	MacAulay, Angus	MacAulay, Angus	Currie, Allan				
2nd	MacAulay, Angus	Steele, John	Steele, John	MacAulay, Angus				
3rd	MacQuarrie, Angus	MacQuarrie, Angus	MacQuarrie, Angus	MacDonald, Angus				
4th	Lindsay, Archibald	Martin, Finlay	MacDonald, Angus	MacQuarrie, Angus				
1931 1st	Campbell, Angus	MacAulay, Angus	Steele, John	Steele, John				
2nd	MacAulay, Angus	Steele, John	MacAulay, Angus	MacDonald, Angus				
3rd	MacQuarrie, Angus	MacLennan, Neil	Campbell, Angus	MacQuarrie, Angus				
4th	MacLennan, Neil	Campbell, Angus	MacDonald, Angus	MacLennan, Neil				
5th	Walker, William	MacMillan, George	Walker, William	Campbell, Angus				
6th	MacDonald, Angus	MacDonald, Angus	MacQuarrie, Angus	Walker, William				
(second piob. event)								
1st	MacQuarrie, Angus							
2nd	Walker, William							
3rd	Lindsay, Archibald							
1932 1st	Campbell, Angus	MacQuarrie, Angus	MacQuarrie, Angus	MacDonald, Angus				
2nd	MacAulay, Angus	MacAulay, Angus	Steele, John	MacAulay, Angus				
3rd	MacQuarrie, Angus	Steele, John	MacDonald, Angus	Campbell, Angus & MacQuarrie, Angus				
4th	MacKinnon, John	Campbell, Angus	Campbell, Angus					
5th	MacDonald, Angus	Walker, William	MacAulay, Angus					
6th	Lindsay, Archibald	MacDonald, Angus	Walker, William					
1933 1st	Campbell, Angus	MacAulay, Angus	Steele, John	MacDonald, Angus				
2nd	MacQuarrie, Angus	MacDonald, R	MacNiven, Owen	MacNiven, Owen				
3rd	MacAulay, Angus	Campbell, Angus	MacQuarrie, Angus	Walker, Malcolm				
4th	MacLennan, Neil	MacQuarrie, Angus	MacAulay, Angus					
5th	MacDonald, Angus	Martin, Finlay	MacDonald, R					
6th	MacMillan, George	MacLennan, Neil	Campbell, Angus					
1935 1st	Campbell, Angus	Bain, Corporal	MacAulay, Angus	MacDonald, Angus				

Appendix

	Piob. (open)	March (open)	S/R (open)	Jig (open)	Piob. (local)	March (junior)	Jig (local)	MSR (local)
2nd	MacAulay, Angus	MacNiven, Owen	Smith, I.	Smith, I.				
3rd	Bain, Corporal	MacAulay, Angus	MacNiven, Owen	MacLennan, Neil				
4th	Kennedy, Hugh	Smith, I.	MacDonald, Angus					
5th	Walker, Malcolm & Smith, I.	MacLean, D. & Walker, W.	Scott, Adam & Campbell, Angus					
1936 1st	Walker, Malcolm	Wilson, John	Wilson, John	MacDonald, Angus				
2nd	Wilson, John	MacNiven, Owen	MacNiven, Owen	Wilson, John				
3rd	Campbell, Angus	Walker, Malcolm	MacDonald, Angus	Scott, Adam				
4th	MacLennan, Neil	MacLennan, Neil	Scott, Adam					
5th	MacDonald, Angus	Scott, Adam	Walker, Malcolm					
6th	Walker, William	Walker, William	Walker, William					
1937 1st	Campbell, Angus	MacAulay, Angus	MacAulay, Angus	MacAulay, Angus				
2nd	MacLennan, Neil	Scott, Adam	MacNiven, Owen	MacLennan, Neil				
3rd	MacAulay, Angus	Steele, John	Scott, Adam	Scott, Adam				
4th	Walker, William	MacLennan, Neil	Steele, John					
5th	MacNiven, Owen	Lawrie, P/M	Campbell, Angus					
6th	Scott, Adam	Walker, William	MacLennan, Neil					
1938 1st	Wilson, John	Wilson, John	Wilson, John	Wilson, John				
2nd	Campbell, Angus & Robertson, J.B.	MacAulay, Angus	MacAulay, Angus	MacAulay, Angus				
3rd		Robertson, J.B.	Robertson, J.B.	Walker, William				
4th	Walker, William	MacLean, D.	MacDonald, Angus					
5th	Scott, Adam	Walker, William	MacLean, D.					
6th	MacLean, D.	Campbell, Angus	Scott, Adam					
1939 1st	Campbell, Angus	MacNiven, Owen	MacNab, Archie					
2nd	MacAulay, Angus	MacNab, Archie	Wilson, John					
3rd	MacNab, Archie	MacAulay, Angus	MacAulay, Angus					
4th	MacNiven, Owen	Wilson, John	Scott, Adam					
5th	Wilson, John	Scott, Adam						

	Piob. (open)	March (open)	S/R (open)	Jig (open)	Piob. (local)	March (junior)	Jig (local)	MSR (local)
6th	MacLennan, Neil	Campbell, Angus						
1946 1st	Campbell, Angus	MacFarquar, Peter	MacKinnon, John	MacDonald, Angus				
2nd	MacAulay, Angus	MacAulay, Angus	MacDonald, Angus	Pearston, Thomas				
3rd	MacLennan, Neil	MacKinnon, John	MacAulay, Angus	MacFarquar, Peter				
4th	Scott, Adam	Walker, William	MacFarquar, Peter	MacNeill, James				
5th	MacKinnon, John	MacLean, Donald	Scott, Adam					
6th	MacLean, Donald	MacLennan, Neil	Walker, William					
1947 1st	MacAulay, Angus	MacAulay, Angus	MacAulay, Angus	MacAulay, Angus				
2nd	Morrison, Roderick	MacFadyen, John	MacDonald, Angus	Scott, Adam				
3rd	Scott, Adam	Scott, Adam	Scott, Adam	Morrison, Donald				
1948 1st	MacAulay, Angus	MacAulay, Angus	MacFadyen, John	MacFadyen, John				
2nd	Campbell, Angus	MacFadyen, John	Lawrie, Ronald	MacAulay, Angus				
3rd	Lawrie, Ronald	Lawrie, Ronald	Morrison, Donald	Morrison, Donald				
1949 1st	Garroway, John	MacLean, P/M	MacLean, P/M	Garroway, John				
2nd	MacLean, P/M	MacAulay, Angus	Garroway, John	Johnstone, Duncan				
3rd	Lawrie, Ronald	Garroway, John	MacAulay, Angus	MacLean, P/M				
4th	Campbell, Angus	Morrison, Alfred	Lawrie, Ronald	Walker, William				
5th	Morrison, Alfred	Johnstone, Duncan	Walker, William					
6th	Walker, W. & Morrison, R.	Campbell, Angus	Johnstone, D. MacMillan, N.					
1950 1st	Garroway, John	MacLeod, Donald	Ramsay, P/M	MacLeod, Donald				
2nd	Morrison, Alfred	MacLean, Donald	MacLeod, Donald	Ramsay, P/M				
3rd	Morrison, Ronald	Ramsay, P/M	MacLean, Donald	MacLean, Donald				
4th	Morrison, D.A.	Garroway, John	Garroway, John	Morrison, Donald A.				
5th	MacLean, Donald	Johnstone, Duncan	Johnstone, Duncan					
6th	Campbell, Angus	Lawrie, D.	Morrison, D.A.					
1951 1st	Burgess, John	Burgess, John	MacAuley, Angus	Burgess, John				
2nd	MacAulay, Angus	MacAulay, Angus	Burgess, John	MacKay, P/M				
3rd	MacFadyen, John	MacFarquar, Peter	MacLean, Donald	MacAulay, Angus				

Appendix

	Piob. (open)	March (open)	S/R (open)	Jig (open)	Piob. (local)	March (junior)	Jig (local)	MSR (local)
1952 1st	MacKay, P/M	MacLeod, P/M	MacLeod, P/M	MacLeod, P/M				
2nd	MacLeod, P/M	MacLean, P/M	MacAuley, Angus	Johnstone, D.				
3rd	MacLean, P/M	MacAulay, Angus	MacKay, P/M	MacKay, P/M				
1953 1st	MacKay, P/M	MacLeod, Donald	MacKay, P/M	MacKay, P/M	MacDonald, Rona		MacDonald, Neil J.	MacLean, Norman
2nd	MacNeill, Seumas	MacKay, P/M	MacNab, Major	MacNab, Major	Campbell, Calum		Campbell, Angus	MacDonald, Rona
3rd	MacGillivray, D.	MacNab, Major	MacLeod, Donald	Johnstone, Duncan	Scott, Adam		MacKillop, Andrew	Scott, Adam
4th	MacLeod, Donald	MacNeill, Seumas	MacNeill, Seumas	Scott, Adam	MacLean, Norman		Scott, Adam	Campbell, Angus
5th	Campbell, Angus	MacDonald, Rona	Johnstone, Duncan					Campbell, Malcolm
6th	Beaton, Calum	MacKillop, Andrew	Forbes, T.					
1954 1st	Morrison, Ronald	MacDonald, William	Morrison, Donald	MacDonald, W.	Morrison, Ronald		Morrison, Donald	Morrison, Donald
2nd	Morrison, Donald	MacKillop, W.	MacKillop, W.	Manson, B.	Johnstone, George		MacDonald, Neil J.	MacDonald, Neil J.
3rd	Campbell, A.	Morrison, Donald	MacDonald, W.	MacKillop, A.	Morrison, Donald		MacKillop, Andrew	MacKillop, W.
4th	Johnstone, G.	Manson, B.	MacDonald, Rona	Morrison, Donald				
5th	MacDonald, Rona	Johnstone, G.	MacInnes, James					
6th		MacDonald, Neil J.	Johnstone, G.					
1955 1st	Nicol, P/M	Burgess, John	MacDonald, William	Burgess, John				
2nd	MacDonald, William	MacKillop, William	MacKillop, William	MacDonald, William				
3rd	Burgess, John	Johnstone, Duncan	Burgess, John	Morrison, Ronald				
4th	Morrison, Ronald	MacDonald, William	Johnstone, Duncan	Johnstone, Duncan				
5th	MacKillop, William	Scott, Adam	Nicol, P/M					
6th		Morrison, Ronald	MacKillop, Andrew					
1956 1st	MacDonald, William	MacDonald, William	MacDonald, William	Beaton, Calum				
2nd	MacLean, P/M	MacLean, P/M	Walker, William	MacDonald, William				
3rd	Nicol, P/M	Nicol, P/M	Beaton, Calum	MacKillop, Andrew				
4th	Walker, William	Walker, William	MacKillop, Andrew	Walker, William				
5th	Beaton, Calum	MacKillop, Andrew	Campbell, Angus					
1957 1st	Morrison, Ronald	MacDonald, William	Brown, P/M R	MacDonald, William	Walker, William		MacKinnon, Angus	Scott, Adam
2nd	Brown, P/M R.	Brown, P/M R.	MacDonald, William	Brown, P/M R.	Scott, Adam		MacDonald, Angus	Walker, William

When Piping Was Strong

	Piob. (open)	March (open)	S/R (open)	Jig (open)	Piob. (local)	March (junior)	Jig (local)	MSR (local)
3rd	MacDonald, William	Young, J.	MacKillop, William	MacKillop, William	Campbell, Angus		MacKillop, Andrew	Beaton, Calum
4th	MacKillop, Andrew	MacKillop, William	Young, J.	MacKillop, Andrew				
5th	MacKillop, William	Fraser, L/Cpl	Beaton, Calum					
6th	Young, J.	Beaton, Calum	Nicol, P/M					
1958 1st	MacDougall, John	MacDougall, John	Morrison, Donald	Morrison, Donald	MacKinnon, Angus		Walker, William	MacKinnon, Angus
2nd	Morrison, Donald	MacFadyen, Iain	Young, James	MacDougall, John	Walker, William		MacKinnon, Angus	Morrison, Angus
3rd	MacFadyen, Iain	Young, James	MacGregor, P/M	Young, James	Scott, Adam		MacCormick, John	Walker, Angus P.
4th	Young, James	Morrison, Donald	MacLean, P/M	MacFadyen, Iain	MacCormick, John		Walker, Angus P.	MacCormick, John
5th	MacLean, P/M	MacGregor, P/M	Beaton, Calum					
6th	Morrison, Ronald	MacKillop, Andrew	Morrison, Ronald					
1959 1st	Brown, P/M R.M.	MacDougall, John	Morrison, Donald	Morrison, Donald				
2nd	MacDougall, John	Brown, P/M	MacDougall, John	Dodds, Allan				
3rd	Morrison, Donald	Morrison, Donald	MacFadyen, Iain	MacDougall, John				
4th	MacLean, Donald	Dodds, Allan	Brown, P/M	MacKillop, Andrew				
5th	Fraser, Ian	MacFadyen, Iain	Morrison, Alfred					
1960 1st	MacFadyen, Iain							
2nd	Burgess, John							
3rd	Morrison, Donald							
4th	MacDonald, William							
5th	MacDonald, Alex							
1961 1st	Young, James	MacCormick, John	Young, James	Young, James				
2nd	MacFadyen, Iain	MacDonald, William	MacDonald, Cpl William	MacDonald, Cpl William				
3rd	MacDonald, William	MacDonald, Sgt William	MacDonald, William	MacDonald, William				
1962 1st.	Lawrie, Ronald	Young, James	Burgess, John	MacDonald, Sgt. William				
2nd	Young, James	MacNeill, Seumas	MacDonald, Sgt William	Burgess, John				
3rd	MacDonald, Kenneth	MacDonald, William	Morrison, Ronald	Lawrie, Ronald				
4th	Morrison, Ronald	Burgess, John	MacDonald, Kenneth	MacDonald, William				
5th	MacDonald, William	MacDonald, Kenneth	MacDonald, William					

Appendix

	Piob. (open)	March (open)	S/R (open)	Jig (open)	Piob. (local)	March (junior)	Jig (local)	MSR (local)
1963 1st	Burgess, John	Burgess, John	Campbell, C.	MacAskill, J.				
2nd	Morrison, Ronald	Campbell, C.	Burgess, John	Campbell, C.				
3rd	MacDonald, P/M Angus	MacKillop, A.	MacPhail, A.	MacKillop, A.				
1964 1st	Young, James	Burgess, John	Young, James					
2nd	MacLellan, P/M John	MacLellan, P/M John	Burgess, John					
3rd	Burgess, John	MacKillop, Cpl William	MacKillop, Cpl William					
4th	Morrison, Ronald	MacDonald, Rona	MacDonald, Rona					
5th	Campbell, Calum	Young, James	Campbell, Calum					
1965 1st	Brown, P/M R.U.	MacLellan, P/M John	MacLellan, P/M John	MacLellan, P/M John				
2nd	MacLellan, P/M John	Morrison, Ronald	MacFadyen, Iain	Morrison, William				
3rd	Campbell, Calum	Brown, P/M R.U.	Brown, P/M R.U.	MacFadyen, Iain				
1966 1st	MacDonald, Kenneth	MacDonald, Rona	MacDonald, Kenneth	Morrison, William				
2nd	MacDonald, Rona	MacDonald, Kenneth	MacDonald, Rona	MacDonald, Kenneth				
3rd	Campbell, Calum	Forbes, Peter	MacCormick, John	Johnson, Norman				
4th	Lindsay, Donald	Campbell, Calum	Campbell, Calum	Campbell, Calum				
5th	Forbes, Peter	Lindsay, Donald	Forbes, Peter					
1967 1st	MacDonald, Rona	MacDonald, Rona	MacAskill, John	MacDonald, Rona				
2nd	MacAskill, John	MacAskill, John	Morrison, William	MacAskill, John				
3rd	MacCormick, John	MacCormick, John	MacCormick, John	Morrison, William				
4th	Campbell, Calum	Campbell, Calum	Campbell, Calum	Lindsay, Archie				
5th	Morrison, William	Lindsay, Archie	Lindsay, Archie					
1968 1st	Beaton, Calum	MacCormick, John	MacCormick, John	MacDonald, William				
2nd	MacDonald, William	MacDonald, William	Morrison, William	Morrison, William				
3rd	Morrison, William	Morrison, William	MacDonald, William	Campbell, Calum				
1970 1st	Lawrie, P/M Ronald	Lawrie, P/M Ronald	MacLellan, Iain	MacDonald, Rona				
2nd	MacLellan, Angus J.	MacLellan, Iain	MacDonald, Rona	MacLellan, Iain				
3rd	MacDonald, Ronald	MacFadyen, Iain	Wilson, Joe	MacFadyen, Iain				
1971 1st	MacDonald, Rona	MacDonald, Rona	MacDonald, Rona	Beaton, Calum				

287

	Piob. (open)	March (open)	S/R (open)	Jig (open)	Piob. (local)	March (junior)	Jig (local)	MSR (local)
2nd	Beaton, Calum	Morrison, Fred	Beaton, Calum	Morrison, Fred				
3rd	Morrison, Fred	Beaton, Calum	Johnson, Norman	Scott, John				
1972 1st	Morrison, William	MacDonald, Angus	MacDonald, Angus	Campbell, Angus				
2nd	Campbell, Calum	Graham, John	Morrison, William	MacDonald, Angus				
3rd	Graham, John	Morrison, William	Graham, John	Morrison, William				
1973 1st	MacDougall, John	MacDougall, John	Morrison, William	Morrison, William				
2nd	Morrison, P/M Donald	Morrison, William	Morrison, Donald	Gillies, Norman				
3rd	Smith, Neil	MacDonald, Rona	MacDougall, John	MacDonald, Rona				
1975 1st	Gillies, P/M Roderick	Smith, Neil	Smith, Neil	Forbes, Peter				
2nd	Smith, Neil	Gillies, P/M Roderick	Gillies, P/M Roderick	Gillies, P/M Roderick				
3rd	Campbell, Calum	MacDonald, Donald	Campbell, Calum	Campbell, Calum				
1976 1st	MacDonald, Kenneth	Duncan, Iain	MacDonald, Angus	MacDonald, Angus				
2nd	Duncan, Iain	Smith, Neil	MacDonald, Kenneth	MacDonald, Kenneth				
3rd	MacRae, Evan	MacDonald, Kenneth	Smith, Neil	Duncan, Iain				
1977 1st	Duncan, Iain	Duncan, Iain	Lindsay, Archie	Smith, Neil				
2nd	Menzies, Jim	Gillies, Roddy	Gillies, Roddy	Duncan, Iain				
3rd	Hoffman, Fritz	Smith, Neil	Not given	Lindsay, Archie				
4th	Gillies, Roddy	Menzies, Jim	Smith, Neil	Hoffman, Fritz				
5th	Beaton, Calum	Hoffman, Fritz	Duncan, Iain					
1979 1st	MacDonald, Kenneth	Burgess, John	Morrison, Iain	Grant, Patrick				
2nd	Duncan, Iain	MacDonald, Kenneth	MacDonald, Kenneth	Wallace, Robert				
3rd	Burgess, John	Morrison, Iain	Burgess, John	Morrison, Iain				
4th	Grant, Patrick	MacDonald, Donald	Campbell, Gordon					
1981 1st	MacDonald, Kenneth	Grant, Patrick	MacDonald, Kenneth	Grant, Patrick				
2nd	Campbell, Calum	MacInnes, Hugh	MacInnes, Hugh	MacDonald, Kenneth				
3rd	Grant, Patrick	MacDonald, Kenneth	MacPherson, Alexander	Smith, Neil				
4th	Morrison, Louis	MacPherson, Alasdair	Campbell, Calum	MacDonald, Donald				
5th	Smith, Neil	MacDonald, Donald	Steele, George	Morrison, Louis				

Appendix

	Piob. (open)	March (open)	S/R (open)	Jig (open)	Piob. (local)	March (junior)	Jig (local)	MSR (local)
1982 1st	Morrison, Louis	MacInnes, Hugh	MacLeod, Roderick	MacLeod, Roderick				
2nd	Smith, Neil	Morrison, Louis	MacInnes, Hugh	MacInnes, Hugh				
3rd	MacLeod, Roderick	Smith, Neil	Begg, James	Monk, Ronald				
4th	Monk, Ronald	Monk, Ronald	Monk, Ronald	Morrison, Louis				
5th	Gillies, P/M Norman	MacPherson, Iain	Morrison, Louis	Smith, Neil				
1983 1st	Wallace, Robert	MacInnes, Hugh	MacBride, Donald	MacLeod, Roddy				
2nd	Morrison, Louis	MacLeod, Roddy	MacDonald, Michael	MacBride, Donald				
3rd	MacKay, Neville	Wallace, Robert	Hutt, Lesley	Morrison, Louis				
4th	Campbell, Calum	MacBride, Donald	MacLeod, Roddy	MacInnes, Hugh				
5th	Monk, Ronald	MacDonald, Donald	Morrison, Louis	Hutt, Lesley				
1985 1st	Duncan, Iain	MacInnes, Hugh	MacKinnon, Angus	Morrison, Louis				
2nd	MacLeod, Roderick	MacKinnon, Angus	MacInnes, Hugh	MacLeod, Roderick				
3rd	MacGregor, Bain	MacLeod, Roderick	Morrison, Louis	Duncan, Iain				
4th	Duncan, Gordon	Duncan, Iain	MacLeod, Roderick	MacInnes, Hugh				
5th	Morrison, Louis	Morrison, Louis	Bilsland, Graham	MacKinnon, Angus				
1986 1st	Morrison, Louis	MacLeod, Roderick	MacDonald, Iain	MacDonald, Iain		MacPherson, Colin		
2nd	MacLeod, Roderick	MacKinnon, Angus	MacLeod, Roderick	MacLeod, Roderick		Burnett, John		
3rd	Smith, John Angus	Smith, Neil	MacKinnon, Angus	Smith, Neil		MacKechnie, Ann		
4th	Monk, Ronald	Morrison, Louis	Smith, Neil	Monk, Ronald				
5th		Monk, Ronald	MacCormick, Iain	MacKinnon, Angus				
1987 1st	MacLeod, Roderick	Cusack, Michael	Gillies, Alasdair	Gillies, Alasdair		MacRory, Iain		
2nd	Matheson, N.	Matheson, N.	MacLeod, Roderick	MacLeod, Roderick		MacDonald, Allan		
3rd	Cusack, Michael	MacLeod, Roderick	Cusack, Michael	Cusack, Michael		MacInnes, Donald		
4th	MacIntyre, Donald John	MacInnes, Peter	MacIntyre, Donald, John	MacDonald, Iain				
5th	Campbell, Calum	MacDonald, Iain	MacInnes, Peter	Henderson, Margaret				
1988 1st	Cusack, Mike	MacDonald, Allan	Cusack, Mike	MacDonald, Allan				
2nd	Reese, P/M A.	Cusack, Mike	MacIntyre, Donald John	Lindsay, Archie				
3rd	Johnstone, Tom	MacIntyre, Donald John	MacDonald, Allan	Cusack, Mike				

When Piping Was Strong

	Piob. (open)	March (open)	S/R (open)	Jig (open)	Piob. (local)	March (junior)	Jig (local)	MSR (local)
4th	Matheson, Neil	Smith, Neil	Smith, Neil	Johnstone, Tom				
5th	Smith, Neil	Matheson, Neil	Johnstone, Tom	Morrison, Louis				
1991 1st	MacLeod, Roderick	MacLeod, Roderick	Matheson, Neil	Morrison, William				
2nd	MacKenzie, John Don	Roach, Andrew	Morrison, William	MacDonald, Dr Angus				
3rd	Morrison, William	Smith, Neil	MacLeod, Roderick	MacPherson, Iain				
4th	Matheson, Neil	Morrison, William	MacPherson, Iain	MacLeod, Roderick				
5th	Morrison, Louis	MacDonald, Dr Angus	MacIntyre, Donald John	MacPhee, James				
1992 1st	MacPhee, Donald	MacPhee, Donald	MacPhee, Donald	MacPhee, Donald				
2nd	Smith, John Angus	MacInnes, Donald	Smith, John Angus	Smith, John Angus				
3rd	MacLeod, Donald	Smith, John Angus	MacInnes, Donald	MacInnes, Donald				
4th	Morrison, Louis	MacLeod, Donald	Morrison, Louis	MacLeod, Donald				
5th	Young, Kenneth	Morrison, Louis	MacLeod, Donald	Lindsay, Archie				
1996 1st	Crabtree, R.	MacInnes, Donald	Crabtree, R.	Crabtree, R.				
2nd	Burnett, John	Smith, John Angus	MacInnes, Donald	Burnett, John				
3rd	MacInnes, Donald	Crabtree, R.	Nicholas, F.	Smith, John Angus				
4th	Morrison, Louis	Burnett, John	MacDonald, Donald	MacDonald, Donald				
5th	Smith, John Angus	MacDonald, Donald	Smith, John Angus	Morrison, Louis				
1997 1st	Smith, John Angus	Smith, John Angus	Hutt, Leslie	Hutt, Leslie				
2nd	Burnett, John	MacInnes, Donald	Smith, John Angus	Smith, John Angus				
3rd	Hutt, Leslie	Burnett, John	MacLeod, Donald	MacLeod, Donald				
4th	Morrison, Louis	Hutt, Leslie	MacDonald, Donald	MacDonald, Donald				
5th	Smith, Alastair	MacDonald, Donald	Morrison, Louis	Morrison, Louis				
1999 1st	MacKay, Donald	Duncan, Gordon	Eade, Brendan	Watt, Robert				
2nd	Houlihan, Margaret	Eade, Brendan	Duncan, Gordon	Duncan, Gordon				
3rd	Roy, Graeme	Watt, Robert	Watt, Robert	Burnett, John				
4th	Duncan, Gordon	Houlihan, Margaret	MacLeod, Donald	MacKay, Donald				
5th	MacLeod, Stewart	MacLeod, Stewart	Houlihan, Margaret	Houlihan, Margaret				

Appendix

	Piob. (class)	MSR (jun.)	Piob. (jun.)	MSR (open)	Chanter, –12	Chanter, –14	Chanter, –15
1906 1st		Smith, John					
2nd		MacMillan, D.					
3rd		Steele, Alick					
1907 1st							
2nd							
3rd							
1909 1st	MacIntyre, Angus						
2nd	MacMillan, Donald						
3rd	Campbell, Neil						
1911 1st	MacMillan, Donald	MacLennan, Neil					
2nd	MacIntyre, Donald	Beaton, Roderick					
3rd	Campbell, Neil	MacLennan, John					
1913 1st		MacDonald, John (1st Div.)					
2nd		MacLennan, Neil (1st Div.)					
3rd		MacLennan, John (1st Div.)					
1st (junr)		MacDonald, Angus (2nd Div.)					
2nd (junr)		Campbell, Angus (2nd Div.)					
3rd (junr)		MacKinnon, Geo. (2nd Div.)					
1st (junr)		Martin, Finlay (3rd Div)					
2nd (junr)		Lindsay, Arch (3rd Div.)					
1914 1st	MacDonald, John	Martin, Finlay	Campbell, Angus				
2nd	MacDonald, Archibald	Campbell, Angus	MacMillan, Donald				
3rd	MacMillan, George	Lindsay, Archibald	Linsay, Archibald				
1922 1st		Smith, Neil		Steele, John			
2nd		*Not given*		MacDonald, Roderick			
3rd		*Not given*		Johnston, Lachlan			
1923 1st		Smith, Neil		Steele, John			
2nd		Smith, John		MacDonald, Roderick			

	Piob. (class)	MSR (jun.)	Piob. (jun.)	MSR (open)	Chanter, –12	Chanter, –14	Chanter, –15
3rd		MacInnes, Donald		MacMillan, George			
4th		*Not given*		Martin, Finlay			
1924 1st		Smith, Neil		Steele, John			Smith, John
2nd		MacDonald, John		MacAulay, Angus			MacMillan, J.
3rd		Smith, John		Martin, Finlay			MacQuarrie, Angus
4th		Walker, William & MacQuarrie, Angus		MacMillan, George			
5th							
1925 1st		MacQuarrie, John		Steele, John			
2nd		MacDonald, John		Martin, Finlay			
3rd		Walker, William		MacAulay, Angus & MacDonald, A.			
4th		Smith, John					
1927 1st		Walker, William		MacAulay, Angus			
2nd		MacMillan, J.		Campbell, Angus			
3rd				MacDonald, Roderick			
4th				MacQuarrie, Angus			
5th				Martin, Finlay			
6th				MacMillan, George			
1928 1st				MacAulay, Angus			
2nd				Steele, John			
3rd				Campbell, Angus			
4th				Currie, Allan			
1932 1st			Walker, Malcolm				
2nd			Smith, John				
3rd							
4th							
5th							
6th							
1933 1st			Smith, John				

Appendix

	Piob. (class)	MSR (jun.)	Piob. (jun.)	MSR (open)	Chanter, –12	Chanter, –14	Chanter, –15
2nd			MacLean, D.A.				
3rd			Scott, Adam				
1946 1st						Campbell, Catherine	MacMillan, Neil
2nd						MacDonald, Rona	Currie, John
3rd						MacKinnon, Angus	Campbell, Neil
4th						MacDonald, Neil	MacKiggan, Samuel
5th						Campbell, Malcolm	MacLellan, Alick
6th						MacKinnon, George	
1947 1st		MacDonald, Finlay					MacDonald, Rona
2nd		Campbell, Catherine					Gillies, Ronald
3rd							Campbell, Catherine
1948 1st		(March only) MacDonald, Finlay & Campbell, Catherine					MacDonald, Rona
2nd							MacDonald, Neil
3rd		MacDonald, Neil					Lindsay, Angus
1949 1st		Campbell, Catherine					MacDonald, Rona
2nd		MacDonald, Neil					MacKillop, A.
3rd		MacDonald, Rona					MacKinnon, G.
4th		Lindsay, Angus					Lindsay, Angus
5th							MacIsaac, Kathleen
6th							MacKay, Neil
1951 1st		MacDonald, Rona	MacDonald, Rona				
2nd		Campbell, Malcolm	MacKillop, M.				
3rd		MacKillop, W.	Campbell, A.				
1952 1st		MacDonald, Rona	MacDonald, Rona				
2nd		Campbell, Malcolm	Campbell, Malcolm				
3rd		Tasker, Robert B.	Campbell, Angus				
1955 1st							MacCormick, John

	Piob. (class)	MSR (jun.)	Piob. (jun.)	MSR (open)	Chanter, –12	Chanter, –14	Chanter, –15
2nd							Campbell, Katie Mary
3rd							Wright, Ronald
4th							
5th							
6th							
1956 1st							MacLean, Jason
2nd							Campbell, Katie Mary
3rd							MacCormick, John
4th							MacEachen, K.
5th							
1961 1st							Currie, John
2nd							
3rd							
1962 1st.				MacDonald, Sgt William			
2nd				Burgess, John			
3rd				MacNeill, Seumas			
4th							
5th							
1963 1st				Burgess, John			
2nd				MacAskill, J.			
3rd				MacPhail, Archie			
1964 1st				MacDonald, Rona			
2nd				Burgess, John			
3rd				MacLellan, P/M John			
4th							
5th							
1965 1st				MacFadyen, Iain			
2nd				Brown, P/M R.U.			
3rd				MacLellan, P/M John			
1966 1st				MacDonald, Kenneth			

Appendix

	Piob. (class)	MSR (jun.)	Piob. (jun.)	MSR (open)	Chanter, −12	Chanter, −14	Chanter, −15
2nd				MacDonald, Rona			
3rd				Campbell, Calum			
4th				Morrison, William			
5th							
1967 1st				MacAskill, John			
2nd				MacDonald, Rona			
3rd				MacCormick, John			
4th				Morrison, William			
5th							
1968 1st				Morrison, William			Steele, Ewen
2nd				MacCormick, John			MacMillan, D. & Campbell, John
3rd				MacDonald, William			
1970 1st				MacDonald, Rona			Campbell, John
2nd				MacLellan, Angus J.			MacLellan, Murdo
3rd				Lawrie, P/M Ronald			MacMillan, Donald
1971 1st				MacDonald, Rona			
2nd				Johnson, Norman			
3rd				Morrison, Fred			
1972 1st				Morrison, William			
2nd				Graham, John			
3rd				Beaton, Calum			
1973 1st				Morrison, P/M Donald			
2nd				Gillies, Norman			
3rd				MacDougall, John			
1975 1st		MacLennan, Murdoch					MacIntyre, Alick
2nd		MacDonald, Donald					
3rd		Monk, Ronald					
1976 1st		MacDonald, John A.			MacIntyre, Donald John		

	Piob. (class)	MSR (jun.)	Piob. (jun.)	MSR (open)	Chanter, –12	Chanter, –14	Chanter, –15
2nd		MacDonald, Donald			MacLennan, Donald		
3rd		MacKenzie, Ester			MacLennan, Rebecca		
1977 1st		MacLennan, Murdoch					MacLennan, Ronald
2nd		MacInnes, Peter					MacLeod, Morag
3rd		MacNeill, Lena					Morrison, Mary
4th		MacRury, Neil					
5th							
1979 1st		Morrison, Angus			MacMillan, Flora		
2nd		MacKenzie, Ester			Burnett, John		
3rd		Morrison, Angus John			MacLeod, Fiona		
4th		MacIntyre, Donald John					
1981 1st		MacPherson, Iain					
2nd		MacKinnon, Angus					
3rd		MacLennan, Ronald					
4th							
5th							
1982 1st		MacIntyre, Donald John					MacInnes, Donald
2nd		MacKinnon, Angus					Smith, Colin
3rd		Henderson, Margaret					MacEachern, Ann
4th		MacLennan, Ronald					
5th							
1986 1st					MacIsaac, Iain		
2nd					MacSween, Donald A.		
3rd					Morrison, Margaret		
1987 1st					MacSween, Donald A.		
2nd					Morrison, Margaret		
3rd					MacAskill, Anne Marie		

Sources: *Oban Times* and *Piping Times*, 1898–1999

DISCOGRAPHY

INFORMANTS

Below are the accession numbers and actual recording dates (the reader will find that the year given in the accession number does not always match the year in which it was recorded) of informant interviews. Original recordings are housed in the Sound Archives of the Celtic and Scottish Studies section, School of Literatures, Languages and Cultures, University of Edinburgh. Copies have been retained by the author. Interviews in 1995 with Angus Campbell, Calum Beaton, Louis Morrison and Neil MacDonald were recorded in writing, as was an interview with Morrison in 1999.

CALUM BEATON, STONEYBRIDGE, SOUTH UIST

30 August 1995
SA 1998.70 (14 November 1998)
SC 2001.025 (20 April 1999)
SA 2001.056 (26 November 2000)

ANGUS CAMPBELL, FROBOST, SOUTH UIST

Several dates through August 1995

NEIL JOHNSTONE, DALIBURGH, SOUTH UIST

SA 1998.71 (26 April 1999)

RONA LIGHTFOOT, INVERNESS

SC 2001.024 (April 1996)

JESSIE MACAULAY, SMERCLATE, SOUTH UIST

    SA 1998.68 (14 November 1998)
    SA 1998.71 (23 April 1999)

NEIL MACDONALD, GARRYHELLIE, SOUTH UIST

    Several dates through August and September 1995
    SA 1998.69 (15 November 1998)

RONALD MACDONALD, DALIBURGH, SOUTH UIST

    SC 2001.024 (August 1995)

LOUIS MORRISON, ORMICLATE, SOUTH UIST

    3 September 1995
    22 April 1999

OTHER SOUND ARCHIVE SOURCES

NARRATIVE AND DISCUSSION

    SA 1952/119: Discussion on Calum Pìobaire, by Angus MacPherson
    SA 1952/146.A/2: *'Pìobairean Smearclait – A' Ghlas Mheur'* by Donald MacIntyre
    SA 1953/36/A1: *'Pìobairean Smearclait'* by Roderick Bowie
    SA 1953/36/B1: *'Pìobairean Smearclait'* by Archie MacDonald
    SA 1959/58/A2: 'Priest cures rheumatic woman with fiddle music and dancing', by Peggy MacDonald
    SA 1960/8/9: *'Pìobairean Smearclait'* by John Campbell
    SA 1960/24/A7: *'Pìobairean a' Chlaiginn'* by D. MacDonald
    SA 1965/115/B3: *'Creideamh a' Bhata Bhuidhe'* by Calum MacRae
    SA 1967/61/B12: 'MacCrimmon receives chanter from fairy woman', by Murdo MacLeod
    SA 1968/116/A and B1: 'Emigration from Benbecula, 1836 and 1843', by D.A. MacEachen
    SA 1970/5/6: Comments on *'Maol Donn'*, by Angus Campbell
    SA 1970/206/A2: Discussion of post-Great-War depression in Uist, by Donald A. Johnson

SA 1971/43/A2: Further discussion of post-war depression in Uist, by Donald A. Johnson

SA 1975/32/A1: *'Pìobairean Bhòirnis: Fear a fhuair ceòl as an t-sithein'*, by D.S. Stewart

SC 87.07.B: Discussing his memories of the Games, by Angus Campbell

Music

These items were all collected by Dr Peter Cooke and Miss Morag MacLeod of the School of Scottish Studies during a research trip through the Hebrides in 1970.

SA 1970/5: 'Old Woman's Lullaby', by Angus Campbell

SA 1970/6: 'I Got a Kiss of the King's Hand', by Angus Campbell

SA 1970/7: *'Fhir a' Chinn Duibh'* (song) and 'Lament for the Children' (*canntaireachd*), by Alasdair Boyd

SA 1970/122/5: 'Prince's Salute' (on practice chanter) and 'Isabel MacKay' (song), by
Calum Beaton

SA 1970/145/2, 3: Strathspeys and reels for an Eightsome Reel, by Calum Beaton

SA 1970/309/3, 4: 'MacIntosh's Lament', by Angus Campbell

SA 1970/309/5: 'My King Has Landed in Moidart', by Angus Campbell

SA 1970/309/6: 'Earl of Seaforth's Salute', by Angus Campbell

SA 1970/309/7: *'Maol Donn'* and *'Cha Till Mi Tuilleadh'* (songs), by Kate MacDonald

SA 1970/334/A, B: Various light music, ear-learned, by Kenneth Morrison

BIBLIOGRAPHY

MANUSCRIPT SOURCES

Celtic and Scottish Studies, University of Edinburgh

Campbell Canntaireachd (c. 1797) Facsimile copy of original held in National Library of Scotland.
Campbell, James (1977) 'History of the Piobaireachd Society' in *Piobaireachd Society Conference Proceedings*, March, pp. 30–48.
MacDonald, Donald John MSS (collected through the 1950s), books 1–69.
Reid, Peter MS (1826).

University of Edinburgh Library, Special Collections

Carmichael-Watson MS.
Campbell, Alexander (1815) 'A slight sketch of a journey made through parts of the Highlands and Hebrides; undertaken to collect material for Albyn's Anthology, by the Editor: in Autumn, 1815', La. III. 577.
Chambers, Christine (1980) 'Non-lexical Vocables in Scottish Traditional Music', unpublished PhD thesis.
Laing Papers.
MacDonald, Allan (1995) 'The Relationship between Pibroch and Gaelic Song: Implications on the Performance of the Pibroch Urlar', unpublished MLitt thesis.
MacInnes, Iain (1988) 'The Highland Bagpipe: Impact of the Highland Societies of London and Scotland, 1781–1844', unpublished MLitt thesis.
Stewart, James A. (1982) 'The Clan Ranald: History of a Highland Kindred', unpublished PhD thesis.

National Archives of Scotland

AD 58/86: Conditions on Barra and South Uist, Highland Destitution.
AF 39: Agriculture and Fisheries Department.

ED 7: Scottish Education Department.
ES 153.57: Lawson, James P., 'Passengers on the Alexander' in *The Island Magazine*, vol. 29, Spring/Summer 1991, pp. 34–39.
GD 1: Miscellaneous Deposits.
GD 50: James MacGregor Collection.
GD 95: Society in Scotland for the Propagation of Christian Knowledge, minutes of General Meetings vols 1 and 2.
GD 201: Clanranald Papers.
GD 221: MacDonald Papers.
HD 16/60: Highland Destitution, minutes of meeting of the Emigration and Employment Committee, 2 March 1847.
RH 2: State Papers Scotland, series 2.
T.60.02: MacKinnon, James N., *The Cathcart Settlers*, Moosomin, Saskatchewan, Canada, 1921.

NATIONAL LIBRARY OF SCOTLAND

Acc 9103: Piobaireachd Society Papers.
Acc 9711: Rev. William Matheson Papers.
Adv 73.1.5–6: 'A Glossary of Ancient and Modern Terms and Expressions Associated with the Music, Poetry, Dancing and Oratory of the Gæil; with quotations from their poetry illustrative of their meaning and use'. By Angus Fraser, c. 1855.

COLLEGE OF PIPING, GLASGOW

Piobaireachd Society Papers, loose committee minutes, various dates.

NATIONAL WAR MEMORIAL, EDINBURGH CASTLE

Rolls of Honour, Yeomanry and Queen's Own Cameron Highlanders.

QUEEN'S OWN CAMERON HIGHLANDERS REGIMENTAL MUSEUM, FORT GEORGE

Crawford, Dick (1999) 'The Queen's Own Cameron Highlanders: A roll of Pipers who have served in the Queen's Own Cameron Highlanders or the former 79th (Cameron Highlanders) since the authorisation of officially recognised Pipers in 1854 and the South African War of 1899–1902', as yet unpublished.

JOURNALS

Am Bràighe.
An t-Uibhisteach.
Cape Breton's Magazine.
Celtic Review.
Dalhousie Review.
Innes Review.
Oban Times.
Piping Times.
Piping Today
Scottish Gaelic Studies.
Scottish Studies.
Tocher.
Transactions of the Gaelic Society of Inverness.
The Voice.
West Highland Free Press.
Yearbook (or *Journal*) *of the International Folk Music Council.*

Secondary Sources

Adam, Frank (1960) *Clans, Septs and Regiments of the Scottish Highlands* (rev. ed. by Thomas Innes of Learney), Edinburgh and London.

Adams, Ian and Meredith Somerville (1993) *Cargoes of Despair and Hope: Scottish Emigration to North America, 1603–1803*, Edinburgh: John Donald.

An Abridgement of the Acts of the General Assembly of the Church of Scotland, from 1560 to 1830 inclusive (1831) Edinburgh: Robert Buchanan.

Anon. (1998) 'Bagpiping revelations' in *Am Bràighe*, Autumn, pp. 6–7.

— (1988) 'Donald Morrison' in *Piping Times*, vol. 40, no. 10 (July), p. 35.

— (1966) 'The Flora MacDonald Cup' in *Piping Times*, vol. 18 no. 6 (March), pp. 7–9.

— (1988) 'John MacDonald' in *Piping Times*, vol. 40, no. 10 (July), pp. 34–35.

— (1964) 'John Steele Contest' in *Piping Times*, vol. 16, no. 11 (August), p. 15.

— (1964) 'Major Finlay MacKenzie' in *Piping Times*, vol. 16, no. 4 (January), p. 6.

— (1984) 'Mr. Alex MacAulay' in *Piping Times*, vol. 36, no. 11 (August), p. 25.

— (1994) 'Neil Angus MacDonald' in *Piping Times*, vol. 47, no. 1 (October), p. 45.

— (1978) 'Pipe Major Robert Nicol' in *Piping Times*, vol. 30, no. 7 (April).

— (1978) 'Pipe Major Robert Nicol' in *Piping Times*, vol. 30, no. 9 (June).

— (1981) 'Roderick MacDonald' in *Piping Times*, vol. 34, no. 2 (November), pp. 18–19.

BIBLIOGRAPHY

— (1967) 'South Uist Contest' in *Piping Times*, vol. 19, no. 6 (March), pp. 10–11.
— (n.d.) 'With Piper Alex Currie, Frenchvale' in *Cape Breton's Magazine*, no. 73, pp. 29–45.
Ansdell, Douglas (1998) *The People of the Great Faith: the Highland Church, 1690–1900*, Stornoway: Acair.
Anson, Peter F. (1970) *Underground Catholicism in Scotland, 1622–1878*, Montrose: Standard Press.
Argyllshire Gathering (results for *ceòl mór* competitions, 1904–present).
Bailyn, Bernard (1986) *Voyagers to the West*, New York: Knopf.
Barron, Hugh, ed. (1985) *Third Statistical Account of Scotland*, Edinburgh: Scottish Academic Press.
Bebbington, David (n.d.) 'Scottish Cultural Influences on Evangelism' in *Scottish Bulletin of Evangelical Theology*, p. 24.
Bennett, Margaret (1989) *The Last Stronghold*, Edinburgh: Canongate.
Blacking, John (1971) 'Deep and Surface Structures in Venda Music' in *Yearbook of the International Folk Music Council* vol. 3, pp. 91–108.
Black, Ronald (1972–4) 'Colla Ciotach' in *Transactions of the Gaelic Society of Inverness*, vol. 48, pp. 201–224.
Blankenhorn, V.S. (1978) 'Traditional and Bogus Elements in MacCrimmon's Lament' in *Scottish Studies*, vol. 22, pp. 45–67.
Blum, Stephen (1992) 'Analysis of Musical Style' in Helen Myers (ed.), *Ethnomusicology: an Introduction*, New York and London: Macmillan Press.
Blundell, Odo (1917) *The Catholic Highlands of Scotland: Western Highlands and Islands*, Edinburgh: Sands and Co.
Brown, Pipe Major Robert (1995) Scottish Tradition Cassette Series, vol. 11: *Pibroch* (eds Peter Cooke and Robin Lorimer), Greentrax.
— and Pipe Major Robert Nicol (1999) Masters of Piobaireachd CD Series, vols 1 and 2, Greentrax.
Bruford, Alan and D.A. MacDonald (1994) *Scottish Traditional Tales*, Edinburgh: Polygon.
Buisman, Frans (2000) 'Double Echoes' in *Piping Times*, vol. 52, no. 6 (March), pp. 39–40.
— ed. (2001) *The MacArthur–MacGregor Manuscript of Piobaireachd (1820)*, The Music of Scotland Series no. 1, Glasgow: Universities of Glasgow and Aberdeen.
Bumsted, J.M. (1978) 'Highland Emigration to the Island of St. John and the Scottish Catholic Church' in *Dalhousie Review*, vol. 58, pp. 511–527.
— (1982) *The People's Clearance: Highland Emigration to British North America, 1770–1815*, Edinburgh: Edinburgh University Press.
Bunting, Edward (1840) *The Ancient Music of Ireland*, Dublin: Hodges and Smith.
Burnett, Ray (1986) *Benbecula*, Torlum: Mingulay Press.
Burt, Edward (1815) *Letters from a Gentleman in the North of Scotland to his Friend in London . . . Begun in the Year 1726*, vol 2, London: Gale, Curtis and Fenner.

Cabar Feidh Collection: Pipe Music of the Queen's Own Highlanders (Seaforth and Camerons) (1983) London: Paterson's Publications.

Cameron, Alexander (1894) *Reliquiae Celticae: Texts, Papers and Studies in Gaelic Literature and Philology*, vol. 2 (eds Alexander MacBain and Rev. John Kennedy), Inverness: Northern Counties Publishing Co.

Campbell, Archibald (1948) *The Kilberry Book of Ceòl Mór*, Glasgow: The Piobaireachd Society.

Campbell, John Francis (1880) *Canntaireachd: Articulate Music*, Glasgow: A. Sinclair.

— (1994) *Popular Tales of the West Highlands*, vols 1–4, Edinburgh: Birlinn (1st ed. 1860).

Campbell, John Lorne (1933) *Highland Songs of the Forty-Five*, Edinburgh: John Grant.

— (1954) *Father Allan McDonald of Eriskay, 1859–1905: Priest, Poet and Folklorist*, Edinburgh and London: Oliver and Boyd.

— (1954) 'The MacNeils of Barra and the Irish Franciscans' in *Innes Review*, vol. 6, no. 1, pp. 33–38.

— and Trevor H. Hall (1968) *Strange Things*, London: Routledge and Kegan Paul.

— and Francis Collinson, eds (1969), *Hebridean Folksongs: A Collection of Waulking Songs by Donald MacCormick in Kilpheder in South Uist in the Year 1893*, Oxford: Oxford University Press.

— and Francis Collinson, eds (1977), *Hebridean Folksongs vol. II: Waulking Songs from Barra, South Uist, Eriskay and Benbecula*, Oxford: Oxford University Press.

— (2000) *A Very Civil People: Hebridean Folk, History and Tradition* (ed. Hugh Cheape), Edinburgh: Birlinn.

— (1984) *Canna: The Story of a Hebridean Island*, Oxford: Oxford University Press.

Campbell, R.H. (1988) 'The Landed Classes' in T.M. Devine and Rosalind Mitchison (eds), *People and Society in Scotland: vol. I, 1760–1830*, Edinburgh: John Donald, pp. 91–108.

Campsie, Alasdair (1980) *The MacCrimmon Legend: The Madness of Angus MacKay*, Edinburgh: Canongate.

Cannon, Roderick (1980) *A Bibliography of Bagpipe Music*, Edinburgh: John Donald.

— (1988) *The Highland Bagpipe and its Music*, Edinburgh: John Donald.

— ed. (1994) *Joseph MacDonald's Compleat Theory of the Scots Highland Bagpipe, c. 1760*, Glasgow: The Piobaireachd Society.

— cons. ed. (2001) *The MacArthur–MacGregor Manuscript of Piobaireachd (1820)*. See Buisman, Frans (2001).

Carmichael, Alexander (1928–71) *Ortha nan Gaidheal: Carmina Gadelica*, vols 1–6, Edinburgh and London: Oliver and Boyd.

Carmichael, E.C. (1905) 'Never was piping so sad, and never was piping so gay' in *Celtic Review*, vol. 2, pp. 76–84.

Bibliography

Carswell, Allan L. (1995) '"The Most Despicable Enemy That Are": the Jacobite Army of the '45' in Robert Woosman-Savage (ed.), *1745: Charles Edward Stuart and the Jacobites*, Edinburgh: HMSO.

Cheape, Hugh (1990) Review of MacNeill and Richardson's *Pìobaireachd and its Interpretation* (1987) in *Scottish Gaelic Studies*, vol. 16, Aberdeen University Press, pp. 201–207.

— (1999) *The Book of the Bagpipe*, Belfast: Appletree Press.

— (2005) '"Get them off his fingers": idioms of piping in Scotland' in *Piping Today*, no. 15, pp. 12–15.

Collinson, Francis (1975) *The Bagpipe*, London: Routledge and Kegan Paul.

— (n.d.) Notes made for cassette, *Scottish Traditional Instrumental Music*, side 1: 'Pibroch'.

Còmhlan Dannsa nan Eileanach (1995) *Hebridean Dance*, Stornoway.

Cooke, Peter (1972) 'Problems of Notating Pibroch: A Study of "Maol Donn"' in *Scottish Studies*. vol. 16, part one, pp. 41–59.

— (1986) *The Fiddle Tradition of the Shetland Isles*, Cambridge: Cambridge University Press.

Dahlhaus, Carl (1982) *Esthetics of Music*, Cambridge: Cambridge University Press.

Dalyell, Sir John Graham (1849) *Musical Memoirs of Scotland*, Edinburgh: Thomas G. Stevenson.

Devine, T.M. (1988) *The Great Highland Famine: Hunger, Emigration and the Scottish Highlands in the 19th Century*, Edinburgh: John Donald.

— (1992) 'Landlordism and Highland Emigration' in T.M. Devine (ed.), *Scottish Emigration and Scottish Society*, Edinburgh: John Donald.

— (1992) 'The Paradox of Scottish Emigration' in T.M. Devine (ed.), *Scottish Emigration and Scottish Society*, Edinburgh: John Donald.

Dickson, Joshua (2003) '"Hiharin" in 1940s South Uist: A Remnant of an Earlier Tradition?' in *Piping Times*, vol. 55, no. 5 (February), pp. 29–33.

— (2003) 'Tradition and change in South Uist, part one' in *Piping Today*, no. 6, September/October, pp. 34–7.

— (2003) 'Tradition and Change in South Uist, part two' in *Piping Today*, no. 7, November/December, pp. 34–7.

Donaldson, Gordon (1960) *The Scottish Reformation*, Cambridge: Cambridge University Press.

— (1972) *Scotland: Church and Nation Through Sixteen Centuries*, Edinburgh and London: Scottish Academic Press (1st ed 1960).

— (1985) *Scottish Church History*, Edinburgh: Scottish Academic Press.

Donaldson, M.E.M. (1920) *Wanderings in the Western Highlands and Islands*, Paisley: Alexander Gardner.

Donaldson, William (2000) *The Highland Pipe and Scottish Society, 1750–1950*, East Linton: Tuckwell Press.

Donovan, Kenneth (1990) 'Reflections on Cape Breton Culture: An Introduction' in Kenneth Donovan (ed.), *The Island: New Perspectives on Cape Breton History, 1713–1990*, Sydney: University College of Cape Breton Press.

Dressler, Camille (1998) *Eigg: The Story of an Island*, Edinburgh: Polygon.

Drummond, Andrew L. and James Bulloch (1973) *The Scottish Church, 1688–1843: The Age of the Moderates*, Edinburgh: Saint Andrew Press.
— (1975) *The Church in Victorian Scotland, 1843–1874*, Edinburgh: Saint Andrew Press.
Dunlay, Kate and David Greenberg (1996) *Traditional Celtic Violin Music of Cape Breton*, Toronto: DunGreen Music.
Dwelly, Edward (1988) *Dwelly's Illustrated Gaelic to English Dictionary*, Glasgow: Gairm (1st ed 1901).
Emmerson, George S. (1972) *A Social History of Scottish Dance*, Montreal and London: McGill-Queen's University Press.
England, Nicholas (1967) 'Bushmen Counterpoint' in *Journal of the International Folk Music Council*, vol. 19, p. 58.
Eyre-Todd, George (1923) *The Highland Clans of Scotland: Their History and Traditions*, vol. 1, London: Heath Cranton.
Feld, Steven (1982) *Sound and Sentiment: Birds, Weeping, Poetics and Song in Kaluli Expression*, Philadelphia: University of Pennsylvania Press.
Finnegan, Ruth (1992) *Oral Traditions and the Verbal Arts: A Guide to Research Practices*, London: Routledge.
Flett, J.F. and T.M. (1964) *Traditional Dancing in Scotland*, London and Boston: Routledge and Kegan Paul.
— (1996) *Traditional Step-Dancing in Scotland*, Edinburgh: Scottish Cultural Press.
Fotheringham, Rev. W. (1917) *Sinclair Thomson: The Shetland Apostle*, Lerwick.
Giblin, Cathaldus (1964) *Irish Franciscan Mission to Scotland, 1619–1646: Documents from Roman Archives*, Dublin: Assisi Press.
Gibson, John (1998) *Traditional Gaelic Bagpiping, 1745–1945*, Montreal and Edinburgh: McGill-Queen's University Press and National Museums of Scotland.
— (2002) *Old and New World Highland Bagpiping*, Montreal and Edinburgh: McGill-Queen's Univ. Press and National Museums of Scotland.
Glasgow Catholic Directory for the Clergy and Laity of Scotland (1889) Edinburgh.
Glen, David (n.d.) *A Collection of Ancient Piobaireachd compiled and arranged by David Glen. With Historical, Biographic and Legendary Notes regarding the Tunes by 'Fionn,'* Edinburgh: David Glen and Sons.
Gray, Malcolm (1957) *The Highland Economy, 1750–1850*, Edinburgh: Oliver and Boyd.
— (1992) 'The Course of Scottish Emigration, 1750–1914: Enduring Influences and Changing Circumstances' in T.M. Devine (ed.), *Scottish Emigration and Scottish Society*, Edinburgh: John Donald.
Gray, William (1995) 'The MacArthurs' in *Piping Times*, vol. 47, no. 10 (July), p. 34 (reprint of 1973 article in the same journal, vol. 25, no. 11 (August), p. 13).
Hammersley, Martyn and Paul Atkinson (1995) *Ethnography: Principles in Practice* (2nd ed), London and New York: Routledge.
Harper, Marjory (1994) 'Crofter Colonists in Canada: An Experiment in Empire Settlement in the 1920s' in *Northern Scotland*, vol. 14, pp. 69–111.

Henderson, Diana (1989) *Highland Soldier: A Social Study of the Highland Regiments, 1820–1920*, Edinburgh: John Donald.
Historical Records of the Cameron Highlanders (1931) vols 3 and 4, Edinburgh and London: William Blackwood and Sons.
Hornsby, Stephen (1990) 'Scottish Emigration and Settlement in Early Nineteenth-Century Cape Breton' in Kenneth Donovan (ed.), *The Island: New Perspectives on Cape Breton History, 1713–1990*, Sydney: University College of Cape Breton Press.
Johnson, Christine (1991) *Scottish Catholic Secular Clergy, 1879–1989*, Edinburgh: John Donald.
Johnson, Samuel and James Boswell (1924) *Johnson's Journey to the Western Islands of Scotland (1775) and Boswell's Journal of a Tour to the Hebrides with Samuel Johnson (1785)* (ed. R.W. Chapman), Oxford: Oxford Univ. Press.
Johnston, Calum and Annie (1995) Scottish Tradition Cassette Series, vol. 13: *Songs, Stories and Piping from Barra* (ed. Virginia Blankenhorn), Greentrax.
Kennedy, Rev. John (1932) *The Apostle of the North: The Life and Labours of Rev. John MacDonald, D.D., of Ferintosh* (ed. Rev. Principal MacLeod, DD), Inverness: Northern Counties Publishing Co.
Kirk, James (1986) 'The Jacobean Church, 1567–1625' in *The Seventeenth Century in the Highlands*, Inverness: Inverness Field Club, pp. 24–51.
Knox, John (1787) *A Tour Through the Highlands of Scotland and the Hebride Isles in 1786*, London.
Kuyper, Abraham (1961) *Lectures on Calvinism*, Grand Rapids, Ohio.
Lindley, Sir Frances (1935) *Lord Lovat, 1871–1833*, London: Hutchinson and Co.
Logan, James (1831) *The Scottish Gaël; or, Celtic Manners, as preserved among the Highlanders...* vol 2, London: Smith, Elder and Co.
McAllester, David P. (1960) 'The Role of Music in Western Apache Culture' in Anthony Wallace (ed.), *Men and Cultures: Selected Papers of the Fifth International Congress of Anthropological and Ethnological Sciences*, Philadelphia: University of Pennsylvania Press.
MacAulay, Alexander (1961) 'The Art and History of the MacDougalls of Aberfeldy' in *Piping Times*, vol. 13, no. 10 (July), p. 10.
— (1961) 'The MacKenzies of Lochboisdale' in *Piping Times*, vol. 13, no. 10 (July), pp. 5–9.
— (1961) 'Pipe-Major John Steele, Late Q.O.C. Highlanders' in *Piping Times*, vol. 14, no. 2 (November), pp. 18–22.
— (1970) 'Alex MacDonald, South Uist' in *Piping Times*, vol. 21, no. 10 (July), pp. 8–9.
MacAulay, Donald, ed. (1976), *Nua-Bhàrdachd Ghàidhlig*, Edinburgh: Southside.
MacBain, Alexander (1890–1) 'Gaelic Incantations' in *Transactions of the Gaelic Society of Inverness*, vol. 17.
McConachie, Jack (1972) *Hebridean Solo Dances*, Kings Langley: Cabar Feidh.
MacDhòmhnuill, Dòmhnull Iain (1973) *Sguaban Eòrna*, Inverness: Club Leabhar.
— (1981) *Uibhist a Deas: beagan mu eachdraidh is bheul-aithris an eilein*, Stornoway: Acair Press.

MacDonald, A. and A. (1896–1900) *The Clan Donald*, vols 1 and 2, Inverness: Northern Counties Publishing Co.
— (1911) *The MacDonald Collection of Gaelic Poetry*, Inverness: Northern Counties Publishing Co.
MacDonald, Donald (c. 1820) *A Collection of the Ancient Martial Music of Caledonia Called Piobaireachd . . .*, Edinburgh.
MacDonald, Donald (1978) *Lewis: A History of the Island*, Edinburgh: Gordon Wright.
McDonald, Fr Allan (1958) *Gaelic Words and Expressions from South Uist and Eriskay*, (ed. J.L. Campbell), Dublin: Dublin Institute for Advanced Studies.
MacDonald, Fr Charles (1997) *Moidart, or Among the Clanranalds*, (ed. John Watt), Edinburgh: Birlinn.
MacDonald, John Angus (1999) *Òrain Dhòmhnaill Ailein Dhòmhnaill na Bainich/The Songs of Donald Allan MacDonald: 1906–92*, Benbecula: Comann Eachdraidh nan Eilean mu Dheas.
MacDonald, Neil Angus (n.d.) *New Bagpipe Collection of Old and Traditional Settings*, Inverness.
MacDonald, Patrick (1784) *A Collection of Highland Vocal Airs, never hitherto published . . .*, Edinburgh.
MacDonald, Rev. Archibald (1894) *The Uist Collection: the poems and songs of John MacCodrum, Archibald MacDonald, and some of the minor Uist bards*, Glasgow:Archibald Sinclair.
MacDonald, Sharon (2000) '"A bheil am feur gorm fhathast?": Some Problems Concerning Language and Cultural Shift' in *Scottish Studies*, vol. 33, pp. 186–97.
MacDonald, William (1999) 'Further Reminiscences by William MacDonald (Benbecula)' in *Piobaireachd Society Conference XXVI*, pp. 1–13.
MacDougall, Rev. James (1978) *Highland Fairy Legends* (ed. Rev. George Calder), Cambridge: D.S. Brewer.
MacEachen, Frances (1995) 'The MacIntyre Pipers of French Road' in *Am Bràighe*, Summer, p. 11.
— (1998) 'A Passion for Piping' in *Am Bràighe*, Autumn, p. 3.
MacGill-eain, S. (1985) *Ris a' Bhruthaich*
MacGregor, A. A. (1925) *Behold the Hebrides*, London and Edinburgh: W. and R. Chambers.
Macinnes, Allan I. (1988) 'Scottish Gaeldom: The First Phase of Clearance' in T.M. Devine and Rosalind Mitchison (eds), *People and Society in Scotland, vol. I: 1760–1830*, Edinburgh: John Donald, pp. 70–90.
MacKay, Angus (1838) *A Collection of Ancient Pìobaireachd, or Highland Pipe Music . . .*, Edinburgh.
MacKay, Iain R. (1963) 'Glenaladale's Settlement, Prince Edward Island' in *Scottish Gaelic Studies*, vol. 10, August, pp. 16–24.
McKean, Thomas (1997) *Hebridean Song-Maker: Iain MacNeacail of the Isle of Skye*, Edinburgh: Polygon.

MacKenzie, Alexander (1883) *History of the Highland Clearances*, Inverness: A. and W. MacKenzie.
Mackenzie, Bridget (1998) *Piping Traditions of the North of Scotland*, Edinburgh: John Donald.
MacKenzie, Compton (1998) 'Catholic Barra' in J.L. Campbell (ed.), *The Book of Barra*, Stornoway: Acair Press.
MacKenzie, John (1904) *Sar-Obair nam Bard Gaelach: or, The Beauties of Gaelic Poetry*, Edinburgh: N. MacLeod.
MacKenzie, William Cook (1903) *History of the Outer Hebrides*, London: Simpkin, Marshall and Co.
MacLachlan-Orme, B.J. (1979) *The Piobaireachd of Simon Fraser with Canntaireachd*, n.p.
Maclean, Alasdair (1984) 'Notes on South Uist Families' in *Transactions of the Gaelic Society of Inverness*, vol. 53, pp. 491–518.
McLean, M.L. (1991) *The People of Glengarry: Highlanders in Transition, 1745–1820*, Montreal: McGill-Queen's University Press.
MacLellan, Angus (1961) *Stories from South Uist* (ed. J.L. Campbell), London: Routledge and Kegan Paul.
— (1962) *The Furrow Behind Me* (ed. J.L. Campbell), London: Routledge and Kegan Paul.
MacLennan, Hugh Dan (1999) 'Shinty and the Celtic Celebration of New Year' in Grant Jarvie (ed.), *Sport in the Making of Celtic Cultures*, Leicester: Leicester University Press, pp. 83–99.
MacLennan, Lt John (1907) *The Piobaireachd As MacCrimmon Played It*, Edinburgh.
MacLeod, Angus (1933) *Sar Òrain*, Glasgow: An Comann Gàidhealach.
MacLeod, Brenda (1950) *Tales of Dunvegan*, Stirling: Aeneas MacKay.
MacLeod, Donald (1999) 'Calvinism and the New Millennium' in *The Realm of Reform*, Edinburgh: Handsel Press.
MacLeod, John (1965) *By-paths of Highland Church History*, Edinburgh.
MacMillan, A.J. (1986) *To the Hill of Boisdale*, Sydney: Music Hill Publications.
MacMillan, Somerled (1968) *Sporan Dhòmhnaill*, Edinburgh: Oliver and Boyd.
McNamee, Peter, ed. (1991) *Traditional Music – Whose Music? Proceedings of a Co-operation North Conference*, Belfast: Institute of Irish Studies.
MacNeil, Joe Neil and John Shaw (1987) *Sgeul Gu Latha/Tales Until Dawn*, Montreal: McGill-Queen's University Press.
MacNeill, Seumas and Frank Richardson (1987) *Piobaireachd and its Interpretation*, Edinburgh: John Donald.
MacPherson, Angus (1954) *A Highlander Looks Back*, Oban: Oban Times Ltd.
MacPherson, Norman (1876–7) 'Notes on Antiquities from the Island of Eigg' in *Proceedings of the Society of Antiquaries of Scotland* vol 12, part 2, pp. 577–97.
Magowan, Fiona (1994) '"The Land is Our Märr (Essence), It Stays Forever": The Yathu–Yindi Relationship in Australian Aboriginal Traditional and Popular Musics' in Martin Stokes (ed.), *Ethnicity, Identity and Music: The Musical Construction of Place*, Oxford and Providence: Berg, pp. 135–56.

Malcolm, Charles A. (1927) *The Piper in Peace and War*, London: J. Murray.
Martin, Martin (1994) *A Description of the Western Isles of Scotland, c. 1695*, Edinburgh: Birlinn.
Matheson, William (1938) *The Songs of John MacCodrum*, Edinburgh: Oliver and Boyd.
Mathew, David (1955) *Scotland Under Charles I*, London: Eyre and Spottiswoode.
Mathieson, William Law (1902) *Politics and Religion in Scotland: 1550–1695* vol. 1, Glasgow: James Maclehose and Sons.
Meek, Donald E. (1996) *The Scottish Highlands: The Churches and Gaelic Culture*, Geneva: WCC Publications.
Menzies, Capt. Robert(?) (1818) *The Bagpipe Preceptor*, Edinburgh: Oliver and Boyd.
Merriam, Alan (1964) *The Anthropology of Music*, Evanston, IL: Northwestern University Press.
Moore, Jerry D. (1997) *Visions of Culture: An Introduction to Anthropological Theories and Theorists*, London: AltaMira Press.
Morrison, Ronald (1963) 'Roderick MacDonald' in *Piping Times*, April, p. 16.
— (1999) 'The Clan Ranald Influence on Early Piping in South Uist' in *An t-Uibhisteach*, no. 4, pp. 19–22.
Moss, George (1983) Scottish Tradition Cassette Series, vol. 6: *Pibroch* (ed. Peter Cooke), Greentrax.
Munro, Jean and R.W., eds (1986) *Acts of the Lords of the Isles, 1336–1493*, Edinburgh: Scottish History Society.
Murray, Col David (1994) *Music of the Scottish Regiments*, Edinburgh: Pentland Press.
— (1997) 'The Maverick: George Moss, 1903–1990' in *The Voice*, Spring, pp. 31–35.
Nattiez, Jean-Jacques (1990) *Music and Discourse: Toward a Semiology of Music*, Princeton: Princeton University Press.
Neat, Timothy and John MacInnes (1999) *The Voice of the Bard: Living Poets and Ancient Tradition in the Highlands and Islands of Scotland*, Edinburgh: Canongate.
Nettl, Bruno (1965) *Folk and Traditional Music of the Western Continents*, New Jersey: Prentice-Hall.
New Statistical Account of Scotland (1845) vol. 14, Edinburgh: Blackwood.
Northern Meeting, Inverness (results for *ceòl mór* competitions, 1831–present).
Ó Baoill, Colm (1999) 'Moving in Gaelic Musical Circles: the root *lu*- in music terminology' in Colm Ó Baoill and Donald E. Meek (eds), *Scottish Gaelic Studies*, vol. 19, pp. 172–194.
— and Meg Bateman (1994) *Gàir nan Clarsach/The Harp's Cry*, Edinburgh: Birlinn.
Pennant, Thomas (1776) *A Tour in Scotland, 1772*, vols 1–2, London: Benjamin White.
Percy, Lord Eustace (1937) *John Knox*, London: Hodder and Stoughton.
Picketts, Anne (1995) 'Pipe Major Angus MacAulay MBE' in *Piping Times*, vol. 48, no. 2 (November), pp. 39–42.

Piobaireachd Society Series (1925–90) vols 1–15, Glasgow.

Poulter, G.C.B. and C.P. Fisher (1936) *The MacCrimmon Family: 1500–1936*, Camberley: Clan MacCrimmon Society.

Purser, John (1992) *Scotland's Music*, Edinburgh and London: Mainstream Publishing.

Ralls-MacLeod, Karen (2000) *Music and the Celtic Otherworld*, Edinburgh: Polygon.

Rea, Frederick G. (1964) *A School in South Uist: Reminiscences of a Hebridean Schoolmaster, 1890–1913*, London: Routledge and Kegan Paul.

Rees, Alwyn and Brinley (1961) *Celtic Heritage*, London: Thames and Hudson.

Rice, Timothy (1994) *May It Fill Your Soul: Experiencing Bulgarian Music*, Chicago and London: University of Chicago Press.

Robertson, Rev. C.M. (1897–8) 'Topography and Traditions of Eigg' in *Transactions of the Gaelic Society of Inverness*, vol. 22, pp. 193–210.

Robertson, Ronald MacDonald (1961) *Selected Highland Folktales*, Edinburgh: Oliver and Boyd.

Rosenberg, Neil V., ed. (1993) *Transforming Tradition: Folk Music Revivals Examined*, Urbana and Chicago: University of Illinois Press.

Ross, Anne (1974) *Pagan Celtic Britain*, London: Cardinal.

Ross, G.F. (1926) *Some Piobaireachd Studies*, Glasgow: Peter Henderson.

Ross, William (1923–50) *Pipe Major W. Ross's Collection of Highland Bagpipe Music*, vols 1–5, Glasgow: Paterson's Publications.

Sanger, Keith (1983) 'The MacArthurs: Evidence from the MacDonald Papers' in *Piping Times*, vol. 35 no. 8 (May), pp. 13–17.

Seton, Bruce and John Grant (1920) *The Pipes of War*, Glasgow.

Sinclair, Sir John, ed. (1791–99), *Statistical Account of Scotland* vol 17, Edinburgh.

Shaw, John (1992–3) 'Language, Music and Local Aesthetics: Views From Gaeldom and Beyond' in J. Derrick McClure (ed.), *Scottish Language*, vol. 11/12, pp. 37–61.

Shaw, Margaret Fay (1955) *Folksongs and Folklore of South Uist*, London: Routledge and Kegan Paul.

— (1957) 'Gaelic Folksongs from South Uist' in *Studia Memoriae Belae Bartók Sacra*, 2nd edn, Budapest, pp. 417–33.

Shears, Barry (2004) 'The fate of Clanranald piper Robert MacIntyre in *Piping Today*, no. 11, pp. 36–8.

— (2001) *The Gathering of the Clans Collection*, vol. 1–2, Halifax: Taigh a' Chiuil.

Stevenson, David (1980) *Alasdair MacColla and the Highland Problem in the Seventeenth Century*, Edinburgh: John Donald.

Stokes, Martin, ed. (1994), *Ethnicity, Identity and Music: The Musical Construction of Place*, Oxford and Providence: Berg.

Strand, Paul (2002) *Tir a' Mhurain: the Outer Hebrides of Scotland*, 2nd edn, Aperture: New York.

Taylor, Alistair and Henrietta (1936) *1715: The Story of the Rising*, Edinburgh and London: Thomas Nelson and Sons.

Telfer, Hamish (1994) 'Play, Customs and Popular Culture of West Coast

Communities, 1840–1900' in Grant Jarvie and Graham Walker (eds), *Scottish Sport in the Making of the Nation: 90-Minute Patriots?*, Leicester: Leicester University Press, pp. 113–24.

Thomason, Gen. C.S. (1900) *Ceòl Mór*, London (1st ed 1893).

Thomson, Derick (1968) 'Gaelic Learned Orders and Literati in Medieval Scotland' in *Scottish Studies*, vol. 12 part one, pp. 57–78.

— (1970) 'The Poetry of Niall MacMhuirich' in *Transactions of the Gaelic Society of Inverness*, vol. 46, pp. 281–307.

— (1974) 'Niall Mór MacMhuirich' in *Transactions of the Gaelic Society of Inverness*, vol. 49, pp. 9–25.

— (1977) 'Three Seventeenth Century Bardic Poets: Niall Mór, Cathal and Niall MacMhuirich' in Adam J. Aitken, Matthew P. McDiarmid and Derick S. Thomson (eds), *Bards and Makars: Scottish Language and Literature: Medieval and Renaissance*, Glasgow: Glasgow University Press, pp. 221–46.

— ed (1994) *Companion to Gaelic Scotland*, Glasgow: Gairm.

— (1996) *Alasdair Mac Mhaighstir Alasdair*, Edinburgh: Scottish Academic Press.

Trevor-Roper, Hugh (1983) 'The Invention of Tradition: the Highland Tradition of Scotland' in Eric Hobsbawm and Terence Ranger (eds), *The Invention of Tradition*, Cambridge: Cambridge University Press, pp. 15–42.

Vance, Michael E. (1992) 'The Politics of Emigration: Scotland and Assisted Emigration to Upper Canada, 1815–1826' in T.M. Devine (ed.), *Scottish Emigration and Scottish Society*, Edinburgh: John Donald.

Wallace, Robert (1996) 'Reminiscences of a First-rate Teacher, Composer and Performer' in *West Highland Free Press*, 6 December, p. 21.

Waterman, Christopher (1993) 'Regional Studies: Africa' in Helen Myers (ed.), *Ethnomusicology: Historical and Regional Studies*, London: Macmillan Press, pp. 240–59.

Watson, William J. (1932) *Bàrdachd Ghàidhlig: Specimens of Gaelic Poetry*, Stirling: A. Learmonth and Son.

West, Gary J (2002–3) 'Land and Lyrics: The Dynamics of Music and Song in Rural Society' in *Review of Scottish Culture* 15, pp. 57–66.

Whyte, Henry (n.d., writing as 'Fionn') 'Historical, Biographic and Legendary Notes on the Tunes' in David Glen, *A Collection of Ancient Piobaireachd . . .*, Edinburgh: David Glen and Sons.

Woolard, Rick (2002) 'Go For the Music: an interview with Ronald Morrison' in *The Voice*, vol. 31 no. 4, Winter, pp. 22–31.

Wright, Andrew (2001) *The MacArthur–MacGregor Manuscript of Piobaireachd (1820)*. See Buisman, Frans. (2001)

INDEX

'A.M.' correspondent to *Oban Times* 117
accordian- and melodian-playing 108, 111, 260(n)
aesthetics, musical 23, 107, 119, 136, 175–6, 179–80, 207–8, 211–35, 270–1(n)
    characterising a 'local' aesthetic of performance in Uist piping 211–19
    impact of literate and aural idioms on construction of repertoire 227–35
    language perceived to influence performance style 23
    performance style as symbolic of identity 175–6, 179–80, 270–1(n)
    verbal aesthetics and surviving terminology in Hebridean community 220–27
Age of Forays (*Linn nan Creach*) 7, 20, 73, 80, 85, 91
Àine Ní Cathan of Co. Derry 40, 176
Alasdair Mac Mhaighstir Alasdair, bard 41, 94, 221, 258(n)
Alexander, the 60, 61, 62, 66
American War of Independence, the 59, 61, 67
'An Spaidsearachd Bharrach' (song) 98
Arnot, Richard, Jesuit missionary 44, 49

Bàl 33, 37, 231, 233
Bàl Suitheadh, the 99–100, 108
Bannockburn Pipes, the 68, 89–90
Barra 42, 43, 44, 47, 50, 63, 65, 83, 87, 99, 109, 120, 130, 131, 139, 145, 146, 164, 191, 195, 238
Bartholomew, Sir John of Glenorchard 272(n)
Battle of Quebec, the 96
Battle of Sheriffmuir, the 148
'Battle of Sheriffmuir, The' (tune) 147, 150

'Battle of the Spoilt Dyke (*Blàr Milleadh Gàraidh*) 147
'Battle of Waternish, The' (tune) 141, 147–8
Bean Eairdsidh Raghnaill – see MacDonald, Kate
Beaton, Alasdair of Stoneybridge 177, 218–9, 233
Beaton, Archie of Stoneybridge 114, 115, 137, 177, 208, 233
Beaton, Calum of Stoneybridge 6, 25–6, 27, 29, 30, 37, 100, 108, 113, 114, 115, 116, 121, 132–4, 137, 142, 143, 145–6, 155, 158, 161, 162, 163, 169, 172, 174, 176–80, 193, 197, 200, 205, 210–11, 214–5, 216, 217–9, 222–3, 226–7, 231–4, 238, 240
Beatons, the, physicians to Clanranald 16, 242(n)
'Beloved Scotland' (tune) 178
'Bells of Perth, the' (tune) 269(n)
Benbecula 44, 48, 50, 58, 63, 65, 86–7, 110, 120, 122, 128–9, 130, 131, 140, 146, 151, 164, 170, 185–7
'*Birlinn Chlann Raghnaill*' (song) 41
'Black Donald's March' (tune) 141, 192
Blàr nan Leine 92
'Blue Ribbon, The' (tune) 165
Bodaich, na (the Elders) 53
'Boisdale's Salute' (tune) 148–9
Bornish Pipe Band 55
Boswell, James, writer 38, 183
Boyd, Alasdair, piper 19, 21–2, 87, 154, 204, 205
Brown, Pipe Major Robert 131, 132, 134, 135
Buchan, Alexander, schoolmaster in St Kilda 49
Buisman, Frans, scholar 81
Burgess, John D. 197

Burt, Edward, writer 18, 97

'*Cailleach a' Ghlinn Dorcha*' (tune) 239
'*Cailleach an Dùdain*' (dance) 209
Calvinism 47, 51, 52–3, 55
Cambuslang, the 1742 communion of 51
Cameron Highlanders – *see* Queen's Own Cameron Highlanders
Cameron piping family, the 125
'Cameronian Rant, The' (tune) 239
Campbell, Alexander, music collector 16, 18–9, 90
Campbell, Angus of Eochar (*an Gighat*) 113
Campbell, Angus of Frobost 20, 131, 45, 155, 156, 158, 162, 163–7, 168, 169, 170, 188, 194, 197–8, 219, 223–4, 226, 229, 269(n), 271(n), 273(n)
Campbell, Calum of Benbecula 155, 163, 197, 198, 238
Campbell Canntaireachd, the 143, 147, 267(n)
Campbell, Fr Alexander of Bornish and Daliburgh 56
Campbell, John Francis, folklorist 17, 33, 161, 223, 243(n)
Campbell, John Lorne, folklorist 3, 17, 48, 54, 85, 98
Campbell, Neil of Frobost 139, 156, 162–3, 191
Cannon, Roderick, scholar 2, 277(n)
canntaireachd 8–9, 14, 19, 22, 23–4, 26, 36, 134–5, 161, 166, 167, 192, 223–4
 as expressive tool 166, 167
 description of 8–9
 Gaelic language a fundamental property of 23–4
 medium for transmission of music from fairies in Gaelic folklore 26
 its use in Piobaireachd Society-sponsored tuition in Hebrides 134–5
caoineadh, the 25–6, 45–6, 244(n)
 as instrumental music 25
 example in historical folktale 45–6
 originating from chirping of birds 25–6
Cape Breton 8–9, 34–5, 54, 65, 70, 71–2, 85–6, 89, 95, 172, 193, 213, 214, 222, 226–7, 242(n), 243(n)
Carmichael, Alexander, folklorist 17, 34, 51, 53, 54, 86, 209
Cathcart, Lady Emily Gordon 65, 189, 271(n)

'Cathcart Settlers', the 60, 65–6, 69–70, 99
Catholicism 38–46, 48–56, 42, 47, 48, 49–51, 50, 54, 105, 151–2, 176, 185, 250(n), 271(n), 274(n)
 'popish' schools in South Uist 47
 anti-Catholic 'oligarchy' of Uist school board, late nineteenth century 48
 attempts to establish a Catholic colony in the New World 61, 66
 Catholic history and social climate of South Uist 39–46, 48, 49, 54, 55, 185
 missionaries' attempts to redress pagan superstition within Christian framework 49–51
 pre-Reformation sees of Argyll and the Isles 42
 tale of priest curing woman of rheumatism with fiddle and dance 54
 visions of Barra folk associated with coming of missionaries 50
'*Cath nan Coileach*' (dance) 209, 277(n)
'Cave of Gold, The' (tune) 20, 25
ceilidh, the 15, 32–7, 52, 53, 99, 100, 108, 112, 113, 119, 146, 171, 172, 174, 199, 201, 203, 206, 208, 215, 228–9, 231, 234, 260(n)
 association with traditional Gaelic social culture and 'worldly excess' 52, 53
 impact of postwar popular culture on 201, 206, 208
 impact of war on 203
 in emigrant Gaelic Canadian communities 34
 memories of piping performance contexts in 100, 172, 260(n)
 suggesting tacit formulaic rituality 33
 traditional context for versatility of Gaelic performings arts 15, 37
 uniformity of activity among *Gàidhealtachds* 33–5
ceòl beag 8, 15, 109, 117, 127, 129–30, 139, 184, 191, 194–9, 234, 238
ceòl cluais 109, 115, 116, 175–6, 178–9, 199, 206, 207–8, 213, 215–7, 219, 225, 229, 233, 234
 – *see* transmission *and* literacy
ceòl mór 2, 7, 9, 13, 15, 19–22, 43, 74, 75, 82, 94, 99, 109, 117, 119, 123, 124, 127, 128, 131–7, 138–53, 154, 157, 162, 163–7, 168, 169, 171, 177, 178, 184, 191–2, 194–9, 223, 224–5, 228, 229, 231, 238

Index

as category of competition in Hebrides at turn of twentieth century 138–9, 184
as category of competition in Uist games 138–9, 168, 171, 178, 191–2, 194–9
as idiom for ceremonial music 15
brief history and description of 7
discussion of repertoire and tune titles 94, 99, 146–7, 266–7(n)
evidence for continuity of transmission in southern Hebrides up to twentieth century 138–46
exclusivity of 2
fears for its future and vitality by Scots gentry in eighteenth century 74–5
interpretation through *canntaireachd* 9, 19–20, 22
its relationship to Gaelic song 2, 13, 15, 19–22, 141, 150–51, 166–7, 243(n)
perceptions of state of *ceòl mór* in Scotland at turn of twentieth century 117
taught by Piobaireachd Society tutors in Hebrides 127–8, 131, 132–5, 162, 229
tunes associated with Uist and Clanranald 146–53
Ceòlas festival, the 238–9
'Ceud Fàilt' air Gach Gleann' (song) 14
'Cha dìrich me an t-uchd le fonn' (song) 98
'Chan eil mi gun nì air m' aire' (song) 54
Cheape, Brigadier-General 272(n)
Cheape, Hugh, scholar 265(n)
'Children, Lament for the' (tune) 22, 141, 273(n)
Church of Scotland Free 51, 52, 53–4, 56, 260(n)
Church of Scotland Reformed 42, 46–8, 51, 250(n)
Clanranald 16, 26, 27, 39–46, 50, 42, 44, 45, 47, 48, 60, 68, 69, 73, 80, 82, 83–96, 141, 147–51, 172, 198, 246(n), 257(n)
Catholic associations 39–46, 50
Iain Mùideartach's reconciliation to Catholicism 42
MacIntyre pipers to 68, 69, 83, 147, 148, 150, 172, 198, 257(n)
patronage of bards 83
patronage of pipers 83–91
patronised pipers in military campaigns 91–6
pibrochs associated with 147–53

Red Book of 16, 40, 92, 246(n)
trade, military and religious links with Ireland 40–45, 46
'Clanranald's Gathering' (tune, various other titles) 148
'Clanranald's Salute' (tune, various other titles) 91, 149
Clearances, the 60, 172
Cluny, Colonel Gordon of 60, 63–65, 91, 172
'Colla Mo Rùin' (song) 20–21
Collinson, Francis, musicologist 146, 147, 150, 265(n)
Colloden, the battle of 40
Comann Phìobaireachd Uibhist agus Bharraigh 238
competition 1, 75–6, 82, 88–9, 91, 107, 109, 110, 117–8, 136, 138–9, 149, 158–9, 164, 171, 174–5, 178, 198–9, 205, 216–9, 225
efforts of the Piobaireachd Society to reform 117–18, 123–4
inherent in Uist traditional life 158–9, 268(n)
role in conjunction with literacy in evolution of Highland piping tradition in eighteenth and nineteenth centuries 75–6
idiom of piping associated with 199, 205, 216–9, 225
Cooke, Peter, ethnomusicologist 2, 21, 22, 151, 166, 176, 207–8, 213, 214, 223, 243(n), 265(n), 266(n), 270(n)
Covenanters War, the 92, 93
'Creagorry Blend' (tune) 140
Creideamh a' Bhata Bhuidhe 61, 82, 149, 252(n)
Crofter's Commission, the 48
Crofters (Scotland) Act of 1886, the 66, 105
Cumming, John, piper to the Laird of Grant 81, 86, 256(n)
Curries of Eochar, the 145, 266(n)

'Dà Làimh sa Phìob' (song) 20, 25
Dalyell, Sir John Graham 113–4
dance 8, 9, 18, 36–7, 52, 54, 97–100, 112, 146, 159, 167–8, 171, 172, 184, 188–90, 192, 193, 208–11, 228–9, 231–2, 234–5
aesthetics associating aurally-learned piping with 207, 211, 213–7, 219, 231–2, 234–5

315

association with traditional Gaelic social culture and 'worldly excess' 52
brief history in Uist of traditional and contemporary 208–11
contemporary observation of transition from strathspey to reel rhythm by Uist dancers, circa turn of twentieth century 99
its functional association with piping in traditional Gaelic community life 97–100, 171, 172, 193
step-dancing 9, 18, 168, 189–90, 213, 241(n)
Daoine, na (the Men) 53, 54, 56
'Donald Bàn MacCrimmon, Lament for (tune), 118 262(n)
'Donald, Willie and His Dog' (tune) 270(n)
'Donella Beaton' (tune) 244(n)
deiseal, the 244–5(n), 248(n)
Devoyer, Fr James 45
'*Diomolodh Pìob Dhòmhnaill Bhàin*' (song) 76
Disruption, the 17, 51, 54, 249(n), 260(n)
Dòmhnall Ruadh Pìobaire, MacIntyre piper of folk tradition 27, 85, 87
'Donald Dougal MacKay, Lament for' (tune) 141, 166
'Donald MacLeod of Grisornish, Lament for' (tune) 141
'*Drochaid Chlann 'ic Ruairidh*' (song) 14
'Duke of Hamilton's Lament, the' (tune) 88

Eairdsidh Raghnaill – see MacDonald, Archie
'Earl of Seaforth's Salute, the' (tune) 167, 243(n)
economy, the Highland 57–60, 106, 149, 151, 245(n), 252(n)
economic and educational conditions in Uist c. 1900 106
instability a source of social unrest 59
kelp manufacture and cattle-dealing in South Uist 58, 60, 106, 149, 151, 245(n), 252(n)
reaction among Highland tenantry to agricultural improvements 58
shift from land-based to commercial-based 57–9
Education Act of 1782, the 105–6

Edward VII, the coronation celebrations of 185
Eigg 42–3, 44, 49, 50
Eilean an t-Sagairt 45
Elliot, Rev., Church of Scotland minister 55
emigration 48, 57–72, 82, 87–90, 106
among patronised piping families 67
due to religious persecution 48, 61–3, 82
economic 'push-pull' argument 58–9, 67
impact on Uist piping community 57, 68–72
major emigrations from South Uist 57, 60–67
Robert MacIntyre's supposed emigration to New World 87–8, 88–90
Uist pipers migrating to Lowlands in search of employment 57
Empire Settlement Act, the 61, 66, 238
'End of the Great Bridge, The' (tune) 135
Eriskay 68, 122, 209, 261(n)
Evangelicalism 51–4, 55, 250(n)
anecdotal destruction of musical instruments by the newly converted 52, 53
reference to piping and dancing as metaphor for evangelical worship 55
viewed as responsible for decline of Gaelic oral literature since nineteenth century 51, 250(n)

'*Fàgail Bhoirnis*' (song) 170
Famine, Great Highland 63–65
'Famous Bridge, The' (tune) 14
feisean 18
'*Fhir a' Chinn Duibh*' (song) 21–22
fiddling 9, 37, 54, 55, 70, 98, 108, 168, 213, 214, 215, 222, 226–7, 234, 242(n), 267(n)
'Finger Lock, The' (tune) 151–3, 269(n)
Flora MacDonald Cup 121, 125, 155–6, 160, 169, 178, 198, 199, 234, 238
Fraser, Angus 220, 225
Fraser, Capt. Simon of Knockie 220
Fraser, Simon of Australia 266(n), 267(n)
Fraser's 78th Highlanders 95–6, 261(n)
function 18, 19, 26, 52, 95, 96–100, 109, 136, 175, 198, 212–19
as accompaniment to group labour, burials and dancing in grass-roots Gaelic traditional life 19, 96–100, 198

canntaireachd as bridge of communication between this world and next 26
  of piping in a ceilidh environment 175
  of piping in association with aural versus literate environments of transmission 212–19

Gaelic poetry 14, 15, 40, 41, 51, 56, 192–3, 204–5, 220, 225, 232–4
  Catholic verse invoking the Virgin and Christ 41
  Donald MacIntyre's legacy as bard 192–3, 204–5
  elegies and histories contained in the Red Book of Clanranald 40–41
  Fr Allan McDonald's appreciation of bagpipe music 56
  performance aesthetics of 14–5
  postmodern example recalling asceticism of the Free Church 51
  satiric verse 14
  schema of traditional bardic development as proposed by Canon J.A. MacDonald 232–4
Gaelic Society of Inverness 49
gaida, the 5, 213, 222, 268(n)
games, Highland 23, 55, 110, 112, 120, 121, 122, 129, 131, 132, 133, 138, 140, 141, 157, 158, 159, 164, 167, 168, 169, 170, 171, 174–5, 177, 178, 181–99, 229, 234
  conservatism of sporting and dance traditions within otherwise artificiality of 187–90
  Georgian and Victorian origins of 183–4
  in Ardvachar 55, 122, 138, 184–5
  in Howmore 186, 187
  in Nunton 185–7
  on Askernish machair 112, 120, 121, 129, 131, 132, 133, 141, 157, 158, 159, 164, 167, 168, 169, 170, 171, 174–5, 177, 178, 181–2, 187, 193, 194, 196, 198, 229, 234
  rising number of non-local competitors taking prizes at Askernish 191, 195–8
Garbh-Chrìochan, na 39, 40
Garbutt, Catriona of Benbecula 155, 161, 273(n)
'Gathering of the MacDonalds of Clanranald (*Cnocan Ailein Mhic Iain*)' (tune) 148

George IV, King 183
Gibson, John, scholar 2, 15, 71, 109, 114, 231
Gillie Phàdruig Duibh 172, 257(n)
Gillies, John MacDougall 123
Gillies, Roderick 238
Glasgow Police Pipe Band 82, 158, 168–9
'Glengarry's Lament' (tune) 125
Gordon, Seton 68, 89, 189, 250(n), 257(n)
Gray, Pipe Major William 82, 169

Hector, the 67
Hegarty, Fr Patrick 42, 44
Henderson, Hamish, folklorist and poet 13
Highland Society of London and its competitions 2, 7, 75, 76, 81, 82, 88, 89, 91, 96, 109, 110, 113, 117, 128, 147, 148, 149, 183
Highland Society of Scotland 2, 75, 76, 110
'hiharin', the 143–5, 223
Houlihan, Margaret, piper 161

Iain Lom, bard 92
Iain Mùideartach – see Clanranald
'I Got a Kiss of the King's Hand' (tune) 76–7, 141, 167, 177
improvement measures 107, 112, 116, 119, 127, 136–7, 261(n)
Ireland 40–42, 43, 44–5, 46, 54, 92, 175–6, 250(n)
  Irish considered by Clanranald to be strategic allies of Catholicism 42
  Irish Franciscan mission of 1619 40, 42–5, 46
  Irish Gaelic antecedents to Hebridean athletic pastimes 187
  links with Catholic Clanranald and Uist 40–45, 46
  pilgrimages from Barra to Croagh Phadruig 41
  reference to 'Irish' character of dance-piping in Uist and its implications 175–6
'*Isbeal Nic Aoidh*' (song) 270(n)

Jacobite rebellion of 1715, the 93, 148
Jacobite rebellion of 1745, the 57, 58, 82, 93–5, 150

Johnson, Donald Alasdair, storyteller 203, 206
Johnson, Samuel 38, 78, 183, 255(n)
Johnstone, Calum of Barra 57, 131, 195, 243–4(n)
Johnstone, Duncan, piper 115, 164, 197
Johnstone, Neil, piper 55, 110, 169, 227–8, 230–1, 234

Kennedy, Hugh 196
Kennedy, Rev. James 55
Kilberry, Archibald Campbell of 22, 141, 193, 196, 262(n), 265(n)
Knox, John, Calvinist preacher 52
Knox, John, writer 18, 97
Knox, Thomas, Bishop of the Isles 47
Kuyper, Abraham, theologian 52

'Latha Dhan Fhinn am Beinn Iongnaidh' (song) 13
Lawrie, Pipe Major William 124, 128–9, 195, 206
Leslie, John, Bishop of the Isles 44
Lewis Pipe Band 52
Lewis 51–2, 65, 184
Lightfoot, Rona MacDonald of Garryhellie 14, 23–24, 57, 121, 156, 157, 159–61, 163, 164, 165, 166, 168, 169, 171, 174–5, 182, 197, 198, 203, 217, 223, 240, 273(n)
Lindsay, Archie 131, 205
Lindsays of Garryhellie, the 155
literacy 16–7, 74–5, 76, 91, 107, 109–112, 127–28, 162, 174–6, 177, 198–9, 200, 205
    emic attitudes among Hebridean musicians toward 91, 107, 167
    impact of British army on literacy among Hebridean pipers 109–12, 167, 198, 200
    mark of elite status in Gaelic society 16–7
    role in altering the nature of Highland piping transmission in nineteenth century 74–6, 199
Logan, James, antiquarian 18, 88, 89
Lordship of the Isles, the 7, 40, 77, 91, 176
Lorimer, Robin, scholar 133
Lovat Scouts the 111, 112, 113, 124, 130, 156, 189, 194, 199, 201–2, 203, 275(n)

MacArthur, 'Professor' John 149
MacArthur, Angus 81
MacArthur, Archibald 82, 90
MacArthur, Charles 77, 78, 81, 149
MacArthur, Donald 77, 81, 86, 256(n)
MacArthur, Fair John 81–2
MacArthurs, the 76, 77–8, 78–82, 86, 88, 146
    accounts of the family in South Uist 78–82
MacAulay, Alexander, piper 107, 119, 122, 125, 228–9
MacAulay, Angus of Benbecula 131, 163, 195, 229, 269(n), 273(n)
MacAulay, Fr Roderick, priest 55
MacAulay, Seonaid 'Jessie' of Smerclate 6, 19, 20, 23, 26–7, 35–6, 40, 69, 85, 100, 108, 110, 112, 113, 114, 127, 155, 161, 171–6, 193, 200, 207, 213–4, 215, 223, 224, 229, 230, 231, 234
MacBain, Alexander, folklorist 49–50
MacCodrum, John, bard 76, 77, 78, 88
MacColl, John of Oban 123, 195
MacCormick, Lachlan, piper 109–110, 112, 122, 125, 139–42, 145–46, 147–48, 164, 167, 184, 186, 192, 197, 219
MacCrimmon, Donald Ruadh 67, 125
MacCrimmon, Iain Dubh 67, 125
MacCrimmon, Patrick Mòr 22, 76–7
MacCrimmon, Patrick Òg 77
'MacCrimmon's Sweetheart (*Maol Donn*)' (tune) 2, 150–51, 163, 167, 243(n)
MacCrimmons, the 25, 26, 30, 76, 77, 85, 86, 88, 124, 125, 134, 147, 150, 161, 193, 244(n), 245(n), 255(n), 268(n)
MacDonald of Kinlochmoidart 68
MacDonald of Sleat 13, 60, 65, 76–8, 80–82
MacDonald, Alexander (*An Dall Mór*), North Uist bard 88, 90
MacDonald, Alexander (*Colla Ciotach*) 20, 44
MacDonald, Alexander of Borrodale 62, 149
MacDonald, Allan of Clanranald 45, 47, 148
MacDonald, Allan of Glenuig 13, 14, 19, 141, 169
MacDonald, Angus of Glenuig 169
MacDonald, Angus (*Aonghus Beag mac Dhòmhnaill 'ic Fhearguis*) 196, 229
MacDonald, Angus Òg, Lord of the Isles 40, 176

INDEX

MacDonald, Archie (*Eairdsidh Raghnaill*) of Garryhellie 2, 28, 156–7, 158, 188–9, 191, 202–3
MacDonald, Bishop Angus 48, 105
MacDonald, Canon John Angus 33, 232–4
MacDonald, Colin of Boisdale 48, 61, 62, 82, 149, 151–52
MacDonald, Donald (*Dòmhnall Roidein*) of Daliburgh 156, 167–68, 189, 219
MacDonald, Donald Allan, bard 14, 232–4
MacDonald, Donald Archie, ethnologist 206
MacDonald, Donald John, collector and tradition-bearer 20, 24, 35, 97, 99, 193, 248(n)
MacDonald, Donald, piper and pipemaker 75, 143–5, 148, 225
MacDonald, Fr Charles 39–40
MacDonald, Hugh of Boisdale 90
MacDonald, John (*Seonaidh Roidein*) 57, 156, 158, 163, 168–9, 177, 191, 205
MacDonald, John of Ferintosh, 'the Apostle of the North' 53, 55
MacDonald, John of Glenaladale 62
MacDonald, Joseph of Durness 2, 15, 54–5, 145, 221, 225, 242(n)
MacDonald, Kate (*Bean Eairdsidh Raghnaill*) of Garryhellie 13, 151, 154, 157, 160, 161–2, 164
MacDonald, Kenneth 169
MacDonald, Neil of Garryhellie 14, 23, 108, 121, 156, 157, 158, 159, 163, 165–6, 168, 169, 171, 203, 219, 226, 271(n), 276(n)
MacDonald, Patrick of Durness 55, 74, 242(n)
MacDonald, Pipe Major Donald Bàn of Benbecula 155, 198, 238
MacDonald, Pipe Major John of Inverness 123, 124–8, 131–32, 134, 135, 139, 145, 163–4, 167, 168, 170–1, 174, 178, 184, 189, 191, 196, 197, 229, 234, 250(n), 264(n), 272(n)
MacDonald, Reginald George of Clanranald 60, 61, 89, 91, 96, 149
MacDonald, Reginald of Ulva and Staffa 82
MacDonald, Roderick (*Ruairidh Roidein*) 14, 57, 163, 168–9, 177, 188, 194
MacDonald, Roderick of Barra 145, 266(n)
MacDonald, Ronald of Daliburgh 122–3
MacDonald, Ronald of Morar (*Raghnall mac Ailein Òig*) 43, 151–2

MacDonald, William of Benbecula 80, 139, 141, 197, 224–5, 240, 277(n)
MacDonalds of Kinlochmoidart 84, 89–90
MacDonells of Antrim 40, 41
MacDougall, Fr Alexander 55, 56, 119–20, 122–3, 136, 184, 186–7
MacDougall, Gavin 124
MacFadyen, Iain 169, 182
MacGillivray pipers of Barra 109, 139, 162
MacInnes, Neil, piper 109–110, 125, 139
'MacIntosh's Lament' (tune) 139, 162, 167
MacIntyre, Angus 192
MacIntyre, Donald Bàn of Rannoch 88, 89, 90
MacIntyre, Donald Ruadh, piper and bard 27, 28, 37, 141, 152, 192–3, 204–5
MacIntyre, Duncan Bàn, bard 221
MacIntyre, Duncan, piper to Clanranald 69, 87
MacIntyre, Pipe Major Donald John of Boisdale 198
MacIntyre, Pipe Major Donald of Boisdale 178, 198
MacIntyre, Robert, piper to Clanranald 27, 68, 87–90
MacIntyre, Sue, piper 161
MacIntyres, the 26, 27, 68–9, 77, 83–90, 147, 148, 150, 155, 171–2, 198
  archers to Clanranald 26, 27, 172, 193
  brief survey of their patrons throughout central and west Highlands 84
  emigration of MacIntyre pipers to New World 68–9
  evidence linking them to MacDonald of Clanranald and to South Uist in particular 84–90
  link to Pipers of Smerclate 26–7
  of Boisdale, South Uist 155, 178
  of French Road, Cape Breton 68–9, 85, 172, 193, 254(n)
  of Rannoch 84, 87, 88–90, 147, 148, 150
  pipers to MacDonald of Sleat 77, 84
MacKay, Angus of Raasay 18, 91, 125, 143, 144, 150, 239, 255(n)
MacKay, Donald 91, 149
MacKay, Iain Dall 67
MacKay, John (*Iain Ruadh mac Aonghuis 'ic Iain Doill 'ic Ruairidh*) 67
MacKay, John of Raasay 91, 125, 161

MacKay, Pipe Major Robert 'Mickey' 178
'MacKay's Banner' (tune) 178
MacKays of Gairloch, the 67, 256(n)
MacKays of Raasay 91
MacKenzie, John Ban 125, 161
MacKenzie, Major Finlay 119, 120–21, 156, 187
MacKenzie, Simon 119–20, 136, 187, 193, 263(n)
MacLachlan, Ewan, dancing master 167, 189–90, 210
MacLean of Coll 78
Maclean, Calum, collector of oral tradition 28
MacLean, Norman 198
MacLean, Pipe Major William 110, 128–9, 139, 186, 204, 275(n)
MacLean, Sorley, poet 14
MacLeans of Duart 78
MacLellan, Duncan of Benbecula 155
MacLellan, John of Eochar 184, 191–2
MacLellan, John Archie 142, 143, 144–5, 161, 177, 233, 266(n)
MacLennan, D.G., dancing authority 190
MacLennan, Pipe Major G.S. 135, 190
MacLennan, Pipe Major Neil 110, 121, 125, 167, 227–8, 230–1
MacLeod, Donald of Lewis 167, 197
MacLeod, Morag, researcher and lecturer 21, 22
MacLeod of Dunvegan 22, 67, 76, 85, 147
'MacLeod of MacLeod's Lament' (tune) 146
MacLeod, Donald, principal of the Free Church College 53
MacLeod, Pipe Major Murdo 'Bogey' 52
'MacLeod's Salute' (tune), 141
MacMillans of Daliburgh, the 155, 164
MacMillan, Somerled 27, 192–3
MacMhuirich, Niall Mór 78–80, 92
MacMhuirich, Niall Òg 16, 79, 87, 93
MacMhuirichs, the 16, 17, 40, 78–80, 83, 87, 266(n)
MacMhurich, Lachlainn 79
MacMillan, Fr John of Barra 115
MacNab, Archie 196
MacNeil of Barra 27, 43, 84, 89, 90, 192
MacNeill, Seumas 146, 265(n)
MacNiven, Owen of Paisley 196
MacPherson, Archie of Eochar 189–90
MacPherson, James, collector of Ossianic lore 16
MacPherson, Malcolm (*Calum Pìobair*) 125, 134, 139
MacQuarrie, Angus 131, 194, 269(n)
MacRae, Fr Angus of Ardkenneth 55
'Maggie Cameron' (tune) 171
'*Maol Donn*' (song) 2, 150–1, 163, 243(n)
'*Marbhrann do Dhomhnall Ruadh Mac an t-Saoir*' (song) 193
'Marchioness of Tullibardine' (tune) 171
Marloch, the 60, 66, 70
Martin, Finlay 194, 205
Martin Martin 16, 48–9, 242(n)
assessment of Uist people and culture 16, 48–9
'Mary MacLeod, Lament for' (tune) 142, 143, 144, 145, 177, 178
Mathieson, Rev. William, scholar 4
McCann, Fr Edmund 42
McDonald, Fr Allan of Eriskay 30, 48, 50, 56, 68, 85, 92, 119, 122, 249(n)
Menzies of Rannoch 68, 84, 90, 147, 148, 150
Merriam, Alan, ethnomusicologist 15, 211–2, 224, 242(n)
military, the 57, 59, 91–6, 109, 110–111, 112–13, 116, 139, 165, 173, 177, 198–9, 200–06, 260–1(n)
aurally-learned piping in 112–13
only recourse to literacy for pipers 110–111, 124, 198
Uist pipers in military campaigns 91–6
Uist pipers joining the Army for employment 57
Moore, Hamish, pipemaker 71, 239, 254(n)
Morrison, Donald A. of Loch Eynort and Aberdeen 135, 143, 170, 197
Morrison, Donald John of Loch Eynort 170, 171, 271(n)
Morrison, Fred Jr 163, 170
Morrison, Fred Sr of Gerinish 57, 170, 197
Morrison, Ludovic 'Louis' 155, 170–1, 178, 198, 217, 229–30, 234, 238
Morrison, Ronald of Gerinish 57, 78, 84, 125, 134, 162, 170, 197, 266(n), 269(n)
Morrison, William of Loch Eynort and Glasgow 121, 170, 197, 229, 270(n), 271(n)
Morrisons of Gerinish (*Clann Sheonaidh Aonghuis Ruaidh*) 155, 170, 197
Munro, Donald, fiddler and catechist, 53
'My King has Landed in Moidart' (tune) 150, 166, 167

Napier Commission, the 66, 105
Napoleonic Wars, the 59, 60, 63, 106, 208
Na Tri Seudan 254(n)
Newfoundland *Gàidhealtachd* 34, 36
Nicol, Pipe Major Robert 124, 131–4, 135, 158
North Uist 60, 65, 77, 78, 81–2, 191, 198, 249(n)
Nova Scotia 67, 69, 71–2, 85, 89, 172–3, 239

òda, the 188, 268(n)
'Old Woman's Lullaby, The' (tune) 166–67, 224
O' Neill, Fr Paul 42, 50
oral tradition, Gaelic 15–6, 17, 18, 19, 20–21, 22–3, 29, 84–6, 87, 94, 119, 138, 157, 167, 176, 229, 232–4
  attesting to Catholic sympathy of Uist's people 45
  complementarity of arts characteristic of 15–16, 18, 19
  continuance of storytelling among emigrants from Uist to Nova Scotia 70
  Fr Allan McDonald's interest in Uist's oral folklore 56
  importance of orality symbolised by Smerclate tales 29
  instrumental music imbued with lexical meaning 20–21
  local account of MacArthur presence in Uist 80–82
  overlapping of speech and song 22–3
  relevance to study of Highland history 4–5
  value of South Uist to study of traditional Gaelic culture 17–8
'*Òran do Rob Dòmhnallach Mac an t-Saoir, Pìobaire Mhic 'ic Ailein*' (song) 88
Ossian and its place in post-Jacobite romanticism 40–41, 183

Pagan superstition 43, 48–51, 248–9(n)
  second sight among Barra Catholics 50
Paisley Bard, the – *see* MacIntyre, Donald Ruadh
'Patrick Òg MacCrimmon, Lament for' (tune) 142–4, 165–6, 197, 269(n)
patronage 74–91, 141, 147–8, 150, 200
  of leading Hebridean piping families 76–82
  of MacIntyre pipers by Clanranald 83–90, 147–8, 150
Pennant, Thomas, naturalist 77
pibroch songs 8, 15, 19–22, 157, 192, 243(n)
Piobaireachd Society, the 1, 80, 107, 110, 116, 117–8, 119, 123–36, 138–45, 154, 158–9, 162, 177, 184, 186, 195, 199, 205, 229, 234, 262–5(n)
  actions to reduce plurality of classical repertoire settings through tuition 123, 263–4(n)
  philisophical origins and aspirations 117–8, 119
  tuition in South Uist, Benbecula and Barra 124–36, 138–45, 154, 177, 184, 195, 205, 229
'*Pìobairean Camshronach anns an Ruaig Mhór*' (song) 204–5
Pìobairean Smearclait 26–32, 68, 83, 84, 85, 86, 92, 152–3, 171–2, 193, 267(n)
  grass-roots comparison between pipers to Clanranald and MacLeod 30–32
  known locally as *Pìobairean a' Chlaiginn* 26
  possibility that they were MacNeils from Barra 26–7
  reference to MacRaes 26
  symbolising importance of orality in Gaelic tradition 29, 32
  the *gille luideach* receives the Gift of Piping 28–30
  thought to have been a family of MacIntyres 26
'Piper's Warning to His Master, The' (tune) 20
Plains of Abraham, the 95
'*Port Bean Aonghuis Ruaidh*' (tune) 26, 244(n)
post-Jacobite era 74, 75, 107, 183
Prebyterianism 44, 48, 52, 53, 55, 73, 247(n)
'Prince's Salute, the' (tune) 147, 150, 270(n)
Protestantism 38–9, 40, 44, 46–9, 51, 54–5, 234
  popular view of Protestant approach to Hebridean folk culture 38, 48–9
  Protestant activity in Clanranald lands 47
  traditional music among moderate ministers and evangelicals 54–5
psalmody 52
puirt-à-beul 9, 18–9, 36, 37, 154, 157, 209, 212, 215, 219, 229, 230, 231, 241(n)
  description of 9

emic categorisation other than as 'song' 9, 241(n)
observed providing rhythm for dance in North Uist 18
survival in South Uist ceilidh performance well into twentieth century 19
traditional context for learning pipe tunes 36, 37, 229, 230, 231

Queen's Own Cameron Highlanders 21, 91, 96, 109, 111–2, 128, 139, 155, 167, 168, 178, 186, 189, 194–5, 198, 201, 203–5, 274(n)

racing in Hebridean athletic tradition 188
Rae, Frederick, schoolmaster 17, 27, 56, 85, 99, 119, 140, 159, 168, 199, 209, 210
Ramsay, John of Ochtertyre 74, 117
Rankin, Condullie 78, 86
Rankin, Ewan (*Eoghainn mac Eachainn 'ic Chon-duilidh*) 78
Rankins, the 76, 78
Reformation, the 39, 42, 44, 234, 248(n)
'Rinn mi mochéirigh gu éirigh' (song) 98
Ross, Duncan, piper 161, 223
Ross, Pipe Major Willie 110, 124, 129–31, 134, 135, 142, 174, 189, 234
Rothiemurchas, Sheriff Grant of 164–5, 194

'79th's Farewell to Gibraltar' (tune) 112
'S mi m' aonaran am beinn a' Cheothain' (song) 98
School of Scottish Studies, the 21, 157, 166, 176, 195, 205
Scotch Reel (dance) 9, 36–7, 99, 136, 188, 209, 215, 235, 276(n)
Scott, Adam, piper 164
Scott, Neilie, piper 217
'Seanchas Sloinneadh na Pìob' o Thùs' (song) 78–80, 82
Seven Years War, the 59, 73, 93, 95–6
'Shaggy Grey Buck' (tune) 229, 277(n)
Shaw, John, scholar 2, 15, 36, 222, 226
Shaw, Margaret Fay, folklorist 15, 17, 20, 119
Shears, Barry, piper and scholar 71, 89, 90
shinty 54, 186, 187, 272(n)
Ships Passenger Act, the 59–60, 63
sithichean, na (the fairies) 25, 28–30

bestows the Gift of Piping to the *gille luideach* of Smerclate 28–30
intervention in human affairs 25
predominating theme of Gaelic piping tales 25
Skye 50, 53, 67, 184
'Smàlaidh mise nochd an teine' (incantation) 50
small pipes, references to performance in Hebrides of 98–9, 259–60(n)
Smith, John of Howmore 142–3, 191
Smith, Neil of Howmore 142, 189
Smiths of Howmore, the 142–3, 145
South End Piping Club, the 55, 178, 238
'South Uist Golf Club' (tune) 140
South Uist Pipe Band 155
South Uist Piping Society 55, 107, 118–21, 124, 126–7, 128, 129, 130–31, 134, 136, 177, 184, 185, 199
actions bespeaking improver mentality 119, 134, 136–7, 185
approach to Piobaireachd Society for tutors 120, 124
its founding members 119–23
Spalding, Anne, piper 161
sports 54, 184, 185, 186–8, 195, 271(n)
associated with games phenomenon 184, 185, 186, 187–8, 195
indigenous to Hebridean tradition 187–8
SSPCK 39, 47, 49, 53
St Columba 39, 43, 44, 50
St John's Island 61, 62
St Kilda 49
Statues of Iona 42
Steele, John of Lochboisdale 125, 194–5, 228–9
Susanna, the 83
Synod of Argyll 44, 47, 49

'Tailor and the Changeling, The' (tale) 24–5
'Taladh Dhòmhnaill Ghuirm' (song) 13
'Tha Thu Mar a Tha Thu, a Bhodaich' (tune) 239
Thomson, Derick, scholar and poet 51
Thomson, Sinclair, 'the Shetland Apostle' 53
'Till an crodh, far an crodh' (song) 31
Tiree 65, 185
Tochradh Nighean a' Chathanaich 40
transmission 19, 24, 35–7, 91, 109–116, 125,

140–46, 156, 157, 160–61, 162, 167, 171, 174–6, 177, 178–9, 199, 205–6, 207–8, 211–35, 268(n), 273(n)
aural and literate 'bi-lingualism' in Hebridean musical tradition 141, 145–6, 162, 167, 171, 216–7, 229–35
aural- and literate-based attitudes to 'false fingering' 114–5, 227
aural transmission of piping 19, 36, 37, 109, 112–6, 136–7, 171, 174–6, 178–9, 198–9, 205–6, 207–8, 211–9, 225–6, 227–35
impact of military context on attitudes toward aural and literate transmission 91, 199
inheritance of musical ability in Gaelic cosmology 157, 192, 273(n)
literate transmission of piping 109–112, 113, 114, 115, 116, 125, 136, 171, 174–6, 177, 179, 199, 205, 207–8, 211–9, 227–35
of Gaelic music from parent to child 24
of Gaelic performance arts in the ceilidh milieu 35
of pipe tunes by listening to songs in ceilidhs in South Uist and Newfoundland 36
women as passive and active bearers of piping tradition 160–61, 174–5, 268(n)

Union of Scotland and England, the 58
Urban VIII, Pope 42
'*Urnaigh Mara Chlann Raghnaill*' (sea prayer) 41

Victoria, Queen 183

Walker, Calum of Garryhellie 155, 196, 269(n)
Walkers, the 155
Ward, Fr Cornelius 42–4, 47, 50, 51, 247–8(n)
'War or Peace' (tune) 274(n)
waulking songs (*òrain luaidh*) 15, 52, 94, 97–9
weddings in South Uist, references to 54, 99, 119, 176
Whyte, Henry, folklorist 84, 147, 149, 151–2
Wilson, John 196
World War I 21, 32, 36, 71, 119, 121, 128, 131, 139, 156, 168, 186, 190, 192, 193, 194, 200–1, 202–6, 274–5(n)
World War II 35, 36, 71, 131, 190, 196, 201, 205, 229, 238

BIRLINN LTD (incorporating John Donald and Polygon) is one of Scotland's leading publishers with over four hundred titles in print. Should you wish to be put on our catalogue mailing list **contact**:

Catalogue Request
Birlinn Ltd
West Newington House
10 Newington Road
Edinburgh EH9 1QS
Scotland, UK

Tel: + 44 (0) 131 668 4371
Fax: + 44 (0) 131 668 4466
e-mail: info@birlinn.co.uk

Postage and packing is free within the UK. For overseas orders, postage and packing (airmail) will be charged at 30% of the total order value.

For more information, or to order online, visit our website at **www.birlinn.co.uk**

Birlinn Limited
IMPRINTS: JOHN DONALD · POLYGON